Strategos: Island in the Storm

Gordon Doherty's love of history was first kindled by visits to the misty ruins of Roman Britain and the sun-baked antiquities of Turkey and Greece. His research expeditions since have taken him all over the world and back and forth through time, allowing him to write tales of the Roman Empire, Byzantium, Classical Greece and the Bronze Age.

Also by Gordon Doherty

Strategos

Strategos: Born in the Borderlands
Strategos: Rise of the Golden Heart
Strategos: Island in the Storm

Legionary

Legionary
Viper of the North
Land of the Sacred Fire
The Scourge of Thracia
Gods & Emperors
Empire of Shades
The Blood Road
Dark Eagle

Empires of Bronze

Son of Ishtar
Dawn of War
Thunder at Kadesh
The Crimson Throne
The Shadow of Troy
The Dark Earth

Rise of Emperors (with Simon Turney)

Sons of Rome
Masters of Rome
Gods of Rome

STRATEGOS
ISLAND IN THE STORM

GORDON DOHERTY

CANELO

First published in the United Kingdom in 2014 by Gordon Doherty

This edition published in the United Kingdom in 2022 by

Canelo
Unit 9, 5th Floor
Cargo Works, 1–2 Hatfields
London SE1 9PG
United Kingdom

A CIP catalogue record for this book is available from the British Library.

Print ISBN 978 1 80436 047 7
Ebook ISBN 978 1 80436 046 0

Cover design by Black Sheep

Cover images © ArcAngel

Look for more great books at www.canelo.co

Printed and bound in Great Britain by Clays Ltd, Elcograf S.p.A.

1

For William.

We'll never forget you.

A set of maps and diagrams to accompany this novel can be viewed
at the author's website: www.gordondoherty.co.uk

PROLOGUE

Friday 26th August 1071 AD: Manzikert

A lone tamarisk tree stood upon a deserted hilltop, bathed in dawn light. The cicadas nearby chattered as if today was just another day. Then the clopping of hooves sounded, scattering a pair of song thrushes from the tree. A lone rider galloped up the hillside, his iron lamellar armour shimmering, his crimson cloak and the black eagle feather plume of his helm flitting in the breeze. He came to a halt near the tree and removed his helm. A gentle wind whipped his silver-amber locks across his face. It was a face furrowed with age and determination: deep-set and saturnine emerald eyes looming under the heavy shade of his brow, a nose battered and scarred across the bridge and taut lips guarded by an iron-grey beard.

Apion slid from the saddle and led his war horse to a trickling brook by the tree. 'Slake your thirst, rest your legs. She will come to me soon,' he whispered, glancing up at the sun-streaked sky as he smoothed the chestnut Thessalian's mane. The gelding snorted in appreciation before gulping at the water. Apion strode over to the tamarisk tree, then sat back against its gnarled trunk and took a long pull on his water skin. Pensively, he looked back to the south, down the hillside from where he had come.

The breeze conducted the tall grass of the slope into a rhythmic dance and at times, when it stood tall, he could see nothing of the plain below – only the Anatolian sky and the snow-capped peaks far to the south. When this happened, his mind wandered in the echoes of the past: those lost days tending the goat herd on the Chaldian hillsides overlooking Mansur's farm. Trapped in a vice of darkness and pain before and after, those few years were the light, the force that kept him holding on, the reason he had wielded his sword to this day.

'Yet it's all… gone,' he mouthed, his whisper carried away by the breeze. He lifted a dark lock of woman's hair from his purse and stroked at it absently. Her name rang in his thoughts. *Maria.* His search for her had been fruitless, and today would surely end any lingering hope.

The shriek of an eagle stirred him, and he realised he was no longer alone. From the corner of his eye he recognised the shrivelled, white-haired crone sitting by his side. 'Wiser men might have kept riding, and fled this land,' she said, her milky, sightless eyes fixed upon him. Then she turned to look downhill with him, extending a bony finger towards the waving curtain of tall grass. 'Look, Apion.'

As if quelled by the frail old woman's words, the breeze died and the grass fell limp, revealing the plain below and the two opposing masses of shimmering warriors there, red dust and woodsmoke pluming above them like a low-lying storm cloud. Romanus Diogenes, Emperor of Byzantium, the *Golden Heart*, was to lead his armies against Sultan Alp Arslan, the *Mountain Lion*, and his Seljuk hordes. The hillside trembled as the last few regiments of Byzantine spearmen filed from their camp and the Seljuk cavalry wings rumbled into place. The air reverberated with the Christian chanting of the Byzantine ranks. Swords, spears, bows, shields and bright standards were held aloft by both armies. The *shatranj* board was all but set. This was the clash these lands had feared for so long. Destiny would be forged on this plain.

Apion glanced from the opposing armies to the nearby, black-bricked fortress of Manzikert by the foot of this hill, and then to the snow-capped mountains far to the south — Mount Tzipan the tallest of them all. These great slopes masked all but a glimpse of Lake Van, sparkling in the sunlight, and the speck on the shore side that was the sister fortress of Chliat. The crone placed a hand on his shoulder, and he recalled something she had foreseen, years ago.

I see a battlefield by an azure lake flanked by two mighty pillars.

The meaning, Delphic then, was all too evident now. His gaze passed across the plain once more, drawn to the heart of the Byzantine ranks where Emperor Romanus sat proudly astride his stallion, defiant in the face of all that had happened in the preceding months. Across the battlefield, behind the Seljuk lines, he could just make out the Sultan's command tent. The rest of the crone's augury came to him:

At dusk you and the Golden Heart will stand together in the final battle, like an island in the storm. Walking that battlefield is Alp Arslan. The Mountain Lion is dressed in a shroud.

He turned to the old woman, wishing to ask her if this meant victory lay in store for Byzantium's forces today, and dreading both possible responses.

But the crone spoke before he did. 'The storm is almost upon us, *Haga*. The answers you seek dance within its wrath.'

Apion felt a stinging behind his eyes, an invisible hand grasping at his heart. 'Do they?' he replied through taut lips. 'All I know is that a vast Seljuk horde awaits, blades sharpened. Alp Arslan, his armies and…'

'And your son,' the crone finished for him flatly.

The truth chilled Apion's blood. He scanned the forming Seljuk lines, unable to discern any of them at such distance but knowing that his boy, Taylan, was there – his heart aflame with a desire for revenge, his sword eager to spill his father's blood. Apion let his head loll back against the tamarisk bark, his eyes shut tight. Death had hunted him for years. Today, death would take him… or Taylan. *How had it come to this?*

'Perhaps you were right – I should have kept riding,' he snorted. 'Then I would not have to clash swords with my boy.'

'Yet Taylan would still seek you out on the battlefield, unaware of your absence. Still he might fall. Still you would be without knowledge of Maria.'

Apion dropped his head into his hands. 'Tell me, old woman: what wickedness has brought today about? Is it Fate, the one you curse so fervidly?'

She shook her head, her face lengthening. 'It is the black hearts and venal curs in the courts of Byzantium and the Sultanate that have brought about this day. Yet it is noble men who will perish down on that plain.'

'Then what hope is there?' Apion said, numbly.

She leaned a little closer. 'While good men do what is right, hope can never die.'

He traced a finger over the faded red-ink *Haga* stigma on his forearm. The effigy of the mythical two-headed eagle there had all but become him and he it. 'You seek good men? Then why do you come to me, old woman?' He turned to her. But she was gone. He was alone once again.

Suddenly, the Seljuk war horns snarled down on the plain. A shiver of finality prickled on his skin. A great empire would be humbled today. All that lay undecided was which.

He stood, walked from the shade and into the sunlight, resting his sword hand on the worn ivory hilt of old Mansur's scimitar. The iron lamellae of his *klibanion* vest chinked rhythmically with each step. He took his gelding's reins and vaulted onto the saddle. From horseback, he could see that the opposing battle lines were almost ready, their destiny ever closer. He closed his eyes to clear his mind, inhaling the sweet scent of jasmine before what was to come.

It was a fine day to die.

Part 1: 1069 AD Two years earlier…

CHAPTER 1

The Rogue of the Black Fort

Psidias the tax collector was an eternally sullen man. The kind of man who would scowl at the sun for being too hot, then curse any cloud that came across it for blocking out the light. In his twenties, he had assumed he would become more at ease with himself as he aged, but now – at forty – he was more irritable than ever. He swept his cloak across his rounded shoulders in an attempt to stave off the chill February wind, his shapeless nose wrinkling in discomfort as the reins chafed on his palms and the juddering wagon pummelled his already numb buttocks. The rugged valleys and mountain passes of Colonea usually made for tedious progress on the route back to the west, but this time they seemed to be making better ground. He laughed bitterly at his momentary optimism. Almost certainly, their swiftness was down to the scant takings and the lightness of the wagon, he mused, glancing over his shoulder from the driver's berth at the half-empty coin sacks. The populace was thin and scattered in this eastern *thema* of Byzantium, many of the taxpaying farmers and townsfolk having deserted the region for areas less prone to Seljuk raids.

He wondered how the poor takings might reflect on him, and his belly began to churn as he imagined his beaky-nosed superiors scrutinising him, questioning him. He looked up to his escort of four *kursores*, riding a few feet before the wagon, wearing felt caps, iron klibanion jackets and carrying spears and shields. These imperial scout riders had performed their jobs, they would receive no scorn when they saw the wagon safely back to the imperial treasury. His anxiety turned to jealousy and he scowled at the riders, only for the hooves of the nearest mount to throw up a cloud of dust that blinded him and coated his mouth with grit. Retching and wiping at his eyes, he made to roar at the rider. But the cry caught in his throat. For the offending kursoris had galloped ahead, his cap falling off as he hoisted his spear. The other three riders rushed ahead with him, all four looking up at the nearby scree-strewn and shrub-dotted rise.

Psidias squinted, leaning out from the driver's berth to look up with them. A shadow loomed up there. No, many shadows. A wall of figures. Iron horsemen. Psidias gulped, his guts at once melting. 'Seljuk raiders? *No!*' he wailed.

But then the kursores before him relaxed their spears and broke out in relieved laughter. Psidias frowned, then noticed the garb of these unexpected horsemen: iron conical helms with broad nose-guards. Mail hauberks and kite shields. Norman mercenaries in Byzantine service. Men who were paid handsomely to protect the outlying *themata*. Twenty of them. One led them down the rise. This one was assured-looking, with wisps of blond hair licking from the lip of his helm. A confident smile grew on his round, red-cheeked face, and his cerulean eyes fell upon the wagon.

'Crispin, of the borderland *tagma*, Lord of the Black Fort of Mavrokastro,' the rider introduced himself to the kursores in his western twang. His tone was haughty but his voice carried well, as if amplified by the walls of the pass. Psidias noticed how his eyes darted back to the wagon as he spoke.

'You are escorting the tax levy from Colonea?' Crispin asked.

'Aye,' the lead kursoris replied.

'Then you can return to your homes, your beds, your wives,' Crispin grinned. 'My men and I will see the taxes safely to the west.'

Psidias heard these jovial words and frowned. They curdled with the ice-cold glint in the man's eyes.

The lead kursoris shared a similar frown with his three men. 'I… I'm not sure we can do that, sir,' the kursoris replied. 'We have orders to see the wagon through to the Thema of Cappadocia.' He held up a wax-sealed scroll.

'Ah, I understand. But if you give me the scroll I will see the wagon safely to that land and I'll make sure that your commander knows you acted appropriately.' Crispin held out a chubby hand, waving his fingers in expectation of the scroll.

Psidias felt his throat dry as he watched the kursores' faces darken. At the same time, the Norman lancers with Crispin exchanged furtive glances. And Crispin himself lost his hearty demeanour. Now his face matched his glacial eyes. He reached out and snatched at the scroll.

But the lead kursoris held onto it. The pair grappled at an end of the scroll each, noses inches apart. 'You know what disobeying an order from a superior entails, don't you? You bloody fool? The lash will lick every last morsel of skin from your back!'

The lead kursoris' face had drained of colour, but he did not let go. 'An order to commandeer tax revenue would come in the form of another scroll, sir,' he replied through gritted teeth. 'And I see no such thing.'

Crispin glared at the rider, then, like the passing of a storm cloud, his face relaxed and he let go of the scroll, leaning back in his saddle with a guffawing laugh. 'Ah, the simplest of misunderstandings!' he beamed. His riders laughed with him. The kursores did not. 'My orders, of course. Here,' he said, rummaging at something under his cloak.

Psidias saw what happened next in a blur. Instead of a leaf of paper, Crispin pulled out a curved dagger. The blade swept up and across the kursoris' neck, and a hot, crimson spray leapt from his torn throat. Gawping, Psidias heard the panicked cries of the other three riders as they were skewered and punched from their saddles on the end of Norman lances. There was a moment of near-silence, with just the skirling afternoon wind and the fading *clop-clop* of the fleeing, riderless kursores' mounts. Then the Norman riders looked to the wagon. They eyed Psidias like ravenous gulls.

Psidias grappled the wagon horses' reins and tried to lash them into a gallop, only for something to flash before him and shudder into his chest. A Norman spear shaft. He looked at the blood haemorrhaging from the massive wound. There was pain for just a few moments, then a numbness raced around his body. He lifted his head with great effort, seeing Crispin dismount and approach, a broad grin etched on his face.

Ah, he thought as his life slipped away, *I should have learned to smile more often.*

Apion hauled himself up and onto the highest branch of the pine, needles showering him, their sharp scent spicing the warm May air. He cocked an apologetic eyebrow to a nestling woodlark disturbed from its slumber, then shaded his eyes from the morning sun to cast his gaze across the land. Here, at the edge of this clearing, he could see for miles. The forest roof – a verdant jumble of ash, poplar, walnut and pine-stretched for some distance. The woods were surrounded by the craggy, burnt-gold and shrub-dotted lands of Colonea and overlooked in the east by the sheer, black-basalt hillside that stood taller than any other. It was practically a pillar of rock, with just a narrow, winding path offering a route to the top. Perched up there, like a rotting but defiant tooth, stood the Black Fortress of Mavrokastro.

He swept his gaze across the rippling heat haze around the fortress, but saw nothing. No movement bar a few lone trade wagons. Then he saw a glint of silver atop the battlements. *Come out, you cur!*

Crispin and his Norman lancers had been pillaging the imperial tax and grain wagons and terrorising local villages with little reprisal since winter. They had come to these lands as allies, taking the emperor's coin and his grant of the nigh-on impregnable fortress in exchange for their service in the border tagmata. They had behaved well and fought nobly at first. Then Crispin had decided to carve out his own little empire.

Stifling a sigh, Apion descended the pine to a chorus of cracking twigs, then thudded to the clearing floor below. Here, a *bandon* of his thematic ranks tried to keep themselves busy. The sounds of chattering and the chopping and hewing of wood echoed around him, while the scent of millet stew and roasting mutton spiced the air. He had led these hundred and seven men from his homeland of Chaldia a week ago, marching from the northern coastal city of Trebizond. They had marched at haste and without complaint, leaving the lush greenery of northern Chaldia behind, ascending into the dryer, hotter highlands of the central Anatolian plateau before crossing into this neighbouring thema.

'Nothing?' a baritone voice asked. He twisted to see Sha, the coal-skinned Malian *tourmarches*, who had been his second in command ever since he had attained the position as the Strategos of Chaldia. At thirty-nine, Sha was five years Apion's senior. His shorn scalp had grown in enough on this march to betray patches of grey and the corners of his eyes were well-lined.

Apion shook his head, brushing the pine needles from his tunic and flicking them from his boots. 'Crispin has grown wary since he was last caught on the field with his men.'

'Not that he came to any harm!' Sha snorted as they strolled amongst the men.

Indeed, the small army sent to tackle Crispin some months ago had caught the Norman and his full force of some six hundred lancers, camped on the flatlands to the north. The imperial army had attempted to sneak upon the camp at dawn while Crispin and his men still slept, hoping for a rout. Then disaster had struck, as – part-blinded by the gloom – the imperial soldiers had tripped on tent pegs and fallen on hidden caltrops, before the Normans rose from their tents and came at them, swords flashing. It had been a rout indeed. Despite seeing off that force, Crispin had since been careful to ride out with just small, swift packs of riders – never more than seventy or so – striking the tax wagons and villages and sweeping back into his formidable stronghold to tally his plunder.

'We can only keep a constant vigil, Sha. Crispin will tire of inactivity soon enough.'

'Just how much plunder does a man need?' Sha scowled.

Apion stopped by the well at the centre of the clearing and drew himself a cup of water from the bucket hanging there. 'Plunder might have been his purpose at first, Sha, but you saw that grain caravan.' His mind flashed with images of the gory stain that remained of the wagon drivers. The grain itself had been left untouched. 'He has come to crave the lustre of blood.'

The pair sat down by the well and fell silent. Sha pulled out a tattered map, plucking a stalk of wheat and twisting it between his teeth as he studied it. Apion fished out a well-read letter from his purse. He read it over once more and frowned. Lady Eudokia's handwriting threatened time and again to drag his mind back to that brief and passionate moment they had shared, just before she had wed the emperor, Romanus Diogenes. Indeed, that she had dabbed her sweet-scented lotions upon it was more distracting still. *Focus, man,* he scolded himself, taking a sip of water from his cup and reading:

Stay vigilant, Apion, for Psellos seems to know of the emperor's every move. You must march to the Black Fortress in the lands of Colonea, where the foul advisor's coins have bought the venal hearts of our border forces. Then I beg you to muster every man you can and hasten to my husband's side on his campaign to Lake Van. Only there can you shield him from Psellos' further ruses…

He looked up at the cloudless morning sky and thought of the black-hearted Psellos and the Doukas family back in Constantinople, of their seemingly bottomless vaults of gold, of their insatiable desire to depose Emperor Romanus and take the throne for themselves, heedless to the toll of lives. Doukas was a swine indeed, but Psellos? Psellos was the jackal-god, so blinded by his quest for power that he would happily set the empire to flame just to be master of its blackened corpse. And Crispin was just the latest in a line of many who had taken Psellos' gold. *So I'm chasing the tail of the snake when the head bears the fangs?*

He rubbed his temples as if trying to massage the thoughts away, then looked over to Sha. The Malian scoured the map intently, but every so often he would pause in his thoughts, trace a finger over the leather bracelet he wore on his wrist and let a faint smile touch his lips. Apion found the smile infectious. Sha had just a year ago been presented with a gift of slaves – a mother and two children – from a trader the Malian had rescued from brigands. Sha had freed the slaves that same day, offering them his home if they would tend to his farm while he was away. Months later, there was no doubting that Sha had found love with the mother, and fulfilment with her children. This threw Apion's thoughts back to the emptiness that awaited him in his own home – the silent, empty keep on Trebizond's citadel hill. He folded up the letter. Memories of his dalliance with Eudokia were but a spark to reignite those of his true, lost love.

Maria.

With his mother and father long ago slain and no children to call his own, he was alone. Even Mansur, the old Seljuk farmer who took him in as a boy, had been snatched from him at the end of a blade. And until last winter, he had long thought Mansur's daughter, Maria, walked with them in the land of the dead. Until the crone had come to him.

You told me she lives, he mouthed into the ether as if addressing the absent crone, one finger sliding into his purse, stroking the lock of sleek, dark hair in there. *But you cannot tell me where, and this world is vast. That, old woman, is a tortuous gaol for a man's mind.*

His gaze grew distant, trawling all that had happened since the crone's revelation. He had sent messengers and hired scouts to scour the borderlands in search of her. Some had searched the eastern themata, others had ventured far into Seljuk lands. All had come back with nothing. He sighed and tried to turn his thoughts back to his next move, thinking of where Crispin might strike next.

A panicked *honk-honk* tore him from his thoughts. He looked up to see two *toxotai* – who had been diligently shooting their composite bows at a nearby tree trunk — now loosing skywards in an attempt to fell the skein of geese that flew overhead. When a fully deserved shower of goose droppings spattered down on their faces and tunics, they stumbled away, cursing, one of them spitting the oily filth from his lips and the other hurrying to put on his wide-brimmed archer's hat to shield him from the onslaught.

'The men are getting restless, it seems.' Sha cocked an eyebrow, folding up his map. 'Perhaps we should move on? Keeping them on the march keeps their minds focused.'

'Move on?' Apion replied. 'If we had an enemy to pursue, Sha, I would have us on the march right now. But until Crispin breaks cover from his fort, we must wait.'

The pair looked around for some form of distraction, both picking up on a conversation between Blastares and Procopius, wandering amongst the men. Blastares was a bull of a man, Sha's age, with a broken nose shuddering between his eyes and a shaven scalp. Procopius was a wiry, puckered officer in his fiftieth year with a pure white, close crop of hair and a face like a dried prune. Apion had known this pair since his first days in the ranks. Now each of them was a tourmarches like Sha, leading a Chaldian *tourma* under his command. Each of them, like Sha, he trusted with his life. And together, this mismatched pair could provide some moments of light relief.

'I hear you've taken on an apprentice artilleryman?' Blastares grunted as he strolled alongside Procopius. The big man curled his bottom lip as if weighing his next words, then a mischievous glint appeared in his eye. 'Good idea. An old fellow like you should be making plans for his dotage.'

'Dotage? I…' Procopius' nose wrinkled as he looked up at his hulking friend, then his eyes grew hooded. 'You know what I say to the lad when I'm training him on *ballista* marksmanship?'

'Nope. Don't care either.' Blastares feigned indifference, pretending to examine the treeline studiously.

'I tell him to imagine that *you're* standing at the target, bollocks out, dangling over the centre.' Procopius walked a little taller as he said this, his age lines multiplied by his growing smile. 'Hits the centre nearly every time.'

Blastares' grin fell away, as if stolen by Procopius. 'Aye? Well at least… at least…' Blastares stammered, his eyes darting as he tried to invent some riposte.

But a cry cut the pair off: 'He rides!'

Apion looked over to the base of the tall pine. The toxotes who had been keeping watch up there thumped down onto the ground. 'Crispin rides from the fort,' the man repeated, taking up his bow and quiver. 'He is headed into the forest, roughly a mile to the south.'

The words were like a whetstone to Apion's senses. He shot to standing. All eyes looked to him, all eager to act at last. His riders had a chance of engaging Crispin before the Norman swept back inside the Black Fortress again, but his infantry would be too slow to traverse the forest floor. Still, he needed their numbers. His mind raced until he imagined the pawn line on a shatranj board. A crooked smile pulled at one edge of his mouth.

'*Skutatoi!*' he yelled to the eighty spearmen as they gathered in a square of rustling iron. Each of them hoisted their spears and crimson kite shields, pulled on their helms and wrapped their iron or leather lamellar klibania around their torsos, then strapped on their swordbelts holding their lengthy *spathion* blades. 'Line the southern edge of the clearing!' He jabbed a finger at the treeline, where a handful of pines had been felled and lay together. 'Be ready.'

'Yes, *Strategos*!' Peleus, the short *komes* at the head of the bandon cried, hoisting the crimson banner of Chaldia.

'And Komes,' Apion added, jabbing a finger at the woodcutting area. 'Take those too.'

Komes Peleus glanced to the pile of freshly hewn sapling poplar trunks – eleven feet in length – then grinned in realisation. 'The *menavlion*? Yes, sir!'

'Toxotai,' he then barked to the eighteen archers – including the two dappled with goose droppings. 'Wait on the flanks of our spearmen. Have your bows nocked and ready.'

'Yes, sir!' the archers replied in unison.

Apion turned to Sha, Blastares, Procopius and the nine Chaldian *kataphractoi* horsemen – already sliding on their iron klibania jackets and greaves, hoisting their lengthy lances. 'Come. We ride ahead,' he said as he swept his crimson cloak across his shoulders and slid his helm on, the black eagle feather plume juddering.

He cast one last look back at the skutatoi forming up in a line by the fallen pines and swept his spearpoint across them. 'Stand firm. You are my anvil.'

'Yes, *Haga*!' the spearmen replied with a roar as Apion and the twelve riders broke into a gallop and vanished into the southern forest.

Crispin crouched in the undergrowth, looking through the trees to a small village in the clearing beyond. A tavern, a kiln, a tannery and a timber grain silo stood at the centre of the settlement with just a few dwellings around them. No walls, no sentries. A hundred or so people milled to and fro, going about their daily business. A peaceful Seljuk settlement within Byzantine lands.

Crispin turned away from the sight and met the gaze of his seventy men, crouched behind him. He fished in his purse and drew out a gold *nomisma* claimed from one of the tax wagons. He bit into it, then threw the coin to the forest floor, the tooth marks clearly visible in the much-debased coinage. 'Pah! Nearly every imperial coin we take is but scrap metal. In there,' he jabbed a finger at the settlement, 'we will find fine Seljuk coin – silver *dirhams* and gold *dinars*.'

Just then, the sound of hooves from behind stirred him. He twisted round looking past his riders. It was a freckle-faced, red-haired rider from the garrison he had left back at the Black Fortress. 'Sir,' he panted, his face pale, his brow knitted. 'One of our scouts came in just after you left; he sighted a detachment of Byzantine soldiers just a few days ago. They were headed south, towards these woods.'

'How many?' Crispin's eyes narrowed.

'A hundred or so, maybe. A thematic levy.'

'A *hundred* thematic wretches – and I will call them farmers, for they are not soldiers – are sent to oppose us, and you shit your robes about it?'

All Crispin's riders jostled in laughter.

'Perhaps they will tangle themselves in our tent ropes and fall upon our caltrops again – like the last lot!' Crispin added. His men struggled to control their laughter now.

Reddening with anger and embarrassment, the rider snapped in reply, 'They are no rabble of ordinary soldiers. They are Chaldians, led by the *Haga*.'

The laughter faded.

Crispin's top lip twitched and he cast a sour glare around his riders. He had heard much of this stubborn strategos. *Heard much, yet seen nothing.* 'So the mention of a man's name is enough to silence you, is it?' He drew out a small purse on his belt and shook it. 'Then perhaps the rattle of good coin will be enough to bring the colour back to your cheeks?' He produced a pure-gold nomisma from the purse – shining with a lustre unlike the robbed tax money. 'Remember what our true paymaster said? Throw the borderlands into chaos. Let them know poverty, famine and fear in equal measure. And if you come by the *Haga*, slay him, and you will never want for gold again.'

A grumble of agreement sounded around his riders, each patting the similar small purses they carried.

'But we can turn our attentions to these Chaldians later,' Crispin said, lifting his conical helm onto his head, the nose-guard sliding into place between his ice-cold eyes. He glanced up through the canopy of leaves to the clear, sapphire sky. 'This fine day is wearing on and I am tired of sitting in the shade. What say you we whet our blades on Seljuk bone before lunch?' He flexed his fingers on his longsword hilt as he said this.

Wordlessly, his seventy men rose with him like a pit of snakes readying to strike. With a rustle of iron, they hoisted themselves onto their nearby mounts and gathered into a rough wedge formation. Crispin took his place at the head of the wedge, then kicked his mount into a trot. When the trees grew thinner, they clustered closer together and sped into a gallop, levelling their spears. When they burst into the settlement clearing, they unleashed a guttural roar that shook the forest.

Crispin set his eyes on the nearest of the villagers; a man, frozen in shock, his arms clutching at his two young sons. 'Ya!' he roared as his spear punched into the man's chest and trampled the two boys while the other riders spilled past him and swept around the settlement like raptors, spearing down terrified Seljuk families who tried to flee, hacking down with their longswords at those cowering in hope of mercy. In moments, the air was alive with screaming and a song of iron. Acrid black smoke billowed from the houses as his men put them to the torch.

'Bring me all they have!' Crispin cried out, tasting the bloodspray on his lips.

Just then, a dismounted Norman lancer emerged from the largest home in the village – a two-storey stone farmhouse. The man's face was spattered red and he tucked his tunic back over his groin as he stepped over a broken, semi-naked and lifeless form in the doorway – the Seljuk woman he had just defiled. In the other arm, he carried a small wooden chest. 'Good coins, sir!' he cried to Crispin, biting one, before taking a blazing torch from a comrade and hurling it into the farmhouse as an afterthought. 'Hundreds of them—'

His words ended in an animal grunt as two arrows thumped into his throat. He gawped at Crispin, then crumpled to his knees, the coin chest toppling and the contents spilling across the earth.

Crispin swung in his saddle, following the flight of the arrows. Thirteen imperial riders had emerged from the northern treeline. The central one – crimson-cloaked with a black eagle feather plume and a beard as grey as his iron armour – was still scowling behind his quivering bow, one eye shut tight, the open one emerald green. First, cold fear grabbed him as he recognised their kataphractoi garb. For a moment, he imagined the forests to be full of these ironclad Byzantine lancers. But he quickly saw that the woods were empty bar these thirteen. His fear melted and his rapacious grin returned.

'Riders!' he bellowed, summoning his seventy from the razing of the village. 'At them!'

His men reformed into a wedge behind him and the earth shuddered as they charged for the treeline. The black-plumed Byzantine bowman and his twelve seemed frozen for a few heartbeats, then they turned and fled, some throwing down their weapons in terror. *The Norman cavalry charge*, Crispin enthused, levelling his lance and training it on the back of the lead rider, *not a soul can stand against it!*

The going underfoot became uneven as they raced into the forest, branches thwacked on his helm and his armour, but the wedge remained together. He saw the lead Byzantine rider glance back at him again and again as the gap closed. The glinting emerald eyes were sharp, but lacking something, he realised. *No fear?* A shaft of sunlight blinded him momentarily and he realised the forest was thinning. Another clearing lay just ahead. At once, the Byzantine thirteen leapt over a fallen pine and into this glade. Crispin heeled his mount into a jump too, then he heard the lead rider cry out.

'Rise!'

From behind the fallen pine rose a wall of imperial skutatoi. Their faces were twisted in fury as they roared and hoisted up spears, the like of which he had never seen before – long and thick. Myrtle, ash and poplar saplings, carved to jagged tips. Crispin gawped helplessly as his stallion plunged onto the colossal lance before him, the tip piercing the beast's breast armour, flesh and heart, the lance barely moving such was its weight and so firmly was it grounded in the soil at the butt-end. Sky and earth changed places as Crispin was catapulted from the saddle. He heard his stallion's dying whinny and many more of his comrades and their mounts. Then, with a crunch of iron that shook him to his core, he thumped down onto the dust, rolling over and over. His soldier's instinct had him instantly grasping for his longsword and struggling to his feet. But he halted as a maw of Byzantine blades and speartips shot for his throat and hovered there. He glanced at each of their faces, pitiless, furious, then locked eyes with the black-plumed, emerald-eyed one with the iron-grey beard who approached on horseback. He walked his mount in a circle around Crispin, hand hovering above the ivory hilt of the Seljuk scimitar he wore on his swordbelt.

At last, this rider dismounted and strode through the teeth of Byzantine blades, coming nose to nose with Crispin. 'I should cut out your heart and throw it to the forest dogs, cur, but I fear your blood might poison them.'

They marched the disarmed Norman prisoners back through the forest, ignoring their foreign curses. When they reached the Seljuk village, Apion thrust his boot into Crispin's back, sending him sprawling, his helm tumbling from his head. Only sixteen of the Norman's fellow riders had survived the menavlion snare and they too were bundled along unceremoniously at spearpoint. The fifty Byzantine skutatoi he had sent on ahead were already working tire-lessly with the surviving Seljuk villagers, hoisting bucket after bucket of water from the village well and fighting the myriad fires that roared in the houses. The stench of burning flesh wafted over him and he fought the urge to retch. Once more, he longed for the satisfaction of slicing this dog's head from his shoulders, or forcing him to walk into the nearest blaze, to be burnt alive. But the brief was for Crispin to be taken alive, lest the many other Normans in imperial service took umbrage.

'How does the scavenger feel, returning to the ruined corpse?' he hissed as Crispin scrambled to his feet once more.

'They're only bloody Seljuks, what do you care?' Crispin snarled, swinging to face Apion, his blond hair dangling in his eyes. 'You'd rather fight men in imperial pay and protect the enemy?'

Apion snorted. 'I hear you're very much in imperial pay – helped yourself to wagon-loads of taxes. And this village is part of the empire. Seljuk blood in a man's veins does not make him an enemy. Black blood pulsing round the body of a so-called imperial mercenary, however...'

Crispin's fleshy jaw squared at this, as he and Apion glared at one another.

All around them, the fires began to dull, and the weak, exhausted coughing of villagers and skutatoi rang out. Komes Peleus and big Komes Stypiotes, faces soot-blackened and dripping with sweat, jogged up to Apion and threw up their arms in salute. 'The fires are quenched, *Haga*!'

At this, Crispin's pale, rounded face creased in a cold smile. 'So it is you?' He laughed with a ferocity that belied his predicament. 'The *Haga* dares to lecture me about virtue. I know of you, I've heard what you've done in your time. A slayer of souls, a burner, a death-bringer. You have no right to judge me.'

Apion felt shame coil around him like the cold hands of a wraith. Well used to its grip, he shook it off, grasping Crispin's collar, pulling him nose-to-nose. 'I have carried out some dark deeds in my time, aye,' he spat. 'I have even plunged a blade into my blood-brother's heart.' Memories of his last moments with Nasir stained his thoughts. 'So do not think I would hesitate to do the same to you!'

Crispin's smile vanished, his eyes darting. Apion could feel the man's heart pounding through his hauberk. Then the pace of the heartbeat slowed and a calmness fell over the rogue Norman once more.

'Your threats grow weaker with every repetition, *Haga*. If you wanted me dead it would be done by now. You have been ordered to take me alive, haven't you?'

Apion growled then shoved Crispin away. Two skutatoi quickly corralled the Norman at spearpoint.

'There is another option,' Crispin cooed, waving a hand in the direction of the Black Fortress. 'There is enough coin in my vaults now to keep a soldier in luxury, even a strategos like you.'

Apion's nose wrinkled. 'When the rest of your riders are prised from that hill, the money will go to the treasury, as intended,' he said flatly then turned away to survey the state of the village. 'To strengthen the border armies, to repair the forts and bolster the garrisons.'

'Ah, so you have no interest in such diluted metals.' Crispin shrugged.

Apion's glare hardened at the implication.

'But what about pure gold?' Crispin continued.

Apion ignored the man, instead accepting a tearful thank you from one old Seljuk woman. He switched to the Seljuk tongue to reply: 'I am only sorry my men and I could not intervene sooner.'

'...pure gold, and there is plenty more of it coming from my paymaster in Constantinople.' Crispin's haughty tones caught his attention once more. He swung round, one eyebrow cocked. The Norman was holding up a small purse from his belt, and had plucked a single, untainted, gold nomisma from it. When the coin caught the light, Apion strode back over to Crispin and grappled the man's wrist, transfixed by the piece.

'Ah, so pure gold is the key to controlling the *Haga*?' Crispin purred, sensing victory.

Apion prised the coin from the man's grasp, then drew his dagger and cut away Crispin's purse. He gave both to the Seljuk woman. 'Psellos' gold serves only to weed out the jackals,' he growled, sheathing his dagger. 'Now shackle him,' he called to his nearest spearmen. 'Ready him to be transported west, where he can answer to the emperor in chains.'

Apion barely noticed Crispin's face fall. The Norman was dragged away and Apion gazed at the spot where the man had stood, eager to flush the black truth of it all from his mind. Duplicity and treachery were still rife, it seemed. He thought of Romanus, the *Golden Heart*, the first emperor in living memory who promised to restore the empire's broken borders and bring peace to Anatolia. The emperor had yet to set out on the long-awaited campaign to capture the fortress of Chliat and secure the Lake Van region, yet already, Psellos had sowed the seeds of destruction in his path. He thought again of Eudokia's plea.

I beg you to muster your men then hasten to my husband's side on his campaign to Lake Van. Only there can you shield him from Psellos' further ruses...

CHAPTER 2

Blood River

It took several months for Apion to fully muster his Chaldians, but by late August they were together, marching under a baking sun as they trekked. Their hooves and boots crunched in time to the cicada song as they marched along the dusty track that wound across desert dry Mesopotamia – the brink of imperial territory. There were fifteen hundred men in all: fifty kataphractoi riders, a smattering of more lightly equipped kursores scout riders plus three vastly understrength *tourmae* of skutatoi spearmen and toxotai archers.

Apion tilted his drinking skin back and enjoyed a mouthful of cold spring water. Mercifully, there were plenty of brooks, wells and springs marked on his map of this eastern land. Mesopotamia was not like Chaldia or any of the other themata. There was no strategos here, no levy of land workers for the empire to call upon – indeed, even the populace was desperately meagre. Instead, this land was ruled by the imperial border *doukes* and patrolled by the mercenary tagmata raised by those men. It was just a few miles more to the south-east and the banks of the upper Euphrates, where they were to rendezvous with Emperor Romanus and his campaign army then finally strike out eastwards, to Lake Van. The sister fortress-towns in that distant land were the prize. Apion had never ventured as far east as that much talked of region, yet he was well aware of the delicate balance of power there: a scant Byzantine garrison already held the northerly fortress of Manzikert, but the lakeside fortress of Chliat was thought to be well guarded by a Seljuk warband. Each faction had long sought to hold both. He heard some of his kataphractoi riding behind him sharing their hopes and fears on the matter.

'Sultan Alp Arslan and all his iron hordes lie in wait by the lake,' one said. 'Many thousands of *ghulam* and *ghazi* riders.'

'Nonsense,' another scoffed. 'I hear that barely a thousand Seljuks man Chliat's walls. We will have that fortress in our grasp in good time.'

'Pah!' another surly rider countered. 'Why so much attention on Lake Van anyway? The land is bleak and far from the hub of either empire.'

Apion fell back a little, listening, eager to see how his men reacted to this. He saw one rider dab out his tongue to dampen his lips. It was Kaspax, a young rider who had recently taken the place of his slain father, Atticus, in the ranks of the precious Chaldian kataphractoi. The young man had an answer but was afraid to speak out against the grizzled veterans. Apion caught his eye and gave him an almost imperceptible nod.

'Because,' Kaspax started, his eyes darting uncertainly, 'because the broad tracts of land that run north of the lake are like a weak spot in our flank. They present an unspoilt path from enemy domains in the east, right into the heart of our lands, our ancient themata. The Gateway to Anatolia, they call it.'

Apion met each man's eyes with a stern gaze. 'And what an apt moniker, for a stronghold is only as strong as its weakest gate. The Antitaurus Mountains sweep along our empire's south-eastern borders and the Parhar Mountains dominate the north and the east,' he nodded to that hazy range, ever present in the horizon, 'like great ramparts that armies cannot traverse without enormous difficulty. But the Lake Van pass is a chink in the armour, a long, flat, broad and snaking route that opens inner Anatolia to all and sundry. The outposts of Manzikert and Chliat serve as fine watchtowers from which to guard the mouth of that route. While our garrison holds the former and the Sultan's men the latter, neither side has the advantage. But should the Sultan seize Manzikert, then he will be master of the gateway. He will be free to pour his armies into these lands,' he swept a hand back in the direction from which they had come, 'and upon our homes.' His men fell silent at the thought. Even the surly rider had paled.

'That is why our emperor summons us and the rest of his armies to march east at haste, to seize Chliat from Seljuk hands and to make Lake Van our own.' He clenched a fist and met each of their eyes. 'So when the Sultan comes calling, he will find only a wall of steel and sharpened spears — and the gateway closed to him and his hordes!'

They cheered at this, rapping their spears on their shields. Just behind, the ranks of the infantry joined in for good measure. '*Haga!*' they chanted.

Apion rode ahead again, satisfied that he had quelled their doubts and fired their hearts. He started to think ahead, glancing to the sun and judging how far they had to ride before they would be at the Euphrates. Just then, Sha ranged level with him, Kaspax coming with the Malian.

'We should probably form a vanguard, sir,' Sha suggested.

Apion squinted into the shimmering golden mountains that lay before them. 'True, we are at the edge of the empire.'

'Kaspax here reckons he's ready to lead the van.' Sha motioned to the lad.

Apion looked Kaspax over. His tanned features and curly, dark locks were reminiscent of the lad's father. But the similarities ended there: while everything about Atticus' demeanour had cried boldness, Kaspax's taut lips and wide eyes reeked of apprehension. He considered sending Sha on to lead the vanguard instead, then wondered what it might do to the lad's confidence. *Maybe confidence, that delicate flower, is all that is missing?* he mused. 'Take ten riders and stay vigilant.' He flicked his head forward.

Kaspax issued a stiff salute and set off, waving a clutch of ten horsemen with him.

'He's a good rider, sir,' Sha said, reading Apion's thoughts. 'He just needs to understand that. Keeps comparing himself to his father.'

'Understandable. Atticus was a boisterous big whoreson,' Apion chuckled, recalling the time the hulking soldier had challenged Blastares to a bout of wrestling after several skins of wine. That had been a messy evening.

With impeccable timing, a snorting noise sounded from behind them. Blastares, leading the infantry there, spat the contents of his throat to the ground then struck up a tuneless chorus to rouse the march-weary men:

'So I woke in a byre one morning.'

The men perked up and joined in. *So I woke in a byre one morning.*

'With me what I thought was a whore.'

With me what I thought was a whore.

'But when I opened my eyes, I got a mighty surprise.'

But when I opened my eyes, I got a mighty surprise… the men continued albeit a little more uncertainly.

'When I saw that I had screwed a boar!' Blastares roared in a joyous crescendo before falling silent, realising he was singing alone.

The column slowed just a fraction, all the riders looking at Blastares in horror. Apion and Sha shared a bemused glance as the big man reddened in shame.

'Eyes front!' Blastares barked to the riders, then twisted to the infantry who had let him down. 'And you lot, stay in line!' Red-faced, Blastares ranged forward to join Sha and Apion, cricking his neck this way and that in an overly vigorous manner. 'Just trying to lift their spirits. Ungrateful bast—'

'How is Tetradia?' Sha cut in.

Blastares' mood lifted at once, his humiliation of moments ago forgotten 'Wondrous,' he beamed.

Apion chuckled, recalling the curvaceous and 'lively' woman the big soldier had met at Melitene in the previous year's campaign.

'Wondrous, aye?' another voice added. Old Procopius rode level too now, barely suppressing a roguish grin. 'And I'm sure the wedding will be too.'

While Apion and Procopius grinned, big Blastares seemed to clam up at the mention of his impending marriage. 'Eh?' he frowned. 'Nah, nah. It'll be a simple affair. One or two guests, that's all. A few amphorae of wine, maybe.'

'For you to still your nerves?' Procopius cackled. 'Though you'd better leave some for me.'

Blastares cocked an eyebrow. 'Who said you were invited?'

Procopius looked shocked momentarily, then smiled, winking at Apion and Sha. 'Tetradia did. Said she'd need me to bolt the door at the church – stop you fleeing like a slinger at a swordfight.'

'Did she say that?' Blastares replied a little too quickly, his face paling.

Procopius, Sha and Apion shared an intrigued glance, then the old tourmarches cocked an eyebrow and replied: 'No, but perhaps I should come along, just in case.'

Spirits high, they came to the golden mountains and a winding valley that led down towards the Euphrates. They enjoyed some shade here, and neither heard nor sighted a single threat, only the recent spoor of a lion in the dust giving cause for caution. Moments later, they crested a saddle of land and a great cheer rose when they saw what lay downhill and beyond: the tumbling blue waters of the Euphrates and the vast Byzantine camp hugging its banks. A sea of tents, serried ranks of steel and a forest of fluttering banners. Apion could not suppress a broad grin as he saw the tall purple imperial banner and the bejewelled campaign cross in the centre, where Emperor Romanus' red satin tent had been set up. Psellos' manoeuvrings had been troublesome indeed, but the *Golden Heart* had marched east, unperturbed.

The camp was a hive of activity. Soldiers milled by their *kontoubernion* tents in groups of ten. They stood or sat by their campfires, cooking and chatting, some painting their shields to match the banners of their regiments, others grooming their mounts. Apion noted the vivid banners of the themata that had mustered here. The green of Charsianon, the sky-blue of Opsikon, the orange of Thrakesion, the tan of Colonea. A good twelve thousand spears and bows in there, he reckoned going by the number of tents. In the centre, he recognised the vivid gold banners of the Vigla and the pure-white standards of the *Varangoi* axemen. These two cavalry tagmata were sworn to protect the emperor at all costs. And then there were the slate-grey banners of the Scholae Tagma, one of the oldest and strongest imperial regiments. Nearly two thousand of these crack kataphractoi had been mustered, it seemed – many new horsemen had been recruited since the near-destruction of that tagma at Hierapolis the previous year. Including Apion's Chaldians, there were possibly as many as twenty thousand soldiers perched on this river's edge camp.

'Strategos!' a familiar voice cut across the babble.

Apion scanned the sea of faces, then broke out in a broad grin. 'Komes!' he laughed, sliding from his saddle to clasp forearms with the scarred figure sporting braided, greying locks. This was Igor, Komes of the Emperor's Household Varangoi. Clad in shell-like, pure white armour, the purity interrupted only by a black spider motif on the shin greaves, a shield strapped to his left shoulder and a huge *breidox* battle axe hanging behind his right, he was a fearsome sight.

'I heard you had ridden on ahead to take Chliat yourself,' Apion jested.

'Pah!' Igor swiped a hand through the air as if cutting with his axe. 'Given half a chance, I would have! But you know how these marches are – slower than a week in Helenopolis. And apparently we had to wait here… for you!' Igor donned a look of mock-rage then cackled. 'Now come, the emperor awaits you.' He beckoned Apion to the imperial tent area.

Apion turned to speak to Sha. The Malian had already pre-empted him, taking the reins of his Thessalian. 'I'll have the men set up our tents.' Then he grinned and added, 'Seems like we got here just too late to help fortify the camp… what a shame.'

As the Chaldians moved off to the eastern section of the camp demarcated for them, Apion and Igor strode on towards the ring of Vigla guards, who parted their pristine golden shields and let them into the emperor's tent area.

Emperor Romanus Diogenes was there, in the stretch of dust beside his tent. He wore a simple white tunic and boots as he drew and aimed a composite bow at a target some sixty paces away within the tent area, left eye screwed shut, the open cobalt eye narrowed as he took aim. Beside him was a tall, lean man with bronze skin, a hooked nose and flowing dark locks that hung to the chest of his rough, black tunic. This one was coaching the emperor on his archery technique, it seemed. Apion and Igor sidled up behind, taking care not to distract Romanus from his shot.

'Exhale and then hold your breath. Nock and raise the bow, begin your draw as you lift. Remember – two fingers and the thumb, no more, no less.' The dark one demonstrated this as the emperor carried out the instructions. 'Draw until your fingers near your face, then roll your shoulder back to stretch a little more until the string is almost at the corner of your lips. The air is dry and the arrow should fly true, so do not aim too high. Now… loose!'

Thock!

Romanus allowed a smile to creep over his face, lowering his bow and admiring the arrow quivering near the centre of the target. The dark man threw up his hands in delight. 'And that, *Basileus*, is the thumb draw – the draw of the Seljuks.'

'A steadier shot, a faster nock, and even a more powerful release,' Romanus mused, running a hand through his swept-back flaxen locks, his gaze lost in the target. 'If we can understand our enemy well enough, then he cannot surprise us.'

'Exactly,' the dark one said.

Apion spoke at last: 'Wise words, but who will teach the stubborn Greeks to abandon their traditional draw?'

Romanus and the dark one swung round to see who had spoken. 'Strategos!' Romanus beamed, his cobalt gaze flashing in the sunlight. Casting decorum aside, he strode forward and embraced Apion. 'It has been hard work keeping my men focused while we waited on you, but I insisted that we would not cross the river until the *Haga* was with us.'

'The ranks are eager, I hear?' Apion said.

'They are hungry to march on to Lake Van, to bolster Manzikert, to take Chliat and to seal the eastern borders. And tomorrow, Strategos, we will set off.' He gestured to the timber jetty on the section of riverbank that formed the camp's eastern perimeter. A fleet of eight round-hulled *pamphyloi* ferries bobbed there.

Apion noticed the dark one by the emperor's side eyeing the red-ink stigma on his arm. Romanus saw this too. 'Ah, permit me to introduce another of my finest officers. Manuel Komnenos, *Protoproedros*, a fine tactician… and a master archer to boot.'

'I have heard many tales of your efforts in these borderlands, *Haga*,' Manuel smiled.

Apion nodded curtly. Bitter experience had long ago taught him to withhold judgement and err on the side of caution whenever he met some new member of the imperial retinue. He managed a smile. That would do for now.

'Perhaps you can share some of your drills with the strategos?' Romanus suggested.

Manuel nodded. 'Certainly. Come, the men are still on the training field,' he said, stooping to feed a clump of hay to his nearby tethered mount — a fine, muscular grey stallion with a white blaze on its face.

The three made their way through the northern sector of the camp, trailed — as ever — by a clutch of Varangoi axemen. A tangy scent of stewing goat meat and a waft of baking bread greeted them as they made their way past the tents of the Thrakesion Thema. Men rose from around their campfires to salute their emperor, some even recognising Apion too.

Next, they came to the workshops, a series of tents where the tink-tink of hammers and sawing of timber filled the air. A small furnace had been set up and the blaze seemed to distort the air around it with its ferocious heat. A smith worked to pattern-weld a spathion, a technique that would give the blade a supple core but a hard edge. A pile of recently crafted weapons lay stacked nearby. This army was indeed well-prepared and eager.

'So we are to leave in the morning?' Apion asked.

'As soon as dawn breaks. I have arranged for Doux Philaretos to remain here as a rearguard.' He pointed to a figure standing atop a small wooden dais by the riverbank, barking his riders into formation.

Apion squinted and spotted the unmistakable doux there. Philaretos had the look of some villainous, murderous type, his face red and scowling under his close-cropped, receding hair. This and his somewhat testy and firebrand nature had troubled Apion when they first met, but he had proved himself valorous and noble in the taking of Hierapolis and Apion had been more than happy to judge him on those deeds during that fraught campaign.

'He will stay at the camp with a third of our forces, protecting us from any attack on our rear as we march east and blocking any westwards Seljuk push into Anatolia.'

They came to the camp's north gate then climbed a ladder to the top of one of the watchtowers flanking it. From this vantage point, he could see the spearmen and archers of the Opsikon Thema going through their manoeuvres on the flatland outside. They worked under an incessant barrage of orders from the *kampidoktores* – a squat, bald man who swished his cane around as if batting the soldiers into line whenever they strayed. The space was overlooked by the towering Mount Taurus, its lofty summit dusted with snow, as if mocking those toiling in the oppressive heat below. Apion imagined himself up there, looking down. His lips played with a smile as he imagined the men like pieces on a giant shatranj board, just as old Mansur had taught him to.

Manuel Komnenos called down to the kampidoktores mid-tirade, halting him. 'Have them practise the square variations,' he said.

'Yes, sir!' the kampidoktores yelled, then flicked a finger at the *buccinator* by his side. Moments later, the *buccina* cry sent the ranks of men scurrying back and forth. Their flat line dissolved and they reformed in a square, hollow in the centre.

'A fine square. It protects our men, and dilutes the front of our enemy,' Apion observed.

'Indeed, Strategos. A square, but with a difference,' Manuel countered.

It took Apion a moment to notice, then he saw it; as usual, spearmen formed the outer layer of the square, three ranks deep. They protected the smaller square of archers inside, again, three ranks deep. This way, the toxotai could loose upon outlying enemies without fear of attack. But there was also another layer of three spearmen inside the square, ringing the backs of the archers and framing the small hollow centre. 'Insurance should the square be compromised?'

'Exactly!' Manuel said. 'Should a pack of Seljuk lancers break inside, there will be no easy slaughter of our archers, just a nest of spears!' He pressed his thumb and forefinger together. 'A hardy formation like this could be the key to staving off our enemies and keeping our borders safe.'

Apion felt a smile touch one edge of his lips, seeing Manuel's eyes sparkle at the notion of bringing peace to the borderlands. An earnest fellow, it seemed. But something troubled him about the square. 'Yet this lessens the number of spears on your front.'

'It would, but should we need their number then—' He stopped and waved to the kampidoktores. Another buccina cry. Another stampede of boots. Almost faultlessly, the spearmen inside the square hurried through the ranks of archers and into the outer ranks of spearmen. In just a few heartbeats, the outside of the square had been bolstered by some three hundred spears.

Apion smiled fully now. 'This is a play on the formations of the past,' he realised.

'Indeed,' Manuel nodded.

Apion scoured the square one more time, then his eye snagged on something. Three spearmen on the front ranks of the square wore mail shirts, and another two donned felt coats, while all the rest on the front were clad in iron lamellar klibania.

'Speak, man!' Romanus chuckled, seeing Apion's eyes narrow. 'Manuel was eager to hear your advice.'

Apion pointed to the mismatched men in the front. 'You should keep your front uniform at all costs. The square will only be as strong as its weakest point. These five should be afforded iron klibania like the men they stand with.'

'Mail is a sturdy armour,' Manuel countered.

'For a sword slash, maybe.' He patted his own klibania-clad chest. 'But the overlapping iron plates on a klibanion help to spread the blow of Seljuk arrows more evenly than mail or felt. And believe me, even then a single arrow can still feel like the kick of an angry mule.'

Manuel nodded with a grin. 'Then the smith will be busy tonight. Is there anything else, Strategos?'

Apion cast his eye across the square again. 'Have the men had a chance to use these manoeuvres in anger – and in particular, against the Seljuks?'

Manuel shook his head. 'That is one part of their training I cannot provide. The lash of a drillmaster's tongue and swish of his cane can only do so much. And I too have yet to face them in the field.'

Romanus clasped a hand to each man's shoulder and looked to Apion. 'That's why we need men like you, Strategos. There is plenty of bread and wine in my tent, not to mention a shatranj board. You should use the rest of today to share your knowledge of our foe. Then tomorrow, we will march, strengthened by it.'

Apion beheld Manuel, Romanus and the sea of serried ranks throughout the camp. For that moment he experienced an odd feeling. All, for once, felt right.

The sun dipped behind the western skyline of Constantinople, bathing the lofty heights of the Imperial Palace in its last light and casting a shaft of deep red inside one set of tall, open shutters there.

Michael Psellos leaned back in his chair, his belly full of lark tongues and falcon eggs and his skin bathed in the fiery sunset. He swirled his cup of well-watered wine, inhaled its sharp, fruity aroma, then took a deep gulp to wash the meal down. He smoothed at his tightly curled, short grey locks, adjusted the purple felt cap on his crown and looked around the grand dining chamber, shivering with delight at the possibilities. The palace was devoid of its emperor. Then he glanced through the tall shutters, his gaze trawling across the Hippodrome, the Forum of Constantine and the forest of marble columns, statues and fine domes. The city was at his behest. He flexed his gem-ringed fingers on the collar of the gold brocade robe he had taken from the emperor's chambers that morning. *With a tailor's skilled hand, this could be a fine fit*, he mused.

A watery belch from the far side of the table stirred him from his reverie. His age-lined, pinched features creased even further in distaste.

John Doukas, tall and black-bearded, simply wiped a hand across his mouth and continued eating, unperturbed. This oaf was to be endured only because he held the key to the imperial throne – the Doukas family having long insisted that they should be returned to the helm of the empire. He wondered who else from that family line might make a more suitable pawn. *Anyone?* he concluded, bitterly.

Just then, Psellos noticed movement at the main chamber door. The two *Numeroi* spearmen standing guard there stepped aside. Before Psellos could rise from his seat to berate them, a figure strode in and stood at the head of the table.

'I bring news that will sweeten your banquet,' the tall, elegant lady said. She wore a dark blue robe that clung to her lithe figure, and her silvery locks were swept together in a swirl atop her head. Her fine-boned features were alive with a smile that was at odds with her cold stare.

John twisted only to glower at her.

'Ah, Lady Eudokia,' Psellos purred, rising now to bow as if in defer-ence. This woman was the widow of the last member of the Doukas family who had held the throne. By wedding Romanus Diogenes and supporting his rise to power, she had broken the Doukid line and caused the rift in power.

Eudokia ignored John's glare and continued as if Psellos had not spoken. 'The rumours we heard have been confirmed; the rogue mercenary of Colonea, Crispin of Normandy, was taken captive by the Strategos of Chaldia some months ago. He now languishes in exile and will trouble my husband's campaign no longer.'

Psellos held her defiant gaze as long as he could, until he felt an incessant itching on his chest. 'That is good news, indeed,' he said, his top lip quivering in suppressed ire.

With that, Eudokia swept from the room and Psellos slumped back to sitting. He glared at the spot where Eudokia had stood, his mood black, the itch on his chest growing ferocious.

John threw down a duck bone and sighed. 'We can eat and drink and pretend we are kings. But when the morning comes, we will wake as mere courtiers.'

'You are unhappy, master?' Psellos asked through taut lips.

John snorted. 'You spent much of my family's money buying off those useless curs in the border tagmata – and what of them?' he roared with a mocking laugh. 'Crispin languishes in exile, and the others you bought were little but an annoyance to Diogenes' march east. What reason have I to smile?'

Psellos issued a terse smile. *Without my wits, oaf, you would already be in exile or dead.* He sucked in a breath through flared nostrils and held John's gaze. More, the itch on his chest stung like fire. This often happened when he became vexed. He scratched and scratched at the coin-sized spot there. Well, it was coin-sized at first, when that crazed old crone had inflicted the mark upon him – with some hidden brand, he guessed – last winter. But in recent weeks it had grown. Now it was the size of a small plate. Angry red, the flesh was blistered and it wept when he scratched at it too much. He felt the skin split as he scratched at it now and this broke his semblance of calm.

John leaned forward and repeated in a flat tone: 'I said; what reason have I to smi—'

'Diogenes is at a critical juncture,' Psellos snapped, grabbing a cup of cool water and holding it against his chest – this seemed to calm the itch. 'He has withdrawn all but the scantest of funding from the cities. Almost every coin from the treasury goes to the armies. The people are unsettled...' he gestured to the Hippodrome, lying empty and unused as had been the case for some six months, '...they need their races and their games!'

John shrugged at this. 'This will not tip the balance. We need Diogenes to fail at the head of his army. When the people *and* the army give up on him, only *then* have we won.'

Psellos smiled coldly, sensing an opportunity to toy with his puppet. 'Yet the balance might still swing against us, master. If he succeeds in strengthening the imperial hold on Manzikert and in seizing Chliat, the eastern passes will be protected and the borders will be safe, the spending can be balanced once more. The people will love him and the army will revere him... and his legacy as emperor will be assured.'

John's jaw dropped, strings of meat dangling from his teeth and a foul look in his eyes. 'If you are trying to encourage me, advisor, then you have failed. Remember, it is your job to ensure that the balance tilts in our favour.'

Psellos ignored the overbearing rebuke. 'If I was to guarantee you that Diogenes will not take Chliat this year, would this calm you?'

John frowned. 'What? No man can make such a guarantee.'

'Oh, but I am no ordinary man,' Psellos smiled. His thoughts flashed to the Numeroi scout riders he had despatched some months ago. *Ride into enemy lands. Spread word amongst our foe of the emperor's planned route.*

'What have you done?' John whispered, a savage grin rippling across his lips.

Psellos simply reached out to pour more wine into their cups. 'I will explain all as we eat and drink, master. As kings!'

Doux Philaretos stood on the edge of the timber jetty as the last of the pamphyloi fleet returned from the far banks to be re-moored there. He ran a hand over his sweat-soaked scalp, burning in the morning sun, then looked across the river and off to the east, watching the last silvery flashes and plumes of dust dissipate at the tail of the departing campaign army. They moved with a broad front towards Lake Van. When they slipped into the heat haze and could be seen no more, he issued a contented grunt, then swung round to look over the camp that would serve as the rearguard's headquarters.

Six thousand men had been entrusted to him. The sixteen hundred toxotai loosed arrow after arrow at a practice range outside the camp's western gate, by the saddle of land in the shady valleys. The rest were inside the camp. Some four thousand of them were skutatoi; the majority of these men had laid down their weapons and iron jackets and now milled about their tents, jabbering, cleaning their kit or praying. Meanwhile, the bandon of three hundred kursores riders busied themselves grooming and exercising their mounts. They were content in their activities in this still and warm land, and rations and water were plentiful. He squinted up at the sun. 'With a little shade, this place will make a fine home for the next few weeks,' he surmised.

When an odd rumbling noise sounded from the north, he instinctively swept a suspicious eye around the camp's mountainous surroundings, then squinted at the shaded face of Mount Taurus. A shower of rocks tumbled from the heights there, the noise echoing across the riverbank. He chuckled and shook his head. Then he remembered the advice of the tourmarches, Procopius, who served under the *Haga*. Before setting off with the Chaldians in the emperor's column, the prune-faced old officer had implored him:

Decrease the size of the camp. Fill in the ditches and throw up new ones that will be more easily defensible for your reduced numbers. You can rebuild the original camp when the emperor returns. And keep a strong watch at all times.

Philaretos snorted at the notion. 'Perhaps, old man,' he spoke into the ether, then turned back to look across the river and east, shading his eyes from the sun. He imagined the emperor's army moving along the broad, winding tracts of land that led to Lake Van. 'But you should first concern yourself with your own marching camp – for it will likely be you who encounters any Seljuk foe.' Then he smirked, drawing his gaze in across the tumbling torrents of the Euphrates. 'And unless they bring ferries of their own, any invading riders from the east might have to content themselves with watching our fine camp from the far riverbanks.'

He jostled with laughter at his own joke, then turned away from the river and strode towards the heart of the camp, where his tent now stood in place of the emperor's. *A cup or two of wine?* he mused as his guards parted. He made to sweep his tent flap open, but his hand froze. He noticed his mount, tethered nearby, scuffing its hooves in agitation. Then it snorted, its ears pricking up.

'What's wrong, boy?' he cooed, stepping over to the piebald stallion.

His question was answered by a chorus of panicked cries from the western valleys. His eyes widened as he saw the archers out there break into a reckless run, racing back towards the camp. He licked his lips and felt his throat shrink as he saw a dust plume and dark shapes cresting the saddle of land in the shady valley. An instant later, the thrum of loosing arrows sounded, and the air behind the fleeing Byzantine archers darkened as a storm of arrows plunged down upon their fleeing backs. Hundreds fell and hundreds more stumbled over the fallen.

'Ghazis!' Philaretos gasped, clutching at the pole of his standard in disbelief, seeing the Seljuk riders swoop like raptors over the saddle of land and down towards the camp. Spiked, conical helms. Iron, horn or leather armour. Nocked bows, levelled spears and raised scimitars. His eyes swept over them once, twice and again. Still, more poured over the saddle. Five, six, no – seven thousand, he realised.

The ghazis unleashed a howling war cry as they caught up with the fleeing toxotai. Without armoured spearmen to protect them, the fleeing Byzantine bowmen stood no chance, falling to the flashing curved blades and sharp lances of these swift riders. Blood spouted and puffed up through the still heat, screams were cut short and the archers were felled like wheat. Those who tried to break away were punched to the ground, backs peppered with arrows.

'Close the gates!' Philaretos roared, pulling the standard from the earth and waving it frantically to and fro as the ghazi mass raced for the open western gate. The skutatoi were in disarray, men tripping over each other as they hurried to find their armour and weapons. Just sixteen guarded the open gate in arms and armour. They threw down their spears and shields in an attempt to close the timber gates. Philaretos rushed to aid them, throwing his shoulder to the stubborn gate. It was inches from coming into line with the locking bar, when his world was thrown upside down. He and the sixteen were cast back through the dust as the gates were barged back open. The tide of ghazis poured inside the camp and spilled across the sea of tents. The unprepared skutatoi threw up what defence they could, jabbing spears, swinging burning firewood or hurling rocks at them. Those who had taken up their shields and spears in time tried to gather together, but the swooping ghazis gave them no time, breaking apart these determined clusters of men and cutting them down. Philaretos, dazed, slumped and unseen by the open western gate, blinked again and again at the rout that ensued. For the first time in his career he was utterly lost. He saw his six thousand fall, limbs shorn, skulls crushed, chests pocked with arrows. Some Byzantines splashed into the shallows of the Euphrates, only to have their skulls split by pursuing Seljuk riders, and soon there were hundreds of corpses drifting off downriver in a crimson wash. One ghazi was the most ferocious of all. A scale-vested rider crowned with a stud-rimmed spike helm. His face was a mask of shadow, with just green eyes glinting, scouring the fray. He cut one man down, then another, swiftly turning to find the next at haste as if searching for the one death that would satisfy him.

Philaretos watched this one, numb with fear. When a gawping Byzantine head bounced past his feet, and a mizzle of blood settled upon him, something changed. He looked up, seeing some other ghazi who had beheaded the soldier. At once, the shame of his folly turned into anger. He leapt up, ducking the thrown spear the rider aimed at him, then drawing his spathion and hacking it through the rider's thigh. Flesh cleaved and bone shattered, the rider fell from the saddle in gouts of blood. Philaretos leapt onto the riderless mount and heeled the beast this way and that, parrying, hacking and ducking a storm of blows as he tried to find some hope of a counter attack. But there was nothing, he realised. He set his eyes upon the western gate. Most of the ghazis had spilled inside the camp's walls now, indulging in the slaughter. The land outside was free of enemies. He filled his lungs and bellowed to all who could hear.

'Retreat!' he cried, helping one skutatos into the saddle behind him. 'Abandon the camp. Head for the mountains!'

A dust plume the size of a colossal thundercloud billowed up in the column's wake. Apion rode with the emperor and his retinue amidst the cavalry head of the column, while Sha led the Chaldians in the infantry body. So far, he had enjoyed high spirits with the rest of the column, chuckling as riders of the Vigla Tagma mocked Igor when the big varangos used his axe blade like a mirror to apply black smudges of kohl on his lower eyelids.

The morning's march had seen them gradually ascend into the Armenian plateau where the air was thinner but still excruciatingly hot. They stopped at noon to eat a hearty meal of fresh bread, mutton and berries. He had seldom seen his Chaldians and the rest of the army quite as eager, yet as the day wore on, a nagging sense of doubt settled upon him. He couldn't quite place it, but he felt something was wrong.

'You look glum, Strategos. Something on your mind?' Romanus asked, his face uplit from the fine silver and white armour jacket he wore.

'Nothing,' he replied. 'Not a thing. This campaign has been impeccable so far, and we are but a week away from Lake Van. Chliat might soon be ours.'

'Then I'd loathe to see you on a bad day,' Romanus chuckled, his white stallion snorting as if in agreement.

'Perhaps it is the absence of struggle that perturbs me, *Basileus*.'

Romanus' brow knitted. 'Aye, not a single Seljuk blade… nor a Doukas snake to be seen.'

Yet. Apion thought. He shook his head, hoping this might cast off his doubts. 'Maybe I seek trouble when there is none,' he offered.

Romanus made to reply, when the pained screeching of an eagle sounded. The noise was so shrill that it cut through the dull thunder of boots and hooves. Indeed, the column slowed just a fraction, all heads looking up and around. The screeching continued. When Apion saw that the sky was azure and marked with neither bird nor cloud, he knew his dread was well-placed. As the cries rang out unabated and the army continued to look to the skies, Apion felt his gaze drawn to the east. There in the dancing heat haze he saw a solitary figure standing in the army's path. Her silvery hair and white robes fluttered in the gentle breeze and her sightless eyes pinned him. She held up the palm of one hand as if barring their way, and shook her head, her features drawn and riddled with sorrow. An instant later and she was gone, as if swallowed by the rippling heat haze.

'What is that infernal—' Romanus started, searching the skies for the absent eagle. But he stopped, hearing the rapid thudding of a galloping horseman approaching from the rear of the column and twisting to look.

Apion tore his gaze from the spot where the crone had been, then turned in his saddle to look back with the emperor. A chorus of chatter broke out, as if conjured by the lone kursoris who swept towards the emperor. The man was wearing a dented helm and a white tunic that was stained brown with dried blood, one arm was clumsily looped around the reins, the hand hanging limp and the tendons of his wrist lacerated. Igor and the varangoi bunched up before Romanus as the injured rider slowed and stopped before the emperor. The column drew to a halt as the rider tried to dismount but instead he fell, panting. His skin was pallid and slick with sweat, and his eyes were black-rimmed.

'*Basileus*,' he gasped, righting himself with his trembling good arm. 'A Seljuk host roams in imperial lands. They came at us from the west. They must have breached the southern borders.'

Apion realised what had happened before the scout could recount the tale.

'They fell upon our camp this morning. Doux Philaretos and the rearguard have been driven into the hills. Scant few survived the attack and now the Seljuk riders have ridden on into our heartlands, to raid the themata.'

The chatter of the ranks rose into panic.

Romanus was silent, his gaze growing distant. Apion saw the sparkle of hope in his eyes fade. In that instant, the promise of the campaign had been snuffed out. 'Raise the standards,' he said to the *signophoroi* by his side, clutching the great purple imperial banners. Then he cast his gaze over the vast ranks of the column. 'We must hasten back to our heartlands, to quell the threat there and avenge our fallen brothers.' The babble died at this. 'God is with us. Let us march with haste!' he cried. The column cried out in approval, the desperate cheer sweeping back across the miles of silvery warriors and vivid banners. Then, like a writhing serpent, they set about turning to face back to the west.

Romanus waited where he was, taking a moment to turn east once again, gazing to the heat haze that blended sky and earth in the distance, to the wide route they would have taken to Lake Van. Desperation and despair danced in his eyes now.

'We will return next year, *Basileus*,' Apion offered.

'A year is time aplenty to see an emperor cast from his throne, Strategos.'

Apion nodded, knowing there was no reply that could sweeten this acrimonious truth.

'What troubles me most, Strategos, is...' Romanus said, turning to him, his face suddenly gaunt and drawn, '...how did they know we were here? Seljuk warbands coming from the south and raiding the rich lands of southern and eastern Anatolia I can understand. But for them to come here, to this dry, dusty no-man's land and fall upon our rearguard? That is no coincidence.'

Apion sighed. 'I regret that I can only agree, *Basileus*.'

Both men instinctively turned their eyes back to the west, beyond the horizon, thinking of the distant imperial capital and the vultures who nested there.

CHAPTER 3

An Elusive Foe

Apion crouched in a myrtle copse at the southern edge of a vast green-gold plain in northern Cilicia. The cicada song grew intense as he scoured the features of the shrub-dotted lands ahead, part-obscured in a gentle heat-haze. A few miles to the east there was a small Byzantine village. He saw the handful of felt-armoured garrison skutatoi standing at the gatehouse of the town's weak timber walls. Half a mile north across the plain was another grove like this one. To the west, there was nothing but open flatland. His eyes scoured the horizon there. *Come on.*

It had been a fraught month since the disaster at the Euphrates. They had returned to the riverside camp to find a carpet of dead and wounded. They had spent the rest of that day and the next burying the fallen. It was on the second night that Doux Philaretos had come out of hiding, leading the pack of nine hundred or so survivors down from the safety of the mountains. The doux had been a sorry sight, his face caked in dirt and blood, and his eyes heavy with shame. The weeks since had been spent chasing the rampaging Seljuk army throughout Byzantine lands. They had hastened through western Colonea, only to find ruined villages littered with corpses and burnt-out forts strewn with mutilated garrison soldiers. The story had been the same as they pursued the enemy riders south through the border themata of Sebastae and Lykandos, then on to the west, into the inner themata of Cappadocia and Anatolikon, where they arrived too late to save the city of Iconium from the raiders' wrath. Indeed, the city walls were blackened with soot by the time they came within sight of it, and the battlements lined with severed Byzantine heads on spikes. This had enraged the emperor. But even when Romanus left Manuel Komnenos and the infantry behind, leading the far swifter cavalry ahead in an effort to intercept the Seljuk raiders, they were still too slow and so the pursuit continued. Just a few days ago, the chase had led them here, to the southern Thema of Cilicia.

He clutched a shard of polished silver in his palm, then shot a glance to the early autumn sun. It was well past noon, and heat and frustration prickled on his skin. The Seljuk host had been sighted a few hours ago, some way to the west, heading in this direction. And this timber-walled village was the only settlement in miles. It had to be where they were headed. *Yet surely they should be here by now?*

'Something's wrong,' Blastares whispered by his side.

'Not necessarily,' Apion hissed, staving off his own doubts. 'We wait.'

Just then, something moved. In the western emptiness, a puff of dust kicked up. All his senses sharpened and he held his breath. When he saw a racing deer, his heart sank. Then, as he made to exhale, his gaze snagged on a lone rider chasing the deer. A ghazi, cutting across the plain on a dark steppe mare, drawing and loosing his bow, his long, braided dark hair billowing in his wake. The rider howled in glee as his arrow punched into the deer's side, felling the animal.

Apion looked behind the lone rider. The horizon rippled in the heat haze. Green and gold danced together. A heartbeat later he felt the ground judder and a blotch of colour appeared, then spilled across the horizon. Thousands of Seljuk riders rumbled into view. Iron helms, brightly painted shields and speartips glinting in the sun. He twisted to Blastares. 'Ready the men.' The big tourmarches rose and scuttled away to the rear of the myrtle copse. Apion shuffled forward, careful not to break cover, then cupped the polished silver shard in his palm. He tilted it up to the sun and caught its rays then flicked it just a fraction. Once, twice and again. He watched the far wood keenly until the three flashes of reply came, then he turned and followed Blastares' path through the undergrowth to meet with the serried wedges of cavalry hidden just behind the grove – some fifteen hundred thematic riders, including Sha, Blastares, Procopius, Kaspax and the fifty Chaldian kataphractoi, the riders stroking their mounts to keep them still and silent. All for this moment. *Mount*, Apion mouthed as he leapt up onto his Thessalian, slipped on his plumed helm and took up his lance. Then he flicked a hand up and forward in silence.

The Byzantine riders broke forward at a walk, moving round the eastern edge of the grove in three fang-like wedges. From the northern wood, another three such fangs rumbled forward – the best of the Varangoi, the Vigla and the Scholae riders with the emperor amongst them. The Seljuk mass spilled along the plain between these two unseen cavalry wings. The jaws of the trap were set, ready to close on the marauding horde. Although numbering only three thousand, the Byzantine cavalry were more heavily armed and armoured than the seven thousand ghazis. And if they could catch them by surprise, fall upon their flanks…

A buccina blared from the emperor's riders across the plain.

'Charge!' Apion roared, kicking at his Thessalian's flanks. At once, he and his three wedges of riders broke forward in a gallop onto the plain. From the northern wood, the emperor's men charged likewise. Apion lay flat in the saddle, levelling his lance, eyes trained on the Seljuk horde. They slowed momentarily, heads switching between the two Byzantine cavalry wings coming for them from north and south. At that moment, Apion was sure the snare had succeeded. So certain was he of coming battle that he saw in his mind the image that had followed him since his earliest days:

A dark, arched doorway, the timbers desiccated and ancient. He heard the striking of flint, saw tongues of flame shoot out from under the door, licking like a demon readying to feast. His grip tightened on his lance and his heart pounded like a battering ram against his ribs.

But in a heartbeat the fire in his heart was extinguished as the Seljuk horde shot apart before him like a flock of birds evading a predator. They split into two groups. The foremost riders bolted forward at a gallop, slipping clear of the two sets of Byzantine riders, and the rearmost riders wheeled away, back to the west. Apion reined in his mount, seeing that the snare had failed, seeing the two jaws of the trap slow to a canter, lances and blades unsullied. Before he had time to look to the emperor for direction, he heard the thrum of Seljuk bows.

The hail was thick but inaccurate, arrows punching down all around the two slowing jaws of the failed trap. It was not meant to be a lethal strike, merely a means to give the fleeing Seljuk horde an extra few moments to make their break. Most of the missiles landed in the dust, but a fair number glanced from the iron coats and helms of the riders, and he heard a thin chorus of cries and whinnies where they found their way in between the iron cladding of horse or rider. As soon as the hail passed, Apion pulled on his reins to swing his mount round.

He watched as the ghazis who had turned to flee westwards arced round the southern edge of the plain, behind the myrtle grove, to join with their comrades in the east. Reunited they rode on to the eastern horizon, mercifully subjecting the timber-walled village to just a shower of arrows as they passed.

A wedge of Scholae riders burst away from the emperor's side, haring after the fleeing Seljuk pack.

'Come back, you fools!' Romanus roared, tearing off his purple-plumed helm and throwing it to the dust. 'You will not catch them. Have you learned nothing in these last weeks?'

A buccina keened to convey this message and the galloping Scholae riders slowed and returned, while the Seljuk horde became but a glint on the horizon. A nauseatingly familiar sight, Apion thought as he joined the emperor.

Romanus was surrounded by Igor, the varangoi and Doux Philaretos.

'Like a whore in oil,' Philaretos grunted, watching the Seljuks slip away.

'It worked at Hierapolis,' Romanus hissed through clenched teeth, punching a fist to his palm as he looked to the northern and southern woods from which his two cavalry wings had sprung.

Apion recalled the move, when he and Romanus had led two wings of cavalry, bursting from the cover of the northern and southern walls of the desert city to ensnare the Seljuk ranks amassed by the western gate, pressing them onto the hardy Byzantine spearmen standing firm there. 'But then our enemy was already engaged with what infantry we had. Those riders,' he flicked a finger to the horizon, 'have never stayed in one place long enough to let us draw up our spearmen and archers.'

Romanus looked north. Somewhere beyond the horizon, Manuel Komnenos and the infantry section of the weary campaign army were marching at haste to catch up, but still nearly a hundred miles behind, going by this morning's report from the scout rider. 'Then we have to find a way to bring our spears to bear.'

'We could try to lure them northwards, onto our infantry?' Philaretos suggested.

Apion shook his head. 'They will not follow us. They mean only to evade us, to sack towns and cause as much disruption as possible.'

'Then we should continue the pursuit. We can only hope that they will slip up soon, surely?' Philaretos grumbled.

'Hope is a fine thing, Doux, but it is not a strategy,' Apion replied as gently as he could manage.

'You are adept at revealing the weaknesses in the suggestions of others, Strategos,' Philaretos snapped. 'Perhaps you might offer an alternative solution?'

Apion looked to the red-faced doux and the rest of the retinue. His thoughts swam as he recalled the terrain of this southern thema. They needed two things; a choke point and a regiment of infantry to block it. There were many choke points to the east, where the Seljuk horde were headed, but no infantry bar a few sparse local garrisons. Then he thought of something else, high up in the Antitaurus Mountains. His eyes glinted and a crooked smile pulled at one edge of his lips. 'This may not be to your liking…'

Apion pulled his crimson cloak tighter around his shoulders as they rode up the winding mountain path. It was mid-September and dark, clear nights like this brought with them a biting cold, especially at this altitude. He wore a long-sleeved tunic both for warmth and to hide his red-ink *Haga* stigma – figuring it might distract those he was to parley with. With him were his trusted three, plus the young rider, Kaspax. They had set off from the imperial army and ridden hard for a day, moving due east to these mountains while the Seljuk horde busied themselves terrorising the Byzantine settlements in the lower foothills just a few miles south.

He glanced to the mountaintop above. It glowed orange, silhouetting a stocky timber palisade wall, watchtowers and sentries. Philaretos' reaction to his plan rang in his thoughts once more.

The Armenian hill princes? Have you lost your senses, man?

Apion chuckled dryly at the memory. The doux was bound to rubbish whatever plan he put forward – the man was still pickled with shame over being routed at the Euphrates camp. As they rounded the last section of path leading up to the hilltop town's gatehouse, he saw the four sentries standing before the gates brace. One of the sentries called out to challenge Apion and his night visitors. Momentarily, Apion wondered if Philaretos had been right. For it was a feral cry, a challenge.

'Apion of Chaldia,' he replied. 'I come on behalf of Emperor Romanus Diogenes.'

The torch near the gates guttered in the chill breeze and for a moment, the lead sentry's face was illuminated: dark-skinned, scarred, with a rich green headscarf on his scalp and a thick beard on his chin. His nose wrinkled and he spat on the ground. 'Byzantines,' he growled, his mail shirt rustling as he squared his shoulders. 'You come to speak with Prince Vardan?' The men beside him laughed. 'I see no reason why I should let you keep your lives, let alone open our gates to you.' As he said this, twelve shadows rose up from behind the palisade walls accompanied by the tune of stretching, creaking bows. The dancing torchlight revealed something else. On either side of the gates, two limp bodies dangled, impaled through the chest on roughly hewn spikes, throats cut, flesh grey, their eyes gone to the crows. It looked as if one of them at least wore the battered armour of a Byzantine spearman.

Apion kept his gaze on the lead sentry. 'You have family in these mountains and the surrounding plains?'

The sentry lost his steely gaze for but a moment, then the scowl returned. 'What is it to you?'

'I come to offer your prince a deal that will see all in these lands, Byzantine and Armenian alike, spared the edge of the Seljuk sword.'

The sentry frowned. 'You speak of the horde? They are some way west of here — I heard they sacked Iconium?'

Apion held his wavering gaze. 'They tore the place apart but we drove them off. I saw the blackened ruin they left behind. Now they are here, only miles away, and they are not yet tired of slaughter and plunder. All I ask of you is that you let me speak with your prince.'

The lead sentry's scowl faded and his shoulders slumped just a fraction. A time passed then, wordlessly, he nodded to his comrades, who hurried forward to strip Apion and his men of weapons. When one of the sentries tried to take the hemp sack from Apion's saddle, Apion clamped a hand over it. 'That is for your prince alone,' he said with the barest of smiles. Next, a creaking of timber rang out and echoed around the Cilician mountains as the gates swung open.

Escorted closely, they trotted along the hay-strewn dirt path that led through the close-packed town. It was a jumble of stone-walled huts and larger villas, clinging to the rounded mountaintop, with a sturdy, high-walled and fortified manor at the apex. Torches sputtered and flickered, lighting their way, and he saw the wide-eyed looks of children and adults alike who peeked from the doors of their homes, eager and anxious to see who had come to their lofty settlement. Towns like this were dotted all across the Parhar and Antitaurus Mountains. Collections of loosely affiliated but notoriously fickle Armenian tribes and federations – more often at war with one another than working together. Again, he heard Philaretos' mocking words.

The lead sentry brought them to the doors of the fortified manor then motioned for Apion to enter, alone. Apion nodded to the others, then slipped from his saddle and stepped forward.

Inside was just one cavernous hall, with a mezzanine of sleeping areas up above. A roaring log fire crackled in a hearth at one end of the hall, and in the centre, a well-weathered man with a thick brown beard and a jacket of leather armour sat at the head of a feasting table laden with wine, fresh and aromatic bread, cooked birds, bowls of blueberries, dates, figs and pots of yoghurt and honey. A motley collection of others lined the sides of the table, cackling and babbling in drunken banter. Slaves scurried to and fro around the dining area and an old, black mongrel lay asleep in front of the fire.

The sentry hurried over to whisper in the brown-bearded one's ear, then came back to him. 'Prince Vardan invites you to join him,' he said, gesturing to an empty seat at the table, a few places away from the prince.

Apion stepped forward, removing his helm and drawing a stool to sit. At once, the chatter ceased. All eyes swung to him. A fawn-skinned bald man with a nose like a sickle frowned. 'What have we got here,' he said, his tone serrated and his demeanour glacial, 'a Rus?'

'My mother was Rus. My father was Byzantine.'

'Aye?' snorted another fellow, plump and ruddy, his teeth stained with wine. 'Then what does that make you?'

'I'm just a man,' Apion replied, refusing the offer of a cup of wine from a passing slave girl. As the slave carried on around the table, he winced as the hook-nosed one seized her by the wrist and pulled her to his lap. He groped her breasts and pawed at her crotch, his bald head wrinkling as he cackled. Most around the table cheered at his lewd behaviour. Only Apion noticed that the man had slipped a tiny clay vial into her bosom.

'What kind of man comes to a mountaintop village in the dead of night?' the plump one scoffed, tearing his attention away from the slave. 'Were you lost?' His cronies hooted in laughter at this. Prince Vardan remained silent.

Apion pinned the plump one with a stare. 'What kind of man drinks himself into oblivion when there is a Seljuk horde rampaging on the fringes of his lands?'

The chatter died again. The plump one gawped, outraged. Prince Vardan's eyes narrowed on Apion.

But it was the bald, hook-nosed one who spoke: 'How dare you speak in such a tone?' His face was pinched as if Apion had just spat on his mother's corpse.

Apion snorted. 'You condemn my tone yet you ignore my words? There is a horde not three miles from—'

'Be careful, wanderer,' hook-nose countered. 'The last man to speak to me so was a slave of mine. I had his throat cut with just a click of my fingers.' He raised his fingers as if to panic Apion. 'Kept his head until it putrefied.'

'Enough,' Vardan spoke in a throaty voice from the end of the table. 'The man is here at the behest of Emperor Diogenes. He is my guest and he will be treated as such.' He clapped his hands, bringing more slaves scurrying from the darkness at the edges of the hall. 'And he is right. It is late, you are all drunk. Leave me!'

With a groaning of chairs and stools on the stone floor, the prince's guests stood to leave. The plump one cast him a mean eye. Hook-nose stepped round behind Apion as he made to leave. 'Be careful, Byzantine,' he whispered, his breath fetid, 'for although Vardan may shield you tonight, tomorrow is a new day. Who knows what it might bring?'

His sibilant words rang in Apion's ears until they were all gone. Now just two spearmen in vivid green-and-yellow tunics and trews stood guard at the door, and a single slave girl remained to prepare some herbal brew for the prince. Vardan beckoned Apion over to sit on the stool beside him.

'What you said, it is true, Apion of Chaldia?' Vardan asked, one hand ruffling his beard, his eyes gazing into the middle-distance.

'Just three miles to the south, over seven thousand ghazi riders roam. They have destroyed all in their path so far. Farms, towns, even walled cities have fallen to them.'

'Many of my kin have been summoned by Byzantine emperors of the past, few have returned,' Vardan replied swiftly. 'I presume that is why you are here – to plead for the help of my army?'

Apion nodded. 'Our infantry are still a week's march away. We need just enough foot soldiers to pin the Seljuk horde, then we can bring our cavalry to bear.'

Vardan smiled wryly. 'So you *do* come to prise away the young men of my villages? You have yet to persuade me why I should grant you this.' He sat back in his chair and sighed, eyeing Apion. 'Who am I speaking to?' he mused. 'Are you a delegate, a learned man of some sort, Apion of Chaldia?'

'I have neither studied the scrolls of the great libraries, nor attended the new universities of the empire far to the west. But I have been schooled in war – the cruellest of mistresses. I have learned many black lessons on the plains and passes of these borderlands. Many times I have been certain that I have seen all war has to show me, yet she still astonishes me at every turn.'

The prince chuckled at this, eyeing Apion's battered nose and scarred features. 'I thought as much. You do not have the look of some soft-skinned envoy. Tell me who you really are.'

Apion hesitated, judging the situation. If hook-nose and his cronies had still been here, he would have lied. But he needed this man to trust him. *Truth breeds truth*, he decided. He pulled up his sleeve, revealing the red-ink stigma of a two-headed eagle.

Vardan's face split in a not altogether reassuring smile. 'The *Haga*?'

Apion nodded.

Vardan laughed under his breath. A laugh that chilled Apion. 'If you had come to my gates and hailed my sentries as so, I would have had you shot through without a second thought. Your trail is black indeed.'

Apion did not flinch. 'I understand. When farmers see me setting light to their village, they do not realise I do it only to deny shelter to invading riders. When I burn or cut down my enemy in their hundreds, I do it only to save the thousands they would otherwise slay.'

Vardan tilted his head to one side. 'Hmm. They used to call me Vardan the head-taker. You know why? Because when I was a boy, the warriors of a neighbouring tribe stopped my father's grain wagon. They raped and killed my sister. They tortured my father, nailing him to a tree. It took him three days to die. It was me who found him, on that last day. His dying gaze was on my sister's corpse. He had seen all they did to her. My grandfather was the prince of this town at the time. He reacted weakly. He demanded the killers pay my mother for her loss. They paid, yet the coins did not soothe our pain one scrap. Only months later, I heard they had murdered again. So I took up my sword one morning, and came back at night with their heads. I never heard of any further suffering at their hands.' He gazed into the fire with a wistful half-smile.

Apion's mind flashed with memories of his early days in the ranks, of his slain parents, of the vile Bracchus. 'Then we may be more alike than you might imagine.'

Vardan beheld him for a moment, then chuckled. 'Perhaps, *Haga*, though my name is known only in these mountains. Yours echoes all across the borderlands.' He sat a little straighter. 'You know much of war, that much is clear. But what do you truly know of my people, of whose lives you ask?'

'I know that your tribe and the others of the hills have suffered as the great empires of east and west have clashed on these lands. Your home has been used as a buffer, your strong young men have been treated like dogs of war, led away to die for some foreign king.'

Vardan laughed heartily now. 'You are doing a fine job in making my decision an easy one!'

Apion leaned forward, holding Vardan's gaze. He reached down to lift up the hemp sack of coins by his feet. 'I was sent to tempt you with this,' he dropped the sack on the table with a thick *clunk*, 'but I know already you care little for coins. I can see you are a prince who cares for his people. My empire's history is stained in places. But for the first time in so long, Byzantium has at its head a man who seeks to end the strife on these mountains, on the plains of Cilicia, in the valleys of Chaldia… in all of the blood-weary borderlands. He strives to seal the borders and end the relentless struggle. Bring your men to fight with us, Noble Prince. Let us drive off these warring Seljuks.'

Vardan said nothing, his face expressionless. He looked in Apion's eyes for some time, then turned to gaze into the fire. The only noise in the hall was the spitting and crackling fire.

As Apion waited on the prince's decision, he noticed something in the corner of the room; the slave girl preparing the herbal brew had a way about her, the swaying hips, the dark hair and dusky skin. For an instant, he could not help but see her as Maria. When she saw Apion watching her, she started, then smiled sweetly, before turning her back on him, finishing the brew-making process before coming over to place the cups down. He noticed now that she looked nothing like Maria and his eye snagged on the bruises around the girl's wrist where hook–nose had grabbed her. She flashed him a swift and nervous smile then scuttled off into the shadows.

'Drink,' Vardan said, pushing one cup towards Apion. 'It clears the head.'

When the prince lifted the cup to his lips, Apion lifted his own. At that moment, he saw the slave girl looking on from the shadows, her face wrinkled with anxiety. His gaze swung to the table where she had been preparing the brew. There lay a small vial, cracked open, its contents gone. Without hesitation, he swung out a hand, grasping the prince's wrist. 'Stop.'

'What is this?' The prince jerked his arm free, brew spilling from his cup and splattering to the floor. At once, the old black mongrel that had been sleeping by the fire woke and hobbled over to lap at the spilled brew.

'Your aide, the bald one who did not take to me. He means to usurp you.'

'What? Hurik is my cousin, one of my most able generals.'

Apion held his gaze. 'And one of your most ambitious, it would seem. For he has had your brew poisoned.'

Vardan looked at his cup and back to Apion, then roared with laughter. 'You are mistaken, Byzantine. Hurik is a surly man, but he would not dare to—' The prince fell silent as the mongrel's whimpering filled the hall. Apion and he looked on as the dog retched, foam bubbling from its mouth. The creature's torment lasted only a few moments before it fell on its side, convulsing, then fell still. The noise of the crackling fire filled the hall once more.

The prince stared at his dead pet, his eyes reddening. After a lengthy silence, he spoke at last: 'You will have your infantry, *Haga*. And Hurik will watch them march from this town. He will have a fine view, what with his head on a tall spike above the walls.'

CHAPTER 4

The Cilician Gates

A pleasant autumn morning bathed the Cilician plain. In the north, the Byzantine cavalry stood in a crescent, facing south, waiting, watching. Somewhere beyond the hazy southern horizon, the Seljuk horde roamed.

On the right wing of this crescent, Apion stood by his Thessalian in just his helm, tunic, cloak and boots – his klibanion and greaves stowed away on one of the *touldon* supply wagons. Likewise, Sha, Blastares, Procopius, Kaspax and the rest of the fifty Chaldians were without their usual heavy kataphractoi armour. He stooped to pluck a handful of long grass and fed it to his gelding. 'I promise you at least a week of grooming, sleeping and eating when we return to Chaldia,' he whispered to the beast. 'But ride swiftly today.'

'The mighty *Haga* and his riders see no need for their armour today, it seems?' Philaretos snorted as he trotted past, looking down from his saddle at Apion.

Apion glanced up, squinting in the sunlight. 'We need to ride fast today, Doux. And if it is merely my armour that panics our enemy, then send it on ahead! Tell it to return when it has brought peace to our borders. I'll be in my tent feasting on goose, awaiting it eagerly.'

The men nearby laughed at this. Philaretos tried to disguise his discomfort at being the butt of the joke by shrugging and laughing too. Then he took to switching his gaze this way and that, before shaking his head and sighing. 'It'll never work,' he concluded. 'What if the horde swings back to the west to ravage the inner themata once more?'

Apion smoothed his gelding's mane and smiled. 'They won't, Doux. They have burnt or overgrazed the lands to the west.' He pointed to the swaying long grass stretched out before them. 'This is the only place they can come to for fodder, and when they do, we must drive them to the east.' He nodded in that direction where in the hazy distance the Cilician mountains loomed.

'Hmm, we'll see,' Philaretos moaned, before turning to walk his mount over to the head of the four hundred Vigla riders who were also on the right of the crescent.

'What an arse!' Blastares muttered by Apion's side.

'An arse indeed, but a loyal arse,' Apion chuckled.

'True. I'd rather have a loyal arse than a treacherous one any day,' Sha added, throwing his saddle over his stallion and buckling it into place.

Procopius hobbled over to join the chat. 'Is that Blastares talking about arses again? Loves the arses, I tell you.'

Blastares frowned as Kaspax and Sha laughed aloud. 'The only arse I'll be talking about in a minute is yours, when it's impaled on the end of my boot!' But the big man's grumbling fell away, melting into a chuckle too.

Suddenly, all of them looked up as the crescent of Byzantine riders bristled. There, coming from the south, was a band of colour and a russet dust plume, heading due north, directly for the Byzantine lines.

'They're coming!' a familiar voice boomed from the centre of the crescent. There, Romanus was mounted and ready on his white stallion. He was clad in his silver-and-white armour, his silver, purple-plumed helm and his purple cloak. 'Ready!' Beside the emperor, the Varangoi and the Scholae horsemen settled in their saddles. On the left, the rest of the thematic riders – a mix of heavy kataphractoi and lighter kursores – readied likewise. Banners were raised, lances levelled, buccinas lifted to lips.

Apion leapt into his saddle as the horns keened. Across the plain, he saw the emerging horde take form. The Seljuk horns wailed as they sighted the Byzantine bullhorn awaiting them. Like a drift of hornets, they swept to the east, towards the mountains.

Yes! Apion punched a fist to his palm.

'After them!' Romanus bellowed, waving the crescent forward.

The ground shuddered as more than three thousand Byzantine riders broke into a trot and then a gallop. Apion watched as the hazy mountains ahead grew larger and larger. *Stay true*, he mouthed, willing the fleeing Seljuk raiders not to divert north or south.

The skyline grew rugged as the mountains loomed ever closer. Directly ahead, two mountains jutted, their adjacent sides almost perfectly sheer, like two limestone walls. A narrow corridor wove between these two monoliths and wound on for some distance like a furrow ploughed by some ancient god. This was it, the only direct path from these lands to the east. At that moment, Apion remembered old Cydones reminiscing: *Many have breathed their last at the Cilician Gates. It is a wonder they are not stained red.*

The Seljuk horde narrowed and funnelled into this corridor, the thunder of their hooves echoing like drums, their hearts confident of escape and further plunder on the far side of the pass. Apion hoisted his lance overhead and waved it to and fro frantically, looking to the tops of the rocky corridor high above. But the high sides of the pass remained lifeless, despite his signal. 'No!' he gasped.

Beside him, Sha snarled, scanning the deserted tops of the rocky pass likewise. 'Treacherous bast—'

'Look!' Blastares cried, pointing up there. First a single spearman rose tall. Then another, then in moments hundreds lined either side of the pass, armoured in felt and mail, some with vivid purple, green and red eastern-style silks wrapped around their heads. The Armenian prince and his army. More than a thousand men. They carried with them bundles of missiles – spears, bows, quivers and slings.

'Loose!' the unmistakable voice of Vardan boomed from up there. It echoed down through the corridor like a clap of thunder, and every Seljuk neck bent to look up. At once, they saw the snare, and a heartbeat later, they broke out in a chorus of panicked wails. Their good order at once descended into horrified flight as each of them grew frantic to race on and out of the corridor. But the Armenian spearmen hurled their lances down on the thick swathes of ghazis and nearly every one struck home with deadly effect. Wails were cut short as men were pinned to their horses, thrashing together in their shared death throes, blood pumping across their comrades. Next, a pack of Armenian slingers hurried to the edge of the mountaintop overlooking the corridor, swiftly loosing volleys of shot. Holes were punched in helms, and blood leapt from the broken heads within. Hundreds more toppled. The remaining ghazis raced now – desperate to be clear of the corridor. However, the Armenians were swift to draw their bows; known as a nation of fine bowmen, they showed their skill, loosing volley after volley upon the Seljuk mass. Many more enemy horsemen fell, writhing, peppered with shafts. Moments later the Armenians took to rolling great boulders from the cliff tops. These monoliths crashed down, pulping clusters of riders like insects, all but blocking the corridor.

Some Seljuk riders broke through the narrow gaps that remained and raced on to the east, but many others – thousands of them – took to wheeling around like a shoal of silvery fish avoiding a preying shark. They swung back to face west, set on taking their chances against the onrushing Byzantine crescent – now galloping to close the door at the western end of the corridor and pen them in. When they threw down their bows, Apion longed to hear them cry out: *Mercy.* But the cry did not come. Instead, they tore out their scimitars and spears, intent on battle.

Apion watched the rider coming for him, and this merged with the pulsing image of the dark door. The man's face was creased in a war cry, his dark moustache whipping in the wind, his spear arm drawn back. The flames roared from behind the dark door, blowing it open. He jinked to his left as the man loosed his lance, the shaft skimming past his neck. A moment later, a flanged mace from one of the Byzantine kataphractoi plunged down into the spearless ghazi's forehead, crushing his helmet and skull like an egg, sending a shower of blood and brains across his comrades and throwing the man back from his saddle. Then the two cavalry lines clashed with a clatter of shields, iron and the screaming of man and beast.

Apion felt the flames of darkness roar all around him as the first few riders that met his lance tip simply vanished, torn through or punched from their saddles, trampled like kindling. Blood whipped across his face in a constant spray, and he smelt the all too familiar coppery stench of death. He ran another three of them through, and saw many more scattering, kicking their mounts into a disordered flight. His Chaldians swept along with him, tearing Seljuk riders asunder, throwing some from their saddles. When his spear was lost, embedded in a Seljuk's chest, he swept his scimitar from his scabbard and lashed it round at those who tried to break past him. He felt Seljuk blades scrape at his skin, death only inches away. He saw throats torn open before him, his sword hand numb yet relentless. *Yield!* he mouthed, sickened at the crunch of bone and tearing of flesh. Yet still they came, maddened and panicked. On the slaughter went.

The sun was high in the sky when at last the Seljuks thinned. Bar a few who had broken past the Byzantine crescent and raced off into the western countryside and the riders who had survived the Armenian hail and forged on to the east, all lay dead before the panting Byzantine cavalry.

Apion gazed around numbly. The Cilician Gates were red once more. Clouds of flies buzzed over the gore, and carrion birds circled and lined the sides of the corridor. Crispin's words rang in his thoughts.

A slayer of souls, a burner, a death-bringer.

A hand clasped his shoulder. 'A fine ploy, Strategos,' Romanus said, catching his breath. 'And not just for today. A lasting bond with the Armenian princes is something that must be forged if the borders are ever to be truly secure.'

From the corner of his eye, Apion noticed the Armenians flooding down the mountainside to meet with the Byzantine lines in celebration.

'Did we finish them? All of them?' Doux Philaretos panted, arriving alongside the emperor.

'No,' Apion scowled, 'but those who made it through the gates are gone. Their raid is over.'

'Gone? Not quite. Some wait to goad us, it seems?' One finger of Philaretos' iron gauntlet stretched out to pinpoint a lone rider, nestled in the shade of one of the giant rocks thrown down by the Armenians. 'I recognise that one – from the camp by the Euphrates… a fierce whoreson, he was…'

Apion squinted along the corridor. The unseen hands of a wraith stroked his neck as he recognised the tall, broad-shouldered warrior's garb. A fine scale vest, a silver helm with a distinctive studded rim and nose-guard – *Nasir?* He mouthed, confused, images of his dead, one-time brother flitting through his mind. Was this some kind of demon? He locked eyes with this masked figure, and his blood ran cold. The stranger's face was bathed in half-shadow, but he was certain the eyes in there were fixed on him. And there was something about those eyes…

Apion's thoughts evaporated when Philaretos grunted and loosed a wayward javelin at the rider. It punched down some twelve feet short, quivering in the dust. Without alarm, the rider turned and rode on to the east.

'Come, Strategos.' Romanus pulled him away from the scene. Apion nodded, tearing his gaze from the sight. As they walked away, he could not help but glance back, sure the shadows had been playing with him.

—

Above the Cilician Gates the sky was jet black, dotted with stars and a waning moon. The Armenian warriors were long gone from this vantage point where they had rained death on the ghazi horde. But the high mountaintops were not entirely deserted.

Having escaped to the east and then doubled back with just his bodyguard, one young Seljuk rider crouched atop the rocky outcrop near the corridor mouth. His skin and hair were coated in dust, his throat parched and his scale armour encrusted in dried blood where his comrades had been struck down around him. He glanced at his reflection in the stud-rimmed helm he cradled, then gazed down to the Cilician plain below, where a thousand torches and campfires demarcated the Byzantine imperial camp. He had heard them pray, now he heard them laugh and cheer their victory, cups clacking together, overflowing with wine. This angered him. When he imagined the *Haga* celebrating with them, the wrath grew fiery.

His bodyguard crept up beside him. 'Sir, our men will have made camp by now, some miles to the east. Should we not return to them? Some of your riders might think you have been captured should you not come back to them before first light. And *Bey* Gulten is known for his fierce discipline.'

The young rider ignored his bodyguard's plea and snorted at the idea that Bey Gulten, the leader of this expedition, was any form of threat. 'After today, Bey Gulten will be known only for his failure.' The howling of some wild dog sounded across the plain. 'Now take my armour,' he said, unbuckling his scale vest and sweeping on a tattered robe, 'then you can return to camp. I have business to attend to first.'

'Sir?'

The young rider looked to his bodyguard, the moonlight flashing in his green eyes. 'Sometimes, to slay a wolf, you must separate him from his pack.'

—

The thick red satin of the imperial tent muffled the jovial babbling from outside. Inside it was muggy, still and tense. Apion sat alone with the emperor, a table between them bearing a shatranj board, a jug of nearly finished wine and a platter of barely touched bread, honey and cheese. He saw the torchlight dance in Romanus' eyes, as if trying to ignite the emperor's vim once more. His veneer of the victorious leader had been shed as quickly as his armour as soon as he had come inside. The white-and-silver klibanion and ornamented silver helm retained their proud, broad-shouldered stance on the timber frame they rested upon, while the man sat in dejection, shoulders slumped.

'I can only liken this campaign to a shipwreck,' he said, his fist coiling and uncoiling as he gazed through the shatranj board. 'Last year, we set out to secure a foothold and a safe border in Syria. We achieved what we set out to. We took Hierapolis and that city still stands firm against the Seljuk threat.'

Apion's mind flashed back to the brutal siege and counter-siege of the desert city. He closed his eyes to block out the memories. The thousands of faces who had fallen there, never to return home. But in the darkness behind his eyelids, he saw one other face. One of the fallen he could never forget. *Nasir.*

'Our losses were great – almost Pyrrhic,' the emperor continued as if sharing his thoughts. 'But when I returned to Constantinople, there was no leverage for my enemies to act upon, for I had achieved what I set out to. This time, I must return to the capital with some tale of woe: routing a Seljuk warband in our own lands instead of taking Chliat and securing the Lake Van region as I proclaimed I would.'

The torch crackled and spat, as if daring Apion to speak. Philaretos and Igor had been present until a short while ago, but the emperor's mood had seen them make their excuses and depart. 'It is vital to the people of the empire that the Seljuks are not allowed to maraud in her heartlands. You achieved all you could and that is venerable. It is futile to brood upon what might have been.'

'I know there is wisdom in your words, Strategos, but I also know you think as I do. I, like you, will lie awake every night, seeing our tenuous hold on Manzikert weakening with every passing month that we do not reinforce the meagre garrison there. Notions of taking Chliat are now secondary – first, we must ensure we do not cede the toe-hold we have on that vital land. And in the west, the heel of Italy is on the brink of falling from imperial control; the city of Barion has been under siege by the Normans of Robert Guiscard for over a year – yet I cannot spare a single regiment to send in relief.'

Apion looked to the shatranj board. Each of them had made just a few moves. Pawns had been advanced, and of the powerful pieces, only Apion's war elephant had been developed. It was then that he spotted the emperor's folly – so plainly visible and unexpected that he had missed it. Romanus' king lay in line to be taken by the elephant on Apion's next move. The emperor's next move would be vital, he thought, then suppressed a shiver as he thought of the reality of the sentiment. He looked up, seeing that Romanus was more focused on the surface of his wine than anything else.

He looked for some crumb of comfort. 'By running down that horde, the heartlands of Anatolia were spared. Psellos and the Doukids cannot twist that reality.'

Romanus stirred from his thoughts at this. 'Psellos? The man has a way with words, as you well know. His grip on power may have diminished in this last year, but he still carries the weight of the Doukas family and all those who sponsor his wiles. The grain and wine magnates of the richer themata bow before me, call me *Basileus*, pledge their private armies to the imperial cause – yet it would be a dark day if ever I was driven to levy those forces... but it is all just a veneer. Worse, some of the strategoi of the imperial themata even still lean to the Doukid cause and heed Psellos' word. And while the tagmata armies are mostly loyal, the Numeroi Tagma still dance to the advisor's tune... and they garrison the capital, their barracks an arrowshot from the chambers in which I sleep!' Romanus thumped a fist on the table, causing the shatranj pieces to jump. 'I rule an empire under the constant shadow of a coup!'

Apion sought words to encourage the emperor, but found none suitable.

Romanus picked up another pawn to move it forward, leaving his king unguarded. Apion winced. He had watched some courtiers play against the man and deliberately avoid advantageous moves so as not to offend their emperor. The thought crossed his mind to do likewise, but he swatted the moment of weakness away. 'Checkmate,' he said quietly, lifting his war elephant piece over to take the emperor's king.

Romanus' eyes widened at this, and he glanced over the board as if in disbelief. The torch crackled and spat as it began to die. 'And in barely a handful of moves,' he muttered.

'Sometimes it serves a man well to be reminded of simple things. Do not let your guard drop, *Basileus*. Psellos might well be planning some intricate coup, but if you return to the capital distracted and melancholy, he might see a far simpler route to achieving his goals.'

Romanus shook his head as if to rid it of the wine's fog. 'I have already doubled the Varangoi presence in the palace and I will do so again on my return,' then he pinged a finger on his wine cup, 'and I would do well to stay clear of this poison.'

Apion's heart lifted as Romanus took to sitting upright, his broad shoulders squared once more and his eyes sharp.

'Now, Strategos, once again after only a short spell in each other's company, we must part. Come the morning, the campaign army will be disbanded. A fleet of imperial *dromons* will arrive at the port-town of Mersin some forty miles south of here. They will ferry the tagmata riders and I back to Constantinople. The soldiers of the themata will be free to return to their lands. You should take your riders home, to Chaldia.'

The pair rose from their seats at the same time. 'Then next spring, we will set out for Lake Van?' Apion asked.

Romanus' brow furrowed. 'Perhaps not, Strategos. If this campaign has taught me anything, it is that a clear and decisive move will be required if we are to seize the Lake Van region. An army so vast in number that it will not be weakened or diverted by the presence of raiding Seljuk hordes. Sixty thousand men or more. Such a venture will take time to organise.'

'So there will be no campaign next year?' Apion asked, masking his unease at this strategy. It was only the tireless campaigning of the last two years that had beaten back the Seljuk incursions.

Romanus seemed to sense Apion's qualms. 'I have told no one of this,' he leaned in closer, 'but I plan to remain in the capital next year, both to appease the citizens and to raise funds to bolster the poorest of the themata. But I will despatch a campaign army eastwards on my behalf. A defensive campaign this time, perhaps stationed in Sebastae to fend off any Seljuk incursions. I plan to appoint Manuel Komnenos as *kouropalates* – leader of the campaign army in my absence. While I sort out affairs in the capital, I will be relying on Komnenos and the few men I trust to protect the empire's lands. Men like you, Strategos.'

Apion nodded. His eyes traced over the pieces on the shatranj board and he recalled the unfinished game he had once played with the Seljuk Sultan in Caesarea. He thought then of the many armies that Alp Arslan could call upon. The innumerable marching spearmen, the heavy lancers and the siege technicians of Persia, the hardy desert warriors of the emirs and the swift and deadly steppe cavalry of the native Seljuk people. He felt fear dig its claws into his shoulder like a hungry crow, then swept the emotion away effortlessly. 'I will do all I can, *Basileus*.'

The pair locked forearms, shared a knowing look, then parted.

Apion slipped from the tent, saluting Igor and the cluster of varangoi guarding the tent entrance. Philaretos was there too with a clutch of the Vigla night guardsmen forming a perimeter around the emperor's tent – resembling an iron palisade of sorts. 'Sleep well, Strategos,' Philaretos nodded.

Apion nodded in return, accepting the salutes of the Vigla sentries, then walked off through the sea of tents – brightly coloured bandon standards hanging limp in the still air over each regimental cluster. The chatter and celebrations of earlier were absent now that the night curfew was upon them – only the night sentries were to be seen. He reached into his purse to unconsciously thumb at the sleek lock of Maria's hair as he walked, and eventually came to the small, irregular bunch of four tents set up for the Chaldian detachment, near the eastern edge of the camp that watched over the mouth of the Cilician Gates. A steady, rhythmic '*hic!*' came from within one tent, followed by a low, painfully serrated and watery belch. This was followed by the thudding of a fist into flesh.

'Blastares, enough!' he heard Procopius hiss, his tone thickened by wine. 'Tetradia'll not stand for your bloody belching.'

'Eh?' came Blastares' groggy reply. Moments later, another hiccup and an accompanying, lasting and forceful emission of wind from an unidentified orifice. 'Plenty more where that came from,' the big tourmarches grunted.

Apion half-smiled at Procopius' muffled gagging and clearly incensed tirade, then slipped into his tent, tying the flap shut with the laces dangling there. While the others shared a kontoubernion tent, with their bedding laid out head-to-toe around the centre pole, armour and weapons by their heads and rations by their feet, this tent was smaller and held only one set of bedding. Isolation was one privilege of a strategos. He wondered what might come to him tonight: dreams of Maria, or the dark nightmares of long-past battles. He lifted a hand to pull the tent flap back when he heard a set of footsteps rushing up behind him. *After curfew?* He swung to the sound, braced, then relaxed when he saw it was just Kaspax.

'Sir, one of the gate guards gave me this.' He handed over a tightly rolled sheet of paper. 'They said some cloaked rider came to the gate just a short while ago and handed this to them. They said the messenger fled before they could question him.'

Apion frowned, then nodded to Kaspax. 'Thank you. And Kaspax, you fought well today.'

'Thank you, sir.' Kaspax nodded and hurried back to his tent, from which a droning snore tore through the air.

'And shove a roll of cloth in Blastares' mouth, will you?' he called after the lad.

'Yes, sir,' Kaspax chuckled.

He turned away, unravelling the scroll, sure this was some jest from the men. But when he unravelled the scroll, his stomach fell away.

It was Seljuk script.

You seek Lady Maria? Then ride east, Haga, to northern Persia, to the silk market in Mosul . . .

Part 2: 1070 AD

CHAPTER 5

Lure

A pack of thirty Seljuk *ghazi* riders thundered across the late winter plains of northern Persia, throwing up a shiver of morning frost in their wake. When they swept across the path of two unusual, woollen-cloaked riders who ambled eastwards, the leader of the Seljuk pack turned to scowl at the pair, the cool January breeze whipping around him. The pair were pale-skinned, one sharp-eyed with amber-silver hair plaited into a tail and an iron-grey beard, the other much younger, with dark locks dangling over his eyes, barely disguising fear.

'Ya!' the ghazi commander yelled, bringing his riders round. He drew the composite bow from his shoulder and nocked an arrow to it.

From the corner of his eye, Apion saw the riders come round. He noticed Kaspax's knuckles whiten on his reins. 'Ride steady, lad,' he spoke under his breath, his lips barely moving. 'As if this was your home.'

'But they've drawn their weapons, sir,' Kaspax croaked.

Apion risked a glance over his shoulder to see the Seljuk rider scowling behind his bow. The thirty that came with him were armed with scimitars, spears and bows and armoured in quilt vests and leather helms. Surely primed for a skirmish. Perhaps even looking for one, and two troublesome travellers might make fine melee-fodder. He nipped the budding fear in his belly and leaned a little closer to Kaspax. 'We are two western traders, that is all. No armour, no military garb, save our swords and daggers to protect ourselves with. These riders will see that and be on their way.'

63

Kaspax's face was riddled with doubt, sweat spidering from every pore. Then the lad jumped as a jagged voice called out from behind them.

'State your business, riders!' the lead Seljuk snapped in his native tongue, his eyes shaded under the rim of his conical helm, his bow creaking.

Apion twisted in his saddle, taking care to do it slowly. He affixed the Seljuk rider with a look of annoyance. 'We come to bargain for saffron and almonds at Mosul,' he said in the Seljuk tongue with a shrug. 'If we can ever find the east road to the city!'

The rider relaxed his bow at this, his scowl melting and a faint look of disappointment replacing it. 'Ride south until sunset. When you come to the twin hills, sleep there then set off eastwards at dawn. You will be at the city by mid–morning tomorrow.'

Kaspax expelled a deep sigh of relief as the Seljuk scouting party thundered away.

—

At dusk, Apion and Kaspax arrived at the twin hills. They stopped at the base of the easterly one, beside a rock pool ringed with soft, green grass. There they tethered their mounts to the desiccated remains of a tamarisk trunk and gathered up the fallen branches to use as kindling. Soon, the chill of night arrived and the fire provided a welcome heat. Above, bats flitted from the caves pockmarking the twin hills, betrayed only by the starlight and the dancing orange of the flames.

Apion skewered a piece of mutton on a twig and held it over the fire. As the meat charred and bubbled, he cast his mind over the last few months. When the campaign army had disbanded at the Cilician Gates, he led his Chaldians north, each of the riders chatting eagerly about returning to their homes within the walls of Trebizond and on the farms across Chaldia. But he had found that he could not sleep. Night after night he had thrown the words of the mysterious letter around in his head. By whose hand was it penned? How did they know where he was? It was over breakfast on the fourth day of their journey home that Sha had come to him. The Malian was one of the few who knew the full story of Apion's troubles.

'You should do what you must, sir. The thema will be in good hands over the winter.' Then Sha had clasped a hand to his shoulder and insisted, 'Go, find her.'

And so he had parted from his Chaldians, their farewell chant of *Haga!* ringing in his ears as he set off south-east, through the Antitaurus Mountain passes, alone. He had only been riding south-east for a few hours when the clopping of hooves alerted him to a follower. Kaspax had ranged alongside him, offering a stiff salute. 'Tourmarches Sha decided you should have a squire. I volunteered.' Apion smiled at the memory. For all his self-doubt and awkwardness, Kaspax was a good rider, a fine swordsman and a valiant soul.

Their journey had been arduous at first. The heights of the Antitaurus Mountains were unforgiving in November and early December. They wore furs and sheltered in caves from the winter blizzards that besieged those lofty peaks, eating hard tack biscuit and strips of salted mutton as they tried to stave off the cold. After a few weeks, they had descended onto the Syrian plain and turned east, into the Seljuk dominion and on into this ancient land. Both men were now saddle-sore and weary.

The bats flitted overhead again, stirring Apion from the memories. Kaspax sat down across from him then, his hair wet and swept back, having washed in the rock pool. He shivered and pulled up close to the fire, and Apion noticed his lips move: *I'll be back to protect you. Until then, let God stay by your side.*

The same words he had noticed the lad mouth every night of their journey. Apion felt a question burn on his lips. A question he had stifled so far, for Kaspax seemed uncomfortable with familiar conversation. Indeed, much of their chat on the journey so far had been focused on matters of the thema, the logistics of their trek and the plans for their return route. Even in the lonely mountain caves. 'Who do you yearn to return to lad? I thought you were without family?'

'I was just praying, sir,' Kaspax said, shrugging, shaking his head then gazing off into the night.

'Come, lad. I can be your strategos again in the morning, but for the sake of keeping us both sane, speak to me as a friend for now,' Apion said, throwing a wineskin across the fire.

Kaspax caught it, licked his lips, then melted into a grin before taking a long pull on it. He let out a contented sigh and wiped his mouth with the back of his hand and tossed the skin back to Apion. 'I have no family. I was speaking to Vilyam.'

Apion cocked an eyebrow.

'My cat,' Kaspax grinned. 'That's my life. My horse, my armour, my home within the walls of Trebizond… and a well-fed ginger tom.' He gazed into the flames. 'The strange thing is that I pray for him every night, yet he barely needs my help – he gets fatter when I'm away. Those who live nearby say he is a menace, raiding their stores and stealing from the market. But when I'm there and I keep him indoors they complain the mice and rats are running rampant and I have to let him out again. I think his system is a fine one,' he said with a chuckle and a fond look into the darkness.

Apion grinned at this, thinking of the affection he had once had for the old grey mare on Mansur's farm, and now, for his Thessalian. 'Animals often make the truest companions.' Then he cocked his head to one side. 'But Vilyam is a Slavic name, is it not? Did he come from a northern trader?'

'No,' Kaspax replied with a blank look.

Apion frowned. 'Then why the Slavic name?'

Kaspax shook his head and held up his sword hand – laced with old claw marks. 'Because he's a vicious bastard,' he shrugged, deadpan.

Apion said nothing for a heartbeat, then roared with laughter, steadying himself at last to take another swig from the wineskin. 'Then we'll have to see you back to Chaldia safely, else Vilyam will be running the backstreets of Trebizond.'

Kaspax grinned, taking the skin for another drink. 'Ha! The *Tyrant of Trebizond*, an apt—' His words caught in his throat as a scuffling sounded from the darkness nearby.

Apion's hand swept round for his swordbelt and scimitar, but halted when he saw the yellow eyes of a desert fox flash and then disappear again into the darkness. 'At ease,' he said. 'Now we should try to get some sleep – we need to be sharp for tomorrow.'

Kaspax let out a tense sigh, then rose and drew two woollen blankets from the packs by their tethered mounts. 'How do you do it, sir?' he asked, throwing one blanket to Apion. 'How do you rid yourself of fear?'

Apion frowned. 'I don't understand.'

'I long to be a fine and brave rider like my father, yet I tremble at the thought of battle. At the Cilician Gates, I thought I would vomit before we even sighted the Seljuk horde. And here, I almost soiled my tunic at the approach of a fox… a damned fox! But you have lived at the edge of death on the battlefield for years. You do not pale or flinch in the face of an enemy. Fear must be a distant memory for you. It would be a fine thing if it could be for me also.'

Apion shook his head with a mirthless laugh. 'Fear has never left me.'

Kaspax frowned, sitting again and throwing his blanket around his shoulders. He hung on Apion's words.

'It rides with me, watches me when I sleep, counts my every breath, waiting for the opportunity to harness me with its talons. If anything it has grown throughout the years.'

Kaspax cocked his head to one side. 'How do you live with such a monster perched on your shoulder?'

Apion prodded the fire with a twig. 'I accept its presence. I accept that fear alone cannot hurt me. I understand that my choices must be truly mine and not guided by fear. And sometimes, just sometimes, fear can be of use – it can hone your senses like a whetstone.'

Kaspax nodded, throwing his blanket around his shoulders and rubbing his hands together for warmth. 'My father used to say that he had never tasted fear. He said that I would be the same when I became a man.'

Apion winced at the lad's words. 'Atticus was a good man and a lion in my ranks… but he didn't half talk horseshit at times.'

Kaspax laughed, taken aback yet trying to mask a spike of grief at the memory of his father at the same time.

'I miss the mottled whoreson too,' Apion assured him. 'But like me, he felt fear. I know. I stood with him on the battlefield many times. I felt the tremor of his spear arm, pressed against my shoulder as we awaited the enemy charge. Perhaps he thought he could set you a fine example with his words. It seems he might instead have left you an unattainable ideal.'

Kaspax still seemed unsure.

'There is always someone who seems braver and stands taller than you. Always,' Apion said. 'You remember old Cydones, don't you?'

Kaspax nodded, a fond smile touching his lips. 'It is hard to believe that frail old goat was once the Strategos of Chaldia before you… a warrior!'

'Oh, but damn, he was. Never a bolder fellow have I met. I swear his balls were made of iron,' Apion smiled. 'Yet even he used to yak on for hours about the heroics of men who had gone before him. The great John Tzimices was his favourite; warrior, battlefield leader then emperor. Could leap over four horses, apparently. Could shoot an arrow through a thumb ring. Could make a ball leap from a vase with a swipe of his spathion – the vase remaining unbroken, of course.' Apion snorted. 'I'm surprised he couldn't shoot Greek fire from his cock!'

Kaspax roared with laughter, rocking where he sat.

'But you see my point?' Apion said. 'Cydones was a hero. He inspired men. He didn't realise how many hearts he touched. He didn't appreciate all that he was, instead he spent his days obsessing over the few things that he was not. Don't waste your life comparing yourself with others. Be all you can be and be proud of your efforts.' Apion met his eyes across the fire. 'You volunteered to come here with me ahead of all the others, into the heart of Seljuk lands. That shows an iron nerve, lad.'

'It is my duty, sir, that is all.'

'You know very well I don't come here on imperial duty,' Apion replied promptly.

Kaspax at first made to deny this, then sighed and nodded. Apion knew that rumours of his nightmares had spread amongst the men. Some had even heard him calling her name, his cries echoing from his chambers in the citadel of Trebizond.

'I knew only that you had some trouble from the past that you had to address. Tourmarches Sha told me about her – Lady Maria. I would be honoured to help you find her, sir.'

He beheld the young rider once more. 'Your father would have been proud of you, Kaspax.'

The fire glinted in Kaspax's eyes as he thought this over. 'Instead I'll have to make do with Vilyam's tepid regards on my return home,' he said with a smile.

'That's if the Tyrant of Trebizond is not too busy ransacking your neighbours' larders,' Apion said with a glint in his eye.

They finished the wine and chatted on until both men felt tiredness weigh on their eyelids. Finally, they lay back on the soft grass, each drawing warmth from their woollen blankets, finding sleep easier to come by than of late.

They rose at dawn to a crisp, cool morning and the sound of a passing Seljuk trade caravan. They bartered for fresh supplies from the friendly wagon drivers, then enjoyed a light breakfast of olives, toasted flatbread and a little honey, washed down with cool water from the rock pool. Replete and refreshed, they set off on the lonely east road to Mosul.

Not long before midday, the road was lonely no more. Silk traders, cattle farmers and grain-wagon drivers joined them as they ambled east. Finally, the outline of the Seljuk fortress-city emerged from the hazy horizon; vast, sun-bleached walls studded with the fluttering golden bow emblems of the Sultanate, wrapping the jutting palaces and domes within. The city was perched on the near banks of the River Tigris, and a thick traffic of trade cogs slipped gently up and downriver through the sparkling turquoise waters, bringing silks and spices to the city's markets and leaving laden with coin.

Apion stole furtive glances to the western gates, where they would enter the city. The gates lay open, yawning as if dismissive of any threat. As they approached, *akhi* spearmen glowered down at them from the gatehouse battlements, eyes shaded by the rims of their conical iron helms, fingers grappling talon sharp spears and tan, turquoise or green shields, bodies wrapped in mail shirts, horn and leather lamellar or brightly coloured felt coats.

'Eyes forward,' Apion whispered to Kaspax once more, acutely aware of the boy's skittishness as they passed under the shadow of the gatehouse. 'Again, we are traders, no more. Don't let fear guide you.'

Inside, they were swept along amongst the throng and the cacophony of shouting traders, jabbering citizens, whinnying horses and the rhythmic patter of drums and twanging of lutes. A tang of spices and cooking meats seasoned the crisp air. Crowds swelled around them, some glancing twice at their foreign features. Apion avoided their stares, looking up and around the street that wound into the heart of the city. Ancient, towering grain silos hemmed one side of the street and a red-brick warehouse had been converted into a covered market on the other side. He dragged his gaze across to the magnificent domed mosque up ahead, tiled in brilliant white with a lacy pattern of turquoise and azure. He shaded his eyes and looked to the four minarets, stretching skywards, spotting the small, white-robed figures up there preparing to make the midday call to prayer. Behind the mosque, on the citadel hill, he saw a sturdy and high-walled keep, with another towering and finely architected building beside it. This other building had tall, arched windows, and silk curtains billowed there in the lofty breeze. For a moment, he was heedless of his surroundings, a strange sense of warmth touching him as he watched the fluttering silk.

'Sir.' Kaspax nudged him, stirring him from his odd musing. He saw that the young rider was nodding ahead. 'Is that it?'

Apion followed his gaze. On its gentle path up towards the citadel hill, the street widened into a market area, thick with islands of stalls shaded under bright canopies. The masses barged and babbled all around. Traders bawled, keen to bring the shoppers to barter for the imported silks and the fine cloth that was the speciality of this city. His mind trawled over the instructions in the letter – *Go to the silk market, seek Danush.*

'Aye, it would seem so. You should hang back once we're in there. Stay vigilant, but try not to draw attention to yourself.'

They dismounted to lead their horses past a pair of akhi standing guard where the street opened out into this thriving silk bazaar. Some commotion was going on around a hulking wagon laden with hewn trunks – two men were arguing about how to safely unload the cargo. Apion led his mount past them and round the thickest of the crowds, then saw one trader, bored and tired of shouting. He gave Kaspax a deft nod and the lad took the reins of his mount and peeled away.

Apion approached the bored trader's stall, lifting and eyeing a silk scarf.

'For your lady?' the trader said, at once alert.

Apion half-smiled at this. 'Maybe,' he replied.

'A dirham and it is yours,' the trader said, a glint in his eye betraying his audacious overpricing.

Apion smiled fully now, pressing a silver coin into the man's palm, but holding onto it. 'Tell me where I can find Danush, and I'll give you another.'

The trader frowned, lost.

Apion pushed a second and third coin into his palm.

Now the trader grinned. 'You look thirsty. Maybe a drink in the tavern would be best for you?'

Apion flicked his gaze to the dusty alleyway sprouting off from the market square. 'Perhaps.'

He approached the tavern alone. The entrance to the tavern was rudimentary at best – little more than a hole in the wall. While the Seljuk conquest had done much to beautify the ancient cities of old Persia, some alleys and corners had remained untouched for many centuries. Indeed, the wall nearby still showed traces of a long-ago bricked-up Sassanid Persian archway.

Inside, the place stank of stale sweat and urine. It was a tavern by function only, its appearance little changed from the trade stable it had clearly once been. A fire crackled in the hearth and the heat in the low-ceilinged space was unpleasant and the air foul. Brick columns divided the tavern-room up into small pockets, with a timber bar at the far end. Hay covered the packed-dirt floor, barely disguising the pools of vomit or lessening the stench. Buzzing clouds of flies seemed determined to draw attention to every such stain. It brought back stark and unwelcome memories of his time as a child slave. Traders and locals were dotted around, babbling in a low murmur, their eyes red with inebriation. A dark-skinned woman with an equally drained look walked from table to table, lifting empty cups and placing down new ones.

Apion frowned, scanning the sea of faces as discreetly as possible, then he stopped on one who held his gaze. A weary-faced old man. A native Persian, fifty years old or more, with lined, fawn skin. Bald, with wispy grey wings of hair above each ear.

'Danush?' he muttered under his breath as he approached.

'I knew it was you,' the Persian said, offering a welcoming smile. 'Sit,' he gestured to the chair by his side. Apion looked to the chair but – still wary of his surroundings – instead took the one opposite to sit facing the man, where he could keep an eye on him. A plate lay before the man, strewn with breadcrumbs of some recent meal. At the adjacent table, a drunken Seljuk lay slumped and snoring.

The barmaid placed down two cups of oily-looking wine. Apion sipped at it and wrinkled his nose – it was hot and vinegary. He affixed Danush the Persian with a solemn look. 'Tell me what you know.'

'What I know?' The man's smile faded. He looked to check that no one else could hear, then affixed Apion with his gaze. 'I'll tell you a story of love and loss. A story of a man who lost his wife to the war.' His eyes grew weary and red-rimmed. 'We met when we were children. We knew love for so many years.' He stopped, placing a hand over his heart. 'Love as I have never known since. My only wish then was that we could be granted the rest of our lives together.'

Apion felt the man's words tease out long buried feelings of his own.

'She bore me three fine boys, we shunned the wars that rolled back and forth across our lands.' Danush stopped, looking up, tears building in his eyes. 'Then she was taken by the Fatimid raiders. They swept across our farm, cut down my boys, took my wife as a prize. I was not there to save them. I thought I already knew grief, but at that moment, I truly experienced it. It was long and lasting.' He shook his head. 'It has never left me. Every day it feels as though my heart has grown whole again only to be torn open by the memories.'

'I'm sorry this happened to you,' was all Apion could offer.

'Ah, if only it ended there,' the old man sighed. 'It was years after they took her – years after I had given her up for dead – that I found out.'

'Found out?'

Tears gathered in the old man's eyes. 'Those raiders had not killed her. She had lived on all those years, many miles away in Fatimid lands, as a slave. And she had died as such. Alone.'

Apion bowed his head and sighed.

'Now do you understand?' the old man asked. 'I cannot right the wrong that was done to me. But when your messengers came from the west talking of a fellow seeking out the whereabouts of his lost woman, I had to act. I missed them, only hearing of their enquiries from others, after they had left. But I had to get word to you.'

Apion nodded, producing the letter from his purse. 'And you did.'

Danush chuckled wearily. 'So my days of waiting for you, drinking oily wine in this sty were worth it.'

Apion reached out and clasped the old man's hands. 'Thank you.'

Danush shrugged. 'It is all I could do.'

Apion waited, senses honed on the man's next words.

The Persian seemed set to tell all, then he sighed. 'Now, let us order some food. Then I can tell you all I know about your woman.'

Apion frowned, glancing to the already empty plate before the man. 'Very well, although I don't have much of an appetite.'

'Be patient.' The old man smiled again, then leant forward, his eyes wide and earnest. 'I know where she is.'

The words were like an elixir to Apion. He barely noticed the barmaid bringing them two plates each with bread, cheese and a blunt knife. He did not touch the fare, instead letting the old man eat in silence while he lost himself in a daze of hope. Suddenly, the foul air was sweet, the dry heat from the fire like a balm on his skin and the vinegar wine like honey. He could have laughed aloud, right there in the middle of the filthy, cut-throat Seljuk tavern, were it not for one odd thing that snapped him from his reverie.

Every time the old Persian carved a piece of cheese from the block on his plate, he would shoot a glance beyond Apion's shoulder, towards the tavern entrance.

–

Kaspax tried to remind himself what inconspicuous meant as he found himself constantly getting in the way of traders and market-goers no matter where he stood. Finally – after he had stood on the toes of a woman and her bull-shouldered husband shoved him out of the way with a mouthful of foreign curses that he was sure might make even Tourmarches Blastares blush – he slunk back into a niche between two stalls. 'This'll do,' he muttered, then set about studying the throng. The two akhi spearmen still guarded the main street leading up into this bazaar, beside the log-wagon and squabbling men. Apart from that, there was little else to keep an eye on. Then he noticed the trader Apion had bought the scarf from was gone from his stall. He scrutinised the crowd again, and saw the trader once more. Talking with someone. A third akhi. Kaspax's eyes narrowed. And when the trader pointed to the tavern, his blood turned to ice.

Kaspax watched as the akhi rushed off towards the heart of the city. His heart battered on his ribs and he felt fear's talons grasp his shoulders.

–

Apion watched the old man finish off his meal. There it was again. A snatched glance to the entrance. He picked up his knife as if to eat his own meal, and furtively angled it so it caught the light. The reflection was dull, but showed enough of the entrance to assuage his fears. Nobody there bar some toothless drunk. *Stow your doubts for once, man*, he chided himself.

'Shall we talk now?' Apion said.

The old Persian nodded. 'Yes, yes. Tell me, is it true what they say? You slew Lady Maria's husband?'

'He gave me no choice,' Apion muttered, that moment atop the citadel of Hierapolis coming back to him like a black wind.

'I hope Lady Maria understands that. I have always wondered what my wife might have said had I rescued her from slavery. Would she ever have forgiven me for letting our daughters die?'

Apion nodded and made to reply, but the breath caught in his lungs. '*Daughters?* A moment ago they were sons?'

The old man stopped chewing, his eyes widening. His lips twitched wordlessly, then his brow furrowed as he scowled at the tavern entrance.

'Sir!' Kaspax's cry filled the filthy inn. 'Run!'

Apion swung round to see the rider at the entrance. Before he could rise, Danush's hands slapped down on his in an attempt to pin him where he sat. 'It is too late,' the old man snarled, his friendly demeanour vanishing like a thin mist, lips curling back to reveal his yellowed teeth. 'It is time to pay for your sins!'

Apion snarled and threw Danush off, then kicked the table back, sending the old man, the cups and plates scattering back across the tavern floor.

Suddenly, as he made to leap from his chair and flee, the slumbering, snoring Seljuk at the next table shot up – not a trace of sleep in his eyes. He swiped an axe out from behind his back, swinging it towards Apion's head. Apion bent back from the blow, then brought his forearm crashing into the man's neck. The big man stumbled forward, stunned. Apion leapt upon him, pressing the giant's head ear-down on the table then drawing and punching down with his lengthy dagger. With a spout of dark blood, the blade plunged into his temple and burst from the other one, pinning his skull to the table. The giant's eyes rolled in his head and his body slackened.

Apion swung away from the scene and leapt over tables and chairs to get to the entrance before the stampede of confused and terrified clientele. Outside, Kaspax pushed the reins of the Thessalian into his hands and in an instant, the pair were mounted. 'What's happening?'

'They're coming!' Kaspax bawled, looking over his shoulder. There, at the east end of the market, descending from the heart of the city, a pack of Seljuk riders were barging through the crowd. Apion's gaze snared on the lead rider. The stud-rimmed helm and nose-guard, the scale vest. It was the wraith-like rider, the one with Nasir's armour from the Cilician Gates. *No!* he mouthed.

The rider roared his horsemen forward, and the crowd in the market square scattered, screaming. 'This way, sir,' Kaspax gasped, urging his mount towards the street leading downhill and off to the western gate. They barged through the throng but Apion saw that they would be caught in moments by their pursuers. As he urged his mount on out of the square, he glanced to the log-laden wagon at the near entrance and, without a second thought, drew his scimitar and swept it across the ropes holding the cargo in place. With a hollow thunder, the logs spilled across the entrance to the square, blocking the oncoming riders.

'The gates are open,' Kaspax panted, pointing through the hastily parting crowds.

'Don't talk, ride!' Apion snarled. He snatched a glance over his shoulder to see the riders trying to clamber over the fallen logs. Two made it, another few fell, then the lead rider leapt over too.

They burst clear of the city's western gates and out onto the vast Persian plain again. For just an instant, there was an illusion of safety, then he heard the rumble of the three riders still in pursuit. 'Archers!' the lead rider roared. A thrum of bows sounded from the gatehouse, then with a whoosh of arrows, a shower of missiles spattered around them. One scored Apion's thigh. He stifled a cry and tried as best he could to lie flat on the saddle, pressing his mount's flanks for every drop of haste.

Every time he glanced back, the city of Mosul was shrinking into the horizon, yet the three pursuing riders were there, just a few hundred paces behind, just out of range to use their bows. The chase continued like this for over an hour. Behind them, a pained whinny sounded as one Seljuk mare foundered, its leg snapping as it fell. But the remaining two did not relent. The rider with the stud-rimmed helm seemed the faster of the two, and took to loosing his arrows as they gained just a little ground. When they thundered down into a dusty hollow, Apion could feel his Thessalian's heart pounding, and noticed its skin was lathered with sweat and foam was gathering at its mouth.

'We have to stop,' he cried over the rush of air to Kaspax. 'Be ready to peel away. We will take on one man each.'

Kaspax nodded hurriedly.

'And Kaspax – stow your fear. Ready... *now!*'

Apion kicked his mount's right flank, bringing the gelding arcing round to the left. Kaspax reflected this move, bringing his stallion swinging to the right. The two Seljuks slowed for a moment as they rode down into the wide hollow, seeing the two Byzantine riders coming round for them. Their confusion was fleeting, as they swiftly snatched up their bows and nocked them.

Apion locked eyes with the onrushing shadowy one, watching his draw. The rider loosed and Apion threw himself from the saddle and clear of the missile's flight. He crashed to the dust, tumbling over and over then pushing himself to his feet. As the Seljuk drew again, only paces away, Apion saw it was his last arrow. He bounded over and leapt up to barge the rider from his mount, the arrow flying off into the brush. As the rider scrambled to his feet, Apion drew his scimitar and the Seljuk did likewise.

The pair circled one another. At this distance, Apion was in no doubt now; this figure wore the armour of Nasir. 'Who are you,' he panted, his scimitar extended.

'I am everything you should fear,' the rider said, his voice a growl. He could see only the dark skin and snarling lips of this one, the eyes shaded under the rim of the helm. 'I live only to slay the *Haga*.'

Apion shook his head. 'Why do you wear Bey Nasir's garb?'

The rider laughed at this. A cold laugh. Slowly, he reached up to prise the helm away. The only noise was the nearby *smash-smash* of Kaspax and the other rider in combat. Apion gawped as the rider's dark locks tumbled to his shoulders, framing the fawn-skinned face of a boy, barely fifteen. His square jaw was lined with the beginnings of a beard. But it was the boy's eyes that pinned him. Sparkling emerald eyes, just like his own.

The boy's face creased in anger. 'I am what you created,' he said as if spitting a lump of gristle. 'I am of your seed.'

Apion shook his head, his mind refusing to believe what his heart was telling him.

'But Bey Nasir was my true father... until you struck him down,' the boy continued.

Apion felt his legs grow numb, his head swam. 'You are my... son?' he said, his voice hoarse and cracking. His mind spun, thinking of those few and precious days he had spent with Maria, many years ago.

'Didn't you hear me? I shun your blood, just as my mother shunned you. I am Taylan bin Nasir.'

Apion shook his head, realisation dawning. 'Then Maria *is* alive?'

Taylan snarled at this. 'Do not speak her name, you godless whoreson!'

'But you must know of her whereabouts?'

'I do, *Haga*, but you never will. She is far from here and she will always be far from you.' The boy grinned a feral grin, his eyes uplit by the light reflected from his scimitar blade. 'Now you will go to your godless realm, *Haga*, and you will tell all the *djinns* there that Taylan, son of Bey Nasir, sent you there.'

When Taylan lunged forward, Apion threw up his blade, parrying the strike. It was deft and strong. They exchanged blows and sparks showered between them as their scimitars sang. At last they parted, panting. 'This is wrong, Taylan,' Apion pleaded, the scene so reminiscent of his final contest with Nasir.

From nearby, a sharp cracking of bone rang out, accompanied by a visceral cry. The second Seljuk rider slumped, Kaspax's sword embedded in his breast. Kaspax pulled his sword clear and staggered away, coming to aid Apion. Apion flicked up a finger to still him.

He turned back to Taylan. 'You are outnumbered,' he said flatly.

Taylan's eyes blazed with indignation at this. With a roar, he surged forward. The boy's blade flashed down for Apion's shoulder, and Apion could only fall back from the strike, throwing his sword arm up for another parry. This time, the two blades met with a dull shearing noise, and the blade of Taylan's sword spun clear of the hilt. The boy staggered back, glancing at his shattered weapon, then glowering at Apion.

'You are outnumbered and you are disarmed,' Apion insisted, then threw down his own scimitar tip-first so it quivered in the dust and held out his hands, palms open. 'The fight is over. Now please, talk with me.'

Taylan shook his head, eyes burning. 'Never,' he hissed as he backed towards his mount. His gaze never left Apion as he swung up and onto the saddle. Then he pointed a finger at Apion as if it was a dagger.

'In every dream, in every waking moment, with every step you take on the battlefield, you should beware. I will be coming for you, *Haga*. I will not stop until I have avenged my true father. And my mother's whereabouts? Never!' With that, he swung his mare round and galloped off, back to the east.

Apion slumped to his knees. No words, actions or emotions came to him. He could only stare numbly at Taylan's fading dust plume.

A crash of iron beside him pulled him from his trance. He blinked, seeing Kaspax had fallen onto his back. The young rider's face was pale, grey even. Blood spidered from his lips and it was only then that

Apion saw the bone-deep thigh wound the other Seljuk had inflicted on him. He shuffled over to lift Kaspax's head and shoulders.

'Sir, I'll need to be getting back home.' The young rider's words were badly slurred and his pupils were dilating. 'Vilyam will be… Vilyam will…' Kaspax's words trailed off with a sigh. At last, emotion came to Apion in a ruthless tide. He tried to stifle the tears as best he could. 'Vilyam will be fine. And you'd better rest, for it will be a long journey,' he said, sweeping his hand over the dead rider's face to close his eyes.

He laid Kaspax down and turned to face the east once more. He had heard much talk of fate and destiny in his time. Much of it he had scoffed at. But at that moment, he knew he had to face Taylan again.

–

White silk veils billowed in the gentle breeze that trickled in through the tall, arched windows of the hospital on Mosul's citadel hill. Maria closed her eyes and let the pleasant air bathe her, taking the fire from her skin and cooling her in her bed. This was as fine a pleasure as any she had experienced. Up here the air was fresh and – apart from some ruckus in the silk market this afternoon – the racket from the streets was barely discernable too. That was why the Sultan's vizier, Nizam, had chosen to build this grand hospital here. The wards were spacious and finely ornamented with marble floors, beautifully tiled walls and fine silks – more akin to a palace than a place where the sick were sent to convalesce. Her train of thought ended at this, and she touched a hand to her abdomen. The hard swelling in there seemed more tender today than it had a few months ago when she had been admitted to the hospital, and her skin seemed more tautly stretched across it. At least now she knew what her future held, she thought, remembering her discussion with the physician that morning.

Just then, that same physician shuffled in wearing a white cap and robes. An old man with a face wrinkled like the skin of a prune, his shoulders rounded and his expression serene. She had often wondered at the strength of those who lived only to care for others in this place. Day after day faced with mortality and locked away from the vibrancy of life elsewhere. The physician carried with him a steaming urn of broth. The elderly lady nearby barely had the strength to refuse the meal, but the man ignored her pleas, instead sitting on her bedside, speaking to her in gentle tones as he filled her bowl then lifted it to her lips. She drank, and as she did so, a tear snaked down her cheek. In all the months Maria had been in here, nobody had visited the lady. The old woman's husband had died and left her a wealthy woman. Wealthy but alone. Now, in her final days, she found conversation only with Maria and a few other patients.

Maria had only one who came to visit her. Her son, Taylan. And every time he came to her he seemed ever more consumed by a burning hatred. That fire had been kindled over a year ago when her husband, Nasir, the man Taylan had long thought to be his father, had been slain. Slain by his true father. She had never regretted telling Taylan the truth about Apion, but she constantly feared what the boy might do with this knowledge. Without the bitter Nasir to scold him and put him down, Taylan had grown strong in this last year, in physical stature and in arrogance. His stock had risen swiftly in the military ranks too. She remembered that day he had come to her after his first battle. In his excitement, he had neglected to wash his fingernails, still clogged with dried blood. His eyes had shone like beacons as he had recounted to her his victory. How he had slain so many Byzantine spearmen that he had lost count. He had not understood why she wept at this. So now he told her little, and they largely sat in silence for the duration of his visits. But she still heard the tales of his exploits from passing orderlies and the occasional soldier sent into these wards. It seemed that Taylan was now leading riders into battle at barely fifteen years of age, and this had even brought him to the Sultan's attention. It seemed that Alp Arslan was to teach him the art of war.

What art is there in war? How many crimson scenes must a man paint to grow tired of battle? She scoffed, her lips curling and her nose wrinkling, thinking of all that was absent from her life. Those lost days when she and Father had lived a simple but happy life in the clement and pleasant valleys of Byzantine Chaldia. Neither Seljuk nor Byzantine, just a farming family. In those days, Apion and Nasir had lived almost as brothers, neither yet sullied by the conflict. But all had been swept up in the ensuing war, all now no more than dust. All except Apion, a legend known across the borderlands, or so she had heard. The *Haga*, one of the few whom the Sultan's armies feared. Some tales labelled him the bringer of death, the burner of souls; others spoke of him as a valiant soul, fighting on in hope of peace.

What have you become, dear Apion? She wondered, thinking of how war and hatred had twisted Nasir into a rancorous and lonely individual. *And what is to become of our boy?*

She sensed him coming at that moment, hearing the clatter of iron armour that rarely echoed in this sanctuary. He came to her, sat by her bedside as usual. The faint beginnings of a beard were now taking shape. His lips were fixed thin and straight. His eyes betrayed some fresh anger, gazing through her.

'Son,' she said, reaching out to touch his hand. This seemed to break the spell and he looked at her now as a son should. But only for a moment. Swiftly, his eyes filled with pity. Maria said nothing. She knew her hair greyed with every passing day, and her once rounded, healthy figure was wasting away. They had to talk today, she thought, placing a hand on the tender lump on her abdomen again. He had to know.

'Come closer, son.'

CHAPTER 6

The Lion's Pride

Muhammud strode through a strange land, his bare feet crunching across a scree of broken bones. A cloudy veil seemed to mask the heavens, with just a watery and weak sun and a featureless sky offering a twilight to illuminate his path. He knew he was on a journey, but he had forgotten its purpose, it seemed. He had no burden, no companions… no reason to be here. The only thing that gave meaning to this trek was the one feature in the landscape up ahead; a jagged mountain, impossibly tall and sheer. Mount Otuken, he realised, recognising it as an exaggerated memory of the mount that marked the heart of the ancient Seljuk tribal homelands on the steppes. But without the long grass, the fresh breeze of the plain and the pleasant heat of the sun on his skin that his ancestors had so often told him of, this seemed hollow, meaningless. Yet still he found himself drawn to it like a moth to a flame, for this represented all that it was to be a noble and legendary Seljuk warrior. Here the khagan would adorn himself in yak tails and bright fabrics, then mark a brave man's face with ox blood and bestow him with his battle name, war drums thundering in the background as all the tribesmen hailed their new heroes. Yet here there was nothing, no sound but the crunching of his feet on the bones, and the mountain seemed to draw no closer no matter how fast he trod.

He stopped, panting. 'I am Alp Arslan!' he bellowed to the lonely mountain. His words died with the faintest of echoes. A silence followed and was then pierced by a cackle. He saw a solitary, white-bearded figure on the mountain's lower slopes. Uncle Tugrul. The Falcon. The Sultan before him.

'Ah, you are tired and weak, Muhammud!' Tugrul boomed haughtily. 'I always suspected you would not be strong enough.'

Muhammud shuddered at this and at the wave of self-loathing the words brought. Then anger took over. 'I have excelled where you failed, Uncle Tugrul. I have swollen our lands and multiplied our armies many times over!'

'Ah, yes, and now the people call you the Mountain Lion, Alp Arslan. When they stand before you, at least… but what does Yusuf call you?'

Muhammud could hear the mocking edge to his dead uncle's voice. Yusuf was one of many who coveted his throne and spread poisoned words about his rule.

'And tell me this, Mountain Lion; why is it that I stand up here on the mountain of legend and you dwell down there?'

Muhammud, enraged, broke into a run. He sucked in breath after breath and soon his muscles burned and his skin was laced with sweat. At last he came to the foot of the mountain. But when he tried to run up its lower slopes, he slipped and slid back down into the bony scree.

'Come now, nephew. Did I not teach you how to climb the mountain?' Tugrul laughed.

Muhammud frowned, then looked around the bones littering the flat ground. Ribs, skulls, femurs and spines, all jumbled together underfoot. Some skulls still wore Seljuk helms, some limbs were clad in rags of Byzantine armour, others in the robes and armour of the enemies he had long ago trampled into the dust; the Ghaznavids, the Daylamids, the Fatimids and the countless hill tribes and desert federations that once ruled the various lands of the now unified Seljuk Sultanate. He looked up at Tugrul, then began piling the bones up to make a ramp. On and on he fetched up the bones until, at last, the ramp was complete, leading right up to where Tugrul waited. He ascended, fixing his uncle with a stern gaze. Yet Tugrul was unperturbed. 'And what else did I teach you, nephew?' he crowed.

Muhammud frowned, slowing, just a few steps from setting foot onto the mountainside. Spots of rain pattered down around him. No, not rain: thick, dark rivulets of blood. Soon it was a rattling downpour, and a coppery stink permeated the air.

'What else did I teach you?' Tugrul repeated, his eyes widening, pointing over Muhammud's shoulder.

Muhammud froze, hearing a foreign clacking noise over the rattling blood-rain, right behind him. He swung round to see that some bones from the ramp had gathered to form a grinning skeleton, its arm raised and wielding a dagger.

Muhammud gasped and fell, the skeleton falling on top of him and the dagger hacking down for his throat.

His eyes shot open and the nightmarish image faded… only to be replaced by another, this time all too real.

A foreign face hovered over his. A leathery-skinned, bearded man, clasping a blade. The stranger's eyes widened and he plunged the blade down. Instinct took over, and Alp Arslan rolled clear of the blow, the blade piercing the pillow. Ostrich feathers filled the air and the assassin wailed in terror, realising he had missed his chance.

'You dog!' the Sultan snarled. 'You rabid son of a whore!' he roared, leaping across the bed and onto the assassin. The pair fell to the floor and he grasped at the man's wrist, twisting at the dagger-hand with all his strength. The brute who had come to slay him was strong, but his fear seemed to beat him. The dagger blade turned until the tip pointed for the assassin's chest. Alp Arslan held his gaze, pushing the blade lower, lower, lower. Then the man gasped as the blade ground through his breastbone and sunk into his heart.

Alp Arslan staggered back from the dark pool of blood that spread out under the assassin's corpse, staining one of the pair of silk carpets on the floor of his fine bedchamber here in the palace at Isfahan. As his breathing began to calm, feathers settled all around him. His long, dark hair was lashed round his neck, stuck there like a noose, and the dangling tails of his moustache were plastered to his face with sweat. Just then, a cluster of guards barged in, spears levelled, switching them this way and that in search of the threat.

'The danger is gone, you fools!' he cried at them. They lowered their weapons and averted their eyes. It was then that another figure hobbled in, wincing, clutching at an egg-sized lump on his scarred, shaven scalp.

'He took me by surprise, my lord,' Kilic said, dropping to one knee and placing his scimitar against his breast. 'I have failed you. Give the word and I shall fall upon my sword.'

'I would, but your blood would sully my silk carpet, and one has already been ruined today. Now put your sword away, you fool,' Alp Arslan fumed, waving his loyal bodyguard up.

The rather sheepish Kilic rose to his feet, then looked at the body of the assassin.

'Yusuf's man?'

'Doubtless,' Alp Arslan replied, his nose wrinkling at the thought of the rival who coveted the Seljuk throne. 'And I am equally certain we will have no trail that leads back to that cur.'

'But this is not the first time he has tried to—'

'For now, we need his armies,' Alp Arslan cut Kilic off. 'I will deal with him when the time is right. Now take the body, throw it in the river. I have business to attend to.'

He closed his eyes. In moments, the slithering sound of the bloodied corpse being dragged away faded, and he heard only the squawking of a parakeet from outside. His head thudded mercilessly and he clutched at his temples, turning his bloodshot, foul glare upon the jug of rich red Syrian wine by his bedside. It had been tart and invigorating when he started it the previous evening, washing away the headaches of many hours of planning. But it had become tasteless before long, and it numbed his mind as quickly as it had numbed his tongue. If those nightmares were the outcome of such indulgence, he seethed, then he would avoid it in future. He contemplated the notion for a moment before rubbishing it, knowing it was the only way he could rid his mind of troubles.

He knotted his hair upon the nape of his neck and slipped on a green *yalma*, the garment absorbing the moisture from his skin, then he strode out of the arched end of the bedchamber and rested his palms on the balcony edge. Grape and ivy vines snaked across the enclosed, vividly tiled courtyard, baking in the March noon sun. He breathed deeply and enjoyed the warmth on his skin, then glanced down to the babbling marble fountain in the centre of the courtyard, nestling in the shade of a cluster of orange trees. The noisy parakeets chattered away in the branches, as if in debate with the incessant cicadas. Suddenly, they scattered when a raptor cried from above. He squinted up and held his arm out for his pet hunting falcon to land. The bird settled on his wrist, its claws sharp on the Sultan's skin. He smoothed the creature's feathers with the back of one finger, then moved his hand to let it hop onto the perch on the balcony. 'Ah, Tugrul,' he mouthed into the ether with a desert-dry grin as he thought of his formidable uncle, 'if only I could have tamed you so.'

He heard the courtyard gate creak open, and saw that it was Malik, his son, and young Taylan. Both had travelled here in preparation for what was to come. The pair were of the same age, and firm friends. He watched as they chattered by the fountain, recalling how only a few years ago they had played together with carved wooden toys. Now they talked of war and commanded wings of riders. A wistful smile arose at this.

He thought of those days, many years ago, after his uncle Tugrul had taken this city from the Daylamids, when he would sit by that very fountain, looking up here and envying his uncle's lot. He looked to the shatranj board sitting by the balcony edge. It had remained untouched since that game he had begun with the *Haga* nearly two years ago in Caesarea. That day, he had sworn to the noble border warrior that the end would have to come for Byzantium. Hubris had fuelled those last words, and he regretted them – or rather, he regretted the truth of them. Like him, the Byzantine Emperor was compelled to cement his place on the throne with military success. And so a great battle was coming. The two great empires would have to clash, and the wheels were already in motion.

The skeletal glares and blood-rain of his nightmare refused to let him be.

The mustering field outside Isfahan was awash with activity. Every spare patch of dusty land outside the beetling southern walls was packed with soldiers. Artisans and engineers stretched and tested ever-more-powerful stone throwers and jabbered about the art of building war towers. Regiments of akhi spearmen clashed in practice bouts, their shields and wooden poles *clack-clacking* and their skin glistening with sweat under the searing mid-afternoon sun. Bowyers worked in the shade of their tent awnings, hewing, boiling and gluing strips of maple wood, then fitting them to horn grips to fashion new composite bows. Thick packs of ghazi riders swept around timber poles, loosing arrow after arrow at great speed, before sweeping for the beleaguered, arrow-riddled posts, drawing their swords and hacking at them as they sped past. At a cry from their lead rider, they would swarm like a pack of darting swallows, only to reform moments later in a pack or a line. The ghulam lancers practised galloping in wedges, spears levelled, man and mount encased in iron. When their lances hit the hay-stuffed sacks they used as targets, little remained bar puffs of straw and scraps of hemp.

Alp Arslan walked to the edge of this field. His aged and wise Vizier, Nizam, walked with him. As always, his great, scarred body-guard, Kilic, followed just a pace or two behind. And today, the two young men from the courtyard walked with him as well. Malik was eager to point out to Taylan the infantry he had already led into battle against the last traces of Fatimid resistance in southern Syria. Taylan seemed oddly quiet – he had been since arriving. Maturity, maybe, or some dark cloud on his mind, perhaps. *Very reminiscent of his father*, Alp Arslan mused, thinking of Bey Nasır.

'The secret to holding our hard-won empire is in the blend of those we choose to defend it, Sultan,' Nizam said. 'The old lands of Persia provide our heavy cavalry and our siege technology.' He gestured over to the ghulam and the men working on the stone throwers. 'The hill peoples of the north and east serve as hardy infantry.' He nodded to the vast ranks of akhi spearmen. 'And those of the true Seljuk blood, from the steppes of the north, furnish us with our swift and nimble ghazi cavalry. No one of the factions we have subsumed has too dominant a position in our ranks. That is a mistake that has been made in generations past, when armies have marched against their masters.'

Alp Arslan smoothed at his moustache. 'A fine strategy, Vizier. I trust you with my life and value your every word. I don't doubt your wisdom and knowledge in all that is non-martial; you have embellished the cities of the Sultanate with fine schools, monuments and palaces, and established an infrastructure of roads, law and trade that will see it last. And I like your policy of limiting the power of the factions within our armies. But I'm not so wary of my army turning against me as I am of the single, hired blades that Yusuf seems to be able to bring within an inch of my throat.'

Kilic hung his head in shame a few feet behind.

'Ah, that seems to be the lot of any great leader, Sultan. Perhaps you should see the coveting of your golden throne as a measure of your power?' Nizam replied.

'Perhaps I should have a timber chair made in its place?' Alp Arslan countered wryly.

They walked on and Alp Arslan's gaze hung on the regiment of ghulam and akhi just off of the mustering field. 'They are ready to ride?' he asked Nizam.

'As you decreed, Sultan.'

'Good, for I am ready to lead them. But equally important is the army I despatch to screen our movements from enemy eyes.'

'Quite,' Nizam nodded.

They paused by the ghazi training area, and he noticed Taylan seemed particularly captivated by these riders. 'You have been training your riders, I hear?'

Taylan started, unaware he was being watched. 'Sultan,' he bowed.

'The future bodes well for you to one day rise to be a bey and lead a ghulam wing, as your father did.'

Taylan shook his head. 'I have no wish to lead ghulam. The ghazis are a finer weapon – nimble and deadly. They ride mares, and a mare is a Seljuk mount. They fight first with bows, and the bow is a Seljuk weapon. My father always said as much.'

'Bey Nasir lives on in your heart, doesn't he?'

Taylan fell silent again. Alp Arslan recalled when the boy was younger and he would come along with Nasir to musterings like this. Young Taylan had hung on his father's every word, always eager to impress and show what he had learned. But there was always something missing; for all Taylan's affection, there was no love shown in return from Nasir. Indeed, Nasir had often shouted Taylan down, regardless of the validity of the boy's comments. His lips played with a dry smile as he remembered his blood-dream.

'I once loved my uncle Tugrul unconditionally. But when I was old enough to understand his flaws, I hated him too. It is a curious thing.'

Taylan avoided the Sultan's gaze, seemingly watching the ghazis intently once more, but Alp Arslan saw him wipe at his eye. Then he thought to ask after the boy's mother, but decided against this, recalling the rumour he had heard regarding her health. This young man would soon be alone, it seemed.

'Break them, then ride them hard for three years,' Taylan exclaimed suddenly as his wing of eighty ghazis swept past. 'Three years pasture after that and then,' he punched a fist into his palm, '*then* you have a war horse!'

Alp Arslan smiled at this. 'You have trained them well, it seems.'

Taylan nodded, the look of a wizened general crossing his face – no doubt learned from the beys he had been serving under in this last year. 'I have put my all into their development. Indeed, they have acquired some new skills, and rediscovered some long-forgotten ones too. Skills that could change the fortunes of our army. Do you notice anything about the stirrups, Sultan?'

Alp Arslan studied one rider as he sped past. The leather straps hanging down on each of the horse's flanks were knotted onto the usual foot-sized iron ring. But the ring was different – flat-bottomed. 'For stability?'

'Exactly. A firmer foothold to rise from the saddle than ever before. It was something Bey Nasir planned to try out, before...' His words fell away, then he cupped his hands around his mouth and called out to one of his riders. The rider's head twisted towards Taylan and he read the command. In the blink of an eye he stood tall on his iron stirrups, continuing to loose arrow after arrow as fast as he had done when seated – one every five or six heartbeats. 'See how he does not quaver when standing tall?'

Alp Arslan's eyes narrowed, his attention snagged.

'And that is not all,' Taylan continued, pointing to one squat and slightly built rider with a yellowish complexion. While the other riders clasped their next few arrows in the palms of their draw hands, this man clutched two arrows in each knuckle of his draw–hand.

'Ah, the mark of an archer who has mastered the reverse shot?' Alp Arslan grinned, noticing this one wore white falcon feathers on the rim of his helm. 'I have not seen those feathers in our ranks for many years.'

'I have reintroduced the custom. This man is the champion of this wing. He can loose an arrow every heartbeat,' Taylan said, then barked a command to the rider. 'He and the others with these skills call themselves the *White Falcons.*'

The rider loosed at a lightning rate, nocking a new arrow from his knuckles in a flurry of dexterity. *Thock-thock-thock-thock-thock-thock!* The arrows rattled into the timber post one after another, barely a heartbeat between each, splinters flying.

Alp Arslan stopped in his tracks. 'You have many riders capable of this?'

'A handful right now, but enough to train the rest,' Taylan nodded, pointing out the sixteen or so riders amongst his eighty who also wore the white falcon plumes. 'Soon, I hope to have a whole regiment of them.'

Alp Arslan looked to the aged Bey Gulten on the training area. This grey-bearded old warrior was to lead the next push into Byzantium – leading the army that would screen his own regiments' movements along the borderlands. Gulten was a fierce old horse, but not one known for his innovation. Perhaps now was the time for new blood to lead. He placed a hand on Taylan's shoulder.

–

While the Sultan strolled off to chat with Nizam, Taylan's mind spun. For a moment his fears for his mother and the swirling gale of angst over his slain father ebbed. Instead, the Sultan's words swam in his mind. He turned to look over his ghazi riders. The swarm swept around again, loosing another quiverful of arrows into the shredded timber post. *Thock-thock-thock-thock!* All hit home bar a few. While most of the riders had over half a quiver of arrows remaining, the squat champion's was empty, and he started on his second quiver as they arced round to the far side of the training field.

Taylan made to stride over to his swarm.

But at that moment, Bey Gulten and his riders nearly cut across Taylan's path, stopping only paces away from trampling him. The old bey's face creased in a scowl, his nose wrinkling as he glowered down at Taylan. 'Move back from the training field, boy!' Gulten snapped, swiping a hand across his path as if swatting a fly. His men chuckled at this.

Gulten had been good to him when he first joined the aged bey's ranks a year ago. Back then, the mottled old warrior seemed to revel in showing him how things were done. It was when Taylan had started to show innovation in how he led his own eighty that Gulten's stance had changed. Jealousy had blackened the man's demeanour like a scudding cloud passing over the sun. Taylan and his riders were soon given the most dangerous sorties – in the vanguard, usually. But when Taylan excelled in these forays, it only served to enrage Gulten further. Then, when he had tried to warn Bey Gulten about the danger of being pressed towards the Cilician Gates last year, the bitter Bey had mocked Taylan in front of the whole army. The very same army that had been shattered the following day in that narrow pass.

'What are you here for?' Gulten continued, eyeing the rough, grubby yalma Taylan wore. 'To shovel horse shit for your eighty cart ponies?' This brought his men into an even rowdier chorus of laughter.

Taylan felt his blood chill under the glare of so many, all significantly older than him. His throat seemed dry and his tongue reluctant to reply, but he steeled himself and ignored the watching masses, focusing only on Bey Gulten. 'How many riders do you have here on the field today?' he asked.

'I do not answer to boys, now get off the field, whelp!' Gulten snapped, then nocked and stretched his bow as if to loose at the ground near Taylan's feet. He trotted forward from his pack, as if to intimidate. His men gasped in anticipation of some clash.

'Aye, you have plenty of arrows left with which to torment me, unlike my champion rider!' Taylan scoffed, gesturing to the far side of the field and the rider with the white plume. Bey Gulten's men shared wide-eyed glances now, some even stifling laughter. Gulten caught wind of this and his bold posture in the saddle faltered as he shot a sour glare over his shoulder at his men. Then, when Gulten came to within a few paces of Taylan, bow nocked and stretched, Taylan found the strength to hold his glower. 'Close enough for you? I watched you and your men practise. I saw that only a few arrows missed every time you swept past that post. I saw that they were yours, every time.'

Now a low murmur broke into a babble of chuckling as the riders failed to contain their amusement.

'And you will address me as Bey Taylan from now on,' Taylan added.

Bey Gulten, mounted and armed yet separated from his pack, suddenly lost his remaining pluck, his bow slackening and his tongue darting out to wet his lips in search of some riposte that Taylan knew would never come.

'You are a bey now?' Gulten muttered, glancing over to the spot where Taylan had been in conversation with the Sultan just moments ago, his face creasing in confusion. 'You are my equal?'

'I am Bey Taylan bin Nasir. And no, I am not your equal. I am your superior. You are to hand over your army to me.'

The man's face now blanched and his eyes widened. 'You, but I...' He frowned, looking from Taylan to the side of the training field, where Alp Arslan stood. The Sultan gave him a nod that spoke a thousand words. Gulten slid from his saddle and bowed before Taylan, casting a foul gaze to the dust. 'Very well. Forgive me, Bey Taylan.'

At the same time, the rest of the riders straightened up, shoulders stiffening, throats bulging as they gulped in realisation. Taylan's eighty riders clustered around them at this point, including the white-feathered champion.

'Stand up, Bey Gulten. Have your men ready their mounts well for the coming days. I will grant you a quarter of the riders, for you are to go south to tackle the ever-rebellious Fatimids.' *Far, far from me, you dog*, he thought. Then he raised his voice so all could hear. 'The rest of you, groom and feed your mares well, for you are to come north-west with me. You will all be part of the sword that sinks into Byzantium's flesh.'

The men roared in delight at this, only Gulten was hesitant, his eyes still smouldering with anger and shame.

CHAPTER 7

A Dagger in the Dark

A hot spring day bathed Constantinople, and every street pulsed with masses of citizens eager to forge their way to the Hippodrome. The tips of the horseshoe-shaped arena were lined with purple imperial banners, rippling gently in a northerly breeze from the Golden Horn that carried a salt-tang with it. The air seemed to crackle in expectation at the races that were to come after so many months of austerity.

Inside, Psellos took his seat in the upper tiers of the eastern stand, with two Numeroi spearmen flanking him. His ears stung at the incessant cheering and babble of the crowd – already some one hundred thousand strong – and his nose wrinkled at their stench. This was the first day of races for nearly a year, yet the wretches of this city who had been dangerously close to rebellion just months ago now fawned over their emperor for bending to their will and reinstating the much-loved spectacle. He glanced across the arena. Beyond the tip of the western stand and across the city skyline, he could see the hazy blackened ruin of the Shrine of Blachernae, jutting like a rotting tooth at the northern end of the land walls. He had paid handsomely to have the holy shrine put to the torch one chilly December night at the tail end of last year. It was supposed to be the omen that would tip the people into outright rebellion against Diogenes. *Yet somehow,* Psellos sighed, *the cur still has the throne.*

Suddenly, the babble died and all heads looked to the *kathisma* – the imperial box shaded by a purple silk awning – perched a few rows behind Psellos on the tip of the eastern stand's midpoint. Following the crowd's lead, Psellos also twisted round to look up to the kathisma. Two varangoi had ascended the spiral staircase leading directly from the Cochlia Gate of the Imperial Palace and entered the box. They stepped to either side of the ornate chairs set up in there and stared out at the crowd like sentinels. Psellos scowled at the two empty chairs, remembering that the emperor had been absent from the city over the previous two summers – on campaign and at the mercy of hired blades and saboteurs. During those precious months he had been seated there in the kathisma's shade with John Doukas, manipulating the fickle people to his own ends, lavishing them with games bought with Doukid money. Now, it seemed, Diogenes was wise to what had gone on, choosing to remain in the capital while appointing Manuel Komnenos to lead an eastern campaign in his stead. This would allow Diogenes' armies to at once fight off the empire's foes and for the man himself to quell the unrest of the citizens. Psellos' spies had told him of the emperor's designs: to empty the imperial treasury in an effort to train and strengthen the themata armies serving under Komnenos – to make them powerful and numerous. Surely, Psellos had thought, this meant the people would still be deprived of their games, for the imperial treasury was nearly bare. How, then, had the cur managed to fund today's races? Such a spectacle was not cheap. Not at all.

Just then, the crowd erupted into a chorus of '*Dio-genes! Dio-genes!*' followed with '*Ba-si-le-us! Ba-si-le-us! Ba-si-le-us!*' as two figures emerged from the back of the kathisma. Romanus Diogenes and Lady Eudokia. The emperor wore a cloak of gold brocade, a chequered klibanion – the small iron squares gold then bronze in turn – that hugged his torso, and the bejewelled imperial diadem on his head, gold crosses dangling from each side. Eudokia wore a green silk robe and cradled her pregnant belly with a gentle hand, but glowered down upon the crowd like a warrior. Cold, austere and aloof as always. Psellos' top lip twitched as they bathed in the adulation. He had backed the Doukas family in expectation that they would swiftly dethrone Diogenes and seize power again. So far, he had backed a losing horse.

The announcer cried out then, bringing the crowd to a sudden hush. 'First, we are blessed to witness the greatest rider of recent years return to the track. After three years of retirement, he will ride for us one last time. I speak of the champion of the races, the breaker of hearts, the swiftest of all Greeks. I give you… Diabatenus of Athens!' The crowd erupted again, confetti blossoming into the air and flitting down onto the sand of the racetrack as a handsome rider drove his gilded chariot out onto the circuit. His fine, almost sculpted nose and cheekbones were framed to perfection by his thick, shiny, dark brown locks, swept across his forehead and tucked behind his ears.

Four stallions snorted and shuffled under the burden — a steeldust, two bays and a chestnut, each of them strong and tall and as fine-looking as their rider. Psellos gazed through the man, bored, while the announcer called the other riders out onto the starting line. Flurries of hands shot up as the many bookmakers dotted around the stands were besieged by eager gamblers, most jostling to place their money on Diabatenus. In moments the horns sounded and the chariots burst forth, conjuring a guttural roar from the spectators that shook the sky over Constantinople.

Suddenly, the lesion on his chest burned. The mere itching was but a distant memory. Now when it came it was as if a glowing brand was being held to his skin. He clamped a hand to it, wincing, feeling the glutinous mesh of unhealing skin stick to the fibres of his robe, peeling away, leaving, raw, pink flesh which burned all the more fiercely. He tried to bury the pain, focusing on the racing chariots.

Just then, another figure barged through the crowd and past the two numeroi to sit beside him. John Doukas wore black robes and a shifty gaze. His eyes flicked over his shoulder to the kathisma. 'Did you hear it? The people's cries are an affront to my name. And that bitch carries the death of my family line in her belly,' he growled.

'The people are fickle and their cries change with the wind,' Psellos whispered. 'And when Diogenes is ousted from his throne, Eudokia will be dealt with also.'

'And her babe too?' John's eyes narrowed.

'Diogenes' line will be extinguished, master,' Psellos nodded.

The pair turned their attentions to the race for a moment. The crowd roared as Diabatenus sped round onto his third lap, leading, of course. The cacophony was spliced by a sudden crack of timber as the lead chariot pitched over on itself. The axel of Diabatenus' chariot had snapped and his mounts collapsed in a whinnying heap. The rider himself was catapulted forward, tumbling head over heels through the sand. A chorus of gasps rang out. Diabatenus scrambled to his knees, disbelieving as he glared back at his ruined vehicle, then gawping in terror as the next chariot hurtled round the bend. The second chariot rider lashed furiously at his mounts to steer them around the felled Diabatenus. Likewise, Diabatenus scrambled back from their hooves. They missed him by inches, only for the protruding spoke of the chariot wheel to tear across his handsome face, putting out an eye in a spurt of blood and white matter. His scream seemed to pierce the heavens. Many thousands of spectators groaned at their lost bets, while the bookmakers punched the air in delight.

'Pah – the fool thought victory was a certainty, it seems. Forgot to check his chariot over.' John laughed heartily, heedless of the horribly injured Diabatenus' sobbing as he was carried from the track. 'Now, why did you call me here? You said there was some other matter?'

'Indeed. A matter that we have neglected for some time. A matter that we should resolve at the outset of our… your journey to the imperial throne.'

John's eyes narrowed. 'Aye?'

Psellos steeled himself and straightened his robe. 'To weaken Diogenes, we must dispose of those troublesome dogs who remain loyal to him. Some more troublesome than others.'

'I don't understand?' John said.

Psellos nodded discreetly to the two figures seated a few rows down. One, a hulking, bearded brute with a jutting brow and a flat-boned face and the other wiry and lithe. Both equally skilled as assassins and torturers. 'Plakanos and Lagudes are the finest of my *Portatioi*. They will leave in the morning.'

'Leave? For where?'

'For Chaldia, master,' Psellos grinned.

–

Apion, fresh from bathing after his morning run, ascended the creaking timber stairs to Trebizond's citadel rooftop, the sun-warmed flagstones soothing his bare feet.

The summer morning sky was cloudless as usual, and up here there were no palms or awnings to provide shade, just the flitting shadow of circling gulls and storks and the salt-tang breeze from the sparkling, azure waters of the Pontus Euxinus, the great northern sea whose coastline the citadel was perched over like a sentinel. The setting did much to lift his soul. He knew the moment would be fleeting – as it always was – and made sure to enjoy it.

The flat rooftop was small – about the size of a modest bedchamber – with a crenelated edge and a ballista mounted at each corner. Several smaller fortified balconies jutted from the two floors below where the citadel widened towards its foundations, set in the bedrock of the grassy citadel hill. His gaze drifted on down the hill and into the lower city, across the broad main street, lined with still palms and packed with sweating faces, shouting wagon drivers, bawling traders, camels, oxen and mules – market day once again. Behind the sweltering masses stood the Church of Saint Andreas. Just looking at the church often triggered an unconscious response, and once again he found himself smoothing at the skin on his wrist where he had once worn a prayer rope, as devout as any of the people in the streets below. He sat down in a crenel at the southern edge of the roof, one leg anchored on the rooftop, then laid down the parcel and water skin he carried. As he shuffled to find a comfortable position, a sliver of steel from the edge of one of the mounted ballistae touched his neck. Despite it being sun-warmed, the sensation sent a shiver through him, and scattered the pleasant thoughts from his mind like a wolf amongst deer.

His gaze drifted past the skutatoi-lined city walls and on to the eastern horizon. Somewhere far beyond the cliffs and lush green woods of northern Chaldia, beyond the borders of the empire, some-where deep in Seljuk lands, Maria lived on. Of that there was no longer any doubt. But shielding her like a sentinel was his son. A boy warped by anger.

In every dream, in every waking moment, with every step you take on the battlefield, you should beware. I will be coming for you, Haga. I will not stop.

He dropped his head into his hands and closed his eyes tight. But in the blackness there, he found only more troubles. He had arrived back from Mosul in February only to hear of grim news from the lands of Chaldia and the surrounding themata. Poor harvests had brought famine in places, and tax revenue had suffered as a result. It seemed that the emperor had somehow managed to stave off these crises, finding funds to cover the loss of revenue and to bolster the themata armies, feeding the people and even putting on games in the capital. As always, Romanus was the beacon of hope.

This brought his thoughts to the as yet unattended task of mustering the men of Chaldia from their farms. Manuel Komnenos and his campaign army would be marching east soon, and Manuel had already sent messengers to Apion, pleading with him to bring as many Chal-dians as he could. He sighed, resolving to begin the mustering later that day, then set about opening the food parcel he had brought with him.

Just then, something bolted up the stairs and out onto the rooftop. Something small. A flash of orange. Apion started, his gaze snapping round. But there was nothing there. He frowned, craning his neck to look behind the ballista, sensing something hiding behind there. Suddenly, a ginger and white paw shot round the base of the ballista, claws extended, batting at the timber. Apion's frown melted into a grin.

'You have followed me, Vilyam? In your adoration of me… or in the hope of yet another feed?' Apion's thoughts drifted to the brave lad he had buried out there in the east. 'Kaspax was right about you.'

As if incensed by this slight, Vilyam the tomcat poked his head from behind the ballista base and glared at Apion, whiskers twitching. With a somewhat demanding yowl he trotted into full view, up to Apion's nearest leg, then his eyes narrowed to slits as he erupted into a chorus of purring, brushing his sun-warmed ginger-and-white coat back and forth against Apion's shin. Then he leapt up, somewhat clumsily, onto the roof's crenelated edge, his eyes fixed on the small parcel.

'Ah, it is like that, I see,' Apion chuckled, opening the parcel to reveal a round of fresh bread, a pot of honey and a small strip of salted duck meat. He put the duck meat before Vilyam, then tore at the bread, dipping it in the honey and enjoying the chewy sweetness before washing each mouthful down with cool water.

Vilyam rolled on the wall's edge, purring shamelessly as Apion stroked his white belly. He made to take another sip of his water when he noticed a familiar sight, approaching on the road from the south. Kursores, riding at great haste.

Wordlessly, he corked his water skin, stood then flitted down through the citadel, descended the citadel hill and came to the squat, red brick barrack compound. Ducking under the narrow arched entrance into the stable yard at the rear of the barracks, he found Sha already with the two newly arrived riders.

'Seljuk raiders, more than two hundred of them. They have slaughtered the garrison at Argyroupolis and now they rampage across the farmlands to the south. Ghazi riders and a small pack of infantry – fierce soldiers with twin-headed spears.'

'Daylamid spearmen,' Apion said, recalling the rugged and ferocious hillmen of the Seljuk armies he had faced more than once. He strode forward from the shade of the archway. 'They are holding Argyroupolis?' he said, his thoughts fleeting with images of the dusty mountain town he had spent his first years of service in.

'Strategos!' the sentry saluted, straightening as he turned to Apion. 'No, they have moved on but they shattered the gates, crippled the defences and slew every last soldier in there.'

Sha offered Apion a weary look. 'There were only sixteen men garrisoning those walls, sir.'

'And even that was more than we could afford, Tourmarches. Other settlements went with less watchmen – some even with none,' Apion replied flatly. Then he turned back to the scout riders. 'And the populace?'

'They too were cut down. Some may have scattered and fled into the Parhar Mountains. But I rode through Argyroupolis' streets, sir, it was a grave sight…' His voice gave out and he looked to the dust before him.

Apion looked to the barrack sleeping blocks. Barely one hundred men were permanently garrisoned here, on watch atop the battlements, patrolling and policing the sweltering city streets or resting between shifts. A handful more men were garrisoning the other settlements, forts and outposts of Chaldia equally thinly, but the vast majority of the Chaldian army were at home, tilling their lands, and would take many weeks to muster.

'We have, what, nine riders?' he asked Sha.

'Seven kataphractoi and these two scouts, sir, yes.'

'Have them ready to ride by noon.'

He saw big Blastares emerge from the sleeping quarters just then, fresh from sleep and eager to know what was going on. Apion pointed to the city walls. 'Blastares, pare the wall guard down from fifty to thirty men. Bring the other twenty here.'

Then he scruffed his beard, realising full well that twenty–nine men would have a hard time besting some two hundred raiding Seljuks, but that was all they could spare. He glanced to the eastern barrack wall and scanned the city skyline beyond it, and his gaze stuck on the tall grain silo and the supply storehouse beside it, where all the grain, meat, wine, honey, textiles and furs were kept. Then he glanced up to the citadel rooftop where he had been moments ago, his eyes locking onto the ballista there where he had eaten with Vilyam. An idea began to form.

He swivelled round to the barrack sleeping block again.

'And will someone wake Procopius.'

Bey Kerim climbed atop the jagged rock to survey the land around him. From here he could see the surrounding valleys of southern Chaldia: burnt-gold and terracotta folds of land, studded with shrubs and beech thickets, shimmering in the heat haze of the late afternoon. Not a Byzantine soldier in sight. Not a sound in the air bar the trilling cicada song. Bey Taylan had sent them on ahead to disrupt this northern thema, and shield what was going on in Armenia and beyond. A plum task it had been, so far.

He had heard much of the tenacious border lord known as the *Haga*, and of his Chaldian forts and armies. 'Pah!' He swiped a hand through the air. 'Crumbling towns with a few malnourished runts on the walls, barely able to lift their spears to my men?' He chuckled at his own hubris, thinking back to the sack of the mountain town, Argyroupolis, the previous day. It had been a procession. He had spared the last few townsfolk until nightfall, only so he could enjoy watching them burn in the darkness while he ate like a king, draining the town's remaining food supplies before laying waste to its defences. 'This feared border lord's reputation is somewhat exaggerated!'

He was interrupted from his reverie by the scuffling of feet and the grunting of men. He sighed, turning, knowing what he would set eyes upon. Indeed, down at the bottom of the rock where his men were camped on the flat ground, two burly, bearded daylami hillmen grappled with a pair of ghazi riders, kicking red dust up in their fracas. One of the daylami grappled a rider by the neck and proceeded to pummel him with a shower of punches. The other hillman seemed bested by his opponent; he was sprawling in the dust with the dark-locked and moustachioed ghazi rider pressing a knee to his neck. All around, the rest of his men bayed and snarled. Kerim sighed and scrambled down the rock, knowing he had to intervene now before it erupted into a miniature civil war. He distrusted the filthy hillmen as much as any of his fellow ghazis, but they had to be tolerated, at least for the remainder of this mission, or at least until he could find some parlous and unwinnable situation to throw them into.

'Enough!' he cried as he thumped down onto the flat ground, sweeping his scimitar from his scabbard and slicing it down into the ground between the two scuffling pairs. They broke apart, shrugging as if their bruises and cuts were painless, eyes glaring, refusing to be the first to look away.

The ghazi who had been on the end of the pummelling coughed and spat a gobbet of blood and phlegm into the dust. His nose was smashed and spread all across his face, and one eye had swollen over shut. Kerim mused over bringing out the lash for this one and his attacker. The words danced on his lips, but they were snatched away by a shout.

'A wagon approaches!'

It was one of the men he had posted to a hilltop opposite.

Suddenly all of them, daylami and ghazi, were united by the prospect of easy plunder and probably some brutal torture of the wagon drivers. They needed little cajoling to clear the flat ground and line up on the hillsides like pincers. The ghazis stilled and quieted their mares, the daylami crouched behind rocks and shrubs, their two-pronged spears poised like fangs. Kerim licked his lips as he watched the bend ahead, hearing wheels grind on dust.

Then it appeared, bouncing as the wheels juddered over a small boulder. Two dark ponies hauled the open-topped cart carrying a canvas-covered heap of *something* round the bend in the hill, then they slowed in fright at the sight of nearly two hundred men flanking them. The wagon came to a halt.

Kerim gawped at it. For there was no wagon driver.

'Bey Kerim, what is this?' one of his men whispered.

One of the daylami had taken it upon himself to approach the vehicle, stalking forward, eyeing the canvas covering the wagon's heaped contents warily. He looked to Kerim, who nodded his assent. *If a Byzantine soldier leaps out of there and runs the bastard through, what do I care, he is only a daylami anyway?*

The daylami swept the canvas back, braced, then cocked an eyebrow at the stack of amphorae there. He lifted one, plucking the cork from it. He sniffed the contents and threw his head back in laughter, before pouring a copious measure of the rich red wine into his mouth.

'The drivers must have got wind of us and fled!' he cried in delight, wiping his mouth with the back of his hand.

Kerim frowned, uncertain, but his men did not wait on his verdict, instead sweeping down from the hillsides to take their share. Just as they were united by the prospect of slaughter and plunder, the ghazis and daylami once again came together in merriment. Red wine showered the air in place of blood, and cries of joy rang out in place of the screams of the stricken. Kerim mused over halting them, but he could see it had solved the problem of their quarrelling, and so he decided not to.

Soon, the sun began to fade, and almost every man bore ruddy-cheeks and hooded-eyes. All except Kerim. He drank slowly, still keen to ensure his men kept a vigilant watch, still making regular trips up to the top of the rock to scour the surrounding lands for himself and check the sentries were not asleep. His men laughed and joked like brothers, they shared rations, toasting bread and eating together, then as another round of amphorae were opened, they sang like a flock of gulls. It was then that Kerim's resolve cracked. The land was as still and empty now as it had been that afternoon. He took up an amphora and guzzled on it. *Enjoy it as a conquering bey should!* he enthused as the wine gripped his mind with a soft, welcome fuzziness.

It was well into night. Under cover of darkness and with their faces smeared with dirt, Apion and his trusted three shuffled on their bellies, snaking forward to the tip of the rock overlooking the Seljuk raiding party. The ghazi guard up here had long since fallen asleep, and then a blow to the temple from Blastares' fist sent him into a slumber he would not wake from for many hours. The four then looked down on the chaotic scenes below.

In torchlight, one daylami stumbled in a stupor to pick up an amphora, one handle already clutched by a slumped ghazi. The daylami tugged at the other handle, bringing the ghazi up onto his feet with a growl, but in their clumsiness, the pair clashed heads and crashed to the ground, groaning. Moments later, a ghazi decided he was a mite peckish, and tried to toast more bread over the fire. It was only when his sleeve caught fire that he realised this was a bad idea.

Blastares chuckled. 'I've never been so glad to be sober.' Then he looked to Sha, Procopius and finally to Apion. 'I'd say now was about the right time, sir?'

'Agreed. Ready?' Apion nodded.

His trusted three nodded back. Sha lifted a small rock. Heavy enough to throw some distance. The Malian winked as if drawing a fine composite bow, then hefted the stone back and hurled it. The four ducked down, only their eyes peering over the ridge of the hill once more. The rock thwacked into the back of a daylami trying to empty his bladder. The big hillman yelped then roared, spinning round, his robe soaked in his own urine. His eyes scanned those sitting around, then he stabbed a finger out at the closest ghazi. 'You, you think… thish… ish funny?' he slurred.

Blastares' desperately pursed lips and watering eyes suggested the answer should be yes. Apion kept his gaze fixed on the pair below. The ghazi riders from the steppes hated the daylami, and the feeling was mutual.

The ghazi shrugged, bemused. Then, when the daylami strode forward, a cluster of ghazis rushed to stand with their comrade. Like-wise, a bunch of daylami crowded round their man. Insults were hurled between the two opposing halves of this swaying, wild-eyed Seljuk warband. Apion found some of the insults beyond his comprehension of the Seljuk tongue, but he did make out one man threaten to kick another's genitals so hard that he would be able to fellate himself. Then the quarrelling voices were interrupted by another sound; the screeching of scimitars being drawn, the growl of the daylami as they took up their twin-pronged spears. Then the two sides advanced towards one another.

It was only when one square-jawed man – the leader of the warband, Apion reckoned – stepped in between the two groups, that the approaching parties halted.

'Silence!' the man tried to calm his charges, hefting a barbed whip in the air. 'The next man to make a move will feel the wrath of my—'

Apion sensed the moment. 'Now!'

At once, Sha hurled another rock. This time it crashed against the forehead of the urine-soaked daylami. There was a hiatus of disbelief and sour glares. Then, at once, the Seljuk camp erupted in chaos. Men screamed, blades clashed, blood sprayed. They fought like desert dogs until swathes had fallen and eventually the ghazis' numerical advantage told. The last of the daylami toppled to the earth, his gut ripped open and his steaming entrails slithering out onto the dust. It was only the brutal reality of what they had done that brought sobriety to the remaining ghazis at last. More than half of their number lay in bloodied heaps, still or groaning, moments from death. Now some of the steppe riders slumped to their knees, dropping their swords, bowing to the earth or clutching their hearts in penance and prayer. Apion felt a black guilt touch him for what he had done; just a single word to loose a rock, and nearly one hundred men were dead. He tried instead to focus on what had happened at Argyroupolis because of those men.

'And now, sir?' Sha asked.

Apion firmed his jaw. The black work was not yet complete. 'And now, we finish it,' he said, then nodded to Procopius. Without a word, the old tourmarches slipped back from the ridge, taking Blastares with him.

Half of his men lay dead around him. Every daylami and thirty-six ghazi too. Bey Kerim shuddered, wondering what might happen if Bey Taylan found out what had happened here. No, he reasoned, he had plenty of time to fabricate a report of some ambush or other that would account for the loss of the daylami. As the stench of blood wafted up from the corpses around him, he scowled. 'Come now, let us be swift, let us be away from this filthy camp before the crows come to feast at dawn. Let us go further westwards to see what more bounty Chaldia has to offer!'

His men broke out in a cheer, and a smile grew on his face once more. Then he heard a crunching of cart wheels on dust round the base of the nearest hill... again.

Without need of a word from their bey, his remaining ghazis swiftly took up their weapons, some drawing scimitars, others nocking bows, some leaping onto horseback, ready to charge this unseen vehicle.

Kerim frowned, his eyes locking onto the wagon that rolled round the bend, trying to discern some detail in the pre-dawn gloom. Again, two ponies led it. No drivers in sight, just a canvas-covered heap in the wagon itself, as before. It stopped next to the wine wagon. 'What is this? *What is this?*'

A few ghazis made to approach the wagon, but Kerim barked them back. 'No!' he roared. 'Nobody touches it this time, except me!' He strode forward, reaching up to lift the canvas, fingers outstretched. But he froze. Had something moved under there?

Suddenly, the canvas was yanked back from his open hand. No amphorae. Just a loaded ballista and two Byzantine soldiers. One with an anvil jaw, built like a bull, one smaller with a face like a shrivelled prune. Both glowered darkly at Kerim, eyes part-shaded under their conical helms. Kerim's last thought was snatched from his mind before it could fully form as the ballista loosed the first of its three bolts. The missile passed through him as though he was not there. Swaying, he touched a hand to the ruin that was his chest, and noticed the absence of a heartbeat. With that, Bey Kerim crumpled into the blackness of death.

Apion watched the ballista bolt ruin the ghazi leader and skewer another man behind him. As soon as their shock had faded, the rest of the ghazis cried out, stretching their bows, all aimed at the two on the scorpion wagon.

Now! Apion mouthed, looking to the other end of the rocky valley behind the angered Seljuks. Sixteen skutatoi flooded into the flatland there. They jogged forward, kite shields interlocked, eyes glaring between the tops of their shields and the rims of their helms, spears jutting forward like fangs. They roared out in unison: '*Nobiscum Deus!*' Behind them, just four toxotai kept pace, nocking arrows to their bows and loosing onto the befuddled ghazi warband. Now, some of the ghazis turned their bows to this miniature phalanx. Arrows were loosed en masse, but the skutatoi shields held firm, just a pair of men falling to the hail as they advanced. Then the spearmen rippled at the call from the man leading them.

'*Rhiptaria… loose!*'

As one, the skutatoi hoisted and threw a volley of the light rhiptarion javelins they carried. The missiles sailed into the ghazis and punched several from their mounts. On the other side of the Seljuks, the ballista bucked and spat another bolt, scything down another four riders. Ghazi arrows pattered onto the wagon all around Blastares and Procopius, but the pair were adept at loading the device whilst sheltering behind its bulk.

The vice was taut, Apion realised. Wordlessly, he waved Sha and the nine other ironclad riders – just a few paces downhill behind him – to their feet and onto their nearby mounts. Likewise, he leapt onto the saddle of his gelding. He clipped his mail veil across his face, then roared with all the breath in his lungs, to be sure that every Seljuk down there heard:

'*Forwaaard!*'

The cry echoed and multiplied. He swept his spear overhead, urging his riders down the hillside and directly at the flank of the ghazis. Sitting as far back as he could in his saddle to balance, he grappled his mount's sides as tightly as he could with his thighs, the beast's every stride covering vast distances of the close-to-sheer slope. He glanced up and over his shoulder to see his riders, the first tinge of dawn light glinting on their klibania and helms, their faces twisted, mouths agape in battle cries, cloaks and plumes billowing behind them, their mounts' eyes white and wide, teeth bared, manes thrashing. Not a single rider had foundered.

The first of the ghazis twisted to look up the steep hillside. His brow knitted in a frown, then his eyes bulged and his mouth opened to cry aloud. The cry did not come, as the kataphractoi ploughed a gory furrow through their ranks. Apion saw the dark door rush for him, crash open and swallow him into its fiery belly. He drove his spear through one ghazi, then threw it at another, knocking the man from his horse. Then he whipped his scimitar from his belt and wheeled around, striking heads from shoulders, dashing skulls open and cutting bodies open at haste. Finally, there were no snarling men before him save his own bloodstained ranks. He stared at the twitching corpses all around him, numb to the dying embers of the fight and the fading flames beyond the dark door, dead to the cries of victory from his own men.

'*Ha-ga! Ha-ga! Ha-ga!*'

—

A muggy summer's night bathed the city of Trebizond and the streets were quiet. High up in the citadel chambers, only cricket-song from the grassy mount outside broke the silence. Apion sat in the map room in his lightest tunic, his chair tilted back against the red-brick walls, his legs and bare feet up on the table, mindless of the map of Chaldia and the small, carved wooden skutatoi and kataphractoi figures carefully laid out there. A scent of roasted goat meat and yoghurt still tinged the room from his evening meal. His gaze hung on the small, arched window that looked out over the city. Pure darkness bar the torchlight from a few homes. He supped on his wine and shuffled for comfort, one wooden figure toppling over from its carefully appointed spot on the map table.

Apion eyed the piece with disdain. 'Cah! Planning can wait until morning,' he muttered. It had been a long day spent huddled over the map with Sha, Blastares and Procopius. The four had shared their thoughts on the raiding party: had it been a lone band, or the first of many? Nobody could offer a convincing answer. Then they had tried as best they could to revise where their scant numbers would be garrisoned for the rest of the year. Even scanter given the eight men lost in the skirmish two days ago. In the end it had been like trying to clothe a beggar in a single thread. And they had still to discuss how to go about mustering the rest of the men of Chaldia from their farms to join Manuel Komnenos and his campaign army — thought to now be marching for the Thema of Sebastae, readying to set up a semi-permanent fort there to ward off any Seljuk incursions from the south or the east. Summoning the Chaldians from their farms was one thing, but getting them in good fighting order within the next six weeks would be another entirely. A throbbing headache blossomed behind one eye.

Just then, like a straggler from a marauding Seljuk horde, Vilyam scampered into the room, purring. The ginger tom then leapt — rather ungracefully — up onto the table, trotting across the map to bat playfully at the wooden pieces left standing. Heedless of the symbolism, the portly cat then took to grappling one piece between his two front paws and collapsing onto his side, biting at the wooden figure's head while kicking at the other end with his back paws, his tail swishing and thumping, sweeping the last few pieces clear of the table.

Apion glared at the cat in horror, then when Vilyam looked up, eyes hooded in pleasure at such wanton destruction, he jostled with laughter. 'Are you telling me our defensive plans were flawed?' As if in some form of reply, Vilyam stood and hurried along the table, over Apion's outstretched legs and onto his lap, where he shuffled and settled in a ball, purring furiously.

Apion stroked Vilyam's ears and supped at his wine once more. He had been too weary to seek out water to dilute this, one of the few amphorae they had brought back after ambushing the Seljuk raid. But he had sworn to limit himself to just one cup of the heady mixture, sending his trusted three back down to the barracks to share the rest with the other men. Yet this one cup was proving to be a potent ration. As the night wore on, the mugginess eased and he felt a slight chill touch his skin. Drawing his cloak over his shoulders and sweeping part round onto his legs and lap to cover Vilyam too, he felt drowsiness come to him. It was a blessing that his thoughts then began to melt away, gently entranced by the cricket melody, Vilyam's purring and the soothing warmth of the wine. His thoughts drifted and memories surfaced – pleasant ones, for once. He imagined the cloak's warmth as Maria's. At last, sleep took him.

Blackness. Pure, dreamless sleep. Then all around him swirled and was swept away. He found himself standing face to face with Taylan once more. His son raised a blade like an accusing finger, and his words from that meeting echoed once more:

'In every dream, in every waking moment, with every step you take on the battlefield, you should beware. I will be coming for you, Haga. I will not stop.'

A rhythmic growl penetrated the blackness. It was faint at first, then it grew fearsome.

The veil of sleep dropped away and Apion awoke, blinking. His mouth was parched and the wine cup had toppled to the floor. It was now pitch black outside – the last of the street side torches having been extinguished. Then, the growl came again, vibrating through his body.

'Vilyam?' he croaked. The ginger cat was poised on Apion's knee, having wriggled clear of the cloak. His eyes were wide, ears back, hips shuffling and tensed to spring. Apion followed the cat's nocturnal glare into the blackness around the window.

'At ease,' he chuckled, 'what harm can a mouse or a bat do you?'

But when the cat reared up, hair spiked, emitting a hiss that split the night air, Apion saw it. A brief glimmer of steel in the blackness, sweeping down for him. He threw himself from his chair, his ankle catching a table leg and sending the table and its contents scattering across the room. He heard the crack of shattering timber and scrabbled round to see the splintered remnant of his chair, cleaved by a blade. Hurrying to the back wall of the chamber he saw the shadow that carried the blade.

'What the… who are you?' he uttered. The images from his dream were still at the forefront of his thoughts. 'Taylan? No!'

The figure did not respond, instead stalking carefully towards him, blade rising to strike.

Apion squared his jaw. 'Tayl—' he uttered again.

At that moment, he heard the gruff laughter of the shadowy figure, and saw the blade in a sliver of moonlight. A spathion. This was no Seljuk.

Apion ducked and the spathion blade scythed round, streaking across the bricks where his neck had been a heartbeat ago. Orange sparks flew in the air, illuminating the assassin's face for an instant. A heavy-browed, flat-faced creature, clenched teeth nestled in a bushy dark beard. He also spotted the knotted rope and steel hook the man had used to scale the citadel wall and climb in the window. Apion heard the assassin grunting and the blade whooshing up to strike again. He kicked out, feeling his heel crack against the man's knee. A yowl of pain sounded and Apion leapt up and headed for the door, Vilyam rushing with him.

His mind reeled. *What a fool!* he scolded himself. *To fall foul of the wine only days after seeing it bring the Seljuk warband to their end. My sword, my armour?* he fretted, looking this way and that down the short, stony corridor outside. Amidst his flurry of thoughts, he remembered stowing his armour in his bedchamber, two nights ago. He rushed past the narrow stairwell that led to the citadel rooftop and on to the small bedchamber doorway that lay just beyond it. But, to his horror, another shadow waited there – this time wiry and lean. It stalked towards him, raising a dagger. Apion backed away from this one, but sensed the hulking assassin coming for him from behind. Nowhere to run except up. He sped up the stairs and onto the rooftop, his eyes at once locking onto the nearest ballista mounted there, glinting in the moonlight. He hefted up one of the unwieldy bolts resting beside the device and levelled it like a spear, spinning round just as the two assassins emerged onto the rooftop as well. He shot a glance over the rooftop battlements. Down below, he saw the lifeless forms of the four guard skutatoi posted at the citadel gate, and another lying in a shattered, unnatural poise – doubtless the corpse of the man posted to this rooftop.

'Sha!' he cried down towards the barracks. Dark and silent like the rest of the city.

'Nobody will save you now, *Haga*!' the burly assassin hissed.

'Shall we gut him, or send him over the edge?' the other said.

'Both?' the big one chuckled icily.

Apion backed away from the pair who held their blades like well-trained swordsmen. His ballista bolt was a clumsy weapon – not quite a spear and not nearly as nimble as a sword. His thoughts were yanked away as his heel struck the crenelated edge of the rooftop. From the corner of his eye, he noticed torchlight sparking into life down below at the barracks. Someone had heard his shout, but he had only moments to live.

The two assassins braced to rush him when suddenly, with a yowl, Vilyam leapt up from behind the burly one, clamping to the back of the man's head and wrapping his claws around to tear at his eyes. The assassin roared out, throwing the cat off, clutching at his bloodied eyes, blinded and staggering.

Apion realised he had moments before the big man recovered. He wasted no time in rushing forward to drive his ballista bolt at the other assassin's chest. But the wiry one was swift, leaping back from the huge, iron head of the bolt and striking down at the shaft with his dagger hilt to throw Apion off balance.

Staggering, Apion just managed to bring the bolt shaft round to parry the man's next blow, the dagger blade scoring Apion's hand, sending the bolt toppling from his grip. The wiry assassin grinned as the pair circled one another, then he swiped out, the dagger scoring Apion's face. Only a sharp punch to the man's gut stopped him from turning the blade down and into Apion's neck.

When shouting and the clattering of rising footsteps from inside the citadel sounded, the man became more desperate, lunging forward. Apion crabbed away from the lunge so the assassin bundled past him. Then he brought his elbow crashing round on the back of the man's head. Stunned, the man swung round, only for Apion to take up the fallen ballista bolt, drive forward and plunge the shaft into the wiry assassin's chest. The blunt force shattered the man's sternum, lodging there and sending him staggering backwards towards the roof's edge. He stopped there, swaying, rasping, blood dribbling from his lips as he glared at the now weaponless Apion. With a look of finality, he raised his dagger, clutching it by the blade, and drew an arm back to hurl it at Apion. But a thrum of loosed bowstrings saw the hand and dagger stilled. Two blazing arrows whacked into the assassin's chest, and in moments his black garb was ablaze. The assassin emitted a shrill, pained death rattle, before toppling over the roof's edge. An instant of silence passed before a thick, wet crunch sounded below.

Apion gawped at the spot where the man had stood, then swung to the top of the stairwell. Sha stood there, panting, his loosed bow clutched with trembling knuckles. A toxotes was with him, bow clutched in similar fashion, and Procopius stood behind them carrying a torch.

'The other?' Apion croaked, swinging round to scan the rooftop.

'Sir?' Sha cocked an eyebrow.

'There was another one – a brute of a man!' Apion growled this time.

'We saw only one, sir,' Procopius frowned.

Apion's gaze caught on the iron hook wrapped over the edge of the rooftop, grinding and sliding as if under great weight. 'No, look, there!' he pointed and rushed over. The others joined him. Down there, near the ground, the hulking assassin shuffled down a rope tied to the iron hook, then leapt down to land on the grassy citadel hillside. Without waiting for an order, Sha nocked and loosed an arrow, the toxotes following suit.

'Wound him!' Apion insisted. 'We won't get much information from the other fellow.'

The arrows smacked down at the assassin's heels as he bounded down the citadel hillside. Blastares and a clutch of skutatoi were flooding from the barracks, racing for the citadel's main entrance. But they were blind to the man's flight and confused by Procopius' shouts to alert them. The assassin went unharmed by Sha's next arrow, then clambered over the squat outer wall of the citadel and out into the lower town. A heartbeat later, the whinnying of a horse and the clopping of hooves sounded as the man sped off along the main way towards the southern city gates.

Wordlessly, Apion led his men down the stairs, raced to meet with Blastares and his men and waved them with him. They rushed along the main way, seeing the handful of night sentries posted along the street startled by the racing horseman.

'Stop him!' Apion cried.

But the sentries' attentions were snared by something else. The horseman took to tossing in his wake handfuls of coins. The coins bounced and jangled as they spread across the street, and the sentries slowed, spellbound by their lustre. Many crouched, scooping up what they could. Apion slowed at that moment, seeing that the side hatch by the main southern gate was already ajar and the skutatoi atop the gatehouse lay slumped and lifeless.

'Sir, come on, if we get our mounts from the stables then we can—' Sha started.

'We will not catch him,' Apion panted, 'he has planned this well.' He stalked over to one coin that the night sentries had missed. He offered these men a dark scowl, and saw the shame in their nervous eyes. 'In any case, we do not need to catch him to find out who his master is.' Apion held the coin so it caught the light of Procopius' torch. The pure-gold nomisma sparkled like a dawn ray.

Apion's jaw clenched. *Psellos!*

'Then what should we do?' Blastares asked, his sword hand clenching and unclenching.

Apion's eyes darted, thinking of Manuel Komnenos and his campaign army. If Psellos was at work once more, then he would not have confined himself merely to an assassination. 'We should bring the mustering forward with haste. I want the fighting men of the thema readied to march for Sebastae by the end of the month.'

—

The streets of Constantinople baked in the summer heat. Babbling crowds writhed in the dockside fish market. A small dromon with a single bank of oars pulled away from the nearby Harbour of Theodosius, leaving behind the hubbub and the foaming, murky waters lapping at the wharf side. Under oar, the ship manoeuvred into the turquoise waters of the Propontis, then the crew hurried to unfurl the purple sail, pulling the boat westwards, skirting the city's southern sea walls and heading towards the green Thracian countryside. Soon the city was but a speck on the eastern horizon.

Psellos stood at the prow of the vessel. Yet he could not enjoy the fresh winds and the gentle noises of the sea, for his chest lesion seared as though a white-hot brand was being pressed to it. It had spread further, he was sure, now covering all of his chest and weeping almost constantly. Great boils had formed over it and just this morning, he had tried to lance one; blood and yellow pus had poured from it, and then a chunk of flesh had come away too. Just a small piece about the size of his fingertip – but it was rotten like spoiled food. Beads of cold sweat scampered down his back at the memory.

What did you do to me, witch? he fretted, remembering the silver-haired old crone whose touch had spawned the lesion.

'I cannot wait to see his gawping, severed head,' a gruff voice interrupted his thoughts.

Psellos swung round to John Doukas, clad in white silks blemished by dark perspiration stains. He wore the look of a man about to sit down to an imperial banquet. His eyes were fixed dreamily on the shoreline, seeking out their destination.

'The *Haga* must surely have put up a fight. How did you say they killed him?' John asked, his eyes sparkling like a child's. 'Tell me.'

Psellos considered his response carefully. 'Plakanos' message only said that the job was done.'

'Where did you say the meeting point was?' John asked.

'We're almost there.' Psellos flicked his eyes to the shoreline: shingle beach then thick forestation beyond, with no signs of farms or settlements nearby.

A fine salt-spray whipped over them as they approached a small, timber jetty. Storks picked their way through the shallows here, bills chattering and occasionally spearing into the water to catch fish. 'Hmm, do you think it was wise to bring only two men?' John nodded past the ranks of rowers to the two Numeroi spearmen. They were clad in fine pure-white tunics, iron klibania hugging their torsos, purple cloaks draped over their shoulders and scale-aventailed helms protecting their heads and necks. Each man carried a kite shield – purple with a white Christian Cross in the centre – and was armed with the finest of spears and spathion blades.

'I think we will be fine,' Psellos said, his eyes narrowing.

When they docked, Psellos, John and the two Numeroi spearmen filed out onto the jetty, wandered up the patchy grass of the shore side to a small timber hut nestled by a thicket of hornbeam trees. A gentle breeze tickled the leaves into a chorus of rustling and a flock of starlings shot to the sky, startled by the newcomers.

Psellos raised a hand to halt his retinue.

He peered at the door of the ramshackle hut. It creaked open ever so slowly. A hulking giant peered out, eyes darting furtively. This one was his finest assassin. The man who had taken over the mantle from Zenobius after that albino agent had been killed on his mission to slay Romanus Diogenes in Syria. Despite his flat-boned, brutish appearance, Plakanos had a shrewd mind, and he had barely suffered a scratch in his duties so far – murdering and sabotaging then fading like a morning mist. But Psellos noticed that Plakanos' eyelids and cheeks were a mesh of scabs and scars, and the whites of his eyes were bloodshot and bleary.

'Advisor, your strongest assassin seems to have had a run-in with… a cat?' John said, chuckling derisively.

Psellos shot his puppet a sour look, then flicked his gaze back to the assassin. 'It is done? The *Haga* is dead?'

Plakanos' eyes darted and a bead of sweat forked across his heavy brow. 'No. He lives.'

'So you failed me?' Psellos said then spluttered with incredulous laughter. 'You failed me and returned to tell me. You, a man who knows full well what happens to those who fail me?'

It was then that the trees rustled again. Seven men in black cloaks and dark-red tunics emerged and stood in an arc with Plakanos. More portatioi. 'My men? What are you doing here?' Psellos asked.

'No, *my* men,' Plakanos said, his shoulders squaring and his demeanour changing. Slowly and silently, the other portatioi drew out weapons from behind their backs. One held a nocked *solenarion* bow, another a small crossbow. One patted a spiked mace menacingly and the others carried clubs and blades. As if reflecting this turn of events, a cluster of grey cloud crossed over the sun, dulling the land and lending just a mite of chill to the coastal breeze. 'Your time is over, advisor,' Plakanos grinned.

'No!' Psellos gasped. He looked to the equally panicked John, then to his two startled numeroi, then to Plakanos and the closing arc of Portatioi agents. 'No!' he cried again. But this time the cry was overly-theatrical, and it tapered off with a throaty chuckle.

Plakanos halted, frowning.

Psellos flicked a finger and the seven with Plakanos suddenly turned on the giant, one striking him on the back of his head with a club. The giant gawped momentarily, realising they were, indeed, Psellos' men. Then he toppled to the patchy grass, unconscious.

'It was as you suspected, master,' the club-wielding assassin spoke in a sibilant tone to Psellos. 'He summoned us here, tried to rally us against you.'

'*Too* shrewd, it seems,' Psellos glowered down the length of his nose at Plakanos' prone form. 'Dispose of him, and make it slow.'

'I have been planning how we might do this all morning, master. Then I remembered that Plakanos once told me of the recurring night-mare he suffers. A nightmare of creatures feasting on his flesh...' The club-wielder grinned and nodded as he ushered the other portatioi to lift Plakanos. They carried their colleague over to a hump of raised earth and placed him beside it, staking his wrists and ankles. One of them tore Plakanos' tunic from his body. Another brought out a jar of honey, then began smearing the viscous substance onto Plakanos' face, all across his torso and around his genitals. The big man was just coming to when he heard them beating at the hump of earth with sticks. He regained consciousness fully just in time to realise what was happening. In seconds, angered ants flooded from their nest under the hump of earth. Myriad creatures, bodies dark and glistening like some nightmarish horde. They swamped Plakanos' skin in moments, and the brutish assassin could only scream with all the power in his lungs as they went to work, devouring the honey, then his skin and flesh. Plakanos' cries were terrible. He thrashed and his limbs strained at the roped stakes, but to no avail. His eyes bulged and seemed set to burst clear of his head. But the ants flooded across his face unimpeded, a cloud of them rushing into his open mouth and nostrils and many more setting to work upon his eyeballs. His screaming grew intense and then fell away, replaced by choking, grunting noises. As the ant-covered mass of Plakanos writhed in the background, John and Psellos turned away, looking back along the coastline to the distant outline of Constantinople.

'So the *Haga* lives on?' John growled.

'The *Haga*'s head will be ours in time, master.'

But John's lips began to twitch. 'The *Haga* lives and Diogenes and his bitch remain unchallenged as the toast of the empire.'

'That Diogenes continues to cower in his palace should not concern you, master,' Psellos replied.

'It is not *his* palace, advisor,' John spat.

'No, he has merely bought himself a stay in your rightful home. By lavishing funds on the games and on the armies of the themata, his stock has risen and his failures on the battlefield have been forgiven.'

'Yet the cur has no vaults of gold, no limitless wealth,' John said.

'No, but he has enough. Enough to allow him this single year of respite from campaign. My spies have been more successful than my assassins. They tell me that he has sold off his manors and great tracts of his family's lands in Cappadocia to pay for his initiatives. He will very soon be a pauper. He means only to have this year in the capital to plan.'

John's pupils narrowed like a preying cat. 'To plan? To plan for what?'

'To lead a campaign grander than any other. Next year, he hopes to raise the greatest army the empire has ever witnessed and to secure the empire's borders… and along with them, the glory that will cement his place on the throne.'

John's eyes darted in panic as he considered this. 'With the revitalised themata, the imperial tagmata and mercenaries too he might well raise an army as vast as—'

'You forget, master, that I am always a step ahead of Diogenes,' Psellos cut him off, ushering him back towards the dromon. 'The themata armies he has poured so much gold into are currently on campaign. They march under the banner of Manuel Komnenos.' He leaned a little closer to whisper in John's ear. 'And we both know how hazardous a campaign can be.'

CHAPTER 8

Field of Carrion

Tepid rain fell in sheets as Apion led the mustered Chaldian ranks through the Sebastae Thema. A thick musty tang of rotting vegetation and wet earth hung in the air and the squelching of boots and hooves sounded behind him. August had brought with it a mackerel sky and then this seemingly never-ending deluge. Every day meant a torrid trek through churning mire in sodden tunics and cloaks and every night was spent under leaking pavilion tents, eating wet rations.

Rainwater drummed on his helm and trickled down his scale aventail, finding its way under the iron collar of his klibanion as he rode. His eyes remained trained on the south, where Manuel Komnenos' army was but a half day's march away.

He recalled the sharp and loyal man he had met at the Euphrates. A good man to lead this campaign – with a brief to stave off any Seljuk advance here in the borderlands while the emperor stabilised affairs in Constantinople. And he had heard good things from his scouts who had been relaying messages between Manuel's campaign army and the Chaldians. Manuel had them marching at a fine pace and morale was high. The Thrakesion, Opsikon and Bucellarion themata had been mustered to provide the bulk of his infantry – and the scouts had spoken highly of their appearance: each man kitted out with fine iron klibania, marching boots, helms, freshly painted shields and good, sharp and true spears, bows and swords. Romanus' funding had transformed them, it seemed. With these refreshed themata rode the Vigla and the Scholae Tagmata. Two fine cavalry corps that would provide a stern hammer to the infantry anvil of the themata.

He held out his water skin to fill it from the vertical drizzle. *Ha! Focus on your own ranks, man!* he mused, taking a sip of water then glancing back over his shoulder. There were his fifty riders, and immediately behind them, a sea of infantry faces stared back, eyes shaded under the dripping rims of their helms or archer's hats, a forest of spear shafts, canvas-covered quivers and soaked crimson banners hanging over their well-ordered lines.

Just over nine hundred infantrymen. None of the three tourmae they were organised into were even close to having the eight banda of two to three hundred men that the military texts recommended. Nowhere near enough, in fact – each division contained barely enough men for one such bandon. They hadn't been at full strength for some years, he mused. Not surprising given the constant Seljuk raids and the major clashes in the past two campaigning seasons. What mattered, though, was that each of these three divisions of spearmen and archers were headed by his trusted three. Sha led his tourma with carefully worded shouts of encouragement, being sure to twist in his saddle and catch the eye of as many of his charges as possible when he did so. Ever the diplomat, Apion thought with a smile. Procopius was a more taciturn leader. The men of his tourma always showed him the greatest of respect and a hint of fear at his stern silence. The aged officer had once confided in Apion that it was all an act, a front. 'Isn't life?' Apion muttered, his smile growing. Then he heard a gruff almost animal-like groan. He twisted to his other side to see Blastares, dismounting, scowling, his face bright red and raindrops dangling from the end of his nose. A pair of skutatoi had stumbled and fallen, sending the front line of his tourma into disarray.

'We taught you how to march *weeks* ago, you bloody fools!' he roared at the pair who had caused the chaos, then wrenched one of them up from his knees by the scruff of his klibanion like a father lifting a mischievous child. 'What the—' the big tourmarches gasped, gawping at the man's boots. The four leather strips that extended above the shin of the boots were stretched up to his thighs, almost as high as his groin, and tied there. 'And we taught you never to march with your boots up. Fold them down, below the knee.' He shook his head in disbelief. 'How can that even be comfortable? Your balls must be rubbed free of skin by now!' The men erupted in a babble of laughter at their shamed comrade, and Apion allowed himself a crooked grin too.

'Unbelievable, bloody unbelievable!' Blastares grunted, ranging level with Apion, Sha and Procopius. 'And this rain is seriously testing my patience. I tried praying for good weather last night... halfway through my bloody tent roof falls in and I get soaked with freezing rainwater. I mean, come on – I've tried to be a good man?' The big tourmarches held out his hands and looked to the sky.

Sha looked to Apion with a devilish sparkle in his eyes. 'You know, back in Mali, we had a saying: the flower accepts the rain because it knows it will be watered.'

Blastares stared blankly at Sha for a moment, his jaw hanging open. 'Hold on. Are you calling me a bloody flower?'

Procopius was the first to break the tense silence that followed, roaring with laughter from the pit of his belly. Sha broke down in laughter too and Apion found it infectious. Blastares' scowl lasted only moments before he joined in too. 'Bloody flower indeed.'

They splashed through a shallow flood-river in one pine-edged valley, then up a snaking path along a mountainous ridge where the land opened out before them. A mile or more to their left stood the city of Sebastae – capital of this eponymous thema. The city's walls were grey and shiny with rain, and there was just a speckle of iron atop the battlements. He had heard that this important stronghold was garrisoned by only eighty men these days.

He noticed his men's heads all twist to the city, no doubt thinking of the taverns and warm fires within those walls. A gentle chatter broke out amongst them.

'Eyes front,' Blastares boomed. 'We're not meeting the campaign army there. It's a camp on a plain for us,' he said, flicking a finger to a ridge on the south-eastern horizon. 'Somewhere out there. Anyway, the wine in that city tastes like rat piss and the whores will leave you with warts on your cock!'

Stunned silence fell, followed by a chorus of chuckling when Blastares swung round on his saddle to flash them a stump-toothed grin. When the big man turned forward again, his grin faded.

'Blastares?' Procopius frowned, seeing the big man's gaze snag on something to the south-east.

Apion looked there too, seeing only the grey mizzle and wet folds of golden land. Then he saw it. The dullest flash of silver out there – maybe two miles distant. An army. Coming north and coming fast.

'Manuel Komnenos?' Sha asked.

Apion shook his head, seeing the dull shape take form. 'See how fast they come? They are all riders. Look, two thousand of them, easily.' The column broke out in a concerned murmur.

'Seljuk raiders,' Procopius growled, switching his gaze from the approaching horde to the grey walled city. 'They're but a few miles from Sebastae.'

'The rain!' Apion cursed the sky. 'The damned rain dampened their dust plume until they were this close.' He looked north-east to the city and south-east to the horde. His nine hundred men and fifty riders were all that stood between the populace of Sebastae and certain slaughter.

'I can have a rider bolt southwards, to reach Manuel Komnenos' camp and call for his help?' Blastares suggested.

'Yes, do that, but be swift,' Apion replied, his gaze flicking to the gorge a few hundred metres to the left of his column. The Seljuk raiders would have to come through that corridor to get to the city – as the rocky land either side was steep and crumbling – nigh-on impassable. 'Then get your men into that gorge!'

The rain-sodden gorge was eerily still, until the silence was broken by the splashing of nine hundred pairs of boots and the clopping hooves of fifty horsemen. The din echoed from wall to wall until the Byzantine soldiers came to a halt. Apion thudded down from his mount. He crouched and held a hand to the ground – rumbling, growing closer, from the south, beyond the kink in the gorge. They had moments, he realised. He stood and scoured the terrain. The gorge was a definite choke point, but it was still fairly wide. Standing three men deep, his infantrymen might just be able to form a blockade long enough for Blastares' messenger to summon reinforcements from Manuel Komnenos. But it would be folly to assume reinforcements were coming, he chided himself.

'Skutatoi!' he yelled, swiping a finger in the air as if drawing out his imagined spear line. At once, the spearmen hurried to form a phalanx from one gorge wall to the other, crimson shields interlocked, spears levelled, eyes glinting with a mixture of fear and battle-hubris. Next, he looked to the hundred or so archers within the infantry ranks, then up to the sides of the gorge.

'I could have the archers up there in moments, sir,' Sha said, reading his thoughts, 'just give the word. They could have the Seljuks in a deadly crossfire.'

Apion shook his head, suppressing a growl of frustration. 'No, the rain will spoil their efforts and the Seljuks will spot them early.' He looked all around the gorge for inspiration. Nothing. The rumbling now seemed to shake the land. He closed his eyes, imagining the Byzantine spear wall and the space before it as a shatranj board. He imagined the Seljuks flooding into the gorge floor as opposing pieces. Their strength was in their number, he realised. His brow dipped as he saw what he had to do.

He swung to the spear wall and saw the two men there who carried with them canisters and siphons. These *siphonarioi* were Greek fire specialists, adept at shooting the blazing liquid across enemy ranks. But today, something different was needed. With a flick of the hand, he beckoned them forward, a hundred paces in front of the blockade. 'Open your canisters,' he said, 'empty the contents across the gorge.' He drew out another line, wall to wall.

The two looked at one another quizzically, then shrugged, uncorking them with trembling fingers. They poured the dark, viscous substance from the mouth, walking carefully in a line as they did so, making a thick stripe that stretched across the soaked floor of the gorge from edge to edge.

Apion looked up, hearing whooping Seljuk war cries, echoing through the ravine as if coming from all around. The thunder of hooves grew rapidly until the Seljuk front rounded the kink and burst into view. They were ghazis, he realised. 'Back!' he cried, waving the two siphonarioi with him back to the Byzantine spear wall.

He shot glances over his shoulder as he ran. Round and round the ghazis came like a deluge of steel. Upon reaching the spear line, he took up a spear and infantry shield then barged into place beside Sha to face the onrushing cavalry. Each and every one of the ghazis raised and nocked their bows. With an ominous and lasting thrum, they loosed.

'Shields!' Apion cried. Like an iron insect, the crimson shields shot up. *Thwack!* A handful of skutatoi fell as blood puffed into the air, but the majority of the Seljuk missiles were wayward, their flight affected by the drizzle. Another volley. *Thrum… thwack!* Again, only a few Byzantines fell and still the Seljuks raced forward, now only fifty or so paces from the spear line.

'Stand firm!' Apion called out, seeing two weak spots in his line where men had fallen.

A komes by his side gasped: 'But sir, our spear wall is thin and they number in their thousands…' The man's words trailed off as the ghazis stowed their bows and drew their lances and scimitars — assured of an easy kill.

'*Allahu Akbar!*' the Seljuk riders roared in a booming chorus, breaking into a full charge.

Apion's gaze fixed on the blurred dark stripe on the gorge floor. The hooves of the first rider crossed it, then hundreds more. Soon, nearly half of the ghazi mass had crossed it and were but thirty paces from smashing into the Byzantine line.

Apion shot a hand in the air. 'Archers…'

From the rear of the spear wall, the hundred archers rose, bows nocked and stretched, each of them wrapped in strips of blazing cloth – the flames fighting valiantly against the rain. 'Loose!' *Thrum*. Apion watched as the volley arced up and over the foremost Seljuks.

A heartbeat later, the thin cloud of blazing missiles dropped, punching into the stripe of viscous fluid underneath the middle of the Seljuk pack. As if a storm had been conjured, the gorge shook with a thunder that drowned out the ghazi battle cries as a broad, billowing curtain of orange fire – a lightning to the thunder – spewed upwards from the gorge floor. The wall of flame dissected the ghazi mass. It sent those to the rear flailing back, reining in their mounts. Those at the front found their charge waylaid by the terrible screams of their comrades behind them. They slowed, glancing back to see the few hundred men caught right in the roaring curtain of fire falling, man and horse ablaze. The charge, a moment ago a maw of levelled lances and scimitars, fell to pieces. Many of them swung their mounts round, seeing that they were trapped in this gorge, between the wall of flames and the nest of Byzantine spears.

The image of the dark door throbbed in Apion's mind, flames roaring beyond it. Before him, the burning gorge was a vile reflection of that haunting image. A wall of thick, acrid, black smoke wafted across him. The siphonarioi cheered out in delight. Apion smelt the overly familiar stench of charred flesh, gazed through the carnage and mouthed into the ether, *forgive me*. To whom the plea was made, he did not know.

The rallying cry of the Seljuk leader saw those trapped on the near side of the fiery wall form into a cluster again, once more ready to attempt a charge on the spear wall. At least now it would be an even fight, Apion thought. They rumbled forward, a madness in their eyes, faces twisted with rage and fear.

'Hold!' Apion cried, seeing the nearest lance tip trained on him. Sha and the komes either side of him pushed a little closer. He felt their heartbeats thud with his own.

'Stay together!' he heard big Blastares roar near the other end of the line.

With a rasp of lance and sword, a clatter of shields and the screaming of man and beast, the ghazis surged into the Byzantine spear line. Apion was driven back several feet as two lances punctured his shield. Blood showered his face as he jabbed out at his attackers with a visceral rhythm. Sparks flew as blades clashed and danced off of armour. All around him, clouds of crimson puffed in the air as steel flashed relentlessly. His spear arm juddered numbly as he scored the gut of one of these hardy steppe riders, the man's yellow-toothed snarl widening into a cry of agony as he toppled from his saddle, trying in vain to close his breached ribcage. Apion saw his Chaldians fall around him, chests run through by Seljuk scimitars or heads crushed under the weight of enemy war hammers. The ghazis were fighting for their lives. There was no route of escape. And nor could he offer them one, he realised. If they broke to the north, then they would fall upon Sebastae. And the south was still a wall of impassable flame. Every Seljuk in this pass had to die, he affirmed numbly, jabbing and swiping with his spear at those who came at him. The Byzantine line bulged at the centre, pushed back by the weight of the mounted pack. Some ghazi riders took to leaping over the spear line, only for their mounts to be pierced in the gut. Apion felt one such animal's entrails spatter down on his shoulder as he hefted his quivering spear arm, looking for his next foe. But there was none. Just a sea of his comrades faces, tear-streaked, bloodstained and trembling. The gorge was painted crimson and carpeted with ghazi corpses. With absurd timing, the drizzle at last faded and the sun came out, bathing them all in its warmth.

'It's over, sir,' Blastares panted, beside him.

He glanced over the gawping, lifeless faces of the dead. He saw them at last as men, and did not try to fight the shame that overcame him. Then, like a brand to his heart, he wondered, what if Taylan had been within this pack? Lost beyond the dark door, might he have slain his own son? No, the chances that Taylan was even part of this raid were slim, surely.

He tried as best as he could to stow the dark thought away, unclipping his mail veil and wiping the blood and grime from his face.

'Sir, what do we do with this one?' a voice called out.

A Seljuk rider had been found amongst the bodies, cowering, hoping not to be discovered. The skutatoi who had found him held his spathion at the man's neck.

Apion dismounted and strode to the man. The man looked up, jutting his jaw in defiance but his eyes aflame with fear. Crows had begun to gather on the sides of the gorge, delighted at this feast of war. They cawed as Apion beheld the man.

'At ease,' he said in the Seljuk tongue. 'You are one man. You will not be harmed. If your comrades had thrown down their lances and bows, they might have been spared too.'

The Seljuk's defiance faded, then he frowned, confused.

Apion hesitated with the next words that came to his lips, but he had to ask: 'Was there a boy rider amongst your ranks. Taylan, son of Nasir?'

None of the other soldiers paid any attention to his words, but Sha, Blastares and Procopius did, glancing over to the conversation. Only his trusted three knew what he had found in his journey deep into Seljuk lands.

'Taylan bin Nasir?' The man's brow knitted. 'He would not ride with a mere vanguard!'

Apion's thoughts spun as the Seljuk was roped at the wrists. 'A vanguard?' he said, glancing round the many fallen riders they had fought.

Now the Seljuk's eyes lit up and laughter toppled from his lips. 'Aye, you fought well today. But you have repelled merely a fraction of the army I ride with.'

Apion's eyes locked onto the Seljuk's. 'Taylan is with them?' His gaze darted up and around the horizon. The southern skyline was still masked by the wall of flames.

The Seljuk snorted. 'Bey Taylan *leads* them!'

'*Bey* Taylan?'

'Aye. He comes to ruin these Byzantine lands and claim the head of some foul border lord… the *Haga*.'

Apion closed his eyes, his heart sinking. When one skutatos lifted his spathion above the prisoner and looked to Apion for permission, Apion shook his head and turned away. The curtain of flames was dying now and he could see that the ghazi riders who had been shut off behind the wall of flame had fled south-east – going by their tracks.

When he looked to the horizon, he felt the breath catch in his lungs. Sha, Blastares and Procopius picked their way through the carnage to stand beside him, gawping southwards too. The clearing noon sky ended there, instead thick with a swirling black mass. *A storm cloud?* He wondered. But when dark shapes swooped and darted from it, he realised it was no cloud. Carrion birds. Innumerable flocks of them gliding through the southern sky, some swooping down onto the unseen ground beyond a ridge. They looked to each other, all thinking the same thing.

Sha said it first: 'Is that not where we were to rendezvous with Manuel Komnenos' army?'

Bey Taylan sheathed his scimitar as he led his horde from the plain behind the jagged ridge and out of the shade cast by the storm cloud of crows. As they galloped south, he wiped the coppery blood from his lips, then looked to the cluster of White Falcons riding alongside him. These few had served him well today, and had set a fine example to the many thousands riding behind him.

'Bey Taylan,' one of his Falcons said, 'the vanguard have not reported back yet.'

Taylan's eyes narrowed, then he shook his head. 'I told them to range as far and wide as they felt necessary. There is little danger to us in these lands now.'

He heard men behind chanting in his praise, and wondered what his battle name might be. Then he thought of the scroll in his purse – the paper given to him by that mysterious, dark-cloaked Byzantine rider just a week ago. It had told him all he needed to know. Where the Byzantine army would be and when. It irked him that the victory wasn't his and his alone, and so he took out the scroll, ripped it into pieces and tossed it to the wind. Still, he thought, amongst the many he had slain today, he had not found the one he sought. The scroll had said nothing of the *Haga*'s whereabouts. The cur lived on.

Anger and confusion tore at him until he hefted his lance into the air and bellowed: 'Onwards, until Byzantium is in flames!'

Behind him, his ten thousand roared in unison.

–

Apion rode south at haste with his trusted three and a handful of his Chaldian kataphractoi. In the open ground, the thick stench of death from the gorge fell away, only the gore plastered to their armour reminding them of it. But when they came to the southern ridge, the reek returned stronger than ever before. The metallic stink curled round the patchy grass here, and the foul odour of spilled guts came and went in thick waves. They could see nothing but the ridge top, and heard nothing but the now deafening cawing of the crows and vultures circling the plain beyond. One of these creatures swooped overhead, an eyeball dangling from its beak by a tendon.

In silence, they dismounted near the ridge, then crept up it until the southern plain came into view. The foremost rider took one look then clasped a hand to his mouth, failing to catch a spurt of vomit. Laments broke out from the others. Apion stared at the scene before him. The plain might this morning have been a dust bowl or a pleasant meadow, but now it was carpeted with blood and broken bodies and bathed in a mist of buzzing flies. Manuel Komnenos' army had been shattered, utterly shattered.

Byzantine spearmen in their thousands lay peppered with arrows. One of these skutatoi was pinned by a Seljuk lance so his corpse knelt, head lolling back over his shoulders, arms dangling. His mouth was agape and his eyes gone as the crows tore at the flesh of his empty sockets. This was the grim fate of the three themata that the emperor had invested so heavily in, every one of those fresh recruits in newly crafted armour was now but a corpse. Then there were shattered piles of man and horse. Flesh and bone. This is where the tagma riders had made their last stand, it seemed. Now they lay still, men with their necks twisted at absurd angles, many with dark, blood-encrusted puncture wounds on their chests where Seljuk lances had pierced their iron klibania and ruined their bodies. The toxotai had clustered together at the last with no other troops to protect them, he realised, seeing the shattered heaps of archers near the centre of the plain. Here the butchery was extreme. The archers, devoid of armour bar the small shields some wore strapped to their arms, lay in pieces. Limbs lay scattered, far from their bodies. Heads were cleaved open like ripe fruit and some had been sliced clear of the neck. Manuel's fine manoeuvres on the training field had brought him little providence. The Seljuk host he faced had given no quarter.

Taylan's face crept into his thoughts again. Could his son really have carried out this atrocity? He thought of the crimson gorge, barely half a mile distant. *Perhaps it runs in the blood?* a cruel voice hissed in his mind.

A groan from the battlefield startled him and the others. A nearby toxotes, lying face-down, shuffled to rise up on his elbows. His back was bristling with arrows. He held a *Chi-Rho* amulet in his trembling grasp, and lifted it to kiss the piece. Apion picked his way through the mire to crouch before the man.

'What happened here, soldier?'

'We came here to make camp, but… but they were waiting for us… in the hills. They knew we were coming. They knew exactly where we planned to stop and make camp.'

Apion's lips trembled in anger. In his mind's eye he saw the shrivelled, gull-face of Psellos. *You foul-hearted bastard.*

'They swept down from the hills and came at us like spirits—' The man stopped and coughed up a lungful of black blood, his face greying. 'They clutched arrows in their fists like the spines of a porcupine… loosed them like demons, one every few heartbeats. They swept past the… infantry ranks. Drew the kataphractoi from us then annihilated them on the hills. I… I managed to loose only half my quiver before we were overrun.'

'All of you fell?' Apion whispered. 'What of Manuel Komnenos?'

'They took the kouropalates… drove him away at the end of a whip like an ox.'

A stiff breeze searched under Apion's armour as he ran his gaze around the edge of the field. What had become of Romanus' trusted man?

'Help me stand, sir. My legs are numb,' the toxotes whimpered. 'I want to find my brother… he's a toxotes too. I heard him calling out during the battle. Sounded like he was in trouble.' The man's voice faded to a wet hiss, and the only other sound was the wind, the buzzing of the flies and the cawing of the birds. Apion saw the arrows had pierced the soldier's spine.

'You sleep, soldier. I will find your brother and bring him to you.'

'Sleep, sir? Yes… that would be a fine thing.' The toxotes smiled weakly.

Apion drew his dagger and reached down to nick the man's femoral artery. The archer felt nothing, his eyelids closing as his lifeblood washed away in seconds. Better this than the hour or more it would take him to bleed to death. Apion lay the man down, clasping the archer's fingers over his Chi-Rho.

He stood, unable to escape the awful scene no matter where he looked. His crimson cloak licked up gently as the breeze came again. The buzzing of the flies seemed to grow louder and louder, the cawing more shrill. 'Let us make haste from this place,' he said hoarsely. 'A Seljuk horde roams nearby. We cannot stay in the field, we cannot face an enemy that has done this. We must fall back behind Sebastae's walls.'

Diabatenus' head spun as he stirred from the blackness of sleep to the sound of drumming rain and the incessant splash of a leak. He came to with a groan, prised open his good eye and felt a headache come on as thunder rolled across the heavens outside. A flash of lightning quickly followed, briefly illuminating his shabby room. It was early morning, he guessed. He poked his tongue through his gummed-together lips and sat up, suppressing a groan as he saw the ruddy features of the whore he had bought last night, snoring by his side. *Tits that taste like honey but a face like a veteran's shield*, he smirked.

He sat up at the edge of the bed. The grim reality of his room in the slums south of the Forum of the Ox greeted him: desiccated timber floors and walls, the shutter hanging on one hinge, revealing Constantinople's iron-grey morning outside, the leaky roof, few possessions bar a trunk of ragged clothes and his old riding helm – plumed with black and red feathers – and a collection of empty wine amphorae. Indeed, he had added two more to the collection last night – or was it three? A foul waft from the nearby fish market pervaded the room and dismissed his curiosity.

He scratched at his scalp and stretched, unsure quite why he had awoken so early on such a foul day. He picked up his helm and, as usual, he held it so he could see only the good half of his face in its reflection. His mother's words came to him then:

So handsome! With your looks you could summon a smile to a dead woman's face.

This memory cut through the fog of the hangover and he grinned. He eyed the fine riding helm and recalled how his looks had indeed guided him down a glorious path. He had been a good rider, no more, but his looks had given him a sturdy confidence, and he had used this to charm women and men with ease. He had worked his way into the racing stables, becoming the champion rider of one stable master while sleeping with the fellow's wife at every given opportunity. At just twenty he had become the famous Diabatenus, Lord of the Hippodrome, swiftest rider in God's City. He gazed into his memories, reliving the glory of his many victories: the cacophonous roar of the crowds, the adulation, the fawning of the city's elite, the prize money that had paved his path with gold. And then his memories juddered to a halt as one image flashed before him: the scything chariot axle that had torn out his eye. He lowered the helm to his lap, the reflection now revealing the craggy shards of bone and pustule-ridden skin that remained of his ruined eye. Anger and pity fought to take hold of him.

It had broken his reputation, stolen his famous looks and snatched away his fortune. Only a fool would bet their all on one race, he had been told. And an overconfident fool he had been: his villa, his stable on Constantinople's sixth hill, his landholdings outwith the city – all staked on that fateful contest. The worst of it was that with only one eye he could race no longer. He could ride swiftly in an open field, yes, but his career at the Hippodrome was over. Four months had passed since that day. Four months of wallowing in self-pity and soaking his mind in cheap wine.

He picked his eyepatch up from the floor and slipped it on. Purple veins shuddered from the edges of the eyepatch, but at least it disguised the full detail of his injury, he thought as he threw on a tunic and pulled on his boots. And in the new career that was due to begin today, he could get by with just one eye. The riders of the Vigla Tagma were eager to have him for his speed, if nothing else. It would provide a paltry wage in comparison with his takings as a racer, but he had little choice; work or starve.

A rat scurried across the floor in front of him as he stretched and chuckled dryly. 'You're welcome to this place, rodent. Like a palace to you I imag—'

Knuckles rapped on the door, cutting him off. He frowned, glancing to the snoring whore. 'I've paid you, you fat dog!' he cried, imagining the corpulent slum landlord out there. No reply. Just another rap on the door. He cocked an eyebrow. Perhaps the Vigla had sent someone to summon him early?

He opened the door and frowned. This guest was entirely unexpected.

Apion stood atop the battlements of Sebastae, gazing out into the dank, cool September night, wrapped in his crimson cloak with a felt cap on his head for warmth. A pan of milk, orchid root and cinnamon boiled on a brazier beside him, but a warming cup of *salep* would be little comfort. Regardless, he poured the bubbling mixture into a cup and supped at the sweet drink, closing his eyes, trying to think.

Two weeks had passed since the clash at the gorge. Of his nine hundred foot soldiers, three hundred and sixty had died. Of his fifty precious kataphractoi riders, thirteen had fallen. To a man, those who survived were scarred, tired and afraid. They had come to little harm inside the city walls, but they had heard the rumours spread by those outlying Byzantine farmers and herders who had fled into the city in that time. Rumours of the Seljuk horde — ten thousand strong — rampaging around Sebastae unchecked, burning crops and slaying villagers, with no Byzantine force left strong enough to face them. Mustering an army to counter them would take months, and so the pillage went on unbridled.

And the rumours had darkened; some said the riders had roved on to the neighbouring themata, sacking and looting with ease. Word spread that they had even pillaged as far west as the city of Chonai, putting the populace to the sword. Tales had been whispered that the young bey leading them had desecrated the shrine of St Michael within Chonai's walls, using the building as a stable for his best horses. Now the towns of Chaldia and even its capital, Trebizond, were at risk of such a fate. Indeed, Apion had heard his Chaldians pray at night for their loved ones, near-defenceless while his beleaguered force was holed up here. He turned to look down into the city. There, standing around another brazier at the centre of an old, oval forum, were his trusted three.

Big Blastares had been uncharacteristically quiet in these last few weeks — no doubt wracked with worry about his new bride, Tetradia, back in Trebizond. The big man's emotions normally ranged from drunk to furious with little in between, and Apion had rarely before seen this battlefield lion so perturbed. Sha stood beside the big man, bending and twisting a sprig of thyme with his fingers, his thoughts faraway and surely on his farm and the freed woman with whom he had found love. Then there was Procopius. The old artillery expert looked gaunt and hollow. Time really had taken its toll on him, but this last fortnight seemed to have etched an extra few years onto his well-lined features. The old soldier had nobody to fret for but his troubled brothers in these very ranks.

Apion let his head loll. Shame crept over him. Shame that his actions, his choices, had brought this about. Taylan had grown into a white-hot coal of hatred because of him. Maria was a widow because of him. Then a fiercer, talon-sharp shame raked down the centre of his heart – shame that he was impotent to do anything to prevent Taylan's marauding horde. The mighty *Haga*, legend of the borderlands – powerless. He ran a finger over the red-ink stigma of the mythical two-headed eagle, shaking his head in disgust. No ruse, no ploy, no subterfuge came to the surface.

Perhaps you could stop him? Offer him your head? A sibilant thought taunted him.

The scuffing of boots shook him from his malaise. He looked up to see Sha ascending the stone staircase. He stood with Apion wordlessly for some time, just gazing out into the night and the countryside of Sebastae, his dark skin glistening in the moonlight.

'This night,' he said at last. 'It seems to be darker and colder than most.'

'It may be the first of many, Sha,' Apion replied. He thought of the Imperial Palace back in Constantinople. After the failed campaign of last year, and now this – an outright defeat – Romanus Diogenes' place on the imperial throne would doubtless come under the gaze of covetous eyes once more. Psellos and his Doukas puppets would be rubbing their hands in glee. On their first day in this city, he had despatched a trio of swift riders for Constantinople to alert Romanus of Manuel Komnenos' defeat – and of his suspicion that treachery lay behind the defeat. The dying archer's words came to him again.

They knew we were coming. They knew exactly where we planned to stop and make camp.

He just hoped that knowledge would be of some use to Romanus in the dark days that would surely come. 'We can only stay vigilant. Trust in the emperor.'

Just then, a commotion near the city's southern gate roused him. He and Sha craned over the battlements and looked down while the city garrison archers stretched their bows. There were just three men out there. Two wore the gold tunics of the Vigla Tagma, but torn and filthy. Neither wore boots or armour. Apion recognised the other man. Tall and lean, but stooped, his long, dark locks clumped together with filth and gore. 'Manuel?' Then he shouted to the archers and the men at the gate. 'Let them in.'

He and Sha hurried down to the gatehouse, Blastares and Procopius joining them as Manuel staggered in. His face was bruised and cut. One eye was swollen and his hooked nose was badly broken.

'Kouropalates?'

'They let me go,' he rasped, his lungs wet with some internal bleeding.

'They are near?' Apion shot his gaze this way and that out into the darkness of night as the gates were hurriedly closed again.

'No, they are gone.'

'Gone?'

'Back to Seljuk lands.'

Apion frowned. While some of the troops nearby took to cheering this news and crying out in prayer, knowing their homes were now safe, Apion felt a creeping sense of doubt. 'Why?'

'Because they have completed their mission. Bey Taylan released me purely so I could spread the word.'

'Word? Of what?'

Manuel's bronze skin seemed to drain of colour at that moment. 'Strategos, you must prepare a messenger immediately. The emperor must be informed. We fought Taylan's horde, thinking they were the Sultan's main initiative for this year. But they were merely a diversion. While we paid them our full attention, something terrible has happened elsewhere.'

Manuel's next words turned Apion's blood to ice.

The late September nights brought with them a chill squall that swept across Constantinople and saw the populace deserting the streets early each night, or wrapping up well in woollen robes and cloaks. The rooftops of the Imperial Palace felt the full wrath of these gales, the winds howling around the domes and balconies there.

Inside his planning room near the top of the palace, Romanus sat on a padded chair with his back to the crackling log fire, studying a scroll again and again, one hand balled into a fist and pressed to his lips. This message had come in from the west, all the way from Italy.

...and so our ancient city of Barion has fallen, and with it, the heel of Italy has slipped from imperial control and into the hands of Guiscard and his Normans. The imperial garrison were executed, the outlying armies were scattered, and those that I have gathered together are ill-equipped to...

The letter rambled on with a tale of woe he had become all too familiar with. The gale outside screamed like a mocking laughter, the shutters rattling like an absurd applause.

'Barion's fate cannot be laid at your feet,' Eudokia said.

He looked up to the darkened corner of the room where she sat, nursing their baby boy, Nikephoros.

'Defeat wanders like an orphaned wraith until it can cling to a man and call him its father. I am that man. Every dent in imperial fortune will be laid at my feet,' he replied. 'The Doukid acolytes will laud this; Barion, the loss of the great slave-trading capital of the empire to the Normans. Just as they heralded the news about the slaughter of Manuel Komnenos' army. Just as they cheered the sack of Chonai. The people are restless. They have gone two years with nothing other than frugal urban spending and tales of defeat or stalemate for the armies that have soaked up their monies.'

He cast his mind back to the recent races. They had staved off the growing threats of riots in the capital. But the money was gone and now the populace were sullen and seditious once more. He had sold all but his armour, a few horses and a small, modest villa in his native Cappadocia to fund those few days of entertainment in the Hippodrome and to equip the themata marching with Manuel Komnenos. They had been furnished with soft leather boots, fine iron klibania, fresh shields, sharp weapons and expertly woven banners. All now – according to the scroll delivered to him from Apion – lying tangled, torn and ruined with the corpses of that slaughtered army. All that remained of that force was the few thousand Komnenos had despatched to the south, to relieve the siege of Hierapolis, before the disaster at Sebastae. His thoughts turned to Apion's suggestion that the ruination of Manuel Komnenos' army had been a result of subterfuge. His lips grew taut, his fists balled like rocks. Then he fell limp with a sigh, his head shaking. 'Soon they will begin to listen to Psellos and the Doukids. Soon they too will loathe me utterly.'

'And so you choose to wallow in this darkest hour?' Eudokia replied calmly.

Romanus looked up, confused by her blunt words.

She held his gaze, her eyes sparkling. 'I never told you why I chose to wed you, did I, when it would have been so easy for me to accept my late husband's demand that I remain a widow?'

Romanus frowned, shaking his head slowly, unsure he wanted to know her reasoning.

'Because amongst the many ranting, black-tongued and venal snakes that moved in noble circles, there was one who was different. One I knew who spoke with his actions and took little pleasure in wealth.' She stared at him, unblinking. 'You of all people can change the empire's fortunes. One swift and decisive move can wash away the doubt, turn the despair into hope.'

He looked to her, smiling despite his troubles. Their son had brought them together in a way he never thought possible. Where once there was only cold convenience, there was now a warmth, a true bond. *But damn, she is still a shrewd one,* he mused.

'The Strategos of Chaldia and others like him will never desert you. Take strength in their faith,' she continued. 'And know that they will take strength from you. It has been so before and it can be so again.'

Her words stirred a tingle of hope in his heart. He rose from his chair to approach her, to hold her, when footsteps rattled from the staircase outside the door.

'*Basileus!*' Igor panted, his face glowing red from exertion.

'Komes?' Romanus cocked an eyebrow.

'Manuel Komnenos lives… but he sends grave news,' the white-armoured Varangoi leader gasped. 'The Sultan has seized the fortresses.'

Romanus shot Eudokia a confused frown which she reflected with one of her own. 'What, where?'

Igor's face lengthened. 'While our armies were troubled at Sebastae and Hierapolis, Alp Arslan has swooped to seize Manzikert. The sister fortresses of Lake Van are united under his rule. The Gateway to Anatolia is in his hands.'

Romanus' mouth dried in a heartbeat. A prelude to an invasion. If the dark hearts within the palace did not bring him to his knees then the Sultan surely would.

He looked to Eudokia again. A swift and decisive move?

Now he had no choice.

Part 3: 1071 AD

CHAPTER 9

Ruthless

It had been a bitter winter, with a thick blanket of snow clinging to the rooftops and domes of Constantinople in the coldest months. Statues of emperors past stood proudly on column-tops draped in a jewellery of icicles. Sentries paced the city walls, shivering, breath clouding in the chill and shoulders wrapped in thick woollen cloaks. Citizens hurried to and from their homes, sharing whispered tales of the Seljuk capture of the eastern fortresses.

Just before dawn on the first morning of February, the snow was joined by a thick and icy shroud of fog. At the tip of the peninsula, the Imperial Palace and the surrounding streets were deserted at this early hour, until the fog swirled and the sound of boots crunching on frozen snow pierced the air. Two figures were being marched by a pair of varangoi, down from the palace towards the Prosphorion Harbour on the north edge of the city.

John Doukas' shoulders trembled with rage, feeling the sword point of the varangos marshalling him resting at the small of his back. Psellos stumbled as the other gruff varangos' axe blade pressed against his back, knocking his purple cap to the ground. The advisor stooped to sweep the hat up again, then swung to face the Rus axemen. 'You are already dead, redbeard,' he hissed, his clouding breaths coiling around the axeman's face. The varangos feigned disinterest at this, twirling his axe, half-grinning and looking on past Psellos' shoulder. 'But not before you have watched your family being torn apart like hogs under a butcher's blade. They live in the south of the city, do they not, by the Forum of the Ox?' Now the Rus' face steeled, his eyes betraying a glint of fear. It was Psellos' turn to grin.

'Onwards!' Igor cried, emerging from the mist behind this party.

Psellos turned and continued down the gentle sloping flagstones, swept clear of snow and glistening with frost, towards the sea walls.

Now he felt the dark glower of John Doukas on him again. The man had insisted on instigating a coup as soon as Romanus' plans had come to light earlier that week. *Rally the Numeroi from their barracks, seize the city and mount Romanus' head on the palace walls!*

Psellos glowered at John. A coup might well have taken the city, but the outlying strategoi and doukes that still supported the emperor would have rallied their themata and tagmata armies and come to the city's walls. But then the delicacies of their situation had always been lost on John.

The walled harbour emerged from the fog like a tombstone, the iron gates keening as they swung open, shards of ice and snow toppling from the movement. A pair of spearmen glowered down on them from either side of the gates. Men from the Numeroi Tagma, Psellos realised. Until a week ago, his men. Since then, the Numeroi commanders had been sent into exile, with the emperor's men taking over the city garrison. Now it was his turn, Psellos realised, seeing the half-rotted dromon that bobbed in the swirl of fog at the wharf side where another group of varangoi awaited them. He and John were to be cast from the city like beggars. They were to be taken across the Hellespont and cut adrift from imperial affairs with immediate effect. Of the Doukas family, only Eudokia's children by her past marriage to Constantine Doukas would remain in the palace. Young Michael Doukas – one Psellos had long hoped to harness – would now be but a pawn of Diogenes and Eudokia. His thoughts began to churn.

They stumbled aboard the vessel closely followed by the varangoi escorting them, then turned to look back across the harbour. There, emerging from the fog of the palace hill, was the white-robed emperor and his harridan of a wife, ringed by more of their Varangoi dogs. Romanus' steely blue eyes were fixed on Psellos, as if John was merely an afterthought. With a ghostly moan from an unseen buccinator somewhere on the harbour walls, the dromon parted from the wharf side, the oars lapping at the waters under the carpet of fog. Slowly, the emperor and his retinue began to fade into the mist too.

'And the last chance of power slips away in utter silence without a blade being drawn,' John said, his voice trembling with rage. He gripped the edge of the ship with wool-lined mits as if trying to throttle the timbers.

'You do not see it, do you?' Psellos replied, never taking his eyes from the emperor's fading form.

'See what? All I see is a bleak future. I will take to my villa in the countryside of Bithynia, and I will no doubt live in luxury. But what good is luxury when my heart and my every thought are cloaked in shame… *shame!*' He thumped a mitted fist on the vessel's edge.

A trio of the fifty varangoi escorting them looked round at this, alarmed for an instant, then melting into gentle and mocking laughter.

'And these *curs* will guard my lands. Not to protect me, but to pen me in like a *dog!*' John panted, then poked a finger at Psellos, wide-eyed. 'And you too, advisor. This is your fate too!'

Psellos did not flinch, refusing to let John's panic take him. 'We have struggled for nearly four years to establish support enough to overthrow Diogenes and reinstate your family dynasty.'

'Aye – four years! You seek to remind me of your failures? *Not* a wise move, advisor. Remember, at my countryside estate I have a company of slaves. They may only number twelve or so, but they will heed my beck and call. One word from me and they will dispose of any soul who displeases me.'

'So already you seem keen to make plans for this countryside empire of yours – a few vineyards, a paltry household slave-guard and a pile of bricks?' Psellos scoffed. 'Will a swarm of cicadas and a field of barley stalks be your army?'

John grappled Psellos' purple collar, lifting him to his toes. 'You know I would give anything to have my rightful throne back, advisor!'

Psellos felt the shower of spittle fleck his face. 'Then you will listen… *master.*'

John set him down, nodding, his chest still heaving in ire. 'Speak.'

'For four years we have tried to garner support to oust Diogenes,' he repeated, 'and for four years the balance has always been too delicate to risk the coup you have long sought.' Psellos leaned his elbows on the lip of the dromon, staring into the dark waters visible through the swirling fog. John joined him. 'Now, it seems, we have pressed the emperor into making this rash move. Sending us into exile will instigate a backlash amongst our supporters… *your* supporters,' he swiftly corrected himself. 'We have a righteous cause, master. And matters are coming to a head, both concerning the throne and the long-anticipated clash with the Sultan and his Seljuk hordes. Romanus has no money and his plans to gather a vast army are listing. Yet he now has no option but to march east, to Lake Van, at the head of what forces he can muster. He must expel the Sultan's forces from Manzikert and Chliat. Only a final victory and an end to the Seljuk threat can steady his trembling grip on the throne.'

Psellos' own words rang in his ears for a moment. More, his chest lesion began itching furiously again. He recalled the night of that winter storm when the old crone had attacked him. Her words from that night now mixed with his own.

On a battlefield far to the east, by an azure lake flanked by two mighty pillars, blood will be let like a tide… and it will be your doing.

The words seemed to usher the chill air in under his robe and across his skin. He shivered, drawing his garment tighter, feeling the glutinous fluid weep from the pitted, bad flesh there. This morning, to his disgust, he had even found a maggot writhing in one of those pits, and when he had plucked it out, he saw just the whiteness of his breastbone underneath.

It was then that something moved in his peripheral vision – along the deck from where they stood. It pulled him from his vile memory. He peered along the deck. A shape swirled in the mist; milky, sightless eyes, grey, web-like hair and one finger outstretched, pointing at him. Her lips were rolled back, her teeth like fangs. Then she swept towards him. With a yelp, he swung to face the approaching shape, only for a cloud of deathly cold mist to sweep over him. Nothing.

John frowned at Psellos' sudden jumpiness. 'A hazardous campaign awaits Diogenes. Yet what influence can we have upon its fate when we languish in exile?' he sighed.

'Probably more than ever before,' Psellos grinned, brushing away the thought of the old crone.

John scowled at this. 'How so?'

'We first heard of the emperor's intentions to exile us a week ago. Do you think I used that time to pack my belongings?' Psellos purred.

'Advisor?'

'I have made arrangements. This time, they shall not fail.'

The corners of John's mouth played with a dark grin, his belief returning. 'Tell me what you have planned.'

Psellos looked up and into the murky wall of fog, back in the direction of Constantinople. He stroked his gold rings, his eyes narrowing. 'When Romanus marches east, he will find that his ranks are peppered with traitors, and his initiatives will be thwarted at every turn.'

The fog cleared from the capital later that day, leaving the air crisp and cool and the sky unblemished. Romanus stepped out from the red dome atop the palace and onto the balcony ringing it. Out here, the snow-covered roofs glistened and the noise of the streets below was faint, contested by the crying of gulls and the lapping of icy waves against the sea walls. He gazed off to the east, across the choppy waters of the Bosphorus Strait to the shores of Anatolia. He needed strength now more than ever. Yet his people were in sedition once more and his armies were in tatters. And the winter had claimed another of his thin band of allies. Manuel Komnenos, shamed yet unswervingly loyal and eager to redeem himself after the disaster at Sebastae, had perished not on the battlefield but in his bed, overcome by a foul ear infection that soon consumed the rest of his body. 'So few good men left to stand with me,' he muttered into the ether. 'And this is truly my last throw of the dice.'

There had been a modicum of respite, however, with the arrival of an offer from Alp Arslan. An offer of temporary truce. It seemed the Sultan aimed to stabilise his hold on Seljuk Syria and wanted to have the spring to seize and garrison the rebellious cities of that baked land. He shook his head and sighed. It was an offer he could not refuse, despite the certainty that beyond the spring it would only result in a greater threat to the few Byzantine holdings in northern and western Syria.

He closed his eyes, attempting to order his thoughts once more. But a dull murmur from the streets down by the Hippodrome suddenly erupted into a chorus of cries. Angst, terror, penance. He frowned, glancing down, seeing a throng of citizens there, heads tilted skywards, fingers pointing. A stark coldness gripped him as he looked up to behold the heavens. A fiery red streak, breaking across the sky, staining the perfect blue. A comet. It shone like a bloody beacon. The cries of the populace rang in his ears. *It is a sign*, one cried. *We have lost God's favour!* Another shrieked. He closed his eyes and clasped a hand over his heart. *Do not desert me in my hour of need.*

'*Basileus*, they have arrived!' Igor's words rang out over the rooftop portico. The big Rus stopped in his tracks, eyes drawn to the omen in the skies. Even this scarred, haggard brute of a warrior gawped impotently at the sight.

Romanus bit his lip in frustration, then strode over to Igor, clasping a hand to the man's shoulder and stirring him from his fright. 'My generals are here? Then we must set to work at once, Komes.' He beckoned Igor back inside the domed roof.

Here, the fine vases and ornaments had been cleared from the large oak table in the centre of the room and a map of the empire was rolled out over its surface. The fire had been piled high with logs and the shelves at the side of the room were well stocked with watered wine, fresh and aromatic bread, cheese and fruit. A pair of varangoi guarded the door and stairwell that led up to the room, and a cluster of thirty or so military men had gathered around the map table. He sought out the three most senior amongst them. 'Bryennios, Tarchianotes, Alyates!' he called out, a broad grin stretching across his face.

Bryennios, the towering doux and *domestikos* of the armies of the west, stepped forward. His dark-skinned face was gaunt and split with a feral grin. He had a thinning peak of dark hair, flashed with grey at the temples. He bowed on one knee and dipped his head. '*Basileus!*'

'Up, up!' Romanus waved him to stand once more. 'It is good to see you again, old friend.'

'I bring with me the best of your Thracian armies. Five thousand riders of the western tagmata,' Bryennios added. 'Steel-skinned, iron-willed, hearts brimming with courage!'

Romanus nodded, heartened, clasping his forearm to Bryennios'. 'I need no reminding of the western riders' valour – indeed, I have missed them since my days riding at their head were curtailed!'

Then the emperor turned to Doux Tarchianotes. This bulky, swarthy individual was some ten years older than Bryennios. The tanned skin of his somewhat unhandsome face was lined with age and spoiled by a bulbous wart on one cheek, a fleshy and shapeless nose and permanently flared nostrils. His dark curls hung to his jaw and a neatly trimmed beard hugged his chin. This man was nominally the commander of the eastern border tagmata, in the hazardous lands east of Chaldia. But in recent years, the armies there had fragmented, with the likes of the odious Crispin of Normandy running riot. As such, Tarchianotes had found himself as a man with a title and little else.

'My friend,' Romanus rested a hand on the man's shoulder. 'Your time has come. The imperial cavalry tagmata – the Scholae, the Vigla, the Stratelatai and the Hikanatoi – will ride under your command,

and the infantry of the Optimates Tagma will march for you too. You will be my deputy for the coming campaign.'

'This is a great honour you have bestowed upon me, *Basileus*,' he bowed.

Romanus nodded in acknowledgement, then turned to the third of his summoned men. 'And you,' he said, 'have grown into a fine leader of men in the years since last we met.'

Alyates, Strategos of Cappadocia, stepped forward, embracing the emperor as a brother would. He was in his early twenties, built like a sapling with lank, dark hair hanging to his cheeks and framing his fine-boned and handsome features. 'The people of Cappadocia, your homeland, are with you in your every coming step, *Basileus*!' Alyates exclaimed. His words were firm despite his soft tone. 'I have mustered what men I could,' he added with a whisper, 'but barely two thousand march with me.'

Romanus felt his heart sink. He had hoped Alyates might raise twice that number from the lands of Cappadocia. He buried his disappointment and grinned, then cast his eyes around the other men he had called here; doukes of the tagmata and strategoi of the inner themata. These men would be his officers in what was to come. The campaign that would seal his destiny. He tapped on the campaign map. All gathered round the table.

'Now, the goal that has eluded us in these last three years of campaigning lies here.' He pointed forked fingers at the two dots lying near a lake, far to the east. 'The fortress-towns of Chliat and Manzikert are akin to watchtowers, overseeing the Gateway to Anatolia. For many years, no one power held both. Now, Sultan Alp Arslan's men garrison the walls of those citadels. He has a dagger poised at our flank. Unimpeded, he could channel his armies into inner Anatolia. In the past, we have suffered raids with bands of Seljuk riders, sometimes numbering several thousand, ravaging our borderlands and penetrating deep into the interior. The forts and watchtowers lie broken and unmanned across the heart of Anatolia in testament. And God will not let us forget what happened to Caesarea and Chonai in these last years.'

At this, the gathered men offered a muttering of prayer for the thousands of souls who died in the sacking of those mighty and once-invincible walled cities.

'But should the Sultan bring the full might of his armies to bear through that eastern gateway, then we will not be hearing tales of ruination from the east. That ruination will befall all Anatolia and might threaten even the great walls of Constantinople itself. God's very city is at risk. The empire could fall in these next months. It could fall, or,' he looked each man in the eye, all faces illuminated in lamplight, 'or we could seize a legendary victory,' he finished, clenching a shaking fist. 'In the past we have held either the desert cities to the south-east – such as Hierapolis, Antioch – or key Armenian fortresses – such as Manzikert or Chliat – in the east. Seldom both. Thus the interior of Anatolia has always been susceptible to invasion. Currently we have both Hierapolis and Antioch garrisoned by imperial troops and standing fastidiously against the Sultan's annual sieges – so the south-east is secure. Bringing Manzikert and Chliat under Byzantine control also would see the eastern border secured.'

It was then he heard a muttering amongst the men.

'What's that you say?' he said sharply, identifying one of the strategoi.

'I... I said how can we secure those two fortresses? For two years running we have set out to do so and failed. And just last year the strongest of our themata were all but wiped out under Manuel Komnenos' stewardship.' The man's words echoed around the chamber until he dropped his gaze, almost ashamed that he had spoken up against the emperor.

'Your words were spoken in earnest, man, do not shy away from them,' Romanus replied. 'He is right,' he said to the others. 'The three themata wiped out near Sebastae last year were supposed to be the backbone of the regional armies we would summon this year. Finely armoured and equipped, they harked back to a bygone era. Now they are part of history. To equip more themata in a similar fashion to replace them requires funding – funding that is simply not there.'

'Then how do we amass a campaign army, *Basileus*?' Another man spoke. 'The themata are battered and broken and the tagmata armies number too few to guarantee victory and seizure of the Armenian forts.'

'Guarantee?' Romanus cocked an eyebrow. 'There is no such thing as a guarantee. I once placed a wager on Xerus and his Phrygian chargers at the Hippodrome. The musclebound rider had won every race he entered – by nearly half the track. This day he was up against Ampelas, a slip of a lad on his first ever race. The boy was trembling visibly as he went to his chariot. But then Xerus turned up, white as a sheet, sweating profusely. He rode like a drunken beggar that day, coming in a full track behind Ampelas. Turns out he ate a bowl of oats shortly before his race that went through him like a blade. Spent the next three days shitting out every last morsel in his guts. So don't talk to me of guarantees!'

A hearty chorus of chuckling rang out at this, even the man who had spoken was grinning. 'Foul gruel for our enemies, then?' he smiled.

'Perhaps,' Romanus nodded with a smirk. 'But first, let us address how we will cope with the shortcoming in the thematic forces.' He swept a hand across the map. 'We can muster but a few hundred from each of the themata shattered in last year's campaign — so I propose the men of those lands are left to defend their homes and tend to their farms. But from the other themata,' he dotted a finger to the themata of Charsianon, Anatolikon and Colonea, 'we will be able to muster a greater number. Perhaps eight or ten thousand spears and bows plus maybe two thousand horse overall, including Alyates' Cappadocians. Doux Philaretos is currently organising the thematic mustering in the upper Sangarios River valley.' He pointed to a stretch of flatland in the north-western corner of Anatolia. 'Philaretos will see what shape he can pull those ranks into. They must be drilled and equipped to form a fine anvil for our cavalry hammer.'

Alyates cocked an eyebrow and he cast his gaze around the room. 'You do not plan to muster the Chaldians? The *Haga*, he is not coming?' Alyates asked.

Romanus looked up with a grin. 'Ah, I had not come to that yet! The Strategos of Chaldia is assembling men in the east as we speak. His numbers are also few, but they are well equipped and expertly drilled. More, I have tasked him with mustering a mercenary army from our Armenian allies in the eastern hills and what nomadic riders he can gather too. He will gather this force and station them in the east at a point on our campaign trail, then come west with his retinue to join us at the mustering ground.'

A murmur of consent rang around the table at this.

'Hmm,' Tarchianotes interjected, 'the combined forces of the themata and the *Haga*'s mercenary armies might still not be enough. Last year, Manuel Komnenos and his twenty thousand were crushed. You have talked of gathering an army thrice that size this year. But with the tagma and themata combined, I foresee only some thirty-three thousand men. Not quite the hammer blow we hoped to deliver to the Sultan, is it?'

Romanus eyed the man carefully. His dark brown eyes were masked in shade. *This one is a shrewd fellow – does he know of my plans already?*

'Indeed. Thus, we must look beyond the themata, or rather, within their lands. The wine and oil magnates own vast tracts of Anatolia. They reap great dividends from their produce.'

'They are self-serving curs, to a man!' Bryennios cut in, thumping a fist to the table. A heartbeat later, he bowed his head. 'I am sorry, *Basileus!*'

Romanus let the outburst pass. He knew Bryennios' son had been slain in some power struggle between the wine magnates of Paphlagonia.

'They have paid vast sums of taxes into the imperial treasury in the past, but you are right, they have also profited greatly from imperial soil. Now it is time to call upon them. Some own sizeable private armies; companies of spearmen, retinues of riders. Many employ Norman lancers from the west or Rus mercenaries from the north. Some even organise their infantry into banda. Others have scant forces – just a handful of thugs and brigands to guard their countryside villas – but vaults brimming with gold. Should they wish to stave off invasion of their precious lands, then now is the time they should seek to spend that money in bolstering their ranks and joining the campaign. I estimate that we could add at least another seven thousand to our campaign army if we call upon them. An army of forty thousand combined. Not quite what I had hoped for, but a strong force indeed. Stronger than the empire has mustered in many years.'

Silence rang around the room, and Romanus could feel the uncertainty growing. Many felt just as Bryennios did about these greedy and proud lords of plenty. A log snapped in the fire, breaking the tension.

'We have no choice, do we?' Bryennios asked.

Romanus nodded earnestly. 'This year demands victory. The Lake Van fortresses must be taken and the Gateway to Anatolia secured.'

'Then I give you my backing, *Basileus*, as always,' Bryennios replied, bowing then looking to his comrades to follow suit. And they did, one by one, some albeit grudgingly.

Romanus felt an all too brief flush of relief. They had bought into his mustering plan. But now he would have to broach a far more contentious subject. 'As you are all aware, I am sure, I must also take measures to protect my throne whilst I am absent from the capital.' He clapped his hands.

The two varangoi at the door parted, and another pair marshalled a young man in. This one wore a leather tunic and a white woollen cloak. He was tall, broad-shouldered, with thick, dark, cropped hair and a flat-boned, fair-skinned face. His dark, almond-shaped eyes lent him a look of openness.

'Andronikos Doukas will be joining us on this campaign.'

'You are taking John Doukas' son on this campaign?' Alyates gasped.

'John Doukas and his acolytes may be in exile, but only a fool would think them content with their lot. Having his son in my ranks will ensure they remain so for the duration of the campaign, at least.'

All eyes fell upon Andronikos. The young man's nose wrinkled. 'Are you seeking out my hidden blade?' he said, meeting each gaze upon him. His voice was throaty and firm. 'I have no wish to join my father in exile. I am to ride with you like a wretch – in chains. And I will do so gladly, if only to prove my valour.'

'Aye, until you can sink a blade into the emperor's back?' one voice called out.

Andronikos came to the edge of the table and stood tall, stretching his neck to see who had spoken. 'I will ride with neither shield nor blade. And I have the courage to do so, unlike you, who casts his words from a veil of shadows.'

The doux who had spoken out leaned forward over the table so his face was fully illuminated. It was Tarchianotes. His bulbous nose was wrinkled in distaste.

'I won't let you out of my sight for a moment… *boy!*'

Romanus leaned in between the pair, cutting through the simmering tension. 'So be it. Now, let us eat and discuss the finer detail. There is much to organise. As soon as the snow lifts from the city, we will make haste across the Bosphorus and meet with our mustered armies on the banks of the Sangarios. Then, with God's will, we will see our empire secured and our people free of strife,' he boomed, lifting a cup of watered wine and urging the others to do likewise.

'*Nobiscum Deus!*' the gathered military men roared in reply, then broke into clusters of conversation, each man taking bread and wine for himself and discussing their roles with their comrades.

At last, Romanus realised, there were no eyes upon him. He slipped from the chamber and out onto the balcony once more. His gaze lifted to the heavens and rested again on the blood-red comet, like a fresh wound in the night sky. His mind tumbled with thoughts of what might happen in this city in his absence, of the patchwork and suspect nature of the magnate armies who would supplement his ranks, of what might happen when they reached Lake Van, far to the east. *And the road to that far flung outpost is long and treacherous*, he thought, his gaze falling to the eastern horizon. A chill wind danced across every inch of his flesh.

The second week of March drove out the last of the ice and snow. Three fresh but clear-weathered days saw the ceremonial gilded shield hung on the gates of the Imperial Palace. This age-old sign meant the campaign was to begin in earnest. Crowds gathered and a thick stench of dung permeated the air as, all that morning, the city streets were flooded with mules, oxen, carts and men, shouting and heckling over the whinnying, lowing and snorting as they guided this, the makings of the touldon train that would supply the campaign, towards the fortified Port of Julian.

When Romanus entered the port gates on foot dressed in his white-and-silver moulded bronze breastplate, white tunic and trousers and fine doeskin boots, all stopped to salute.

'*Basileus*,' they called out.

He saluted in return, then motioned for them to get back to their business. He took just a moment to glance up and over the walls of the port, across the fluttering banners atop the Hippodrome and up to the red dome at the pinnacle of the Imperial Palace. He saw her there, the woman he had come to love. He stroked the golden heart pendant she had given him as a wedding gift, then tucked it inside his armour and thought of her and young Nikephoros.

'Until I return to your side,' he whispered. *If you return*, a cruel voice countered in his mind. He ignored the voice of doubt, slipped his purple cloak over his shoulders and boarded the imperial flagship, his escort of varangoi flooding onboard with him.

Igor and his men were resplendent in their pure-white armour, fine silk cloaks, shell-like shields clinging to their shoulders and battle axes slung over their backs. Most wore simple helms or none at all – letting their blond and red braided locks hang free. The sight of one thousand of these hardy and ruddy-faced curs filled his heart with hope. Another two thousand such men were to remain here in the city with a brief to stay vigilant of any manoeuvrings. For although Psellos was in exile, the man's claws were long and insidious. His gaze had unwittingly drifted to the form of Andronikos Doukas, being led on board the flagship, his wrists bound in chains. The young man had done nothing to suggest he was of the same ilk as his father, and this brought a dark cloud of guilt over Romanus' heart. *A hard choice, but the right one*, he affirmed.

'We are ready to embark, *Basileus*,' the ship's *kentarches* said, panting, his hands lined with rope-burns from working the rigging.

'Good. Take us out,' Romanus nodded, then moved over to the prow, resting his palms on the edge of the ship to look ahead as the vessel moved under oar out through the sea gates and into the Propontis. Then the purple-and-white Chi Rho sail was unfurled – at once billowing proudly in the stiff sea breeze. Romanus inhaled deeply. The salt spray made it all real – always the first step of a campaign to the east. The scent of the ocean, the stinging chill of the water, the sight of the foaming, choppy surf offering the first hint of defiance, the crash of the waves against the hull and the crying of gulls and cormorants.

Let's see what you have for me this time, he said with a nervous but defiant grin.

All around him, clusters of round-hulled pamphyloi bobbed, ferrying horses, fodder, supplies and artillery components. Just ahead, dromons – each with three banks of oars – brimmed with spearmen and riders from the imperial tagmata. The completion of this small but fine fleet was one of the few rewards for abstaining from campaign the previous year.

He looked east in the rough direction of Helenopolis, the small port-town in Bithynia that was their destination, then up to the sky, taking heart at the unbroken blue that promised of the spring and summer to come. His memories of the grim comet had faded. Even the populace seemed to have gotten over the spectacle without too many predictions of doom. The voyage continued throughout the morning, swift and steady. It was only when they cut away from the coast and out across the Propontis that the skies greyed. The turquoise waters turned sombre in reflection, the choppy peaks growing higher and causing the timbers of the vessel to groan. Some soldiers, unused to the buck and swell of the sea, took to throwing down their bread rations and retching overboard. Then the grey clouds conspired to unleash a chill rain that swiftly turned into a hailstorm. Chunks of ice as large as a sword pommel smashed down on the deck. Soldiers yelped and ran for cover, clustering under the sails.

Romanus braved the storm until it became ferocious, some chunks of hail even splintering a barrel of wine stowed on the deck. At this, he hurried to join his men under the precarious shelter of the sail, slipping and sliding through the slick of red wine. There, he watched as the sky continued to hurl down its wrath, turning the water all around the boat into a foaming cauldron. The stench of sweat and damp clothing soon filled his nostrils.

'It is a sign,' he heard a squat Vigla soldier say, behind him. 'We should be going to Pylai, not Helenopolis. The men of my bandon, they all have been on campaign before, and they say they have always travelled to Pylai and then set off overland from there.'

Romanus made to contest the man's fears, but another voice cut in;

'And if the men told you they always drank each other's piss on campaign, would you yearn to do likewise?' the voice said. It was Andronikos Doukas, his haughty posture and calm expression untroubled by the squall.

The Vigla soldier scowled and grappled Andronikos by the throat. 'Close your mouth, cur! You are in shackles, remember. Be thankful you still have your tongue!'

Andronikos gazed down upon the man, barely flustered.

'Enough!' Romanus stepped in. The pair parted. Romanus offered Andronikos a barely noticeable nod of appreciation, then turned to the Vigla soldier.

The Vigla soldier gawped, meltwater running from his nose. He saw the emperor's features, flaxen hair plastered to his face, cobalt eyes glinting, and at once paled.

'*Basileus*, I… I apologise,' he stuttered over the rattle of the hail.

'Why? Because I am your emperor or because you understand this man's point?' Romanus countered, opening a hand towards Andronikos. 'Tell me as you would any of your comrades; why would Helenopolis be any sort of cursed move?' He shrugged. 'It is some ten miles more easterly then Pylai. Ten miles less to march!' he cocked an eyebrow, awaiting an answer.

The Vigla soldier gulped then nodded. 'Yes, *Basileus*, that is true. But it is a damp and unpleasant place. The miserable city, some call it. Campaigns that have been victorious in the past have all gone via Pylai.'

Romanus snorted. 'As have many disastrous ones!'

The men chuckled at this, and the Vigla man nodded in acceptance.

'Think not of omens and portents.' He clasped a hand to his breast. 'If we are showered with hail today then we will drink chilled water with our meal tonight!'

At this, the men broke out in a cheer. Then, as if the storm had been conquered by his words, the sky brightened, the hail lessened and then stopped. He strode from the shade of the sail, welcoming a modicum of warmth from the watery sun. As he gazed up at the thinning clouds, he saw a bird in trouble up there in the zephyrs. He walked to the prow of the vessel again, seeing the creature flail to right itself. It tumbled lower and lower. Finally, just a few feet above the deck of the boat, it caught the breeze and began to glide. Romanus watched as it then arced round and came to land on the prow right before him. It was a grey dove – rarely seen this far from land. He frowned at the creature's boldness, then started as it hopped forward along the rim of the ship and onto the back of his hand. Romanus lifted his hand back, drawing the creature closer to examine it. An ordinary dove, bar the distinctively grey feathers and almost laughable impudence. Just an ordinary dove.

But he heard the murmurs from the deck behind him, and knew all eyes were upon him.

'Another sign from God. He chooses to send a grey dove and not a white one. A truly ill omen,' they whispered.

Romanus set the creature to flight once more, then bowed his head in frustration.

–

The weather had turned back to mizzle when the fleet reached the grassy headland of Helenopolis – a tiny promontory jutting into the Gulf of Nicomedia. Soon, the campaign army had disembarked at the broad timber wharf side, where a few round-hulled pamphyloi listed in the shallows, badly in need of repair. The small port–town itself was indeed rather sorry–looking. Unwalled, with a collection of timber shacks and a few dilapidated stone buildings that served as the offices of the local tourmarches, it had the look of a muddy stain on the otherwise verdant countryside surrounding it. A handful of garrison skutatoi in grubby tunics and rusting armour stood guard around the streets and atop the rickety watchtowers that overlooked the town and the disembarking fleet.

The army flooded through the town to set up camp south of the settlement. Romanus strode around the earthworks as the men busied themselves preparing the camp's ditch and rampart, the scent of damp earth and sweet woodsmoke spicing the air. He stayed out in the relentless drizzle for the rest of the day, helping to erect the gates at the camp's eastern side. By dusk, he was filthy, sodden and exhausted, but the camp was complete. Men settled down to pray and to kindle cooking fires, melting down cakes of dried yoghurt, sesame seeds and honey or cooking meaty stews. His appetite awoke at that moment, and he swung round to see the red satin dome of his tent at the heart of the camp. He strode towards it, then stopped before the ring of Vigla skutatoi demarcating the imperial tent area, turning to sweep his gaze around the rest of the camp in the fading light. More tents than he could count. Myriad vivid banners standing proudly albeit soaked. And by his sodden imperial tent stood two symbols of greatness – the glittering campaign Cross and the blue–gold Icon of the Holy Virgin of Blachernae. The core of this campaign army was ready to stride forth and make history. 'It seems the omen of the dove was somewhat exaggerated!' he chuckled to himself.

He acknowledged the salutes of the Vigla guards, who parted to let him through, then nodded to Igor and the eight varangoi who formed the inner layer of sentries, dotted around the edges of the imperial tent. Sweeping the tent flap back and entering, he saw that his bed had been prepared. A lamp glowed beside it, casting the tent in a warm and inviting orange. He slumped down, sliding off his cloak and boots with a sigh. A dull rumble emanated from his belly, and he realised he had not eaten all day. He noticed a tray in the corner of the tent, containing his evening meal of stew, fresh bread and more wine. He pulled a chunk of bread from the still–warm loaf and dipped this in the thick, delicious–smelling stew. The warm, meaty meal swiftly innervated his weary limbs and he finished the lot soon after. He washed this hearty meal down with a cup of watered wine from the jug. The wine had a bitter edge to it, spoiling the drink somewhat. 'Pah,' he scoffed, 'you're too used to the finest Paphlagonian, man!'

With that, he slipped off his tunic and sunk back onto his warm, dry bedding. The tension in his muscles seeped away and sleep overcame him in moments. It was dark and dreamless.

Until he heard something crashing like a war drum.

He sat bolt upright; all was dark – the lamp having burnt out – and the camp was silent outside. Had it been a trick of the mind? Then… *Boom! Boom! Boom!* The blood hammered in his ears rhythmically. He clutched the sides of his head, wincing, feeling a wave of nausea rush over him. He stumbled from his bed, falling to his knees, retching. Only a thin, acidic bile came up. The floor seemed to melt away before him and he was overcome by a terrible sense of falling endlessly. He cried out, flailing, lurching to his feet in order to grasp out at something, anything. He crashed against the centre pole of the tent and heard a dull and distant crack amidst the rapid drumming of blood in his head. He barely noticed the pole shredding or the canvas of the tent falling down around him, covering him. He barely heard the cries of alarm from outside when this happened. He scarcely recognised Igor and the other varangoi who pulled him out of the collapsed tent. He did, however, recognise the panicked mutterings of the vast number of soldiers who had rushed from their tents to the scene of the incident and now stood, gathered and gawping in torchlight.

'The tent pole snapped and nearly saw our emperor suffocated. God have mercy on us. Another dark portent!'

'No… I…' he croaked, reaching a hand out to the staring masses. But a rush of nausea snatched his words away and sent him spinning into the blackness.

CHAPTER 10

Adnoumion

The first weeks of April were dry and hot. Spring had arrived and the once barren inland hillsides of the Opsikon Thema were now alive with the chirruping cicada song and dappled with thick green grasses, wheat fields and shady groves of ash and poplar.

A flock of starlings scattered from one such thicket as four horsemen rose over the tip of a grassy hill, silhouetted in early morning sunlight. One of them, sporting three black eagle feathers in his helm, raised a finger and pointed downhill.

'Let your weary eyes rejoice,' Apion grinned, scratching at his iron-grey beard.

Sha, Blastares and Procopius looked with him, gazing across the vast army camp that spread across the banks of the Sangarios, interrupting the tracts of wheat that clung to the sides of the calm, teal river. The camp was just downriver from the Zompos Bridge, an ancient-looking stone structure that had long allowed imperial armies to march east without the need of a ferry fleet. This was the *adnoumion*, the ritual mustering. The land where the emperor assembled his armies, summoning the regional themata to join his tagmata corps. He spotted the bright banners of the imperial tagmata; the Scholae, the Vigla, the Stratelatai and the Hikanatoi. And the fluttering emblems of the Cappadocian Thema and the Anatolikon too. Then there were stand-ards he did not recognise – western tagmata, it seemed. More than twenty thousand here, he reckoned on a rough count of the tents, and doubtless many more to come. This was the emperor's response to the news of Alp Arslan's taking of Manzikert. Once more, the *Golden Heart* filled Apion with that precious commodity; hope.

Realising his trusted three had never witnessed the mustering before, he pointed to the sturdy fortress that sat on a small hillock overlooking the vast camp and was framed by a backdrop of tall, rocky hills. 'That is the fortress of Malagina. That is where the last blades will be forged, the last garments woven and the supplies will be gathered, ready to be loaded onto the mules and wagons of the touldon before the campaign continues eastwards.'

Next, he pointed to the rows of timber stalls that hemmed a patchwork of lush green meadows, dotted with horses. 'And here we have the imperial stables. Thousands of the finest battle horses are reared, broken in and put to stud and pasture right here.'

'Hmm. I wonder if they'd be interested in a trade?' Procopius grumbled. His grey stallion snorted and shook its head as if in protest. 'This one gives me nothing but a mean eye and blisters on my arse!'

Sha chuckled. 'Perhaps your mount means to trade you in?'

'Ha,' Blastares cut in, 'for what, a sack of hay?'

Procopius' eyes widened and he squared his shoulders indignantly. 'Alright, alright, you pair of bast—'

'Look, to the south!' Sha cut in.

Apion blinked and peered to the green hills there. From a fold in the land, another column snaked towards the camp. He spotted the silver banners they carried. And a mile further south again, another column sporting green banners. 'The Colonean Thema and the Charsianon Thema! They must have some two thousand men each. That is a fine sight.' Then he eyed his trusted three with a mischievous grin. 'Still, I'm not in the mood to let those beggars beat us to the gates. Ya!' he cried, heeling his Thessalian downhill towards the camp.

Apion noticed many things inside the camp. There were many soldiers moving to and fro in the full glare of the mid-morning sun. The tagmata men seemed well prepared and equipped for this campaign, but the themata armies seemed to present a jumble of issues. The Anatolikon Thema and the Cappadocian Thema were already encamped, but their ranks seemed to consist of very old men with good armour and weapons but lacking the physique of soldiers. When the Colonean and Charsianon ranks came in, it was a different story; they had indeed mustered nearly three thousand young men, but in such haste, they had found little time to provide basic kit for these recruits. Most had shields, spears and felt caps or helms, but many marched in bare feet and few had swords.

'Ah, there is much organisation to be done,' he muttered to himself, sliding from his saddle. Amongst the sea of tents, the incessant babble and the packs of men hurrying this way and that, Apion realised one thing was missing. The campaign Cross was nowhere to be seen. Indeed, the usual central compound with the emperor's tent was missing. 'Sha, set up our tent. I'll be with you soon.'

'Sir,' Sha nodded, waving Blastares and Procopius with him.

Apion frowned, stalking over to the centre of the vast camp, where the emperor's tent would normally be. There was nothing bar a pile of crates and barrels. A man of some fifty years was sitting on one of these crates, cross-legged, with a slat of wood on his knees, a pot of ink in one hand and a quill pen in the other. He had a bookish look about him, his eyes shaded under his mop of curly silver locks and his slender frame draped in some grey silk robe. He seemed to be taking in all that was going on around him, gazing across the sea of tents, over the surrounding hills and up to the pleasant sky. Then he took to scribbling furiously on a sheaf of paper stretched across the timber slat.

'A fine place you choose to write — this is the place where the emperor's tent should be, is it not?'

The man looked up, as if having been awoken from a daydream. 'Indeed it is.'

Apion cocked an eyebrow. 'And you are?'

'Michael Attaleiates. I am the emperor's scribe. It is my job to capture every detail of this campaign. I don't know where he is — I only know that there has been some… confusion.'

'So you choose to sit and write?' Apion frowned, scanning the goings-on nearby for some familiar face.

Michael smiled. 'Future generations must know what transpires — virtuous or wicked,' he said with a wry grin.

Apion snorted, recalling old Cydones' disdain for the scribes and chroniclers. 'Virtuous or wicked? Surely that depends on the eye of the beholder… and his agenda.'

Michael's grin grew a little taut at this. He looked Apion up and down. 'And you, you must be an officer?'

'Apion, Strategos of Chaldia.'

Michael's eyes sparkled shrewdly at this. 'Ah, the *Haga* is here? I have heard your name mentioned by more than a few. Perhaps I should write of you in my chronicle?'

Apion smiled and shook his head. 'I am but one blade amongst thousands. Save your ink for those who matter, writer. For now I'd like to know where the emperor is. Who here can help me?' he asked, looking round but seeing only unfamiliar faces striding to and fro.

'Perhaps the Komes of the Varangoi might be best placed to explain.' Michael pointed over Apion's shoulder.

Apion twisted round to see Igor stalking towards him, his armour brilliant white, his face lobster pink – almost blending in with the vertical scar that ran over one eye – and his braided locks bobbing with every step.

Apion held out an arm, ready to greet the big warrior as he had done at the Euphrates camp two years ago. But this time, Igor's face was a picture of dread. '*Haga!* You are here at last,' he said, clutching Apion's outstretched arm. 'And not a moment too soon.'

Apion frowned. 'The emperor, what is—'

Igor held their embrace, whispering, 'The emperor is not himself.'

Apion saw the dark look in the Rus' eyes. Igor's gaze stayed locked with Apion's and then flicked up, beyond the fortress of Malagina to the cluster of rocky hills that loomed over the mustering plains.

'Come, ride with me, I will take you to him,' the Rus said, hefting up a cloth-wrapped parcel from the pile of crates and looking to the hills.

—

Apion mounted his Thessalian and followed Igor out of the camp, trotting through the long grass around the Malagina Fortress hillock. The Rus remained silent as they passed a pair of varangoi who seemed to be guarding the dirt track that led up into the hills. They picked their way up this track until they came to the rougher ground near the cliffs at the top of this range.

The path was mercifully shaded by the cliff face, but the going was treacherous, the track winding up around the cliff side, growing steeper with every stride. They came to a perilously steep section. Apion's Thessalian stumbled in the scree here, sliding to the side of the long-disused path and halting only inches from the edge. Apion's eyes bulged as he clutched at his reins and swayed in his saddle to balance, catching sight of the sheer drop into a rocky gully he had only just avoided. A vulture swooped by overhead and screeched as if thwarted of its chance of a meal.

'Igor, for pity's sake, will you tell me what is going on and why you are leading me into the sky – preferably before I fall and break my neck!'

Igor looked all around, his eyes narrowed in suspicion as if looking for some observer.

'We are alone, I can assure you,' Apion spat. 'No other cur would be so mad as to come up here!'

Igor snorted at this. 'Ah, if only that were true. But no, our emperor languishes atop these cliffs.'

'What, why?'

'Walk with me,' Igor said, dismounting.

Apion followed suit, patting his Thessalian's neck and crunching on up the scree.

'There have been ill portents in every direction since the start of this campaign. Blood comets, freak storms at sea and grey doves suffering from wanderlust,' Igor panted as they neared the top of the cliffs. 'All brushed aside by the emperor's hubris and his stirring homilies. But when we camped at Helenopolis, something changed. In the dead of night, his tent collapsed, the centre pole shredded and it fell in upon him.'

Apion sighed, knowing full well how such incidents were usually perceived by the Christian ranks. 'And the men think it was a sign from God?'

'They do. But the worst of it is that God had no hand in this. The emperor himself brought his tent down in some blind fit, throwing himself around.'

Apion cocked his head to one side. 'But surely a few words from him, would have remedied the situation? A dash of humour and bravado?'

'They would, had he not been acting so strangely since. After we pulled him from the tent, he was suffering some blinding headache. He said nothing to the men before he blacked out. Then, when he awoke the next day, he was – as I said – not himself. He was sullen and highly irritable.'

'Has he been seen by an *archiatros*?' Apion asked, knowing full well that the emperor would have brought some of the fine physicians from Constantinople along with him.

'They tried to examine him, but he would not have it. He lashed out, blackening the eye of one orderly. When we deconstructed the camp, he then insisted on riding as part of the vanguard.'

Apion's gut tightened at this. The emperor was a brave soul, but not a fool. Even in firm imperial territory, he would never risk riding in the van in case he might fall to some enemy ambush.

'And when we came here, he watched the men build the camp, but insisted the imperial tent should not be pitched. And then... then he rode from the camp at haste, alone. We pursued him, all the way up here.'

Apion looked up to see they were approaching the clifftop. 'Here, why?'

The steep path levelled off and the shade fell away as they stepped onto the clifftop. Apion squinted in the sunlight at what lay up there. Three huts stood, all of them ruins, deserted long ago. Hovels at best. The roofs had caved in, the clumsily piled stone walls lay tumbled and broken in places, and the remnant splinters of what had once been a door hung from the entrance to the nearest one. Cicadas sang in the weeds. Clouds of flies buzzed in the shade of the doorway, next to which the emperor's white stallion was tethered. Then Apion saw smoke puff from this roofless abode.

'Because the emperor insisted he preferred to be away from his men. He said he favoured these hovels over the fresh and open wheat banks of the river. He has slept here for the last week and has had food brought to him.' Igor tapped the parcel.

Apion heard a scuffling from inside the tumbledown ruin then.

'*Basileus*,' Igor called out.

Apion removed his helm, readying to salute his emperor, the one man who promised to bring an end to the empire's constant struggles. But his blood iced when he saw the figure that emerged from the hovel. Romanus' flaxen locks were unwashed and tangled, his skin was awash with profuse sweat and his chin was covered in unkempt bristles. His lips were taut and twitching, his cobalt eyes darting. His white tunic and trousers were encrusted in filth.

He barely made eye contact with Apion or Igor, instead seemingly more interested in the ashes of a fire. He crouched beside it and poked at the ashes with a stick, sighing and muttering to himself.

'*Basileus*, the *Haga* is here,' Igor said, crouching by the emperor's side, placing the parcel down. 'Only weeks ago you talked of how glad you would be to see him.'

'Hmm, the *Haga*? I don't need him. I just need to be left alone. Away with you both. *Away!*' he snarled.

Igor stood back, blanching.

'*Basileus*,' Apion said. 'The men need you. But I understand you are not well. You need to allow the archiatros to examine you.'

'I am well. I have my home...' He gestured to the hovel, then unwrapped the cloth parcel to reveal a round of cheese, a loaf of bread, dates, honey and a small amphora. 'I have food in my belly and the sun on my skin.' He looked up to the sky, then winced, looking away and clutching at his temples. 'I need no physician.'

Igor and Apion shared a wary look, then bade the emperor farewell.

'Perhaps tomorrow you will feel better,' Apion said.

Romanus said nothing, remaining crouched, his eyes screwed tight shut with a hand on his forehead.

'He is unwell, there is no doubt about it,' Apion whispered to Igor as they made their way back down to their mounts.

'What are we to do?' Igor shrugged. 'My men are guarding the tracks up here, so he is safe from attack, but the armies are becoming restless.'

Apion tucked his hair behind his ears and slid his helm back on. 'If tomorrow, he still insists on dwelling in that ruin, then we must take matters into our own hands – have the archiatros see to him whether he likes it or not.'

Igor smoothed his moustache and shook his head. 'I truly hope it does not come to that.'

Apion sat on a log under a clear and starry summer night sky at the heart of the camp where the emperor's tent should have been. The fire before him was dulling. The cooks who had prepared food to be taken to the emperor cleared away their implements and stored their supplies. The other men of the emperor's retinue sat alongside him, jabbering about what should be done.

He glanced around each of them. Alyates, the young, lean, Strategos of Cappadocia seemed a good sort if a little naïve – insisting that the emperor just needed time to come back to his senses. Doux Bryennios, on the other hand, seemed a shrewd and bullish character, keen to assert his authority in the emperor's absence. Meanwhile, Doux Philaretos was eager to force the emperor to return to the camp. Doux Tarchianotes was the most aged and seemingly the most balanced individual; he listened to the arguments of the others while stroking his tidy beard, then countered their thoughts with his own. Each of them pitched their ideas as to how to deal with the emperor's strangeness, each of them jabbing fingers up to the dark silhouette of the cliffs that loomed over the camp.

Only one other around the fire remained silent. Andronikos Doukas. The young man sat there, staring into the fire, one arm chained to a post and constantly under the glare of the two varangoi permanently assigned to watch him. The flames illuminated his broad, flat-boned face and betrayed a sadness in his eyes. Apion thought of the man's cousins – Eudokia's sons; young Michael Doukas and his younger brother, Konstantious. In his time in Constantinople, Apion had got to know them both; one a confused young man and the other an innocent and scared boy. Being a member of the Doukas family did not make Andronikos an enemy, but Apion felt a distinct discomfort at his presence in the camp. *No man is born evil*, he reminded himself, then countered: *nor into virtue.*

Suddenly, a scream rang out. The chatter ceased and all heads swung round. 'Fire! Fire!'

Apion looked this way and that. There were no flames, no clouds of smoke.

'God have mercy!' Alyates gasped by his side, shooting to his feet and pointing to the cliff tops.

Apion followed his gaze. Up there, an inferno raged. The outline of the hovels were just visible in the blaze.

'The emperor!' Bryennios gasped.

'Take water, form a chain!' Tarchianotes cried.

Men rushed to and fro. A pack of varangoi hurried up the narrow dirt track that clung to the cliff side, focused on rescuing Romanus. Several banda of infantry formed a line from the river's edge all the way up to the hill track, passing buckets of water hurriedly. 'More, we need more!' Alyates yelled, beckoning more men to the end of the chain which barely reached the lower slopes of the rocky hills.

The faint cry of the varangoi rang out from the cliff top. 'We cannot find him!'

Apion looked up to see their tiny, silhouetted forms up there, arms waving. Then he heard a chorus of laments from the chain of men now winding up the steep dirt track. That and hooves thundering and a horrific, pained whinnying. Apion's eyes locked on the dirt track just as the source of the commotion burst into view. The emperor's white stallion charged down and around the track, its coat and saddle utterly ablaze. It shook and thrashed its mane, bucking and kicking, biting, knocking water-bearing soldiers from the dirt path and into the treacherous gullies. The beast's struggle only intensified the flames. The stallion barged down onto the flat ground and raced into the camp. The stench of burning hair and flesh was rife, bringing memories of the dreadful Greek fire to Apion. Swathes of soldiers fell back and gawped at the sight of their emperor's horse in flames. The tortured beast circled the camp, setting light to tents, then charged from the northern gate and into the imperial stables beside the fortress of Malagina. There it took to throwing itself against the stable pens, terrifying the other beasts in there and setting the timber structures ablaze too.

Apion saw from the sea of dumbstruck faces all around that somebody had to act. He ran for the gate, plucked a spear from the trembling hands of a skutatos on sentry duty, then rushed to the stables. The stallion charged for him, maddened. Apion braced, thinking of the many battles this brave creature had fought in with Romanus. Then he plunged the spear into the beast's breast. At once, the stallion slumped, pulling the spear down with it. Apion crouched by the dead war horse, his eyes moistening. Moans and laments rang out all around.

'Get water to these fires!' Igor cried over the tumult.

A flurry of crunching boots, splashing water and shouting ensued. Apion felt distant from it all. He stared into the stallion's burnt-out eyes and wondered if this was it. With Romanus burnt alive on the cliff top, the campaign was over. The enemies of the *Golden Heart* would seize the throne.

The next voice he heard spoke calmly. Oddly so, given the circumstances.

'Ah, *Haga*, you made it at last!'

Apion looked up to see Romanus, soot-stained and dishevelled, his knees and elbows bloodied where he had somehow scrambled down the mountainside to escape the blaze up there. Yet he was smiling as though this was an ordinary night, his eyes sharp. '*Basileus?*'

Romanus looked around the camp, seeing the panting, gawping men of his army, the half-ruined stables, and then the corpse of his beloved war horse. 'It seems we should move on from here?' he said, showing little emotion. Then he nodded as if agreeing with some inner voice. 'Yes, yes, we will move on tomorrow.'

After a sleepless night, Apion rose before dawn and set off on a run, barefoot. He jogged along the main way through the camp, where the dewy air was still spiced with the tang of charred wood, and the burnt remnants of the stables and tents blackened his peripheral vision. When he slipped from the camp's southern gate, he ran south, along the western banks of the Sangarios, on past the Zompos Bridge.

He had run some seven miles when the sun broached the horizon and cast a purple-pink light across the sky. Normally, a morning run would purge his mind of troubles. Today, though, the jabbering thoughts seemed eager to cling to him. Even when he pushed himself into a sprint, they followed like wolves chasing a bloodied deer. Frustrated, he slowed, panting, then waded into the shallows of the river, throwing off his tunic and ducking under the surface. When he rose, he swept his silver-amber locks back from his face and inhaled deeply. Here, at last, he felt his troubles fade. Here, he could see only the grassy hills and valleys, hear only the chattering cicada song. For the briefest of moments, a treasured memory came to him. He saw the valley of Mansur's farm, imagined himself as a boy, leading the goat herd onto the hills, watching Maria as she went about her business, pretending she didn't know he was watching her.

The first shafts of full daylight bathed him at that moment, and a smile stretched across his face. He splashed out of the river and tied his hair back in a ponytail, then threw on his tunic and dug out the lock of hair from the purse sewn onto his belt.

'I don't know anymore what terrifies me most, Maria; not finding you, or finding you,' he whispered, settling on a fallen hazel tree by the riverbank. 'For if I have to come face to face with Taylan again to learn of your whereabouts, I fear that only one of us will walk away.'

He listened to the sounds of nature, as if waiting for an answer. Instead, he heard something on the log beside him: the scratching talons and rustling feathers of some settling raptor. From the corner of his eye, he saw a metamorphosing shape, growing, changing. Finally it settled. The crone's silvery locks lifted in the gentlest of breezes.

'Yet if you do not face Taylan, he will pursue you evermore,' she said.

'I know this. I know we must meet,' he sighed.

'It is a choice, Apion. Likewise, young Taylan has a decision to make. Together, your choices might still confirm or confound my nemesis, Fate.'

'Fate has ploughed a crimson furrow through my life,' Apion said flatly. 'I spit in Fate's eye.'

She placed a gnarled hand on his forearm. 'And that is why I always return to you.'

'I am but one man. Your faith in me is misplaced.'

She shook her head. 'The deeds of one man can inspire the hearts of others. You know this.'

Apion looked north, downriver to the horizon in the direction of the camp. 'Ha! Then I will need to perform many deeds to right things. Thousands of men wait back there – confused, angry...' His words trailed off with a sigh. He looked to her, seeing her milky eyes fixed on the rippling waters of the river, now sparkling and illuminated in a rich teal. 'I should know better than to ask you for answers, old woman, but tell me: are these omens that have riddled my emperor's campaign mere coincidence?'

'Cah!' she swept a hand through the air then broke down in a wheezing cackle. 'Omens help weak men make poor choices.' She extended a bony finger, pointing to a calm spot amongst the reeds. 'See how the sunlight bathes the shallows on the far bank?' While the morning shadows had yet to retract from the rest of the eastern banks, a wedge of morning sunlight had, indeed, conspired to shine through two eastern hills, casting a shaft of rich yellow–orange on this part of the bank. Tiny rainbow trout leapt from the surface, biting at the clouds of mayfly gathered there, and the light betrayed larger, silvery carp darting under the surface. 'Bountiful, is it not?' the crone said.

Apion resisted the temptation to answer, noticing a crane stalking over to the reeds, attracted by the sunlight and the leaping fish.

'A good omen if ever there was one?' she continued, eyeing Apion in search of an answer.

Apion remained tight-lipped.

The curious crane plucked a trout from the water at will, stopping every so often to look this way and that, somewhat disbelieving its luck. Then the bushes nearby shuddered and a leopard leapt from the undergrowth, clamping its ferocious jaws around the crane's neck and snapping it like a dry reed.

'I take your point,' Apion replied.

'Then take my next words with you as well. Not omens, but two things I have foreseen. They will not help you find your woman or confront your son, but they are vital.'

Apion looked to her. 'I may not always comprehend your words, old woman, but I will always listen to you.'

She smiled, her age-lines fading, her whole being exuding warmth. 'When you come by the boy on the dead man's horse, choose your words well.'

Apion frowned, nodding.

Then, like a cloud masking the sun, her demeanour changed, her face fell grave, her gaze glacial. 'And then beware. Beware the serpent with the amethyst eyes!' she hissed.

Apion frowned. 'The serpent with…'

Suddenly, a shrill cry rang out from the far riverbank. Another leopard, far larger than the first, had arrived to challenge the kill. Apion looked to the confrontation then back to the crone. But she was gone, the log beside him was empty. The angered keening of an eagle rang out above, and this seemed to scare the fighting leopards into flight. Apion glanced up and all around the morning sky. Unblemished. Empty.

He set off back to the camp, enjoying the cooling dew of the pasture-lands on his bare feet as he jogged. His thoughts began to gather like clouds as he tried to work out how to approach the emperor when he got back.

The camp was still a few miles distant when he noticed movement on the western track. A lone rider, emerging from the heat haze. An eerily familiar-looking military man with long, dark locks, tanned skin and a hooked nose, his fine bronze klibanion vest sparkling in the sunlight. And the grey stallion with a distinctive white blaze on its face – he had seen that fine steed once before, at the Euphrates and on the march through Mesopotamia two years previously.

Manuel Komnenos? Apion mouthed in disbelief.

He slowed to a walk, peering into the sunlight, knowing it could not be true. For Komnenos had perished – the reports had come to Apion only in the last month or so, but they had been clear; a vicious, malignant growth inside one ear had claimed the emperor's man, and this had saddened Apion greatly. He squinted, seeing the rider behold him too. Shades had long plagued his dreams, were they now haunting his waking hours also?

But as the rider came closer, he saw that this was not Manuel Komnenos, but a young lad cast in the dead general's image.

When you come by the boy on the dead man's horse, choose your words well…

As they came to within a few paces of one another, the boy's eyes narrowed, seeing Apion's faded red military tunic. He cast up a hand in salute. 'Perhaps you can help me, soldier?'

'You seek the mustering fields of Malagina?' Apion guessed, saluting in reply.

'Aye,' the boy said, peering down his nose.

'Where is your escort?' Apion asked.

The boy shrugged, maintaining an aloof gaze. 'I have no need of an escort.'

Apion cocked an eyebrow. The lad's mount and armour were fine indeed, and brigands would happily rob a lone traveller of both. 'Very well, but if you refuse to be escorted then how can I guide you to the camp?'

The lad's aloofness cracked for an instant as he grinned impishly. 'Good point,' he said, sliding from the saddle to walk his stallion. 'So who is my escort?' he said, the loftiness returning.

Apion could not help but chuckle at the boy's pluck. 'Apion, Strategos of Chaldia,' he replied.

The boy's face brightened and his eyes flashed with realisation, darting to the red-ink stigma on Apion's arm. '*You?*'

Apion feigned a smile, unconsciously shielding the stigma with his other hand.

'Then I can speak freely,' the boy said, his reserve fading and a look of relief washing across his face. 'I have no escort because the emperor meant to keep me from this campaign – for my own safety, apparently. It is a shame that the guards posted to retain me in Constantinople did not have the wits to match my determination.' He said this with a grin, then his look grew earnest. 'But I worried who I might meet first upon arriving at the mustering fields. Before my brother died, he told me that there were few men I should trust. One was the emperor, another was the *Haga*.'

Apion nodded, swatting away the embarrassment. Then realisation dawned as to how the lad had come by the arms and war horse. 'Ah, so you are Manuel's *brother*?'

The boy nodded, standing a little taller. 'I am Alexios. I live to wipe the black stains from the Komnenos family name. My brother died in shame. Rumours spread that it was his poor generalship that saw his army wiped out by the Seljuks last year at Sebastae. Worse, the chance to rectify his mistakes were taken from him by disease—'

'Your brother was one of the most astute and loyal souls I have ever come across in all the lands of our empire,' Apion cut him off, but kept his tone gentle. 'In the end, he was vanquished by a hardy Seljuk foe and a venal cur in the imperial court who betrayed him and his army to the enemy. There is no shame there for your brother, only for the cur.'

A silence passed.

'I can see why he liked you,' Alexios said sheepishly at last. 'He said your name and your symbol were signs of hope to the armies of Anatolia.'

'Ha! When I first met your brother, I felt just the same about him. His armies were in awe of him. A fine leader, a fine man. One of so few.'

Apion noticed Alexios' eyes reddening. So he changed tack, instead asking the lad about his military experience. They ambled up the track towards the mustering fields, chatting as they went. Eventually they came back to more sensitive matters.

'Manuel used to say that Romanus Diogenes is the last ember of hope for our empire,' Alexios said, feeding his grey handfuls of grain as they walked. Then he lowered his voice, darting glances this way and that before adding: 'And that the Doukas family are like a dark thundercloud, eager to extinguish it.'

Apion smiled dryly at the description. 'You think the Doukas family will bring ruin to the empire?'

'I am sure of it.'

'I am certain they will try,' Apion snorted.

'But if Psellos and John Doukas ever find their way onto the throne…'

'They will not,' Apion countered, willing his words to be true. 'They are in exile and there they will remain.'

'How can you be so sure?' Alexios frowned. 'Neither of those dogs will ever stop in their efforts to dethrone the emperor.'

'The empire has endured many foul characters in the past. Wolves constantly watching the throne. Some have even managed to claim the seat of power. Yet the empire *has* endured. That is not down to good fortune, Alexios, that is down to good men.' He took a stalk of wheat from the trackside and twisted at it, thinking of the crone's advice, seeking his next words carefully. 'Most men are a blur of light and darkness, good and evil, swinging from one to another like a dead man on a noose. But there are some who refuse to let blackness tip the balance. Good men like the emperor... like your brother.' He fixed Alexios with his gaze. 'While good men stand firm and refuse to buckle under tyranny, corruption or lies... there is always hope. Always.'

Alexios held his head a fraction higher. His eyes reddened once again and tears escaped, yet these tears came with a smile. When the lad looked skywards and mouthed a prayer, no doubt for his lost brother's soul, Apion looked away to afford him some privacy.

They walked on until they came over a rise in the track, then onto the plain of Malagina and the approach to the camp's southern gate. They slowed only when a pack of Pecheneg steppe riders thundered to the gate before them, filing inside two abreast. These stocky men rode on equally squat and hardy ponies. They wore leather armour and animal hides, and each man had two or more bows on his back, plus a clutch of arrow-filled quivers. Apion counted some four hundred of them. A fine addition to the campaign army, he thought – if they stayed loyal.

'Come,' he said to Alexios as they entered the southern gate of the camp, 'I will take you to the emperor.'

He picked his way past the clustered tents of each thema and tagma army, and saw that a wing of mercenary Norman riders had arrived also. Nearly five hundred men in mail hauberks and iron helms with broad nose-guards, grooming their tall, powerful battle mounts or honing their lances. They bore emblems of their homeland and symbols of God on their garments. Apion could not help but think of that Norman dog, Crispin, still roaming somewhere in Byzantine lands. He thought also of Dederic, a Norman he had trusted with his life, and still missed every day, despite the little rider's betrayal.

He stirred from the memories when he saw what lay up ahead. His eyes lit up as he beheld the red satin imperial tent, erected at last at the heart of the camp. All looked as it should, with the bejewelled campaign Cross mounted nearby and the blue-gold Icon of Blachernae sparkling in the morning sun. The emperor's cooks were busy preparing some sweet-smelling stew. Andronikos Doukas was chained to his post nearby, pretending he was not interested in the delicious fare. Best of all, the emperor was there, talking with his retinue, looking over maps, pointing this way and that, his movements sharp and determined. He had washed the worst of the soot from his face and hair and he wore his white tunic and trousers, purple cloak, doeskin boots and his fine white-and-silver armour breastplate. The *Golden Heart* was back, it seemed.

'Ah, Strategos,' Igor called out, stepping away from the discussions and beckoning him over. 'And… Alexios?' Igor frowned. 'I thought you were supposed to be—'

'I am exactly where I am supposed to be,' the lad replied swiftly, donning his haughty mask again.

'Ha!' Igor said in an effort to disguise his discomfort. The big Rus frowned, then added, 'Perhaps it would be best for you to wait here and speak to the emperor later?'

Alexios made to protest, then looked to Apion.

'It will only be for a short while, lad.'

Alexios stowed his complaint, nodding and leading his horse to a nearby trough.

Apion and Igor walked together towards the emperor. 'To see things in their right place is encouraging indeed,' Apion whispered.

'Things are still not right, despite how it might look…' was all Igor had time to whisper in reply.

'*Haga!*' Romanus laughed heartily, extending an arm, his eyes sparkling. Gladly, Apion clasped his arm to the emperor's. Then they embraced. 'Damn, but it is good to have you here at last. I trust your journey from Chaldia was smooth?'

Apion disguised a frown; so the emperor remembered nothing of their meeting at the cliff top hovels, or last night, standing over his burnt war horse? And he noticed Romanus was still unshaven, his cheeks gaunt and ruddy, his skin bathed in sweat and his hair unkempt. 'And damn, it is good to be here,' he offered in as genuine a tone as he could muster. 'I bring only my three tourmarchai, but my two thousand Chaldians, another two thousand Armenian spearmen under the command of Prince Vardan and nearly eighteen hundred Oghuz horse archers wait just south of Ancyra, eager for the campaign column to come by, eager to join your ranks, *Basileus*. Though I see those forces will be but a grain of sand on a bay, given the numbers that have been gathered here?'

Romanus nodded, sweeping a hand around. 'The mustering is almost complete – we have nearly twenty-seven thousand men gathered. The iron riders of the tagmata, the myriad spears of the themata, and the lancers and archer cavalry of our allies. All that remains is your forces and—'

His words were cut off by a cry from the southern gate. 'They're here!'

All heads looked south. Over the camp's southern palisade, the Zompos Bridge was just visible. Writhing like a silver snake, myriad warriors poured across the river there. They moved not in ordered formations, but in a mass of riders and foot soldiers combined. More akin to a horde than an imperial army.

'There must be four, no five thousand of them,' Igor gasped.

'Closer to seven thousand,' Romanus marvelled. 'Now we can move east with almost forty thousand men altogether. The Sultan, or any other who might choose to stand in our way, should be sure to devise a plan of retreat.'

'You chose to call on the magnates and their private armies, *Basileus*?' Apion said in a hushed voice. He had heard this rumour, but dismissed it as apocryphal. In previous years, he and Romanus had discussed the possibility but rejected it on the basis of the dubious character of these private levies.

'Seven thousand men, Strategos,' Romanus said brashly, not observing Apion's quieter tone. 'They'll make up for the losses from last year.'

The riders at the head approached the camp's southern gate now. He could see that they wore a mish-mash of armour and carried a selection of unorthodox weapons. Some of them wore just tunics and boots and carried simple spears – no doubt levied farmworkers from the magnates' lands, men who should have been serving with their local themata anyway. Others were clad in mail, some in scale. The cavalry amongst them carried axes, clubs and short stabbing swords – totally unsuitable for mounted warfare. The magnates themselves were easy to spot. These leaders wore ludicrously ornate and antique breastplates of moulded bronze and silver – some outshining even the emperor's armour. Most bore helmets with garishly ostentatious plumes. One even had a plume of ostrich feathers – dyed red and glued to stand proud nearly a foot higher than the tip of his helm – and a caged faceguard. When he lifted the faceguard, the expression on his face said it all. A smug, defiant grin and a dark trident beard. He glared disdainfully at the imperial regiments through bloodshot eyes.

'Well this lot will surely provide much entertainment on the march,' Apion muttered, seeing that the bearded one rode on a stiff and barely used leather saddle. 'He'll be counting the blisters on his arse by this evening.'

'Ah, yes, Scleros will be in charge of the magnate ranks,' Romanus said, clasping a hand to Apion's shoulder and nodding to the trident-bearded one. 'Now, come with us to the fortress. There is one piece of business to attend to before we set off.'

Apion nodded and fell back as Romanus took the lead, beckoning Philaretos, Alyates, Tarchianotes and Bryennios along. He leaned in to Igor's ear as they followed. 'Has he said anything about the fire and his behaviour in these last weeks?'

Igor pulled a perplexed frown. 'Not a word. As I say, he wears a veneer of normality this morning, but…'

Romanus boomed over his shoulder: 'This might just be the most important choice of the entire campaign.' The emperor strode up the short ramp leading to the gates of the Fortress of Malagina. The gates swung open before them to a chorus of salutes from the wall garrison. Inside, Apion looked to the *armamenta*, the three-storey arms warehouse – perhaps they would be calling in there to pick up extra supplies? Or the granary, for more rations? But instead, the emperor veered towards the small, domed church nestled in the corner of the fortress walls.

'*Basileus?*' Apion frowned, seeing the confusion of the others in the retinue.

But Romanus continued as if he hadn't heard. 'The final part of our campaign route has yet to be finalised. When we march east, beyond the themata, how should we approach Lake Van? Do we take the more northerly route, into the Armenian highlands and through Theodosiopolis – mountainous but direct. Or the southerly route we used two years ago, across the Euphrates and through Mesopotamia – flatter ground but many more miles through hostile territory?'

'I would opt for a smooth march over a fast one, *Basileus*,' Apion answered. 'But in any case, I would suggest this is a matter best decided over a map table as opposed to in a church.'

Romanus seemed oblivious to his words, coming to the tall arched doors of the church and sweeping them open. Inside, candles flickered on the altar. Two scrolls lay before them, pooled in the dim orange light.

Apion stepped inside, his footsteps reverberating like the echoes of his past. He felt the flesh on his wrist where he had once worn the Christian prayer rope tingle, as if trying to conjure guilt from him. Mosaics on the domed ceiling glared down upon him sombrely, the faces of the Apostles and the Virgin Mary unsympathetic. *And where were you in my darkest hour?* he mouthed, glaring back with equal austerity.

He, Romanus and the retinue stopped before the altar. All but the emperor shuffled uncomfortably, glancing around the cold, shadowy and otherwise deserted chamber. Finally, a scraping of sandals sounded from behind a screen. A trembling, ancient-looking priest hobbled into view, his shoulders crooked and his head bowed awkwardly. The old man shuffled over to the altar. When the aged priest looked up, Apion saw straight away a distant dimness in his eyes. It was clear that the man was absent in all but body.

'Now, as we agreed; let God direct us,' Romanus coaxed the old man, pointing to the two scrolls.

Apion felt his blood cool.

'*Basileus?*' Igor gasped.

'Select a map, priest,' Romanus said, again seemingly unhearing.

The old man lifted a badly shaking hand to clutch his Chi-Rho necklace, and then reached out with the other to lift the leftmost scroll. Romanus took it, unfurling it and grinning broadly. 'We take the northerly route – past Theodosiopolis!' he said, flashing his grin around the gathered generals.

Apion felt his optimism of earlier melt away. As pious as any other Byzantine, Romanus had never in the past let his faith and his rational, military judgement collide. Now he was asking God to make his choices. The emperor was clearly still not himself. A glance to the others confirmed they shared his thinking.

Romanus was oblivious to their doubt. He marched from the church as boldly as he had entered, then back down to the camp.

Reaching the central tent, he stopped, frowning, rubbing at his temples and blinking, sweat lashing from his ruddy skin. Finally, he swung round to Apion and the others following. 'Tell me, where is my horse?'

CHAPTER 11

The Strangeness

The Byzantine column marched on past the great cities of Dorylaeum and Amorium, and by late May they had reached the plains south of Ancyra's walls. Here, they rendezvoused with the six-thousand-strong army Apion had left stationed there; two thousand Chaldian infantry and fifty precious kataphractoi riders, Prince Vardan and his two thousand hardy Armenian spearmen and a swathe of Oghuz horse archers. Now complete and numbering forty thousand overall, the campaign army journeyed on eastwards and entered the lands of the Cappadocian Thema, the column now resembling a giant silvery serpent, nearly twenty miles from tip to tail, scales glinting in the baking midday sun and vast plumes of gold and red dust spiralling skywards as it moved along this arid highland. The vanguard – composed of a bandon of iron-vested kursores and the five hundred mercenary Norman lancers – led the way. Fine and well-ordered wedges of the tagmata riders rode a quarter of a mile behind the van, with the white-armoured varangoi forming a circle around the emperor. Behind them marched seemingly infinite ranks of iron-helmed skutatoi spearmen and their bobbing banners. Dotted amongst them were packs of toxotai archers mercifully shaded from the sun in their wide-brimmed hats and enjoying wearing only light linen tunics and boots. The touldon of supply wagons and mules rumbled along in the midpoint of the column, giving the serpent a swollen belly. The Pecheneg horse archers rode wide of the column, as flank-screening outriders. To the rear, a mass of mercenary cavalry rode. The heterogeneous rabble of the magnates were nominally led by the trident-bearded Scleros, but in truth their armies were kept in order only by the fifty Chaldian kataphractoi led by Apion and his trusted three.

One cluster of the magnate riders strayed from the column, trotting nonchalantly to the south to squint at the ruin of a farmhouse. One of them wore ancient, baked leather armour, no doubt harvested from some battlefield years ago. The others wore just ragged tunics and sported untidy beards and rotten teeth.

'Get back in line, you dogs!' Procopius howled, the sinews in his neck straining and his eyes bulging. 'You can turn your mind to plunder once you've ridden as far as the emperor demands, and risked your bloody necks against the empire's enemies.'

The leather-vested leader of this pack turned to look Procopius up and down with disdain, his lips wrinkling as if preparing to fire back some venomous retort. Only when Scleros called to him did he halt, the words remaining unsaid. With a dipped brow and a barely disguised grimace at Procopius, the leather-vested one and his small band of cronies heeded their master's words, falling in with the main pack again. Once there, they instantly set about bickering and arguing amongst themselves.

'Unbelievable,' Procopius growled, riding back to join the head of the wedge of fifty.

'This lot are supposed to be a rearguard,' Blastares grumbled, slapping a fly from his wrist, then lifting his helm to sweep a sheet of sweat from his stubbled scalp, 'and at seven thousand strong, they *should* make a bloody formidable one.'

'I'd rather have a single lion watching my back than a pack of quarrelling wolves,' Sha said, chewing on the flesh of an apple.

'True,' Apion commented, digging out and biting into an apple himself. 'But in any case, I fear our greatest danger lies not here, but at the head of the column.'

Sha, Blastares and Procopius followed Apion's gaze into the eastern horizon. Somewhere beyond the cloud of dust and the iron snake, beyond the shimmering haze where land and sky melted together, and nearly a half day's hard ride ahead, the emperor and his retinue led this vast column.

'You speak of the Seljuks... or the narrow-eyed dogs who ride with the emperor?' Sha asked with a hint of a grin.

Apion snorted, thinking of Alp Arslan, Taylan and the hordes. That ever-present threat hung like a blade in the sky over Byzantine Anatolia. Then he thought of the men the emperor had surrounded himself with. Philaretos was a firebrand, but a loyal one. There was Tarchianotes, the gnarled and guarded doux. Bryennios, the lithe giant with the grin of a sly hunting dog but the reputation of a military genius. And then there was Alyates, a loyal and well-meaning young man on the surface. *But what colour is his core?* Apion wondered, the words stoked by bitter experience. He then thought of Andronikos Doukas, riding in chains alongside the emperor too. He shook his head, his thoughts tangling. 'Both trouble me equally, but not as much as the emperor himself,' Apion replied at last. 'He is suffering from some illness still, I am sure of it.'

'The madness from the mustering?' Procopius cocked an eyebrow. 'That was unsettling, aye. But now we are on the march. I have heard of no incident since. Even when we camped near Cryapege, all was quiet.'

'This is true,' Apion mused, stroking his beard. Camp had been still and peaceful that night and in the nights since. The last flashpoint had been the sight of young Alexios Komnenos being led back to Constantinople, escorted by a troop of determined varangoi. Alexios' howls of protest had unsettled many of the watching soldiers. Apion regretted that he would not have further chance to talk with the lad. But perhaps it was a sensible move by the emperor. Alexios, a steadfast ally, would be a fine asset to have back in the capital.

'And you haven't heard anything from Komes Peleus or Komes Stypiotes since we set off from Malagina, have you?' Blastares added.

Apion thought of the loyal pair of skutatoi commanders who marched near the column head with the Chaldian infantry. He had insisted that they were to relay any news of the emperor's behaviour to him via a kursoris scout rider. 'No, but then I do not equate silence with surety.'

'I could ride ahead, check on them?' Sha offered.

'No, I need you here,' Apion replied, leaning forward to feed his apple core to his mount. 'But watch the horizon, watch for the kursoris.'

Near the front of the column, Komes Stypiotes marched at the head of one bandon of Chaldian spearmen. The hulking soldier fought to suppress a groan. Despite being afforded the 'luxury' of marching without their heavy armour jackets, the going was tough. Dust coated his skin, his mouth was parched, his feet were blistered and swollen and his head throbbed from the *crunch-crunch* of marching boots. Tiring rapidly of the sight of swaying horse buttocks in front of him, he glanced to either side of the column to the shimmering heat haze that blended dust with sky. To the south, there was a faint sparkle of blue. Lake Tus. He watched the rippling air and imagined the cool, clean waters rushing towards them. Most of the infantry in the campaign army would have welcomed such a relief from the blazing afternoon sun.

The *bandophoros* was the only one to enjoy a sliver of shade, offered by the crimson Chi-Rho standard of the bandon. Stypiotes eyed the patch of shade jealously, then winced as the linen cloth that acted as padding between his helm and his scalp slipped, the hot metal stinging his skin. Feeling the irritation growing in his chest, he shot a glance over to Komes Peleus, leading the adjacent bandon. 'How long since we last stopped for water?' he hissed.

Komes Peleus shot him a glare in return, frowning, nodding faintly to the men who marched behind him. Then he barked an order for his own bandophoros to take the lead before sidling over to march with Stypiotes 'Why? Oh, let me guess, because you're thirsty and too hot?'

Stypiotes made to retort, but a waft of dust kicked up by the hooves of the kataphractos before him caught in his throat and he broke down in a coughing fit. 'Look,' he stabbed a finger ahead at the swaying cavalry, 'I'm bloody sick and tired of watching a collection of horses' arses, complete with flies and regular consignments of turds, in this bloody inferno.'

Peleus smirked sardonically. 'Really? That's odd, because we all love it. Anyway, I told you not to drink all that wine last night.'

Stypiotes thought of the game of dice after evening prayer that had seen him gleefully collect in the wine rations of four of his skutatoi. It had tasted ever so sweet… last night at least.

'That's why you're so thirsty,' Peleus continued, 'and testy.'

Stypiotes grumbled and sought a reply, when suddenly, the men of the Chaldian Thema broke out in a murmur, necks craning to get a view of some activity ahead. 'Hello, what's this?' he cooed.

'The emperor, he's leaving the head of the column,' Peleus gasped.

Sure enough, a silver-and-white-armoured figure with a purple-plumed battle helm saddled on a dark stallion emerged from the many wings of cavalry at the front of the column. He moved at a trot, riding off at a tangent to the south. A clutch of Varangoi riders hurried to follow him. Over the gasping of the ranks, the emperor's booming laughter rang out as he kicked his stallion into a gallop across the dusty plain heading towards the distant, sparkling waters of Lake Tus. Then he tore off his helm and tossed it to the dust with a metallic clunk.

'What the?' Peleus gasped. 'What is he doing?'

'Look at the colour of his face – seems like *he* was on the wine last night,' Stypiotes mused, squinting at the emperor's florid skin.

'Why would I want to ride with a shower of sweating men and horses,' the emperor's distant cry was only just audible, his arms outstretched to the sky. The varangoi pursuing him caught up and gathered around him, Igor remonstrating with him most fervently.

'I can sympathise with him… but I'd say it is time to send the kursoris back to the strategos?' Stypiotes nodded to the lone Chaldian scout rider trotting with the column on the northern flank.

'Hold on,' Peleus said. 'He's coming back.'

Sure enough, the emperor had turned his stallion around and was now trotting back with Igor and his men. One of the Rus guardsmen stopped to collect the discarded helmet.

They marched on until late afternoon without further incident until they came to the banks of the River Halys. As arranged, a fleet of round-hulled pamphyloi were already waiting there to ferry the column across the river. The operation would take the rest of the day and most of tomorrow.

The tagmata were first to cross, those reaching the far banks setting to work on a camp over there, while those who waited on the near bank did likewise there. When the last of the tagmata were safely on the far banks, the varangoi turned to Romanus and gestured to the next free pamphylos, expecting the emperor to lead them on board. But Romanus looked at them blankly, then snorted.

'I'll not be crossing today. I think I'd prefer to remain here,' he said. Then he took to squinting at the shingle banks and poplar groves downriver. 'Yes, I think that shady dell there would make a fine spot for a new imperial manor.' His eyes swung round and rested on Stypiotes and Peleus. 'You, Chaldians. You will set to work on this immediately. You can quarry good limestone in these lands. I know this,' he patted his silver-and-white breastplate with pride, 'for Cappadocia is my homeland!'

Stypiotes stared back, stunned. Until now he had been in awe when in the emperor's presence. Until now – or a few weeks ago at least – the emperor had commanded such awe. But this? This was lunacy.

'You will find strong and supple timbers in the valleys further downriver. Some of you will have to go to the hill town of Nyssa, of course, to buy textiles and furnishings.' His gaze swept over to the far banks of the river. 'And perhaps we should bring the Scholae Tagma back, denude them of their horses. Those mounts could seed a new imperial stud farm here.'

Igor and the other varangoi pleaded with the emperor in hushed tones, but he waved their appeals away with an arrogant sweep of one arm. 'Enough!' he snarled, his hands shooting up to rub his temples as if some crushing headache had overcome him. He heeled his mount into a walk to stand and face the shimmering body of the vast column, stretching off to the west as far as the eye could see. His eyes fell upon Stypiotes and Peleus. 'Well? I asked you to quarry me fine stone and fell me the tallest trees. Be about your duties, soldiers!'

Stypiotes and Peleus hesitated only because of their incredulity. It lasted just moments. Then, as one, they turned and barked to their men. 'You heard your emperor. Drop your weapons, take up your axes and picks. Make your way for the trees and the limestone cliffs.' In mute disbelief, the Chaldian infantry did as they were told. Spears, shields and bows clattered to the dust. Two thousand men trudged off, heads bowed in disillusionment. Stypiotes shared a wide-eyed glance with Igor, then turned with Peleus to follow the ranks.

But Romanus was not finished. He jabbed a finger at Prince Vardan and the Armenian spearmen, mustered by Apion, who had been marching just behind the Chaldian ranks. 'And take those eastern, godless whoresons with you!'

Prince Vardan bristled at this. Teeth bared, he swept a hand towards his swordbelt. It was only the cooler-headed men by his side who calmed him, persuaded him to play along. Vardan lifted the trembling hand to adjust his gold silk headscarf, then nodded, albeit with twitching lips and fire in his eyes. 'Spearmen, follow me,' he bawled hoarsely, then led them towards the groves and cliffs.

'Now… we must get word to the kursoris,' Peleus hissed under his breath as they walked from the column.

'It is taken care of,' Stypiotes replied, glancing over his shoulder to see Igor already whispering to the lone rider.

Apion hurried his gelding along the side of the column, passing rank after rank of thematic infantry as night fell. The closer he came to the head of the column where the ranks were spilling into the vast camp on the Halys' western banks, the more troubled the voices around him became.

'He has truly lost his mind!' one cried out. 'Gave the lash to an Armenian soldier for accidentally shredding a plank of timber. The man's back is hanging in strips.'

'He refuses to cross the river with us. The campaign is dead in the water.'

Apion scowled at this talk and turned to wave his trusted three on at haste. 'Ya!' he yelled, heeling his own mount. He slowed as they reached the western gate of this riverbank camp. Men babbled in confusion now. As he pushed through the masses, he saw that many men had left their tents unconstructed, their attentions on something going on by the river. Sha, Blastares and Procopius flanked Apion as he dismounted and barged through. Here, the air was spiced with shouts of anger and the gloom speckled with torchlit faces twisted with ire. The ranks had gathered in a dense crescent around the end of the camp adjacent to the riverbank with just Igor and a wall of varangoi holding them back.

The camp ditch and palisade running along the bank broke for a short distance to allow access to the basic timber jetty and the pamphyloi docked there. The crew on the boats watched from the decks, mouths agape, as Emperor Romanus strode back and forth through the empty crescent of shingle, hurling objects into the bubbling rapids. He strode over to the thin wall of varangoi holding the crowds back, then shot a hand between two of the Rus to grapple the wrist of the nearest skutatoi, tearing something free.

'A bronze bracelet?' he gasped, holding up the trinket. 'Nonsense! It will only slow you down, hold us all back.' Without decorum, he turned to toss the piece into the river. The skutatos gawped, his lips twitching to cry out, his soldierly training only just keeping his ire in check. Igor and the varangoi struggled to keep the mass of men at bay with their shields as they cried out in a fresh wave of confusion and anger.

'Hold us back?' one voice said as Apion barged closer and closer. 'Yet only hours ago he was all for remaining here to build a villa!'

Apion winced. So the kursoris' report had been true.

He saw Romanus reach through the Varangoi wall again to tear a silver-embossed shield from one skutatos. Clearly an heirloom this soldier's forefathers had carried to war. The man's hands remained outstretched, fearing the shield would be thrown to the depths as well. But Romanus eyed the shield, then shrugged, taking it instead to a wagon parked nearby, heaped with such goods. 'Yes, this shield will make a fine addition to my collection. Without all the other litter to weigh the boats down, my wagon might just get across the river,' he chirped, as if ignorant to the thousands of eyes burning upon him. Apion caught Igor's eye just then. The big, haggard Rus' face was blanched and weary.

'It has been a grim day, Strategos. I prayed you might get here earlier,' he called out over the baying crowd, putting his shoulder to his shield in an effort to keep them back.

'Why has nobody intervened?' Apion hissed, seeing that amongst the onlookers from the docked boats, the retinue of Philaretos, Alyates, Tarchianotes and Bryennios watched on, bereft of words or actions. And shaded beside them stood Andronikos Doukas, wrists in iron.

Just then, the emperor's eyes sparkled and snapped onto something happening beyond the mass of onlookers. Apion twisted to see that, in the far corner of the camp, one Byzantine toxotes was being bundled along by a superior, who was berating him mercilessly. The cowed soldier led an ass by a tether.

'You!' Romanus cried. Like a parting sea, the mass of men at the riverbank split, the varangoi opening a channel to the pair.

The archer leading the ass looked up, startled. The superior, a komes, looked equally sheepish. '*Basileus?*' he croaked.

'What is this?' Romanus boomed, then winced and pinched the top of his nose as if in great pain.

The komes' eyes darted in confusion. 'He... he stole this ass from a local farmer. I'm making him return it.'

'And then what?' the emperor spat.

'And then he will be put on half-rations, latrine detail and double-watch for the next two weeks,' the Komes said.

Romanus' eyes locked onto the shame-faced soldier with the ass. 'Bring him to me.'

Two varangoi took the man by the shoulders, shaking the tether from his grasp and then marching him to stand before the emperor, the corridor closing up behind them. The soldier fell to his knees in obeisance. The two varangoi took a couple of steps aside, eyeing the confrontation with a sense of dread.

'Do you know what used to happen to criminals?'

'Not the lash, *Basileus*, I beg of you,' the man whimpered.

Romanus was oblivious to the man's pleas. He plucked a dagger from his belt and held it up so the polished blade sparkled in the torchlight. '*Rhinokopia*. Once a thief, always a thief.'

Apion's heart froze and gasps rang out all around, some men falling to their knees lamenting or praying. Was the emperor ill or utterly possessed? The punishment of slicing off a man's nose had not been used in hundreds of years. In the blackness of night, a flicker of torchlight betrayed the nightmarish scene clearly for just a moment; Romanus lowering the dagger blade and pressing it to the bridge of the wretch's nose. He pressed against the wall of varangoi. 'Igor, we must stop this.'

Igor shook his head. 'We obey the emperor's word, be it good or loathsome.'

Apion shoved closer, so only the Rus komes could hear. 'Let me through. Nobody will lose face, I swear it. If we let this happen then morale will be shattered.'

Igor beheld him momentarily, then nodded, nudging the varangos by his side. The pair parted briefly and let Apion through onto the crescent of shingle.

'Stop!' Apion cried out.

Romanus looked up, one cheek twitching, his eyes scouring Apion's form with disdain. 'Who dares to interrupt the emperor?'

'The Strategos of Chaldia, *Basileus*,' he replied, bowing a little and moving close enough to whisper. 'Your friend.'

Romanus frowned, fixing his unrecognising gaze to Apion's. It was then Apion saw just how lost and distant the emperor's eyes were, how bloated and ruddy his sweat-soaked skin was – rashes now creeping across his neck from the collar of his armour. And the emperor's hand trembled, ready to slice down with the dagger and cut off the kneeling archer's nose. Apion stepped back at that moment, realising he would have to call upon a force long lost to him.

'Then I cite the Intercession of the Holy Victory,' Apion said, stepping back. 'Bring forth the icon of the Holy Virgin of Blachernae.' The gasps from all around fell silent. Then cheers broke out in support of this move. The Intercession of the Holy Victory could see any man spared such a fate. Moments later, a clutch of varangoi brought forth the blue-gold icon, holding it aloft for the gathered crowd to see.

Romanus looked to this and blinked hard, shaking his head.

'*Basileus?*' Apion whispered, hoping the emperor had come to his senses.

But Romanus now shook his head firmly. 'No. The punishment will be carried out, as planned.' His knuckles then whitened on his dagger blade. A rivulet of blood spidered from the bridge of the kneeling man's nose and the emperor's arm tensed to push the blade down through the cartilage. Apion grasped his arm before he could do so.

Romanus shot an animal glare at him. 'Unhand your emperor.'

'*Basileus*, it is not becoming of you to become sullied in blood. Allow me to do this.'

Romanus stared into Apion's eyes as Apion prised the dagger from his grip. At last, the emperor stood back, nodding, somewhat bewildered.

Apion strode to stand before the kneeling skutatos. He placed the blade on the man's nose, then looked up and met the eyes of the watching thousands. The gathered ranks of the skutatoi, the varangoi looking over their shoulders, Scleros and the first horsemen from the magnate armies just reaching the camp. He gritted his teeth… and swept the dagger blade down. It chopped through flesh. Hot blood spurted and bone crunched. Then the wretch fell back, clutching his bloodied face. 'Take him away,' Apion growled, throwing a strip of bloody flesh to the dirt.

The sea of faces gawped at Apion. Some in fear, many in disgust.

Apion cradled his hand in the dull lamp light of his tent. Sha, Blastares and Procopius looked at him, searching for the right words.

Just then, the tent flap rustled and opened. Komes Igor ushered the wretch who had stolen the ass inside. The man sat opposite Apion. His face was still encrusted in dried blood, his nose badly broken but all still there. Komes Igor sat next to the fellow, then nudged him.

'God bless you, sir,' the man said quietly to Apion.

'God blesses foul hearts and fair with little distinction. I'd rather listen to a dog howl at the moon than take a blessing from God,' he snapped in reply, cradling his palm and wincing.

The man's head dropped at the admonishment.

Sha let a desert-dry laugh escape his lips. 'He accepts your gratitude, soldier. Now be off back to your tent before curfew begins, lest you end up in more trouble.'

'Aye, sir,' the skutatos nodded. He turned to Apion one more time as he left. 'Thank you, *Haga*.'

Apion nodded silently.

'Word is already spreading around the ranks that the man did not lose his nose,' Sha said as the tent flap fell closed again. 'The men know their emperor is unwell, but had that wretch been mutilated...' The Malian's words trailed off and he shook his head. 'Now let me see the mess you made of your hand,' Sha insisted again.

Apion uncurled his cradled hand, revealing the red raw strip on the heel of the palm. When he had swept the dagger down, he had broken the skutatos' nose with his knuckles and sliced this strip of flesh off his own hand with the blade's edge. The blood had spattered over Apion and the man's face, disguising the fact that the man's nose was only broken and not mutilated, and the thrown-down strip of palm-flesh had diverted the eyes of the emperor and the onlookers.

The Malian took a rag doused in vinegar and cleansed the wound. Apion did well to limit his discomfort to a teeth-grinding grimace. 'It'll heal within a few weeks,' Sha said, wrapping a length of linen bandage around the palm tightly. 'But if you have to lift a shield in that time it'll sting like fire.'

'Then I won't dwell upon it until I need my shield,' Apion grumbled. 'And in any case, I feel we have more important things to set our minds to.'

'What has happened to him?' Igor muttered aloud. 'He was sharp, brash and noble until we arrived at Helenopolis. Even on the crossing to that miserable town, he cajoled the men amidst a grim hailstorm, had them defying the hail and chanting his name.'

Apion looked up. 'And what has changed since then?'

Igor's eyes swept across the lamplit floor. 'Much has changed. We have come far from the capital, through the verdant coastal trails and now across the dry inner plateau. Spring has become a foul and hot summer and...'

'No, what has changed about the emperor. His habits, his routines?'

'An emperor on campaign follows a strict routine of sleeping, bathing, eating and riding.' Igor looked up, his eyes glinting. 'You suspect treachery, Strategos?'

'I find it a suitable default stance, Komes.' Apion offered a wry half-grin in reply. His mind flashed with memories of his night-visit to Prince Vardan's hilltop town, to Hurik the poisoner. 'Now, does anyone have access to his garments, his bathing waters or his food?'

'A few men tend to his clothes and prepare his washing water, yes, but they are beyond suspicion, Strategos.' The big Rus' eyes were earnest, almost longing to believe his own words.

Apion cocked an eyebrow. 'Such men make the best traitors, Komes. And his food?'

'Ah, poisoning? Yes, I thought so too. But it is impossible,' Igor said, his eyes narrowing and the vertical scar across one wrinkling. 'Those who cook his meals are watched by the Vigla sentries and the best of my axemen. No poison could make it past all of them.'

'But if it did?' Apion persisted.

Igor laughed aloud. 'It simply could not, Strategos. And besides, even if it did, we have a man who tastes a small portion of every meal before it goes to the emperor. A humble eunuch by the name of Symeon. He would have fallen ill by now if the emperor's food had been poisoned.'

Apion balled his good hand into a fist. 'There must be something, someone…' His words trailed off as he remembered the one man on this march who had almost become a forgotten figure, shackled only feet from the cooking area by the emperor's tent.

Igor's eyes narrowed in realisation, then they hissed in unison:

'Andronikos Doukas!'

Apion and Igor strode through the night, picking their way around the clustered pavilion tents and accepting muted salutes from the night watchmen. Up ahead, the emperor's red satin tent glowed brightest of all, surrounded by a ring of torches, vigilant Varangoi axemen and Vigla skutatoi bearing grim and alert scowls.

The Vigla sentries parted at Igor's command, then the varangoi in the inner circle recognised their leader and saluted silently.

'The emperor is asleep?' Apion asked in a hushed tone.

'Fitfully, but yes,' the Rus by the tent flap replied. Through the canvas, Apion could hear Romanus' dull moans.

'And he has eaten tonight, I presume?'

'Heartily,' the Rus replied. 'And he drank like a man who had been lost in the desert. Five cups of watered wine!'

Apion and Igor shared a narrow-eyed glance. 'Bring me his wine jug,' Igor ordered. The big Rus at the tent flap ducked inside then reappeared with the near-empty jug.

Igor took it, sniffed at it, shrugged, then tilted it to catch the light. There was nothing suspicious about it, it seemed.

'The cooking area?' Apion suggested.

'This way,' Igor beckoned, leading Apion round to the rear of the imperial tent. Here, a smaller set of tents were erected in a semi-circle. They all faced onto a blackened campfire, over which hung pots and kitchen implements. A squat, bald man ambled around the kitchen area, gathering up washed implements and stowing them away. 'Symeon,' Igor muttered to Apion, nodding to the food-taster. But Apion's attentions had fallen on the only other figure in the space, sitting on a stool, irons shackling one arm to a post.

Andronikos Doukas gazed listlessly into the black remains of the fire before him, his flat-boned features sullen. Apion eyed the length of the chain, then the closeness of the kitchen area.

'He has always been kept this close to the cooking fires?' Apion whispered to Igor.

'Yes,' Igor sighed.

'And when the emperor insisted on living in the hilltop hovel – his food was prepared here and taken to him?'

Igor sighed again. 'It was. And in all that time this one has been but a few paces from the emperor's meals. The chains are too long.'

Andronikos shot to standing, his eyes flashing with ire as he overheard them. 'You assume I am responsible for the emperor's madness?'

Symeon, ambling nearby, started at the outburst, dropping the pans he carried then apologetically gathering them up.

'Convince me otherwise, boy,' Apion snorted.

A silence ensued until the fire left Andronikos' eyes and he slunk back to his stool, his chains clanking as he dropped his head into his hands. 'I see. So you judge me on my father's deeds. I should have expected as much.'

'Men are fickle and I am no judge,' Apion snorted. 'All I know is that our emperor has fallen to some madness, and I find you within arm's reach of his kitchen.'

Andronikos looked up, his eyes meeting Apion's. 'I care little for the emperor. Also, why would I care for the cur who calls himself my father?' He snatched up the chains and shook them, teeth gritted. 'His meddling has seen him cast into exile… and me brought along on this campaign, tethered like a rabid jackal.' He shook his head, dropping the gathered chains. 'So if you are looking for an answer to the emperor's madness, look elsewhere.'

Apion watched Andronikos as the young man dropped his head back into his hands. Words were ever so cheap. He had seen some fine actors in his time. Was this young man another such?

'What do you think, Strategos?' Igor whispered beside him. 'We will have him removed from the imperial tent area, that is for certain. But as to his punishment…'

Apion heard little else of what Igor said. His eyes hung on Andronikos but, like a hunter, he noticed something flash in his peripheral vision. He looked over to see the squat Symeon waddling to and from a storage tent, humming some tune. Then he saw it again. A flash of silver. He saw that the man wore a bracelet on his wrist, with an amulet dangling from it – a tiny, silver cylinder with an asp coiled around it. As Symeon turned, the moonlight glinted on the tiny purple gemstones that were the serpent's eyes. The sight stole Apion's breath away and the crone's words hissed sibilantly in his thoughts.

Beware the serpent with the amethyst eyes!

'Komes,' Apion said, cutting Igor off. 'I think we have our man.'

Igor frowned, following Apion's gaze, then gawping as Apion strode over to stand before Symeon. 'Symeon? Never! The man is as loyal as they come.'

'A simple test will prove it.'

Igor shook his head, sighing. 'Do what you will.'

The squat food-taster looked up to Apion, a pleasant smile spreading across his face.

'You taste the emperor's food, yes?' Apion asked him.

'Not a morsel goes to him without me sampling it first,' Symeon nodded.

'Show me,' Apion said, gesturing for Igor to give the food-taster Romanus' wine jug.

Symeon took the jug and a cup, pouring a little wine and then sipping at it. 'It is a pleasant task,' he grinned. 'And I can assure you I have had no ill-effects in these recent weeks.'

Apion did not return his grin. 'Now hand me your amulet.'

Symeon frowned, clutching his bracelet. 'My amulet? Whyever would—'

'Just do as he says,' Igor cut in, albeit reluctantly.

Symeon lifted the bracelet from his wrist and placed it in Apion's hand. Apion eyed the piece. It was the size of his smallest finger and it was finely carved, the snake's body etched with individual scales, the mouth open, fangs bared as if striking. Within the mouth was a tiny stopper. Apion plucked it out, then held the amulet over Symeon's wine cup. As he tilted it, he watched the food-taster's face, saw a bead of sweat dart down the man's forehead. Finally, a glimmering, silvery globule dropped from the mouth of the amulet and splashed into the wine.

Igor gasped beside him.

'Care to drink some more?' Apion asked Symeon.

The food-taster hung his head.

'What was it?' Apion asked.

'Quicksilver,' Igor answered for him, snatching the amulet and tipping another drop from it. The silvery bead splashed on the ground and divided up into several smaller beads. 'Symeon, why?' he demanded, grabbing the little man by the shoulders and shaking him.

'They told me to make it look like some sort of illness,' Symeon confessed to the big Rus. 'They have my sister... in the torture chambers under the Hippodrome,' he said with a trembling voice, his eyes rimmed with tears.

Apion knew there was no need to ask who. He closed his eyes and bowed his head as he tried to block the memories of those dark chambers where Psellos and his Portatioi agents tormented and mutilated their political foes.

'Now they will kill her,' Symeon whimpered. 'Unless...'

A rasp of iron tore Apion from his thoughts. He looked up to see that Symeon had stolen the sword from Igor's scabbard and pushed back from the big Rus. The little man swiped out with it clumsily, slashing the Rus' chest armour and sending him toppling backwards. The food-taster spun round, his eyes wide, fixed on the red satin sides of the emperor's tent.

'No!' Apion cried.

'I have to,' Symeon wailed, then made for the side of the tent, hefting the sword back to cut through and buy a chance to slay the emperor inside.

Apion leapt to block him. Without shield or armour, he could only draw his scimitar, grappling it two-handed, readying to parry. But his raw, wounded palm stung like fire and the hilt fell from his grasp. Defenceless, he could only watch as Symeon's wild sword strike swept down for him and the side of the tent.

A stinging pain slashed across Apion's cheek and he heard a sudden clanking of thick iron. He staggered back, blinking. He touched a hand to the spot on his cheek, where hot rivulets of blood trickled. The blade had only nicked it. And there, right before him, was a terrible sight. Symeon, gagging, eyes bulging, face reddening, Andronikos Doukas stood tall behind him, wrist chains wrapped tightly around the food-taster's neck. The little man thrashed like a fish trapped in shallow water. The sword toppled from his grasp and his face grew purple as Andronikos wrenched tighter and tighter. A moment later, and Symeon's body fell still.

Igor was back on his feet now and came to stand with Apion. They both watched as Andronikos set the food-taster's corpse down, then settled back on his stool. He looked up with a sardonic half-grin. 'Seems it was a good thing that these chains were long.'

The campaign army had marched on into fine June sunshine and now they were at the eastern edge of the Charsianon Thema. Three days had passed since Symeon's death, and Apion struggled to take meaning from what had happened. He thought over it as he rode. A seemingly good man had been outed as another of Psellos' pawns – but then his motives were valorous. The grim truth was that the food-taster's sister was now doomed to die in those dark torture chambers. And Andronikos, the one he had suspected initially, had proved to be a noble man. *Noble? By virtue of choking a man to death?* And so the thoughts continued in this grey loop.

At dawn on the fourth day after Symeon's death, Romanus and Apion sat alone in the imperial tent, playing shatranj. The emperor was – for the first time in weeks – clean-shaven and freshly bathed, his flaxen hair still-damp and neatly swept back. More, the pink-red tinge to his skin and the copious sweat were gone. The poison was fading from his system. Apion had taken over as food-taster, and this morning's meal of eggs, bread, honey and yoghurt was delicious and free from any uninvited ingredients.

Apion watched as the emperor made to lift a pawn forward, a move that would expose his king within two moves. But Romanus hesitated, replacing the pawn. The emperor looked up, cocking a wry smile.

'Proof enough that I have recouped my senses?' he said.

'You never lost them, *Basileus*. They were simply tainted by quicksilver.'

Romanus sat back, gazing at the tent flap, beyond which the purple-orange of dawn was growing, promising another day of fiery heat. 'Yet it seems I did my damnedest to dispirit the men. It is a wonder that they did not think to cut me down for my deeds. Throwing their belongings in the river, having them build some manor… and the fire at Malagina – I have little memory of how that started, other than a vivid recollection of walking through the flames, laughing like a drunk. My stallion, after years of charging bravely into battle, bearing my burden… burnt alive without an enemy blade in sight. The Armenians are better men than I – forgiving me for the slurs I cast at them shows they are noble allies indeed.'

'I have explained what happened to Prince Vardan. And the armies are simply relieved to have their emperor back, *Basileus*,' Apion insisted. 'That is why none tried to depose you or relieve you of your post – because they need you to lead them, to make them believe.' He cast his mind back over Romanus' speech the previous day – the first time he had addressed the men since his poisoning. They had stopped at noon near a fresh spring and an orchard. They waited there for the rest of the afternoon until the majority of the column had caught up. The men unburdened themselves of their armour and sat in the tall grass, speckled with roses and lilies, nourishing themselves on cherries and icy-cold water. Romanus took that moment to stand before them and lay his soul bare.

I will forever carry the guilt of my actions in these last weeks. That you still heed my word is a testament to your strength and will. Be angry not at me for my times of madness, but at the cur who poisoned my food and those who compelled him to do so. They have hurt us all, but they have not broken us. This campaign set out to march east and seize the Lake Van fortresses, and it will not be waylaid by treachery! I look over you and see nigh-on forty thousand faces. I listen and I hear forty thousand beating, noble hearts. I know we will be victorious. God is with us!

The cheering of the gathered men had seemed to rock the land for miles. Apion felt a gentle smile creeping across his face at the memory.

'But the rhinokopia,' Romanus continued. 'If I had actually gone through with it I don't think I would be able to face them...'

'But you didn't do it, *Basileus*. I knew there was something else at play here. No man turns from a noble and brave leader into a mindless tyrant without a cause. Psellos. *He* is the one who forced Symeon to do what he did. *He* is the one who slew your stallion. *He* is the one who tormented the troops.'

Romanus sighed. 'The dog still operates from exile, it seems.'

Apion felt his dark memories surface again, remembering the many slain at the advisor's behest. Old Cydones the most prominent. 'Perhaps you should consider nullifying his threat more permanently?'

Romanus shrugged. 'And then what? Watch while another black crow flutters down to perch on the shoulders of the Doukas family? No, best accept the enemy I know and understand than some new force.'

'True. The Doukas family and their supporters are widespread and entrenched in imperial lands. But not all of them are black-hearted. The one you have in chains, outside. He is no lover of his father's scheming.'

Romanus stroked his jaw in thought. 'Andronikos is a decent man with a shrewd eye for the battlefield. He has led men in wars past and shown himself to be a strategos in the making. It does not please me to see him led with us in chains like some exotic animal. But he is John Doukas' son, and as much as the young man despises his father, John covets the lad, sees him as a protégé yet to fall into line with his thinking.' He toyed with the pawn again as he said this, then changed his mind, lifting his knight out over the pawn line and into play. 'Yet I brought Andronikos along thinking it might stop Psellos and John's attempts to dethrone or slay me. How wrong I was. It seems that John cares as little for Andronikos as he does for his father?'

Apion swept his war elephant across the board, taking the emperor's knight with a dry grin. 'Still, be on your guard. Every man has it within himself to be at once noble and despicable.'

Romanus grinned. 'You can be sure of it, Strategos. Andronikos will earn no sympathy until this campaign is over and the Lake Van fortresses are ours. Then, perhaps, I might offer him some respite from his vile father. Until that moment, he can ride in chains. And when we go to battle, he will remain in chains and line up within the magnate armies.'

Apion whistled at this, thinking of the rabble of infantry and cavalry. 'I would hesitate to send my darkest enemy into those ill-ordered ranks.'

Romanus leaned over the shatranj board, his face stern. 'I brought them along to swell our ranks and fend off the detractors who would otherwise say my army was far less numerous than I proclaimed it might be. Seven thousand men. Seven thousand men led by a clutch of self-serving dogs. Cut them and they would bleed avarice. That is why they will not be used in this campaign unless desperation overcomes us.'

Apion nodded, thinking of the clutch of overly proud men who led these private militias. 'They have taken to giving themselves grand titles. I've heard the one with the trident beard – Scleros – calling himself doux and strategos, when I'd wager he has never once been in battle – no doubt too busy sucking wine from a jug and growing fat as he watched his slaves toil over his crops.' He lifted a pawn out in an attempt to lure the emperor's chariot piece.

Romanus swigged at his cup of watered wine, gazing out through the tent flap as the sun broached the horizon, casting his face in orange. 'Always a balancing of risks, is it not? Who would have thought that upon assembling an army of this strength, we would still face such choices? We must not fail this time, Strategos. Manzikert and Chliat must be taken, at any cost. If I return to the capital without these prizes, the people will not support my reign any longer. Psellos, John Doukas and their many agents and sympathisers will pluck me from the throne like an overripe fruit.'

'The Lake Van fortresses can be taken, *Basileus*. And done well, there should be no need for great bloodshed.'

'I pray for better than that, Strategos. Our army is capable of taking the fortresses by force if needs be. But I have been thinking, thinking of a way to obtain the fortresses with no bloodshed at all.'

'*Basileus?*' Apion frowned.

'I have taken a measure for the greater good… though it may rankle with you and some of my retinue. Ah, here they come.' Romanus stood as a collection of men entered the tent. Igor came in first, still dressed in his pure-white armour having been on night watch. Tarchianotes entered next, wrapped in a woollen cloak and wearing an ugly scowl that accentuated his cheek-wart and suggested he had just been awoken from a deep sleep. The lithe and fresh-faced Alyates was dressed in his finely polished iron klibanion, tunic and boots, his chin freshly shaven and his lank, dark hair neatly combed as if he had risen early to be ready for this. Doux Philaretos entered next, halting only to hurl some volley of abuse at a soldier outside. Then he came in, his face sullen and inches from ire. Bryennios came in last, running his hands through his greying peak of dark hair to neaten it, then flashing his wolfish grin around the gathered men. The five sat around the table with Apion and the emperor. Romanus lifted the shatranj board away, careful not to disturb any of the pieces, then unfurled a yellowed, well-used map of the empire. He tapped the blue outline of Lake Van, sliding his finger between the two dots there that represented Manzikert and Chliat.

'I summoned you five — and only you five — because I trust each of you with my life.' Romanus said flatly. 'I want our men to remain vigilant, but, should things go to plan, we may find that the Lake Van fortresses can be acquired without facing the Sultan's armies. Even without bloodshed.'

Bryennios gasped. '*Basileus*, that is a fine aspiration, but—'

'I have not taken to the quicksilver again, I can assure you,' Romanus cut him off with a raised hand and a firm grin.

'But Alp Arslan will not relinquish his grasp on those fortresses without a struggle, *Basileus*,' Alyates added.

'No he won't. Unless we offer him something more attractive than a fight.'

Apion felt a warm glow in the pit of his stomach as he caught on to the emperor's thinking. *A trade!*

'The Sultan is having difficulty in securing his hold on Syria. Just when the Fatimids seemed beaten, they have raised their heads again. I believe we have something in those lands that he covets.' Romanus' finger lifted from the Lake Van area of the map and swept down to the south, to Syria.

'Hierapolis,' Apion whispered, thinking aloud.

Romanus flashed him a grin, his finger falling right on the city in the sands.

Tarchianotes gasped. 'You propose we trade the desert city? The city we fought so hard – and lost so much – to take?'

'Unlike you, Doux, I was there. Memories of the fighting within those walls, and the faces of the many lost, do not evade me, nor my nightmares,' Romanus said, an edge of terseness in his reply.

'Yes, *Basileus*,' Tarchianotes bowed his head in apology.

'Holding Hierapolis for these last three years has allowed us some respite on those borders. Antioch and our coastal holdings in Syria have been strengthened. Fortresses have been constructed in the Anti-taurus Mountain passes, and are now garrisoned by our Armenian allies. Edessa's walls have been bolstered, the towers heightened and the garrison doubled. Indeed, I hear reports that the Sultan has been bombarding the city with his war machines since the start of the month, but is unable to break the walls. Antioch, Edessa, and this line of mountain fortresses can be the basis of a formidable chain of defence for our south-eastern borders. Hierapolis has served its purpose. Now it could serve another, of equal if not greater significance.'

'We withdraw our Hierapolis garrison, and station them instead in the mountain fortresses?' Apion suggested.

'Exactly.' Romanus swung round, pointing at Apion.

'So Alp Arslan will walk into Hierapolis and suffer no opposition,' Bryennios frowned. 'Then what? We simply march east and take the Lake Van fortresses likewise?'

'Perhaps. If the Sultan sees sense,' Apion mused.

'Alp Arslan fought hard to win Manzikert from our hardy garrison last year. I heard he lost two wings of his finest veteran ghulam riders in the process,' Alyates said.

'And he fought even harder to establish Seljuk control in Syria,' Apion countered. 'The emperor is right. The Lake Van fortresses are more valuable to us than to Alp Arslan, and Hierapolis is more valuable to him than it once was to us.'

'We are some six weeks away from reaching Lake Van, *Basileus*,' Tarchianotes said, his morning scowl having relaxed a fraction. 'Official parley and agreement of such a trade will take significantly longer, I would imagine. So do we halt the march, put the campaign on hold?'

Romanus' lips lifted in a wry smile. 'Sometimes, in the name of expediency, decorum and pomp can be dispensed with. All we need is a fast rider. The fastest of them all. Someone who can hasten to the Sultan and propose this trade.'

Apion listened as they chattered over the possibilities. The warmth in his belly was an unfamiliar feeling. Powerful men discussing the real possibility of sealing Byzantium's borders from attack at long last. But something nagged at him. If there was to be no confrontation with the Sultan's armies, then he would not face Taylan. Maria's whereabouts would remain elusive. *But I will not have to face my boy*, he reasoned. A bittersweet swirl of emotion played with his heart.

Then he thought of something. Words that had long hovered in his thoughts. The crone's shrill tones echoed in his mind as his gaze fell upon the map. Lake Van and the two fortresses near its shores.

I see a battlefield by an azure lake flanked by two mighty pillars. Walking that battlefield is Alp Arslan. The mighty Mountain Lion is dressed in a shroud. Then his eyes drifted to the golden heart pendant Romanus wore around his neck. *At dusk you and the Golden Heart will stand together in the final battle, like an island in the storm…*

The warmth in his belly faded, and a chill took its place.

The burnt-gold Bithynian countryside basked in a serene summer's day. A villa stood at the crest of a gentle hill, surrounded by orchards and crop fields. Cicadas trilled and a pair of nut-brown hares hopped across one orchard floor, nibbling at seeds, play-fighting as they went. Neither noticed the osprey perched on the branches above. Starved of its usual diet of fish, it swooped, scooping up the smaller hare in its talons, piercing the creature's heart.

John Doukas observed from a bench overlooking the orchard, heedless of the remaining hare's keening for its lost partner. He watched the osprey rise and soar away with its prey, gliding off to the east. His hands flexed on the ball-shaped top of the knotted walking cane he had come to need, imagining it as Romanus Diogenes' heart in his grasp. His mind pulled in myriad directions at once. He longed to stand and stride to the palace wing he had once called his home, to call together his shrewdest minds and plot their next move. He yearned to visit the Numeroi barracks and the dark chambers underneath, where the Portatioi would doubtless have another foe in chains for him. He hungered to hear the crowd in the Hippodrome rise for him, cry out for the Doukas family, laud his every movement. Instead, he could opt only to stroll in this pleasant estate, or shuffle around the corridors of this white-walled villa, with the advisor, Psellos, his only company. The dusty lands beyond the orchard flashed momentarily, and he glanced to see the pair of white-armoured varangoi there, their breidox axes glinting in the sun as they let the bread boy into the estate – bringing fresh loaves from the bakery in the nearby village. And so it was every hundred paces; a pair of stony-faced, iron-willed Rus. Not just at the perimeter of their exile, but within the estate and inside the villa too. He saw another of the big Rus axemen from the corner of his eye, standing in a shaded villa doorway, studying him as the osprey had watched the hares just moments ago.

They wanted none of his gold, none of his promises of riches. He had even given one of these surly wretches a purse-load of pure-gold coin – nearly all he had. The red-bearded cur had taken it too. He had revelled in the possibility that his games of power were alive again, only to return to his bedchamber that evening to find an ass tethered there, the empty purse lying on the floor beside it. *Your coins will not tempt the Varangoi!* Redbeard had snorted, then the ass had started braying and the rest of the Rus nearby had erupted in laughter. And when he had told Psellos of this, the shrivelled advisor had worn a mocking glint in his eye too.

The cicada song seemed to grow deafening, and his knuckles whitened on the cane. There had to be a way, a way to gather the Doukas supporters, to break him and Psellos free of this powerless tedium of exile.

A crunching of boots in scree sounded as Psellos came from within the villa to sit by his side then. He braced himself for some caustic, wordy rhetoric – that had been Psellos' speciality in these last months, usually accompanied by frenzied scratching at the mysterious affliction that burgeoned on the advisor's chest. But this time, something was different. He was grinning. 'Advisor?' John whispered.

Psellos waited until the watching varangos turned away, then leaned a little closer. 'The lines of communication are open once more, master.'

John frowned, then saw the bread boy descending the gentle dusty slope to leave once more.

'And he did it for just a bronze nomismata.' Psellos' shoulders jostled in mirth.

'He brings news of Diogenes' campaign?'

Psellos' grin widened. 'It seems there was some dark soul who brought the emperor to his knees with poison.' The grin faded a fraction. 'Yet the poisoner was outed and slain.'

John's hopes sank. 'Then your ploy failed,' he said flatly.

'Did it?' Psellos replied, the grin returning. 'The bread boy told me how close the campaign army had been to revolt. Word of this has spread across imperial lands. The people are doubting Diogenes once again. More...'

John made to interject, but Psellos raised a finger, silencing him. The advisor's eyes shut tight for a moment, his face wrinkled in agony and paled. He reached a hand up to his chest and made to scratch at the lesion under his linen robe, but hesitated, wincing at the lightest touch. A patch of pinkish-red, sticky fluid blossomed from the point where he had made contact. John's skin crept as he saw something else under that translucent patch of linen; something writhing. Shuddering, the advisor composed himself, pulling his robe clear of his skin. The grin returned, albeit pained.

'...more, the boy brought me word *and* will take word with him. Riders will take that word to your followers, master. To those in the capital and those all around the empire's lands. Prime them, ready them for what is to come.'

John's brow knitted. 'What is to come?'

'I planned for many eventualities before we were sent into exile, master. The poisoner was but one string to my bow. The first of many.'

CHAPTER 12

The Lion's Fury

The Seljuk artillery groaned and creaked. The Byzantine garrison on Edessa's battlements gawped. The searing hot midsummer day was silent for but a moment. Then the artillery commander threw a hand forward like a catapult arm. 'Loose!' he roared, a thick spray of spittle clouding before his lips.

At once, the air was filled with the thwacking of ropes, the bucking of vast timber war machines – nearly thirty onagers and six trebuchets, lined on the crest of the war-scarred hills nearest the city's southern walls – and the whistle of colossal rocks hurtling through the ether. With a crash that shook sky and earth, the rocks battered the city walls. Thick clouds of dust puffed into the air as sections of the battlements were gouged away where the rocks struck. Skutatoi were crushed on the walkway or punched like insects into the city streets below, leaving just a crimson stain where they had stood. The foundations shuddered where the rocks landed lower down, cracks snaking from the point of impact. But it had been this way for twenty-three days now. And still the beetling and ancient bulwark remained tenaciously unbreached.

Watching from behind the artillery lines, Alp Arslan calmed his panicked mount. As the beast stilled, he felt his blood pound like thunder in his ears. He had woken that morning, annoyed by the rich red wine he had consumed in an effort to bring on sleep, needled by the knowledge that Edessa, this thorn of a city, awaited his attentions for yet another day. The city, garrisoned only by some three hundred Byzantine spearmen, had withstood all his artillerymen could throw at it. The Byzantine ballistae mounted on the high towers had been broken almost every day by the longer-ranged Seljuk trebuchets, only to be repaired at night. The sapping tunnels he had ordered to be dug had been countermined and destroyed, killing hundreds of diggers in the process. The horde of some fifteen hundred akhi spearmen he had assembled to storm the city had sat and watched, idle, their spears untarnished. As the days had worn on, he had even taken to leaving his battle armour, helm and weapons in his tent, so sure was he that each day would pass without a conclusion to the siege. This had been planned as a swift siege, the first of many, breaking the easternmost of Byzantium's cities in order to prise open their southern borders just as he had gained a foothold in the Lake Van region. But then the cursed Fatimid boil had risen once again. Cities all across Syria had turned upon their Seljuk garrisons and declared themselves under the protection of the *Fatimid Caliphate* – Aleppo the biggest loss of all. All his progress from recent years was close to crumbling, and his rivals watched on with glee.

As the artillery stretched once more, the Sultan pinched the top of his nose and bowed his head. For a blessed moment, he was spirited from the chaos all around him. He thought back to February, just a few months ago. Before turning his attentions on Edessa, he had sought first to assimilate or conquer the defiant Marwanids, one of the rebellious factions holding out against him in the city of Amida. They held out for four days. When the gates were smashed open, his armies sped to pour inside, eager to sack the homes and temples and put the populace to the sword. But he had ridden to their head and halted them with a raised hand.

His men had looked at him in disbelief, but he had defied any of them to challenge his order. 'Today is not a day for slaughter,' he had told them, thinking of his son, born that morning, 'today, the battle is won. It ends here.'

And he had ordered just a handful of his finest beys to ride inside and negotiate a surrender. Then he had twisted in his saddle and looked up to the battlements of the city. The Marwanid prince stood there, smoke-stained and beleaguered. Alp Arslan simply raised a hand, then passed the palm over his face, showing his desire for a peaceable end to the day. And so Amida had fallen into the Seljuk dominion, swiftly and with minimal bloodshed. He gazed at his palm – the same one that had halted his army and granted mercy on all those citizens.

A scream rang out, tearing him from his reverie. He looked up to see that the latest bombardment of Edessa had brought down another section of the battlements. A Byzantine soldier was responsible for the screaming, his legs and pelvis crushed by a rock, the rest of him propped there in a dark pool of blood, arms thrashing.

Just then, hands barged him from his horse. He landed on the ground just before a Byzantine ballista bolt plunged into his horse's throat. The beast reared up and collapsed, thrashing in a pink froth. The unseen hands dragged the Sultan back.

'They have done something to increase the range of their weapons,' Bey Taylan said, his sparkling green eyes shaded under the rim of his helm, 'we must draw the lines back.'

Kilic, the other who had pushed him from the path of the bolt, helped him to his feet.

Alp Arslan cursed himself for being so negligent, so certain of dogged but eventual victory, that he missed this. Seljuk war horns blared all along the noose of men encircling the city, and the lines drew back. As he buckled on a coat of leather armour handed to him by Kilic, he noticed a lone rider emerging from the city gates. Another on foot slapped the horse's rump and sent it galloping towards him. The rider was unarmed, his tunic sweat-slicked and his dark face dominated by his wide eyes and dark moustache. A Seljuk prisoner of war, Alp Arslan realised as he came closer, seeing his wrists were roped together. 'Speak,' he said flatly as akhi spearmen helped the man from the saddle and cut his bonds.

The man gulped and bowed. 'My Sultan. The Byzantines send you this…' The man rose gingerly and reached for an amphora tied to his saddle. 'Iced water. They said the River Scirtus' waters are pleasant at this time of year and that there is plenty to go around.' And then he produced a parcel of salted meat and bread. 'And their storehouses are… bountiful.'

'So they can hold out for weeks, months?' Alp Arslan shrugged. 'I can wait just as long to see their wells run dry and their food spoil,' he lied. He traced the snaking silver course of the River Scirtus across the land, cursing it for entering the walls of the city under a ferociously protected culvert and lending the defenders such an advantage. While his men could also drink until their hearts were content downstream from the city, food was much less abundant. He saw the two akhi who bookended the wretched rider. These, his finest spearmen, looked like beggars, their cheeks gaunt and their eyes black-ringed. The Edessan garrison had done well to burn the farms and orchards of the countryside in advance of his arrival. He sighed, squinting into the sun, then glancing around for inspiration. He looked over his shoulder to the line of Byzantine soldiers roped together there, kneeling. 'I could send one of them into the city to tell the proud Byzantines that their hubris will be their downfall. I'd wager that they in fact have very little food left. Did you see these full storehouses?'

'No, I…' the man stammered.

'Then you have been blinded by their words.'

Another day passed, and the bombardment continued. The walls of Edessa began to resemble a haggard cliff-face – scarred and pitted, jutting from the green–gold land. But they would not fall. Alp Arslan came once more to the ridge across from the city's southern wall.

'They will break today, I can feel it,' the Sultan muttered.

'They seek parley, it seems?' Bey Taylan said, again by his side, pointing to the wagon that came from the gates.

The driver was an aged, bald man. A Byzantine this time.

Alp Arslan sat taller in his saddle. 'Their stores are empty at last!' he hissed.

'How can you be so sure?'

'Look at the driver's skin – pallid and sickly.' *Just like so many of your own men*, a voice hissed in his mind. 'Let us hear what he has to say.'

The man slid from his horse and croaked: 'The Doux of Edessa will turn the city over to you, Sultan. He asks only one thing: that you end the bombardment and put your siege engines to the torch.'

'Never!' Taylan spat.

'Silence, young Bey!' Alp Arslan snapped, cowing the snarling Taylan.

'It is a trick!' Taylan insisted.

'*Silence!*' the Sultan repeated.

'It is no trick,' the bald man pleaded. 'We are running short of food and so are you. Let our people leave the city without the threat of being dashed on open ground by your stone-throwers. Please, destroy your artillery and we will leave. As a token of our good faith, here is all we have in the city treasury.' He swept the canvas from the back of the wagon to reveal twelve barrels brimming with gold and silver coins. 'Fifty thousand pieces.'

'They are dinars and dirhams, Sultan. Coin collected – no, stolen – from our people at some point,' Taylan insisted, squinting at the bounty.

Alp Arslan shot him another glare of reprimand. 'Gold is gold and silver is silver. It exists to compel men and stoke their greed. It was doubtless once Byzantine coinage and before that Persian or Roman.'

He turned back to the wagon driver. 'If this *is* some ploy, Byzantine, I will have your head,' he growled.

The man nodded, holding the Sultan's gaze earnestly. 'I understand.'

Alp Arslan gazed upon the gold and silver. *Should they renege on their word*, he thought, *this coin will allow me to hire a mercenary army that I can leave behind to finish the siege*. Once more he remembered the good faith with which the siege of Amida had ended. He heard the first cries of his son again. A warmth touched his heart. *But let there be no treachery, let this be the last day of this dogged standoff*. He turned to his artillery lines. 'Burn the siege engines.'

The engineers protested at first, but their commanders soon noticed the fire in their Sultan's eyes and put their men to the task. Within the hour, the siege lines were ablaze, thick coils of black smoke staining the sky and the flames bending and distorting the air. A cluster of akhi spearmen laid down their weapons and shields to lift the barrels of coins from the Byzantine wagon onto one of the Sultan's. They strained and puffed at each barrel's great weight, then, when they came to the last one, one man stumbled and fell. The barrel tumbled with him. The gold and silver coins spilled across the sand before Taylan and Alp Arslan – but not a barrelful… just a smattering. Below the rim, the barrel was filled only with wet sand.

Alp Arslan's skin prickled. The stench of his blazing war machines taunted him, and he felt the gaze of all nearby who had witnessed the ruse. He swung to the Byzantine wagon driver. 'You deceived me.'

The man clasped his hands together and knelt. 'I did what I had to in order to protect my people. God's people. There is enough food left in the city to last a few more days. Your men cannot hang on that long, we know this. So my people will not be leaving the city. You will, however, abandon these lands in search of forage. The siege is over. The city remains in imperial hands.' With that, he bowed his head and muttered in prayer.

Alp Arslan's chest rose and fell faster and faster with every heartbeat. He looked to Kilic, his battle-scarred bodyguard, standing just a few feet behind the kneeling man. One word to the giant killer and the treacherous Byzantine's throat could be opened to his spine. Alp Arslan's mind spun with the possibilities. A quick death? Maybe slow, wicked torture? Or acceptance, acceptance that he had been outsmarted. This last possibility irked him most of all. He turned to Kilic and Taylan.

'Do with him what you will, then ready the army. We must depart for the south at once. There is fodder and game to be had there. Then we will turn our attentions upon rebellious Aleppo.'

He stalked away. Behind him, he heard a scimitar being unsheathed, then the thick, familiar hiss of slicing skin and bone and the *thud* of a severed head hitting the dust.

A week later, the Sultan and his army came to Aleppo. The tall, sun-bleached walls of this desert city shimmered, the battlements packed with jeering Fatimid troops. The Sultan's head pounded. His nostrils and throat were parched and coated in dust, and his mind was thick with the fog of the copious volumes of red wine he had consumed in these last nights. He looked along his armies. They were well fed and watered now, but without the means to breach Aleppo's towering walls. He looked to the pair of trebuchets his engineers had cobbled together in an effort to replace the burnt artillery – flimsy, weak-looking devices. They bucked and spat forth rocks no bigger than a man's head. These rocks sailed through the swirling desert air and smacked into Aleppo's gatehouse. A puff of white dust. Barely any damage to the walls. A moment of silence. Then more haughty cheering from the garrisoned Fatimids.

The beys nearby began chattering anxiously, offering him advice, each sure they were correct in their words. Alp Arslan was focused on something else entirely though; on the tallest of the city's gate towers, a handful of Fatimid soldiers were scurrying to and fro, drawing some vast, black cloth with them. They then draped the cloth like a veil over the tower top as if to shade it from the blistering sun and hush the intermittent din of the siege. The laughter that followed echoed from the city and washed out across the Seljuk siege line.

'What is this?' he spat.

'I believe they are trying to goad us, Sultan,' Taylan growled. He was the only one who had refrained from offering jabbering advice.

'Goad us?' he said.

Taylan nodded to one of the enemy soldiers up there, clasping his hands to his head and pretending to swoon, bringing more laughter from the others with him. 'They mean to tell us that our siege engines have served only to give their towers a headache.'

Alp Arslan snatched his wine skin from his nearby mare, uncorking it and lifting it, eager to drink hungrily.

'We must hew more timber to fashion proper stone-throwers!' Bey Gulten yapped, barging in between Alp Arslan and Taylan.

'Send the ladders forward!' another shrieked.

The Sultan paused, the skin at his lips. Then he threw it down, the wine spilling into the sand. 'There is no timber in these parts, you oaf!' he roared at Bey Gulten. 'And you, feel free to take the ladders forward!' he bellowed at the other. 'When you reach the top and find they are five feet short of the wall tops, then perhaps you can ask the Fatimid garrison for a helping hand onto the battlements?'

Both beys dropped their gaze from Alp Arslan. Bey Gulten did snatch a swift and fiery glare at Bey Taylan, by his side.

'This siege has failed. This year of campaigning was supposed to deliver Syria to me. Instead, my reward is humiliation,' the Sultan snarled. He drew his gaze around each of the men there. How many here were truly with him? How many were as eager to see him fail as his rival, Yusuf, the dog who had tried to assassinate him?

He felt all semblance of self-control crumbling at that moment, his head thundering and his chest rising and falling in ire.

—

In a niche upon a craggy hilltop east of Aleppo, Diabatenus crouched on one knee, adjusting his eyepatch as he surveyed the scene below. He could see the Seljuk siege lines wrapped around the city like a noose and he had watched the bold move to ire the Sultan with the black veil. A weighty move that played with the lives of the citizens, he mused, then weighed the scroll he held. With this one sheaf of paper, he too might save many thousands of lives. To trade cities rather than blows with the Sultan was a noble aspiration. He glanced to the dying embers of the small fire he had kindled to cook his midday meal of thick porridge and let his mind wander.

The emperor had asked for the fastest rider amongst the ranks of the army to carry this scroll to the Sultan. From the Scholae, the Vigla, the Stratelatai and the Hikanatoi, one name had echoed: *Diabatenus, Champion of the Races!* He smiled, thinking how times had changed since that thundery, grim morning in his slum-hovel back in the capital. It seemed that fortune had befallen him once again.

Then he heard hooves rounding the hilltop. A lone Seljuk scout was racing downhill for the Sultan's siege camp, unaware of Diabatenus' presence in this nook. Diabatenus looked to the rider, then to the scroll once more, weighing it again. 'Such a shame,' he smiled as he pressed it into the embers of the fire. He didn't wait to see it blacken and burn, instead he stood tall and hailed the rider.

The Seljuk scout swung his mount round and drew his sword. 'Byzantine?' he snapped, his eyes flicking this way and that, wary of more enemy soldiers.

Diabatenus held up his hands. 'At ease, I am alone!' he pleaded as the rider ranged around him, sword levelled. 'I come only to pass on a message to your Sultan.'

The rider eyed him in suspicion.

Diabatenus noticed the rider's tatty garb and the poor welding of his blade. 'A message that he would be glad to hear. I'm sure he would reward you well for it.'

The rider flicked his head up briskly. 'Very well. What?'

'The Emperor of Byzantium is on the move. Right now he marches east… and he means to take the Lake Van fortresses. He plans to slay the Seljuk garrison there to a man, and then to march down the upper Euphrates valley, striking directly into the heart of your realm. His goal is to seize your capitals and lay waste to your lands. He spoke at length of it. He regaled his men with promises that they would soon be dining in the halls of Tus and Isfahan, their boots wet with Seljuk blood and their seed in as many of your women as they wished.'

The Seljuk rider's eyes widened. 'You bring this news to us… why?' he snarled.

Diabatenus grinned. 'Because I will be rewarded for it also,' he said, plucking a pure gold nomisma from his purse, flicking it up and catching it mid-air. He thought back to that grim day when he had joined the Vigla for a paltry rider's wage. Then he recalled the rap on the hovel door one morning that had changed everything. While all others had forgotten him, Michael Psellos, advisor to the imperial throne, had not.

The rider galloped on down to the camp and he settled to watch. From here he could make out the area where the Sultan sat with his courtiers – at a row of chairs near the north of the camp by a grand yurt. The Sultan seemed to be gulping down vast quantities of wine.

The Seljuk rider dismounted before Alp Arslan, and there was a hiatus as he bowed and relayed the message. Alp Arslan seemed cast in stone for some time afterwards as the rider backed away, his step faltering. Then, like a demon awakened, the Sultan stood, hurled his vase of wine to the ground and bellowed a primal cry into the ether.

Taylan slid off his mail vest and unbuckled his swordbelt, handing them to his attendant. He crouched and frowned, examining the cracks in his mare's hooves, then stood tall to stroke her mane. 'Many months of war take their toll on us all, do they not?' he whispered to her. All around him, the men of the akhi force sat slumped, gratefully devouring their bread and cheese rations. Felt and mail vests had been cast aside and spears and shields lay in piles. War was the last thing on the minds of these men. Taylan's thoughts too turned to his growling belly, his eyes flicking to the large terracotta urn of yoghurt and the small pot of dates laid out for him on a blanket nearby. He sat to eat, resting his back on a sun-bleached rock. The sweet, sticky fruit and the cooling yoghurt felt like an elixir to his tired flesh.

His comfort faded when he saw in his mind's eye the scarred, pale face of the cur who had sired him. The *Haga*, the poison-filled boil yet to be lanced. Anger licked at the sides of his heart.

He clasped his hands to his temples and thought then of Mother. Thinking of her brought a cooling calm to his mind. He vowed to visit her as soon as the Sultan disbanded this army. It had been some months since last he set eyes upon her pale and emaciated form. He prayed he would be able to return to her soon, before…

The crunching of boots and a sudden flurry of murmurs snapped him from his thoughts.

The Sultan strode towards him, eyes ablaze, his long dark locks and his flowing moustache tied back, the ends knotted at the nape of his neck. A sure sign that the *Mountain Lion* was readying to ride once again.

'Sultan?' Taylan cocked an eyebrow.

'Pick up your armour, Bey. Ready your mount.'

'We are to ride?' Taylan asked, seeing the Sultan's eyes drift to the northern horizon.

'Aye, we are to ride,' Alp Arslan replied. 'Byzantium's armies have marched east and must be tamed.'

'You had best be getting back to your bed, Lady Maria, the sun is weakening,' the physician said.

Maria clasped the sun-warmed marble balcony edge at the top of the tiled hospital roof, closed her eyes and inhaled again as the zephyrs licked at her greying locks. 'And when it drops, the stars will be revealed. Why would I hide from such beauty?'

The physician shuffled awkwardly. 'We have talked of this before. You must not stay on your feet for too long. You are not strong enough. You may only have days—'

'My limbs may be weak, but my heart is strong,' she cut him off. 'Give me more time. And take that foul paste you call medicine with you.'

'Very well,' the physician sighed, surreptitiously placing the clay bowl of chalky paste he carried down nearby. Maria noticed this, but felt too weak to argue. 'But I will be back before twilight,' the physician added as he turned and descended the stairs into the hospital building.

Alone at last, she savoured everything around her. The sprawl of tiled palaces, mosques and the timber slums filling Mosul's walls. The dull orange light bathing the dusty plain beyond. The hazy sky, stained with streaks of purple. The sweet scent of cinnamon from some nearby kitchen. The gentle babble and laughter of unseen families. The soothing mix of the day's heat and the coming night's chill, dancing on her skin. Each and every detail beautiful to her. She felt at peace, without pain. Then a dull ache in her abdomen called her back to reality. She touched a hand to the hard, jutting growth there – almost the size of a melon. The ache became a lancing pain. She winced, clutching at it now, staggering back from the edge of the rooftop, her robes suddenly awash with a tide of cold sweat. She stifled a scream of agony, sure that the physician would hear and take her back to the lonely ward and never let her leave again. But the pain came on again like a dagger, driving into her core. She opened her mouth to scream out, but the noise was drowned out by a screeching eagle passing overhead. At the same time, a deep, healing warmth touched her, dissipating the pain like a morning mist.

She blinked, realising she was prone on the rooftop. And she was not alone. The old crone who was with her held a warm hand over her growth. 'You?' she stammered, recognising the withered, hunched old woman. The milky, sightless eyes were unforgettable. She had come to her in the moments after she had learned of Nasir's death.

'I comforted you then and have come to do so again.'

She helped Maria to her feet.

'You refuse your medicine?' the crone inquired, nodding to the untouched bowl of paste.

Maria almost smiled. 'The last time I was up here, I watched a crow with a broken wing. It stood just paces from the fouling corpse of a hamster. It could have eaten and prolonged its suffering. It chose not to.' Her eyes drifted to two small piles of bones on the far side of the roof.

'Then you may not thank me,' the crone said, backing away and lifting her warm hand from the growth.

Maria frowned and touched it. A wave of disbelief washed over her – the growth was half the size it had been moments ago, and she was sure she could feel it shrinking further. 'It's different. Smaller. What did you do?' she said, her eyes brightening with hope.

'Ah, not enough. Never enough.' She waved a hand dismissively. 'I merely staved off the inevitable, gave you a handful more sunsets like this. It seems I am not as wise as the crow.'

'But you did not come just to soothe my cancer, did you?' Maria realised.

The crone's face sagged, the deep furrows of time magnifying. 'No,' she sighed. 'I came to tell you that they will meet. Of that there remains no doubt.'

Maria frowned, then she understood. 'No,' she shook her head in denial. 'Apion and Taylan? They cannot. Taylan will not rest until he spills Apion's blood. Yet he is but a boy, blinded to his own weaknesses. If he faces his father then…' She broke down in a chorus of sobbing.

The crone cupped an arm around her shoulders. 'But then, if he did not face his father, imagine what he might become. Remember what happened to Nasir? A spark of hatred left unchecked can become an inferno given time.'

Maria clasped her hands to her heart, following the crone's sightless gaze, off to the distant north. 'What will become of them?'

The crone shook her head in resignation. 'Fate sharpens his blades and grins at his own reflection. The hearts of men are all that stand against him now, Maria.'

CHAPTER 13

Field of Bones

The column marched on into the Sebastae Thema. The mid–July heat was intense, and this dry and dusty land offered little respite as they trudged through the endless valleys to the cicada song, the taste of dust and the absence of moisture on the tongue.

Apion tucked his sweat–slicked hair back onto the nape of his neck and shuffled to adjust his equally sodden tunic. Relieved of his task of monitoring the rearguard of the magnate armies, he now led his handful of Chaldian riders at the head of the column alongside the tagmata cavalry. And the emperor was always in sight – something that gave him great comfort, especially as the *Golden Heart* was at all times surrounded by a thick ring of Varangoi riders, Igor leading them, eyes vigilant. Even his retinue of Philaretos, Alyates, Tarchianotes and Bryennios were not allowed to ride within this protective circle of Rus riders.

Only the varangoi and the vanguard, some half a mile out in front, wore armour in this heat – much to Igor's annoyance. Apion and all the others carried just their spears, shields and swords – all helms and armour stowed on the lumbering touldon of mules and wagons. He glanced back over his shoulder, over the winding body of the serpent. The heat haze offered up a shimmering sea of faces, bobbing helms, spears and banners, and melted into the horizon many miles short of where the rearguard would be riding.

For the next few weeks, the march through Byzantine lands continued without incident. They moved at the planned ten miles per day, drinking vast quantities of water as they went. This water came from natural springs, wells and imperial supply dumps marked out on the emperor's route map.

One morning, they went some three hours without a stop. But when the route took them past the banks of a small freshwater lake, the purple imperial banner was at last raised for a halt, and sighs of relief rang out. 'Fill your skins, slake your thirst!' A cry rang out from the signophoroi wielding the banner and was echoed back down the miles of the column.

Apion slid from his saddle with a groan, waving the Chaldian ranks from their marching positions, over to the lake's shores. He looked west along the lake's banks. The rest of the column hugged the shore for miles like a great herd. He watched as the men enjoyed the chance to quench their thirsts fully and splash themselves with the cool water. Some filled their skins and then emptied them into the collars of their tunics to soothe their tired bodies. Apion waited his turn to fill his water skin. He had seen countless barrels of water drained in the space of an hour on previous campaigns, with ten or twenty thousand men, but these forty thousand men and nearly twenty-five thousand mules and horses drank so much that he was sure the waterline of the lake visibly dropped as he waited his turn.

'Half a pint of water per hour for every man?' Sha croaked, draining his own water skin by the lake's shores and filling it again. 'This lake will be a puddle by the time we're done.'

Apion nodded as he saw a space and stooped to fill his skin. 'That's at a minimum too – a pint per hour when we leave imperial lands and have to march in armour.'

'Pah!' Procopius snorted, throwing water across his wrinkled face then blinking it away. 'Onagers and trebuchets need no water!'

'Aye, but the poor mules pulling the carts they are laden on do!' Apion laughed.

Procopius shrugged, then looked over his shoulder and grinned. 'Talking of mules…'

Apion and Sha looked to see Blastares, hobbling to the lakeside. The big man had the look of a shaved mongrel that had accidentally bitten into a lemon, his shorn scalp and skin glistening with sweat and his eyes like slits. 'This is brutal, sir. Every year, I swear that it will be my last campaign,' he grumbled as he crouched stiffly to dip his water skin into the lake. 'That I'll buy up a good farm and settle down with Tetradia. *Get fat, get old*, I tell myself. Though not as old as this one.' He jabbed a thumb at Procopius and roared at his own joke. His laughter faded as Procopius' face wrinkled in a scowl of indignation. Then the old tourmarches' face bent into a mischievous scowl, and he started prising his boots off.

Blastares continued, 'But every year I find myself at it again, cooking in the midday sun, wandering through the dust, breathing the scent of stale tunics and sweaty arses.'

'It could be worse. You could be marching with the infantry, Tourmarches,' Apion pointed out.

Blastares' face puckered just a little more. 'Seems like a distant memory – no, a nightmare! Still, riding is hard work. March and get blistered feet. Ride and suffer sore balls and a raw backside.'

Apion chuckled. 'Anyway, to ride in just tunics and boots is luxury. Soon we'll be in borderland territory. Then we'll have to ride in full armour, our bodies cooking and our brains baking inside our helms.'

'Thanks for the encouragement, sir,' Blastares grunted sarcastically. The big man gulped his skin of water dry, then made to fill it once again. But he halted, glancing to his side. 'What the? You filthy old bugger!'

Procopius looked up with an air of innocence, pausing only momentarily from lancing the next of the blisters on his gnarled, dirt and sweat-coated feet with his dagger, only inches away from the water Blastares had been drinking from. He flexed his toes a few times, prodding at one angry-looking blood blister. 'Ah, this one'll have to go as well. What's wrong? Not thirsty?'

Sha stifled his laughter as best he could as Blastares stomped away to find another drinking spot.

Apion cocked an eyebrow and patted Procopius' shoulder. 'What need for artillery, old horse, when your feet can send a soldier like Blastares running?'

It was in the third week of July when they came to an area that Apion recognised, but he couldn't quite place it. 'Tell me,' he said absently to Sha, riding by his side, 'we are in the eastern reaches of Sebastae. The sun might be playing tricks on my eyes, but is this…?'

'I fear it is,' the Malian sighed, then pointed to the heat haze before them. 'See the ripples in the land up ahead? That is the route to the gorge, I am sure of it.'

Apion's blood chilled. Memories of the gorge and the wall of fire from the previous year were but an echo. Worse, that meant that somewhere near here was the grim flatland where Manuel's army had been massacred. He tried to blank out the thought.

'That field will have long since been cleared and planted with crop,' Sha said, his thoughts attuned to Apion's, his lips taut. 'The garrison of Sebastae will have come from their walls to tend to the dead... surely.' The doubt in his tone battled with the words. Apion knew as well as he did that the garrisons of these eastern cities were thinner than ever, and were not prone to wandering the countryside in such scant numbers.

When they rode up and over a gentle range of hills, a series of laments rang out. All heads twisted to the right. There, just a stone's throw to the south, lay a terrible sight. The field of the massacred, untouched since the previous year. Bones, stripped of every last morsel of flesh, bleached pure-white by the sun. The bloody, staring eyes of that day were now empty, gaping sockets, sprigs of rye grass sprouting through rib cages, trembling in the delicate breeze. The mouths locked in death cries were now lolling white jawbones. The vicious flesh wounds were absent – now just brutal scores and holes in the skulls and limbs, some with semi-rotted arrow shafts still lodged where they had struck. Rusted spathions, faded shields and crumbling fragments of armour speckled this grim sight.

Up ahead, the imperial banner rose, swishing twice, and a series of buccina cries confirmed it. 'Time to don arms and armour,' Apion said, reading the signal. He had been in the discussions where it was agreed that they would march unencumbered until they reached the unstable lands of Theodosiopolis, still several days away. The bones, it seemed, had served to highlight how far inside Byzantine territory the Seljuk scimitar could swing. With a rustle of iron, leather and felt, the men of the column dressed as if for battle.

They rode on in sombre silence until late afternoon. The next voice they heard was a sharp cry. A jagged Norman twang.

He and Sha twisted to the sound. Two riders hared from the east, coming for the head of the column at pace. One was a Norman of the vanguard. The other a tagma horseman in a fine iron klibanion, no helm and armed only with the spathion strapped to his swordbelt. And he wore an eyepatch, purple veins shuddering from its edges. The emperor, Apion, Igor and his clutch of varangoi were quick to react to the shout, coming forward to intercept the pair. Romanus sat straight in his saddle. 'It is Diabatenus, my rider. The exchange!' he gasped.

Apion's ears pricked up at the words. He eyed the tagma rider. Bar his disfigurement, he had a handsome face and thick, sleek and swept-back brown locks.

'*Basileus!*' the rider called out, dismounting and saluting nimbly.

'Report,' Romanus said.

'I found the Sultan. I spoke with him. I tried as best I could to underline your sincerity… but he seemed uncertain of the trade. He doubted you. Indeed he…' Diabatenus dropped his gaze, 'he said it was a pity you did not send two riders to him, for then he could have sent the other back to you with my head by way of reply.'

Romanus looked around the men of his retinue, then to Apion. Sadness lined his eyes. 'How can a man dismiss an offer of a bloodless trade? He must surely know that I will now march on the Lake Van fortresses and seize them by force. His garrisons will be slain should they not surrender.'

Apion sighed. 'I played shatranj with him once, after his horde took Caesarea. I sat across from him, unsure of whether I would end the night free to leave… or with his dagger in my belly. Fortunately, he let me and the citizens leave unharmed, but I saw then that he was two beings within one: a valorous leader and a dog of war.'

Romanus' expression darkened. 'Then we will be compelled to seize Manzikert and Chliat by force, it seems. And I presume the Sultan will bring his armies to those lands too, in an effort to block our armies?'

'No, *Basileus,*' Diabatenus replied, a beaming smile replacing his prior sobriety. 'His sieges of Edessa and Aleppo failed. He was outsmarted by the doux of our city and the Fatimid governor of the other. His army was on the brink of starvation and he had to disband them. As I rode away from our parley, they were already melting away in small groups, hurrying back into the eastern sands to their homes. The Sultan and the few riders he had left were set to follow them and return to the heart of the Seljuk realm.'

Romanus' eyes darted. 'So after years of smashing against our borders and expanding his realm, the *Mountain Lion* has foundered?'

Apion leaned in to the emperor's ear. 'Do not be fooled by some ruse the Doux of Edessa might have pulled off, or take confidence from our number. Remember, the Sultan's armies are founded on the principle of the feigned retreat.'

Diabatenus flashed a grin at Apion, his sense of hearing evidently as sharp as his looks. 'I assure you, *Haga,* this was no ordered retreat. The Seljuk armies were panicked and eager to be gone from their regiments.'

Romanus seemed to mull over the report for what felt like an eternity. The column had halted, every man gazing at their emperor. At last, Romanus looked up, meeting the eyes of his retinue and then coming to Apion. 'Then it seems that circumstance favours us. We continue east, to Chliat, to Manzikert.'

CHAPTER 14

The Gathering of the Horde

In a pine forest north of the plain of Khoi, a bleak and barely populated border district at the north-western edge of the Seljuk dominion, Bey Soundaq crouched by the rock pool, lifting and tossing pebbles into the shallow waters absently. He paused for a moment and gazed at his reflection as the water stilled, seeing the lines that dominated his face and the wispy, white strands of his thinning hair. *An old man in a young man's fighting garb*, he thought, clutching a hand to the mail shirt that now hung loose on his withering frame. Feeling every one of his years and more, he swiftly lifted and threw another pebble to disperse the reflection.

He looked through the canopy of branches above into the unblemished afternoon sky and recalled the times in his youth, as the son of a lowly steppe rider. He had risen from his lot to prove his valour in the wars of Sultan Tugrul. He had become a bey – a leader of men – before he was twenty. Images flashed through his mind; of the many battles along the Byzantine borderlands, the epic clashes with the Fatimids, the thunder in his heart in the heat of battle. He remembered the end of one such clash. He had fallen to his knees and pressed his forehead to the blood-stained dust, praying to Allah. But, with a mixture of guilt and anticipation, his thoughts were not on his god, but on the path to glory that awaited him. It had seemed almost certain then. Tugrul had suggested he might be raised to lead a ghulam wing. A prestigious post indeed, and only a few steps away from the Sultan's throne.

But in the years that followed he had been forgotten, swept aside by the countless other brave young warriors who had caught the eye of Tugrul and then Alp Arslan. Thus, at forty-nine years old, he had moved no further forward. He spent his days patrolling these far-flung forests and mountain passes. He had a fine villa, slaves, and a brave band of ghazi riders who fought at his word. He wanted for nothing. Nothing bar the lost glory of his youth.

'Where did it all go wrong?' he sighed. Then he chuckled. 'I still taunt myself with that question, when I know the answer full well.' His mind's eye flashed back to the day, sixteen years ago. Tugrul had despatched him and his riders to the Byzantine Thema of Chaldia, with a licence to ravage that border province. *Plunder all the wagons that dare to travel their roads, break their trade networks, terrify the citizens and thin the garrisons!* Tugrul had enthused. And so they had done as was asked. Within weeks, he and his men had woven a trail of desolation through the mountain passes of that land. Then they came to a small, hilltop village. An insignificant little settlement with barely a hundred or so farmers dwelling there. He had seen it as an easy picking that day. Yet he had left with his confidence shattered. A young Byzantine soldier had orchestrated a desperate and ingenious defence of the town, thinning his riders by drawing them onto a line of stakes, then scattering them with tarred pigs set aflame.

'Set your mind at rest, old fool,' he smiled bitterly at his reflection again, 'the *Haga* has vanquished many men sharper than you.'

He twisted away from the rock pool and cast his gaze over his men. One hundred and forty-three ghazi riders. They sat around, polishing their mail shirts and horn lamellar vests, darning their felt jackets or grooming and feeding their mounts. Some honed their scimitars and axes, others loosed arrows into a fallen pine. Some of these men had been with him that day. Others were the sons of men there that day but lost to the sword since. Time, it seemed, was slowly sweeping his name into the dust.

'Ah, glory, perhaps we will meet after death?' he chuckled with a shake of the head.

He made to stand to join his men who were cooking up a pot of salep. But he hesitated, noticing the horses' ears prick up. He put a hand to the ground. Rumbling. His eyes narrowed, flicking around the surrounding treeline. His mind, still plagued with memories of that long-lost skirmish, conjured images of Byzantine riders. *Surely not out here, beyond their realm?*

He rose and peered into the shade of the trees, seeing the branches judder, the dull outline of thrashing hooves and the shadow of an iron rider. The blood seemed to halt in his veins as the rider passed under a shaft of sunlight. Sparkling emerald eyes glowered at him from a shadow of a face. Memories of that day grappled his heart. Cold fear had him. His men rushed to take up their weapons, stretch their bows. Soundaq grappled the hilt of his scimitar and bared his teeth. 'Come on then you—' His nascent roar fell away. His men relaxed.

The rider was in Seljuk scale armour, and the handful of men riding behind were clearly ghazis. The lead rider prised his stud-rimmed helm from his head, revealing youthful cinnamon skin, a tuft beard on the chin, sleek dark locks held in a ponytail and those piercing green eyes.

What's your story, lad? he wondered, edging forward, noticing that his escort wore white falcon feathers in the rims of their helms – like the steppe riders of old.

'Bey Soundaq?' the boy warrior said.

Soundaq nodded. 'Protector of the northern passes. And you are?'

'Bey Taylan, son of Bey Nasir,' the lad replied.

Soundaq's eyes widened. 'Nasir?' he uttered in realisation, glancing once again over the familiar armour he wore. The high-ranking Bey Nasir had been one of the young warriors who had swept him aside. 'Have your men dismount, Bey Taylan,' Soundaq said swiftly, bowing as he realised the gap in rank between he and the boy warrior. 'I will see to it that you are fed and that your mounts are watered.'

'We have little time to sit and eat,' Taylan replied curtly, drawing his scimitar and sweeping it through the air once, twice and again, as if slicing up an imaginary opponent, before drawing the blade close to his face to examine the edge. 'In the south, on the plains of Khoi, the Sultan musters an army. To the west, the Emperor of Byzantium wanders eastwards blindly. And with him,' he paused, his eyes growing distant, 'is the *Haga.*'

'The scourge of the borderlands?' Soundaq replied. His heart thumped in a way it had not done for many, many years. Like a war drum.

—

Alp Arslan stood by his tent at the centre of the vast, sun-baked and writhing mustering plain, hands clasped behind his back, his green silk yalma fluttering in the breeze of the oft-passing clusters of horsemen. He wore a leather band around his head to keep his hair from his eyes, and the ends of his flowing moustache were knotted on the nape of his neck. The drills were rotated to allow every ghazi wing to have a chance to show their prowess, while those not in practice would rest and have their mounts graze on the fine pasturelands near the river that bordered one edge of the plain. He cast his eyes across the many thousands of his mustered cavalry. Apart from a small wing of a thousand ultra-heavily armed and armoured ghulam and a regiment of a few thousand finely armoured akhi spearmen – all collected from Baghdad by Nizam – the rest were ghazis. Some twenty thousand of these nimble and deadly riders. And there were more to come, he realised, seeing the small bands of border patrols trotting down the paths of the surrounding mountains, flooding into this plain like meltwater streams to join the horde.

'It reminds me of long past days,' Nizam said, shuffling from the tent to stand beside him. The aged vizier nodded with a wistful look in his eye. 'When your uncle Tugrul and your father formed the hordes that won the first of the Sultanate's lands. Those lands were won almost entirely with steppe cavalry. Master archers who bewildered the foot soldiers and lumbering riders of Persia.'

Alp Arslan smiled dryly at this. The unattainable days that Tugrul had taunted him with were here again, it seemed. 'Aye, but then we had hunters in crude leathers and furs; now we have finely garbed soldiers.' He proffered a hand to the nearest sweeping wing. Each man wore horn, iron or felt armour, a thickly padded cap or a conical helm, fine leather boots and linen trousers. Each man carried a composite bow, a scimitar, a teardrop shield and a short, light lance. Some had lasso ropes dangling from their belts, others had war hammers or axes. 'None of them finer than Bey Taylan's White Falcons.' He nodded to the nearly five-thousand-strong wing who outshone the rest. Each of them were now well-trained or training in the art of the reverse shot and the knuckle hold – five or more arrows clasped between the fingers of their draw hands. Indeed, many of them now boasted the feathers that marked them as master archers.

'The nock and draw is an impressive spectacle, but the reinforced stirrups...' Nizam nodded. 'I am no strategist, but they have been something of a masterstroke.' As if prompted to justify this praise, a cluster of some one hundred White Falcons swept past and stood tall and steady on their stirrups. The dark-skinned and moustachioed riders each closed one eye behind their nocked, stretched bows, their dark locks and falcon feathers fluttering in the slipstream. Then they loosed. *Thwack!* Not a single arrow missed the target board.

Nizam nodded in approval: 'Exceptiona—' *Thwack!*

His words were cut off as another volley hammered into the target, the archers nocking another arrow from their knuckles an instant after loosing the last. Then another, and another. *Thwack! Thwack! Thwack!* And so it went on until their quivers were empty.

'Bey Taylan deserves much praise for his initiatives,' Nizam concluded, shaking his head in near-disbelief. 'He has revived near-forgotten arts and blended them with new ones.'

'Well you can lavish praise on him now, Vizier,' Alp Arslan grinned, pointing to the nearest of the mountain tracks to the north. There, winding down the rocky mountainside was Bey Taylan. In his wake, some seven hundred more ghazi riders followed. They headed straight for the Sultan's tent.

'Sultan!' Taylan barked, sliding from his saddle and dipping to one knee before Alp Arslan in one motion. He scooped his helmet from his head, the mail aventail rustling, then looked up. 'I bring the riders of the northern borders, and Kurdish mercenaries from beyond, as instructed.'

'Fine work again, Bey Taylan,' the Sultan said.

Nizam nodded. 'Now this force can march west with confidence.'

'But we do not yet number enough to tackle the Byzantines. We have twenty-four, maybe twenty-five thousand horse. They have forty thousand in their ranks,' Taylan countered.

Alp Arslan smiled. 'You never stop thinking, probing, looking for a weakness, do you? You will make a fine second man to a Sultan one day, Taylan. Perhaps when my son, Malik, inherits my throne, you will be by his side?'

Taylan seemed oblivious to this praise. His brow was knitted in a frown as he looked over the horde. 'I will think of the future only once this clash is over. We must address the shortfall in our numbers.'

Alp Arslan tried to disguise his own doubts over this very matter. 'There is no time for such deliberation, Bey Taylan. We ride for Lake Van tomorrow.'

The armies retired to the sea of yurts nestled in the shade of the surrounding mountains, and Taylan was the last man at the heart of the dusty mustering plain, his chestnut mare snorting and shuffling a few paces away, munching on the remains of some fodder. His shadow stretched long across the flat ground as the sun began to sink below the western horizon. He watched a thin coil of red-gold dust whip up in a light breeze, then dance across the deserted field.

It had been a good day, he mused. And tomorrow? Tomorrow would be the first step in his journey to confront the *Haga*. His mind raced and his heart rapped on his breastbone.

A lone eagle shrieked high above, stifling his growing hubris. But he glanced up to see only an empty, dusk sky, streaked with pink, orange and sapphire. The bloodlust returned. 'I will play my part,' he called into the ether. 'I will form the spear that pierces the beast's heart! The *Haga* and his empire will burn!'

'To hear those words makes me wonder if Bey Nasir is still alive and well,' a frail voice spoke, only inches from his ear.

Taylan swung round. The dancing plume of dust had taken form as an elderly woman. Her spindly frame was wrapped in a white robe. Her silver, wispy hair framed a face puckered and lined with great age. Her sightless eyes were milky yet utterly fixed on him.

'And if only he had listened to my words, perhaps that might still be the case,' she added.

Taylan's fingers moved to his scimitar hilt but, as if guided by a warm, invisible hand, they fell away again, all alarm swiftly draining from his veins. 'You knew my father?' he asked.

The crone smiled wryly at this. 'Which one, Bey Taylan… which one?'

Taylan frowned at this, expecting shame to wash over him at the implication. But for once, it did not come. 'Bey Nasir. My true father. You knew him?'

'I did. I also know your blood father, Apion.'

Taylan shook his head. 'Do not use his name. Father hated his name.'

The crone's face lengthened. 'When a father bestows nothing upon his son but his own hatred, something has gone terribly, terribly wrong. And hate is such a poisonous word. Bey Nasir once thought he hated everything about Apion. He talked only of destroying the *Haga*. Words almost identical to yours today.'

Taylan looked to the dust, his eyes darting. Finally he looked up again. 'If someone had taken all you had, would you rest until you had redressed the balance?'

'Apion took nothing from you. He gave life to you. Nasir died on Apion's blade only because of his own mule-headedness,' she said, frowning now, one bony finger wagging. 'And your mother lies ill – growing frailer by the day – and you choose to whittle away your time clashing swords and snarling about men you know little of.'

Guilt clutched at Taylan's heart. It had been so long since he had visited Mother. Too long. Every time he visited, he longed to speak to her as he had once done. As a boy, he could talk with her freely. They would spot birds and butterflies in the gardens of their home, go to market in the mornings and cook together in the afternoons. A lost age, he realised. And soon she would be but memory.

Come closer, son, there is something I must tell you…

A volcanic sorrow threatened to erupt at that moment, and he only just suffocated it with a mask of ire. 'So you expect me to forgive him… the *Haga*?'

'I expect nothing of any man,' the crone snorted at this. 'And I repeat, you have nothing to forgive Apion for. But know this: I was with Nasir at the last. I walked with him into the grey land. He lamented his years of bitterness, longing to return to them and relive them well. Longing to bestow something upon you other than his hatred.'

Taylan contemplated her words, seeking out an answer in the dust around his feet. 'But I swore to avenge his death.'

'By slaying Apion, your blood father? One of the few men your mother still cares for? You would break her heart.'

'But she has not spoken to the *Haga* in many years,' Taylan replied.

'Yet she has never forgotten him. She would mourn him and her grief would be strong. More,' she stabbed a finger at him, 'she would mourn you, Taylan, were you to lose yourself to war as Nasir did. That grief alone might be too much for her.' She placed a hand on his shoulder. 'Men are defined by their choices, Taylan. Now it is time for you to choose: slay the *Haga* and break your mother's heart, or stow your blade and let go of this false vengeance.'

Taylan felt a stab of panic in his breast, memories of Mother in her hospital bed flashing before him. 'But… the hatred has become me and I it. Without it, what would I be?'

'Find out, Taylan. Find out.'

He looked up. She was gone. The dust plume danced once more and then the breeze faded and it was gone. A fading eagle's cry sounded.

At once, his emotions went to war, combing over her reason and seeking fault with her every argument. At last, he strode with purpose for his mare, vaulting onto the saddle. He drew his scimitar and glowered at his reflection in the blade. He saw nothing but his sparkling green eyes. A pang of grief and unspent anger broiled in his veins as he glanced up into the empty sky.

'You cannot ask a man to go against his heart, old woman!'

CHAPTER 15

City of Echoes

The early-August sky was grey and the air intolerably muggy, and the gloom seemed to rob the armoured column of its lustre as they marched up into the Armenian highlands via the northerly passes. This was the route decided by the befuddled old priest in the church at Malagina. As they ascended, the air grew mercifully cooler, but thinner too, and the pace of the march slowed. This eastern land – beyond the themata – was nominally in Byzantine control, presided over by the border doukes and their mercenary armies. In truth, there was little sign of imperial control. No waystations, forts or patrols.

Soon though, they were on the uphill road towards the city of Theodosiopolis. That fortified, moat-ringed city was a solid Byzantine holding, and it would serve as a final staging post before the campaign column struck out on the final leg of the march to Lake Van. Vitally, its stores would provide the grain and water required for man and horse to make this strike into enemy lands.

'There she is!' Igor bellowed, stretching out a finger.

All necks craned to see the towering Mount Drakon up ahead, one face carpeted in green shrubs and grass, the other a haggard, rocky and arid tumble of scree. The imperious vista inspired the men, and they took to cheering as they approached; for at the foot of this mount was the city of Theodosiopolis.

Apion had been there just once, many years ago, to help plan the new moat system. But as they approached and came within sight of the city, he realised that something was wrong. The city's walls seemed to be a shade of grey, reflecting the mood of the sky, and even the red-tiled roofs visible within seemed dulled with dirt, weeds sprouting from the cracks. And there was a distinct lack of movement on the walls. Yes, the purple imperial banners fluttered up there in the breeze, but they were ragged and filthy, and the usual glimmer of helm or spear was absent. The emperor saw this too and gave a nod to the signophoroi, a tacit command to bring the column to a halt, some five hundred feet from the city walls. As the campaign banners were waved and the ranks crunched to a standstill, the emperor and his retinue scoured the scene. Silence, bar a faint and whistling breeze.

'Where is my vanguard?' Romanus spoke testily, scanning the road ahead, as deserted as the city that it wound past.

They gazed ahead, each man imagining the Normans and the kursores of the vanguard lying slaughtered and unseen, ahead, destined to become another field of bones. But, with a thunder of hooves, the Normans and kursores of the vanguard burst round from the rear of the city, having circled the walls. They were calling out to the battlements, receiving no reply, only echoes.

'Look, the gates have taken a battering recently.' Alyates squinted ahead. The tall, arched timber gates were splintered around head-height, the tell-tale marks of a ram-head impressed on the planks. More, they lay slightly ajar.

'But the walls remain intact,' Tarchianotes replied. 'Though not for want of trying.' He nodded to the piles of rubble and earth that had been tipped into the moat channel to form a bridge. Below it lay a broken siege ladder, and the stonework here was charred black from fire.

'Look.' Bryennios pointed to the grass by the roadside. Hundreds of arrows lay embedded in the soil, like some foreign crop.

'Seljuk raiders,' Apion said, recognising the fletching immediately.

'Aye, and incessant, they were too!' a croaking voice startled them all.

Apion turned to see a withered old fellow in a coarse grey robe at the roadside. He led a single oxen and his twig-like legs looked painfully bowed.

'The trade dried up first,' the old man said. 'They burnt any wagons that came near the city and slew the drivers. A shortage of jewels and fine pots is no great hardship, but when they started attacking the grain wagons... well, enough was enough. The populace left this cursed place nearly six months ago. They fled south to seek protection from the Armenian princes, or north to live in the countryside and help work the farmlands to earn their grain.'

'And the garrison?' Romanus said, barging through the men of his retinue.

'*Basileus?* So the rumours are true,' the old man said with a half-smile, casting his eye over Romanus' armour and then sweeping his gaze down the road along the column. 'It has been a long time since an emperor made it this far east. I spent my career as a skutatos, praying to see such a sight. Yet it never came. And now I am too old to ma—'

'The garrison!' Igor barked, shaking the old man from his musings.

'Ah, yes. The shower of cowards who walked these walls dissolved into the countryside too. Seventy men, *Basileus*, just seventy men were spared to guard this place. I could say I don't blame them for running, just as I wouldn't blame mice for scattering before a wildcat. But there is nothing to fear here. Just as the populace left long ago, the raiders did too. The danger for you and this fine army lies further east.'

'East?'

'I have heard word that the forts near the great blue lake are modestly garrisoned by their Seljuk masters. They have heard of your approach and are right now putting the crop fields west of Chliat to the torch. They mean to offer you not a single grain and not a drop of encouragement.'

'They seldom do, old man,' Romanus smiled, heeling his mount forward.

Apion followed the emperor, his retinue and the varangoi forward to the gates while the rest of the column waited a few hundred feet from the city. The riders of the vanguard pushed the gate open. It groaned on its hinges and revealed the deserted streets within.

'Be vigilant,' Romanus said, beckoning them forward.

The clopping of their mounts' hooves echoed through the broad way that led to the heart of the city and the many narrow alleys that sprouted off from it. Cups, clothing, bags and trinkets were strewn on the flagstones, entangled with the weeds that had shot up through every crack.

'They must have been swift to desert their homes,' Igor noted grimly.

Apion recalled the last time he had been here. The place had been vibrant – thick with traders and shoppers and well-kept by the militarily minded doux who had once commanded the garrison. Now, it seemed like just another cadaver. Forgotten, abandoned.

They trotted into the centre of the city. Here, a sturdy limestone keep sat astride a man–made mound. Untouched by rock, blade or flame, it seemed.

'They just gave up,' Alyates said, his words unintentionally amplified by the walls of the church and granary that boxed in the keep square. Apion looked up and around, seeing the serpentine, green tendrils of nature that clung to every wall, weaving through open windows and infiltrating homes. Claiming back the once–proud city. They came to a fountain that lay dried up and filled with dust. In the centre, a pair of marble legs sprouted and then halted at the thigh, the top half of this ornamentation lying in the dust in the fountain's basin. It was an ancient statue of Emperor Justinian. Romanus stared at the broken effigy, wordless.

'Have the men set up camp outside the wall. We will use the keep as a planning room.'

When night fell, a vast band of flickering orange torches illuminated the flatland outside Theodosiopolis, wrapping round the city and touching the lower slopes of Mount Drakon. Incongruously, the only lights within the city walls came from the lonely keep at its centre.

Six men were gathered around an oak table there, poring over the campaign map and a sheaf of papers. A fire crackled and spat in the hearth behind them, casting dark shadows on the walls and spicing the air with woodsmoke. Apion watched on as the debate raged, still weighing his thoughts.

'We cannot split the army, *Basileus*!' Alyates pleaded. 'It goes against every military maxim.'

Tarchianotes was swift to counter: 'But if that old goat's word was true, then we face a great danger of starvation if we do not. The grain supplies we expected to find here are absent, just like the population and the garrison. And this...' He jabbed a finger at their current position on the map, then dragged it east to Lake Van and tapped it there. 'This is not Byzantium. We will find no supply dumps, no friendly – or deserted – settlements from which we can levy food and fodder. We *must* split the army and send our fastest regiments to drive off these rogues around Chliat before they leave the earth there burnt and barren. Forty thousand well–fed men might well bring victory, but forty thousand starving men will ensure defeat – regardless of whether we come face to face with the Seljuks.' He looked to Romanus. 'Take half with you to Manzikert, *Basileus*, to begin the siege. Take the infantry and those who will be able to storm that sturdy fortress. Send the other half – the riders and the foot archers who will be able to move swiftly – to the fields around Chliat. These men will clear the land of Seljuk rogues and secure the grain and forage that is to be had there. Then, when Manzikert falls, we can be reunited to take Chliat as well. Is that not the objective of this campaign?'

'Have you lost your mind?' Philaretos slammed a fist on the table in challenge to Tarchianotes. 'Stay together, there will be forage enough! Some may perish. But is that not expected on such a great expedition?'

Bryennios shook his head. 'A few dead or dying from hunger swiftly becomes a hundred, and then a thousand. I have seen such a sight before, and I pray I never have to see it again. Should our men perish, then let it be by the sword and not meekly, crying out for bread. We should separate the army. One half takes Manzikert, the other half secures the grain at Chliat, as Doux Tarchianotes suggests.'

'I hear two voices for staying together and two for splitting,' Romanus said. Then he turned to Apion. 'Well, Strategos, what is your view?'

Apion balanced both views. There was danger in each. But Tarchianotes was right. The supply train was low on rations. Dangerously low. He had checked inside one of the touldon wagons and noted that they had grain enough only for a few days' bread at best. Their stores were due to be replenished here in this dead city, but the empty grain silos offered nothing other than cobwebs and dust. If they moved on as a single column, their pace would be slow and lumbering. If the old man's reports were true then the grain fields near Chliat would be ash by the time they reached them. Every fibre of his being screamed at him, demanding that he listen to the memories of old Cydones and old Mansur, two military giants of their day. *Never divide your forces. Sooner split your own head with an axe than send half of your army away,* Cydones' stern words echoed in his mind. Then Mansur's gravelly tones interrupted, as if challenging his old foe: *Who would clad his men in fine iron coats and boots and give them bright shields and tall spears, but neglect to keep their bellies full and their spirits high? Who, but a fool?* Apion gazed into the fire. *There is no correct choice, is there?* he answered the memories, then looked to the emperor and met the eyes of the others. 'We cannot risk splitting the army,' he said. 'Yet we cannot risk marching on as one force.'

Philaretos snorted at this. 'Such wisdom!' he spat. 'What else can you bring to this discussion; that night will be black and day bright?'

Apion resisted the urge to snap back at the firebrand doux. 'Night is black, day is bright… and dusk is grey.'

Philaretos' scowl deepened.

Apion tried not to let the man's ire hurry him. 'The men tire because of the march, Doux. Marching is an exhausting detail, especially in the thinner air of these highlands. Every infantryman requires a pint of water per hour and a pouch of grain, salted meat or cheese morning and night. We have talked only of two options; split the army or keep it whole. But there is a third option. Abstain from the march, and the men would require less.'

'Stay here?' Bryennios cocked an eyebrow. 'Why – to solidify our borders in this region? But again, what would we eat?'

At once, another squabble broke out. 'Impossible – the Lake Van fortresses must be taken,' Tarchianotes rasped. 'We cannot stay here!'

'But the empire has clearly lost control over this city and these lands. We need to consolidate!' Alyates snapped in riposte, stabbing his finger at the table-top map around the area of Theodosiopolis.

Romanus hushed them, both hands raised, casting a stern glare around the table. 'Strategos – perhaps you should explain your thinking.'

Apion nodded. 'We should stay here, but only for a few days. Long enough for our kursores to sweep the countryside, bring in what rations they can from the farmlands where the populace of this city now dwell. Grain *is* out there.'

'Enough to feed nearly forty thousand men for the week of marching that will take us to Lake Van?' Tarchianotes frowned.

'Why not? This city was once populous enough to have grain silos overflowing with surplus – and that was when just a portion of the locals worked the land. If even a quarter of those who lived within these walls have fled to the farmlands in the north, then now they will certainly have grain and fodder aplenty. There is no certainty that this approach will work, but if it does, then we need not consider splitting the army, and our well-fed and united force would be primed to sweep over Manzikert and Chliat. You know this, all of you.' Apion looked up, his face uplit by the flames. He held the gaze of each of the retinue until they looked away or nodded. He looked to the emperor last.

Romanus gazed back for what felt like an eternity. 'Then that is what we must do.'

Tarchianotes stood back from the table. 'Folly,' he muttered under his breath. 'We should split the forces and move on – at haste!'

'If we fail to gather the grain and rations, *Basileus*...' Bryennios added his dissent, albeit more graciously.

'Then we will be compelled to split the army.' Romanus glowered at him. 'But first, send out our champion rider with a wing of kursores. Speed is of the essence.'

Diabatenus admired his beauty, reflected on the flat of his spathion. If he squinted enough, he could not see the purple veins snaking from his eyepatch. God truly favoured him, it seemed. 'Lead the kursores to the farmlands in the north, you say?' he grinned, looking up to the gruff Rus axeman who had come to his tent.

'At first light,' the varangos confirmed, handing him a weighty sack of coins. 'Use this to buy whatever the people can spare. The emperor prays that you will ride as swiftly as always.'

'It will be done,' he nodded.

When the Rus left, Diabatenus turned his gaze back on his sword blade. A broad, white-toothed grin now split his features. An alternative brief had already been supplied to him by the other man from the emperor's retinue who had come to him only a short while ago. The lost riches of his racing career would be dwarfed by the gold he would earn from this. He lifted his eye patch to reveal the cracked bone, the welt of pustules and the scarring that lined his empty eye socket. His grin faded into a sneer.

Yes, it will be done.

Genesios halted his oxen, seeing the dust cloud coming from the south. Fear gripped him instantly. *Another Seljuk raid?*

'Father?' his boy whimpered, sitting astride the plough.

'The raiders rarely venture this far north, Nicholas,' he lied. 'There is nothing to fear.'

His guts turned over as the dust cloud came closer. From the many farmsteads and shacks around his, he heard wails of distress, saw women gathering the hems of their robes and running from the fields, men throwing down their hoes and tools or grappling them like weapons, some trembling. They had fled the great stone walls of Theodosiopolis to leave behind raids like this. *Let the Seljuk raiders have the city and the trade route, we desire only to be left in peace and safety with our families*, he had implored the doubters. He clutched the Chi-Rho on his breast and prayed he had not led them all to their doom. He glanced to the barely started earthworks they had planned to develop into some form of defensive barrier, and cursed their lack of progress on this.

'Father!' Nicholas cried, a smile like a breaking dawn spreading across his fresh face. 'They are imperial riders!'

And indeed they were. Kursores, he realised. Light and swift cavalrymen, torsos wrapped in iron or leather klibania, heads crowned in glistening iron helms. Genesios shuddered with a sigh of utter relief, then followed it up with a lungful of laughter as his fear melted away, leaving him shaking and drained. *Thank you*, he whispered skywards.

The handsome, eyepatch wearing lead rider pulled up before him, clods of dew-damp earth spraying as the man's mount circled. 'The people of Theodosiopolis?' he mused, casting his good eye over the fertile strip of land, his gaze coming to a rest on the timber grain silos and storehouses. 'I am Diabatenus of the Vigla. Who governs this community?' the man asked, stroking his wind-ruffled, dark-brown locks back into place.

'I do,' Genesios replied. 'The governor and the garrison of Theodosiopolis fled and bought residence in the hilltop towns of the Armenian princes.' He pointed a finger to the southern horizon. 'The people without such means needed a leader.'

'A brave man it is who steps forward in treacherous times.' Diabatenus nodded firmly. 'Now, you have surplus food, I understand. Grain, salted meats, fish, cheeses, honey, nuts?'

Genesios hesitated before replying. 'We have stockpiled for the winter, yes, but we are likely to need it in those cold, harsh months.'

'I find coin often supplants the need for other things,' Diabatenus grinned, lifting the heavy sack of coins from the back of his mount. 'The emperor and his campaign army lie camped outside the walls of your old city, some ten miles south of here.'

'The campaign army is in these lands? I had heard only rumour of this.' Genesios' eyes widened. 'Then he means to buy our surplus?'

he looked to Nicholas and thought of the boy. He and many others would go hungry this winter without the surplus in the storehouses. But with coin they could replenish the stores over the next few months by visiting the northern market towns. He looked up to the handsome rider. 'When I left Theodosiopolis I brought with me God and all that I love about God's empire. I will do anything for the emperor, God's chosen one, anything for Byzantium.' He smiled at the rider and beckoned him over to the silos.

'In here you will find maybe a hundred wagon-loads of food and fodder.' He opened the storehouse doors to reveal tightly bound bales of hay, hanging meats, various amphorae and brimming barrels of grain. 'You should bring your wagons round from the west, as the ground is rough and...' His words trailed off as the acrid tang of burning resin curled into his nostrils. He turned around, frowning. The handsome rider was grinning, the kursoris beside him had lit a torch.

'As I said, coin can bring about almost any possibility.' Diabatenus' grin grew. He turned to the kursoris, clapped a hand on the sack of coins then nodded towards the silo. 'Put it to the torch. Earn your share.'

The kursoris looked uncertain, glancing back over his shoulder from whence they had come, then to the faces of Genesios and little Nicholas, then to the sack of coins. His expression hardened.

'No!' Genesios roared as the man tossed the torch onto the hay bales inside the silo. Several more riders did likewise to the other buildings nearby. 'What have you done?' He crumpled to his knees as angry flames and thick black smoke billowed from the silos and storehouses. 'You have killed us all. Now we will not last even until the winter, let alone through it.'

Diabatenus grinned down at him and shrugged. 'Then let me offer you some mercy.' He nimbly swept out his spathion, hung low in his saddle and swirled the blade round in one stroke, hacking into the side of Genesios' neck. The farmer shuddered where he knelt, the blade cutting deep, a spray of red showering his son before dark blood came in sheets.

Genesios reached out to his son, longing to protect the lad, but the blackness of death swept him away.

Diabatenus took a rag from his belt to clean the blood of his first ever kill from his blade. *Damn, but that felt good*, he realised. He had missed the raw, visceral power of the Hippodrome, but this was a fine substitute. He kicked his mount into a walk around the rising inferno. *This will do it*, he enthused. *I will forge a chariot of solid gold once Psellos pays me for this.*

At that moment he felt utterly invincible. His charm, his looks, his wits and his abilities. Even his skin felt like cold, hard steel. So it was a surprise when he felt a dull blow in his flank. He turned round, frowning, expecting that one of his fellow riders had clumsily barged into him. Instead, he looked down to see the drawn, haunted eyes of the farmer's little boy, gazing up at him. The lad's face was smoke-stained and tear-streaked. He held the shaft of a hoe in both hands. Diabatenus' gaze ran up the hoe shaft to where the blunt blade rested under the hem of his iron klibanion. Blood washed from his flank in waves. He felt the urge to correct the lad, tell him he had been mistaken. *You can't hurt me*, he thought, *I am Diabatenus, Champion of the Races, Breaker of Hearts, Best of the Vigla…* His thoughts fell away as he slid from the saddle, thudded to the ground then gazed up at the sky, his body growing terribly cold.

The last thing he saw was the farmer's boy standing over him with a heavy rock in his hands. A heartbeat later, the rock crashed down, and Diabatenus' beauty was crushed into the dirt like an egg.

—

Apion stood on the battlements of Theodosiopolis, clasping his helm underarm as he gazed into the clear, unspoilt morning sky. But his thoughts were dark and murky. Two days had passed since Diabatenus and his riders had been sent out. And it seemed that they had simply vanished into the ether. Romanus had insisted they keep word of this from the rest of the army. *We bury this news and we split the army. It is our only option now. Tarchianotes' regiments will forge south-east towards Chliat, and I will lead the rest at a slower pace towards Manzikert.*

He looked down to the vast camp outside of the city. Half of the site now lay empty. To the south, the rumbling was just beginning to fade as eighteen thousand men slipped over the horizon, despatched on the most direct route to Chliat to seize the fields, forage and fodder there. Not just any men either – the cream of the campaign army. The Scholae Tagma, the Hikanatoi Tagma, the Stratelatai Tagma and the Vigla Tagma – more than eight thousand cavalry, many of them the precious heavy kataphractoi. The hammer of the campaign. Supplementing them were the four hundred strong pack of Pecheneg riders. The infantry of the Optimates Tagma, the Anatolikon Thema and the Charsianon Thema, plus the bulk of the foot archers from the other themata had been despatched behind them at a quick march. Doux Tarchianotes had been entrusted with this fearsome and fast-moving corps.

'Strategos,' Sha called from the end of the battlements. 'We are to leave within the hour.'

Apion turned and nodded to the Malian. So it was to be that Romanus and the remaining half of the army – twenty-two-thousand strong – were to march directly for Manzikert. The make-up of this half was troubling.

There was a solid core. The infantry of the Chaldian Thema, the Cappadocian Thema and the Colonean Thema along with Prince Vardan and his two thousand Armenian spearmen. These men would happily bleed for the empire, without question. And the siege engines loaded onto the wagons would be well utilised on Manzikert's walls by Procopius and the artillerymen.

The make-up of the cavalry presented more issues. He saw Igor readying his Rus riders, polishing their white armour and honing their axes. These thousand riders were fierce and loyal, but as cavalry, they were not the most nimble. There was Bryennios' western army – five thousand strong. One in ten of these men were heavily armoured kataphractoi. The rest were the more lightly equipped kursores. These western riders were brave and skilled, but they had yet to face a Seljuk foe in full battle. This fact tossed up memories of Manuel Komnenos' over-confidence the previous year. Then there were the two thousand Oghuz archer cavalry and the five hundred Norman lancers; men with no love of Byzantium other than for the gold coin minted in her treasuries. Lastly, there was Scleros and the seven thousand of the magnate armies. They busied themselves strapping their overly ornate weapons to their belts and backs, supping neat wine and boasting with each other as to how they would smash the skulls of the Seljuk garrisons. This rabble were yet to be tested in a battle of any kind.

They had been involved in skirmishes with brigands along the way, but had never been seriously challenged. Would they stand firm and charge hard, should the need come? His gaze snagged on the one who stood solemnly amongst them. Andronikos Doukas. The young man was something of an enigma. Heedless of his shackles, he polished his armour and checked his horse's snaffle bit and scale apron. Probably the best soldier amongst them. Yet the son of John Doukas would ride into this battle with not so much as a dagger to wield. *Your father has a lot to answer for*, Apion mused, batting away the sliver of sympathy he felt.

Just then, the buccinas blared and the standards were raised above the myriad banda of infantry – assembled now in an offensive formation to present a broad front nearly a mile across. The priests raised the campaign cross, chanting as they walked before the formed ranks. He flitted down the stone steps and gladly departed the ghost city of Theodosiopolis, taking the reins of his Thessalian from Sha then riding to the front of the column where the emperor sat astride his dark stallion.

'*Ha-ga!*' the men of Chaldia chanted as he passed them, men from other themata joining in.

Romanus beheld him as he approached. Apion nodded, sliding his helm on his head. Romanus nodded in return, then raised his bejewelled spathion overhead. The chanting fell away. 'Forward – to our destiny!' the emperor cried.

They headed east, turned south to cross the Araxes River then journeyed through the broad Murat Su valley. It was early afternoon six days later – six days with scant half-rations but otherwise without incident – when they came to the top of a green hill. On the brow, the emperor halted the column. He raised a hand and pointed south, down the slope that lay before them.

'Look. At last we are on the cusp of all we have strived to achieve,' he said to his retinue, his voice but a whisper in the dry, hot air.

Apion gazed south, fixated on the black-walled fortress town, less than half a mile away, standing proudly where the hills faded into a dry, dusty flatland.

Manzikert!

A pack of swallows swooped and darted above the compact, tall and well-architected structure. The tiny silver dots of Manzikert's Seljuk garrison strolled back and forth on the battlements. The fortress was small – not much bigger than the citadel of Trebizond, but it was well situated on top of a small hill by a fresh brook.

He gazed on past the fortress. The dry plains of Manzikert stretched out for many miles to the south. They ended somewhere in the heat haze, and from that same haze sprouted an imperious mountain range. The tallest of these, Mount Tzipan, was snow-capped and rugged, and just behind its slopes, Apion noticed a shimmering sliver of blue. *Lake Van*. His mind turned over all he had been told of this land and the many maps he had scoured on this march. Somewhere, behind the mountains on that lake's northern shores lurked Chliat and its fertile farmlands. Hopefully those lands would soon be under the control of Tarchianotes and his men, and grain and fodder would be forthcoming. But it was the nearer fortress that drew his gaze once more. He beheld Manzikert and felt a chill of the unknown on his skin.

Destiny, he mouthed.

As he knew they would, the crone's words came to him.

I see a battlefield by an azure lake flanked by two mighty pillars.

He looked to Romanus, his eyes falling to the golden heart pendant on his breast.

At dusk you and the Golden Heart will stand together in the final battle, like an island in the storm. Walking that battlefield is Alp Arslan. The Mountain Lion is dressed in a shroud.

He scoured the horizon and frowned. The land was empty and at peace. Bar a modest Seljuk garrison on Manzikert's walls, oblivious to their observers, neither the Sultan nor his forces were anywhere to be seen. He had seen to it that Komes Peleus and Komes Stypiotes – two of his most loyal men from the Chaldian ranks – had ridden with Tarchianotes' half of the army, and had implored them to make sure that any signs of danger were communicated to the emperor at haste. There was nothing in the scene before him to rouse fear. But he recalled something he had forgotten from his childhood, before he had first walked the dark road to war. On a day as fine as this one, he had watched a family of robins working tirelessly in the clement air to construct a nest of twigs and feathers atop an old poplar tree near his parents' farmhouse. The mother robin had flitted to and fro, bringing twigs to the branch, while the hatchlings clung to the branches near the trunk and cheeped as they watched on. The sight had captivated him and he had remained fixated until nearly dusk. The nest complete, the birds had settled in their new home. Apion had turned to go back to his own home, when he felt a stiff breeze pick up. Moments later, it was a gale and then a storm. Grey clouds scudded across and then filled the sky, bringing night in moments. A stinging, chill rain battered down. The gale and the deluge served to bend the poplar in its wrath, casting the new nest from the branches. The hatchlings were dashed on the ground or swiftly pounced upon by foxes. In the end, only the elegiac song of the mother robin remained, piercing through the roar of the storm.

He cast another glance across the idyllic, summer-bathed countryside and shivered as if it was the dead of winter.

—

Tarchianotes scoured the green valleys ahead. It had been a hard march, but his many wings of kataphractoi and regiments of skutatoi and foot archers had nearly reached the shores of the great lake – and in good time. The towering mountains either side loomed over them like giants, casting them in shade as if separating them from the fine day above. He watched every bend ahead, wondering when he would see the blue waters.

'Chliat is but a mile away, sir,' Komes Peleus, riding by his side, shouted over the thunder of so many hooves. 'Does it not worry you that we have yet to sight a single Seljuk rider?'

Tarchianotes nodded by way of reply, casting the small komes a dismissive look. They had found some of the wheat fields burnt to ash and some still ripe with crop. But he wasn't looking merely for small parties of terrified Seljuks. When they reached the end of the valley, a murmur of excitement and anxiety broke out as a pleasant waterside breeze wafted over them and the land ahead revealed the azure waters of Lake Van, bathed in sunshine. And there, nestled just a few miles away along the lake's shores, stood the dark-brick fortress of Chliat. A small but sturdy fortress that resembled something of a boil on the pleasant bay. Tarchianotes raised a hand for a full halt, just at the edge of the valley's shade. The thunder of hooves and boots ceased at once.

Peleus gawped at the fortress. 'We have come too far. The emperor was clear that we were not to approach the citadel.'

'We have come just as far as I wished,' Tarchianotes sighed, his gaze fixed on the fort. Just a few hundred helms and spears glinted atop Chliat's walls.

Peleus frowned, seeing Tarchianotes' gaze remain on the fortress. 'Sir, the emperor was adamant we should not attempt to take Chliat until the two halves of the army are united again. They have all the artillery and the bulk of the infantry. We should turn back, harvest what crops are still left. Grain and fodder are our priorities.'

Tarchianotes ignored the little komes, his eyes now drifting beyond Chliat and eastwards along Lake Van's shores. There, the land seemed to be writhing, shapes spilling from a col between two mountains onto the broad shores to ride along the waterline, moving towards Chliat.

Peleus saw it too, his eyes bulging. 'Sir… is that…?'

Tarchianotes' eyes narrowed. Riders, hundreds of them. He made out their conical helms, mail shirts, spears and vividly painted shields.

'A raiding party? Perhaps it's the field burners returning to Chliat?' Peleus stammered. A hundred other voices of the riders just behind them made similar suggestions.

'These are no mere raiders,' Tarchianotes replied. 'Look,' he pointed a finger at the tall golden banner bearing the double bow emblem that bobbed out from the col, carried by many hundreds more riders. 'The Sultan has come to protect his holdings.'

Hundreds became thousands and thousands more followed. Peleus' eyes danced over the mass of Seljuk riders. 'There must be twenty or thirty thousand of them – at least as many of them as there are us, sir. They are coming this way. Shall I give the order to take up battle lines?'

Tarchianotes gazed at the thick swell of enemy horsemen, now almost dominating Lake Van's shores. He shook his head. 'No. The risk is too great. We don't know what other forces they have in the vicinity.'

'Then what—' the komes started.

'We are as yet unseen. So we withdraw,' Tarchianotes replied flatly. 'Turn the column around and back into the valleys before the Seljuk riders sight us.'

Peleus stared at him, lips quivering as if to contest the order.

'Did the emperor not say we were to avoid any major engagement?' he said, parroting Peleus' earlier words.

'Aye, he did,' Peleus nodded as the signophoroi silently waved their banners, herding the column into a gradual turn back into the shaded green valley.

Peleus rode alongside him as the mass of Byzantine riders and foot soldiers hastened back the way they had come. When they came to a forked valley, the komes seemed to slow, looking up the northerly fork which led to the flatland and Manzikert.

'Fall into line, Komes!' Tarchianotes barked at him, guiding the column to the westerly fork.

Peleus' brow knitted. 'But sir, the north track is the swiftest one that takes us back to the emperor?'

'And the west track takes us away from the enemy. Many, many miles away and back into safe imperial territory. It takes us to Melitene,' Tarchianotes snapped.

'Melitene? But… does the emperor know of this plan?' Peleus frowned, thinking of that faraway Byzantine city, his gaze switching from west to north.

'No, Komes. I am using my experience as a doux. A battlefield commander should know when it is right to stay and fight and when it is right to withdraw.' Then he stroked his neat beard.

'But the emperor must be told of our retreat, and of the threat that hovers nearby,' Peleus insisted.

'You are a swift rider?' Tarchianotes asked.

'Swift enough,' he beckoned Komes Stypiotes, another Chaldian, to him. 'I will take my fellow komes too, if you will permit it?'

'Very well. Ride, and ride at haste. Tell our emperor of this unexpected Seljuk presence and urge him to make haste back to the west likewise.'

'Yes, sir!' the komes nodded hurriedly, before heading north towards Manzikert with his comrade.

Tarchianotes watched the pair go, then, when they had slipped out of sight, he turned to four riders who served as his personal bodyguards. He nodded to them. In silence, the four peeled away from the column and headed north too.

Tarchianotes allowed himself a hint of a smile, then waved the vast column of men with him, back to the west, leaving Lake Van behind.

'Something's not right,' Stypiotes growled over the rush of air as they galloped along the valley floor.

'I had that one worked out some time ago,' Peleus yelled in reply.

'We should have tried to rouse the men in the column, urged them to stay.'

'No, Tarchianotes' men would have stamped out any undermining of his authority. We must forget the man and think only of getting word back to the emperor.' He jabbed a finger ahead at the end of the valley, the flatland and the distant speck that was Manzikert. 'Half of his army has just deserted him!'

Stypiotes did not reply. Peleus looked up to see the big komes was gawping up at the valley side on their left. Now Peleus saw it too. A pair of kataphractoi. Tarchianotes' men. They trotted down the hillside, hailing Peleus and Stypiotes. Each bore a gruff, haggard grin. 'Riders, you set off too soon. Doux Tarchianotes had more yet to brief you on.'

Peleus frowned, then saw that one's gaze was darting between himself and Stypiotes, and his sword hand was falling away from his reins. At the same time, he heard a thundering of hooves behind him. He and Stypiotes twisted to look up the other valley side to see another pair of kataphractoi racing down this slope, spears levelled.

'God be with us!' Peleus gasped.

'Draw your blade!' Stypiotes cried, pulling his mount round to face these two.

Peleus swung to face the first two, now rushing for him, spears level. He managed to swipe the spearhead from one, then the second lance punched through the iron plates of his klibanion vest and tore his heart in two. He toppled to the ground, where his big friend, Stypiotes, already lay. The pair shared a wordless, dying gaze.

As life slipped from Peleus, he heard one of the four grunt. 'Hide their bodies, just in case.'

All his thoughts turned to God. He prayed with his last moments of life that he had not let the emperor, the *Haga* and the rest of the army down.

Part 4: Manzikert

CHAPTER 16

The Taking of Manzikert

The morning after surveying the plain of Manzikert from the faraway hill, Romanus Diogenes, Emperor of Byzantium, led his twenty-two thousand men south. They poured down from the hills and onto the plain, just a few hundred feet from Manzikert's gates, then spilled around the citadel's base. At once, the sturdy black-walled fortress seemed dwarfed. The Seljuk garrison squabbled and rushed to and fro around the battlements as a massive, noose-like Byzantine siege line was set up in the blistering morning heat. A line of palisade stakes faced the fortress like fangs, and a sea of tents and banners sat behind this. When Romanus offered the Seljuk garrison terms, they rejected them outright. And so the tap-tap of the siege engineers' hammers rang out along with the singing of iron weapons being honed, the jabbering of eager men and the whinnying of horses.

Apion, shorn of his armour, chewed on a desert-dry chunk of hard tack biscuit as he strode behind the palisade, squinting and shading his eyes from the sun as he eyed Manzikert's high battlements on each of its four walls. The biscuit was foul and he only had two more of these meagre rations and a half ball of dried yoghurt and almonds remaining before he would be bereft of food. The rest of the army were on the same precipice of starvation. But with such a prize in their grasp, the men's hearts had soared, sure that victory and the spoils of Manzikert's stores lay only the breadth of a swift and effective siege away. Indeed, he heard Blastares rousing the Chaldian infantry ranks into a hearty – and so far clean – chorus as they worked away on honing their spathions.

Apion returned to counting the Seljuk helmets and speartips up on Manzikert's walls.

'Two hundred,' a voice concluded for him somewhat breathlessly. It was Procopius – the old Tourmarches having already circled the walls to take a rough count.

'So there are probably less than five hundred akhi within those walls,' Apion surmised.

'There could be ten thousand in there, it doesn't matter. Just wait until the trebuchets start swinging.' The old tourmarches winked, once again judging the distance to the walls.

Blastares roared with laughter at this, striding over, cutting off his song midway through a line that was due to rhyme with 'rock'. 'You deaf old bastard – didn't you hear the emperor say the fortress is to be taken intact? We came here to seize the strongholds, not reduce them to dust.'

Procopius swiped a dismissive hand through the air. 'We don't have to hit the walls with rocks. A few deliberate near-misses and that lot inside will be joining the brown tunic club. And if that doesn't work, then we'll send men to the walls.'

'Siege towers?' Sha asked, joining the conversation.

Procopius shook his head, nodding to the rubble- and shrub-strewn hillock the citadel sat upon. 'The slope is too uneven. Towers would topple over. It'll have to be ladders. Get a few men up to the walls to engage those on the battlements. When they're fighting, they're not raining arrows down on us, so we can quickly get a good few hundred more up there. Ha!' He dusted his hands together and grinned. 'When do we begin?'

'As soon as the emperor gives the word.' Apion nodded past the shoulders of his trusted three.

They turned to follow his gaze; the emperor and a trio of varangoi trotted towards them, having completed a circuit of the palisade on horseback. Romanus' locks were swept back, his eyes sparkling and his jaw set in determination. He carried a purple shield with a single arrow jutting from it. 'Seems we underestimated their archers' range,' he shrugged, snapping the shaft off and throwing it to the dust.

'There is nothing else of note?' Apion asked.

'Nothing, Strategos. Archers abound but there are no ballistae up on those walls to trouble us,' Romanus smiled. 'We are on the cusp of all that we have worked towards. Now, as we discussed earlier, a small, direct infantry assault will be the best approach. Your men are ready?'

Apion looked to Blastares, who had already darted off to ready the Chaldian skutatoi and the Armenian spearmen. 'Their blades are sharp and they are waiting on your word, *Basileus*.'

'Then mount your horse, Strategos. You can watch from the saddle with Alyates, Philaretos, Bryennios and I.'

Apion shook his head. 'With your permission, *Basileus*, I will march with my men today.' The Chaldian ranks heard this and broke out in a confused murmur that quickly developed into an excited chatter. Many were new recruits and had never fought alongside their legendary leader. '*Ha-ga!*' some of the older veterans cried.

'You wish to walk into the Seljuk arrow hail and meet your fate?' Romanus cocked an eyebrow, seeing Apion take up his klibanion from one soldier and buckle it on over his torso.

Apion squinted up at the sun, seeing the swallows swooping high above the fortress. 'I have heard many stories of Fate in my years — how man dances to his whims like leaves in a gale. Today, I'm of a mood to seize Fate by the balls.'

Romanus gawped, then roared with laughter.

'Hoo-*ha*! Hoo-*ha*! Hoo-*ha*!' the men of Chaldia chanted as they shuffled forward in *foulkon* formations, protected under a shell of shields. They moved like three great tortoises across the few hundred feet of desiccated no-man's land between the Byzantine palisade siege line and the hillock upon which Manzikert sat, converging on the black-walled fortress. Apion moved at the head of the central foulkon, his shield interlocked with Sha's and those of the fourteen other men on the front line. The men behind held their crimson shields overhead, the Seljuk arrows rattling off this protective roof. A gurgling cry rang out just behind him as a man fell. 'Slow and steady!' he bawled. 'Their arrows cannot penetrate the foulkon unless we present them with gaps.' He glanced to the interlocked shields on the left of his foulkon: a sliver of daylight between two shields there revealed Blastares' foulkon a hundred feet or so away, moving at a good, steady pace. To his right he saw Procopius' lot moving forward likewise. Immediately behind these three giant tortoise shells, packs of Armenian spearmen ran, crouched, carrying with them two tall ladders per pack.

'Ready for the hill!' Sha bellowed.

At once, the grass and dust of the plain underfoot changed as they moved onto the slope of the fortress mount. Scree and shale slid under each footstep, causing more than a few to slip or stumble, prizing the tight tortoise shell open in places and leading to more wet punches of arrows plunging into flesh. Gorse bushes scraped past legs and the men's breathing grew heavier as they climbed. Apion glanced up to see that the wall was but feet away. 'Fill your lungs, we are almost there!' Then he barked back over his shoulder in the direction of the Armenians. 'Ready to bring the ladders forward!'

But as soon as the words had left his lips, a grinding of rock on rock sounded from high above. A heartbeat later, the tortoise was smashed apart by his side as a hulking rock crashed down through the front line of shields. The man by his right shoulder and two more beside him disappeared under the rock with abruptly strangled cries. Blood spurted up over him and Sha as the rock rolled on down the slope, pulverising the ranks behind, leaving a crimson trail of crushed men, pulped like ants under the heel of a boot. Another crash. The men wailed in terror and instants later the left side of the foulkon was ripped away as another great boulder rolled past them, crushing the shields, feet and legs of those unfortunate enough to be on that side. Another crash. Then another and another.

'Back, back!' he cried. 'Dissolve the foulkon, but keep your shields up!'

The tortoise disintegrated as the men fell back from the bombardment. Apion saw the Seljuk akhi atop the walls heaving the great, rounded boulders over the battlements and onto the fleeing Byzantines. Pockets of men lay dashed along the crimson smear of each boulder's path. As the Byzantine soldiers fled, the Seljuks took to throwing tightly bound balls of hay, ablaze, down from that great height. Unlike the lumbering rocks, these flaming bales bounced and raced after the fleeing Byzantines, flattening some, setting others ablaze. Their screaming lasted all too long and soon the dry, hot air was spiced with the foul stench of burning hair and flesh.

They retreated to the palisade line and fell in behind it, panting, shaking. Apion turned to see that more than ninety of his men had perished in the failed assault, and their ladders lay abandoned at the foot of the walls.

'We need protection, Strategos,' Prince Vardan insisted, tearing off the bright green and now somewhat charred silk scarf he wore round his head, nodding to his slain Armenians on the ground between the siege line and the walls of Manzikert.

Apion nodded, tugging at his beard as he raked over the possibilities. He turned to Procopius. The tourmarches winced, clutching his shoulder. It was badly bloodied where one of the boulders had scraped past him, and his sword hand trembled, unable to clasp his blade firmly.

Procopius offered a half-grin. 'It's not that bad. Another few inches and it would have been different.'

'That's what Tetradia's sister said about you,' Blastares chuckled, poorly masking his concern for his old friend.

'Your fight is over for today, old horse,' Apion insisted.

'Never,' Procopius hissed.

'You'll still play your part in the battle. We need you to direct the artillery crews.' He nodded to the workmen standing nearby, tools lying around their feet. 'We need some form of protection against the rocks and flaming bales.'

Procopius' defiance faded a fraction at this, his interest piqued. 'Aye, well... perhaps.'

It was late afternoon when the foulkon formations marched forward again, crossing the ground between the Byzantine siege line and the fortress mount. 'Hoo-*ha*! Hoo-*ha*! Hoo-*ha*!' From the front line of the central foulkon, Apion again watched through a sliver-gap between the shields, seeing the Seljuk garrison readying great boulders and hay bales once more.

But this time, several smaller clutches of Armenians ran out ahead, carrying giant four-pronged caltrops and mantlets – strapped, portable palisade barriers.

'Get 'em up onto those slopes!' Procopius' hoarse cries rang across from the siege line.

Apion watched as the small packs of Armenians fleet-footedly stole up onto the fortress mount's slope, arrows hissing down around them. There, the first of them threw down a giant caltrop – three of its four lance-like spikes digging deep into the ground and the fourth jutting skywards. They crouched to hammer the three grounded spikes a little deeper into the dust. Job done, their leader stood tall to wave them back to the siege line, when a Seljuk arrow punched him to the ground. He shuddered where he lay, his neck craning up, head trembling as he clasped at the arrow shaft embedded in his chest. With his other hand he made a feeble attempt to stand until another arrow took him in the eye and his head dropped back like a stone. Then another of the boulders came crashing over the battlements, thundering down the slopes at great pace towards the rest of the small party. They wailed in terror, falling to the ground and throwing up their hands as if to shield themselves. When the boulder was but paces away from crushing these few, it thwacked into the upright caltrop prong with a dull thud of rock on iron, and was still. A sharp cracking noise followed, then the boulder split in two halves. The Armenians cried out in glee, then hurried to retreat back to the siege line, breaking past the central of the three advancing foulkons.

'It's working!' Apion hissed, shaking a clenched fist as the Armenians flooded past his tortoise-shell. Each of the other small packs of artillerymen took to dropping and bashing their mantlets or caltrops into the earth, progressively higher up the slope, gradually fashioning a rudimentary, diagonal barrier running from one end of the fortress' south-westerly corner to the south-easterly base of the fortress mount. Some fell, shot down by Seljuk arrows before they reached the slope, but many made it. Soon, they were done. The boulders and flaming bales tossed down from the southerly battlements crashed to the ground and rumbled downhill, only to be snared on the crude barrier or channelled downhill to the south-easterly base of the slope.

'Give the order,' Apion said to Sha, his eyes narrowing.

'Pick up the pace!' Sha cried. The central foulkon crunched onto the slope and up to the discarded ladders at the south-west corner. Boulders and flaming bales were thrown hurriedly, only to be innocuously corralled down the crude barrier and away from the giant tortoise of men. The Seljuks' cries of alarm multiplied as more Armenians, crouching behind the foulkon, rushed to take up the abandoned ladders and swing them up to the wall tops. In moments, the men of the Chaldian Thema were streaming up these two ladders, crimson shields strapped to their backs as they climbed, spathions clenched in one hand, ready for battle.

Sixty or more Chaldians had spilled onto the wall tops when Apion and Sha climbed and leapt over onto the battlements in unison. They pressed together, back to back, as the skirmish up there raged around them. The stone walkway was wet with blood already, and part-carpeted in twitching, thrashing men clutching opened throats or torn-open bellies. The cacophonous song of iron upon iron was incessant. Apion saw the pulsating image of the dark door, heard the thunder of an angry fire blazing beyond it, heard it creaking open, sensed it drawing him in, felt the flames lick at his skin. He heard his own nightmarish growl like that of a crazed hound.

A dark-skinned, moustachioed akhi spearman wearing a gold cape came at Apion with a howl, lancing forward with his spear. Apion jinked to one side and the spear tip ripped across the breast of his klibanion, dislodging one of the square iron plates. He grappled the spear shaft and used it to pivot his foe round on his own weapon, tossing the man like a child's toy from the wall, down into the cramped interior of the fortress town. His shrill cry was cut short by the dull crunch of bones where he landed.

'*Haga!*' a familiar voice roared over the din.

He swung to see Blastares hurling a spear right at him. Reading the big man's eyes, he ducked, then twisted round to see the akhi who had been rushing for his back, scimitar raised, now halted with Blastares' spear lodged in his breast. A heartbeat later, the butt of another Seljuk spear shaft bashed Blastares' head, dazing him momentarily, the towering, dark-bearded attacker swirling his spear overhead to bring the tip down for the big man's neck. Apion lunged forward, striking down with his scimitar to deflect the blow, then hacking forward, driving the akhi back. The man ducked under Apion's next swipe, then threw down his spear and tore out his own scimitar. Sparks flew as they clashed blades again and again. Then, with one swift and clean swipe, he cut through the wrist of his opponent. The man's sword hand and blade spun through the air with a spurt of blood. The dark-bearded Seljuk crumpled to his knees, wailing, clutching the stump of his arm. Apion snarled again and hefted his blade overhead ready to swipe the cur's head away, feeling the fire of battle sear his skin. A moment later he was unseeing of his foe. In his mind's eye he saw a face in the blackness beyond the dark door. Taylan.

What would you do to find out the truth, Father? the lad mouthed.

A hand clamped onto his shoulder, wrenching him from his dark reverie. 'We have the walls, sir!' Sha cried.

The blaze of battle dulled and then hissed in his mind, extinguished as swiftly as it had come on. His heartbeat slowed and reality trickled in once more. The dark door faded. He blinked, seeing the black-bearded akhi still crouching before him, cradling the spurting stump of his sword arm, roaring in agony. He lowered the blade, catching the beaten akhi's eye furtively, fighting off the familiar sense of shame as he heard the warrior hurriedly offer prayer before he was slain. Apion tore off a strip of his tunic, tossed it to another beaten Seljuk nearby, then nodded to the humbled, bleeding akhi. 'Tie this tightly around his arm or he will be dead in moments.'

He turned away from the gawping Seljuk pair and followed Sha's sweeping hand.

'But while we have the walls, they have that.' The Malian's finger stopped, pointing at the sturdy, tall but slender keep in the heart of the fortress. The last of the Seljuk akhi were rushing from the smattering of houses, timber stables and shacks around the fortress interior to get inside this stronghold. It had a small, crenelated roof and was taller than the fortress walls by a good ten feet. The thick oak, iron-strapped door at its foot slammed and the clunk of many iron bolts inside suggested it was to remain closed.

'We'll need new ladders,' Blastares panted. 'Or perhaps we could lay the ladders we have from the battlements across the gap? Heh, old Procopius' constant prattle about siege theory seems to have rubbed off on me.'

'Or perhaps we need to bring a ram up to break that door down – though it would take some doing,' Sha mused.

'No. The siege is over,' Apion said, wiping the grime of battle from his face and beard. 'These men are terrified, a few words will suffice to end this.' He eyed the clutch who had spilled out onto the keep's roof. They babbled, panicked. He made out their words. *We will die if we surrender. We will never see our families again.*

Apion filled his lungs and shouted across in the Seljuk tongue. 'Brave akhi, your fears are misplaced. If you surrender, you can set down your weapons and go free. If you resist, I will certainly see to it that, once we take your keep, each and every one of you is beheaded within these walls.'

The akhi atop the keep visibly blanched as they heard their own tongue being spoken by their attacker. The leader of them came to the lip of the keep roof, eyes wide, mouth agape. 'It is the *Haga*,' he muttered, his whisper carried in an echo around the fortress walls, 'the slayer of men.'

Apion's skin prickled with shame at this epithet, aware also that it was this blackened reputation that would carry his plan through.

They babbled amongst each other, then the leader came to the walls again, nodding hurriedly with no more words.

Apion descended the stone steps into the fortress interior where the Chaldian ranks were assembling round the base of the keep. When he, Sha and Blastares came to the main door, the iron bolts within clunked once more. The door creaked open and the lead akhi was revealed.

The weaponless man beheld Apion, then walked from the keep, doing his best to hold his head high, leading his men with him. Each of them paled under the gaze of their enemy as they filed out of the fortress. At the last, just two moustachioed akhi remained inside, standing in the shadow of the doorway. They wore stiff and defiant looks, their eyes ablaze, their jaws squared and lips pursed, spears clasped firmly, levelled at Apion and his men.

The taller of the two spoke first: 'My brothers may have chosen foolishly. To throw down their weapons and turn their backs on the scourge of the borderlands is folly. We will fight you to the last. So come, take our heads, but we will cut many of you down before you better us!' he panted, his chest rising and falling rapidly, as if expecting to be set upon by Apion and the mass of Byzantine soldiers.

Apion looked to Blastares, and they shared a tacit nod of affirmation. Like leaping cats, they plunged into the doorway. Apion ducked under the spear thrust of the tall one and then brought one hand up to grasp the spearshaft, the other coming round in a right hook to crash into the man's jaw. The akhi stumbled backwards, dazed and dropping his spear. Likewise, Blastares sent the other akhi spinning with a jab and then took the man's weapon.

The tall one came too, stood gingerly, then flopped to his knees in resignation. 'Very well,' he said, 'extending his neck, 'take your prize, you godless dog.'

Apion took up his scimitar, swirled it in his grasp then brought it swinging round to bash the flat against the back of the man's head. The man blinked and yelped, then looked up, confused.

'Get up, both of you. Go and join your brothers on their journey home. I have no wish to take your heads, you fools.'

By the time sunset came, crimson banners fluttered from Manzikert's keep and corner towers and two hundred skutatoi now manned the battlements. Apion led the rest of the Chaldian ranks as they crunched down the hillside from the fortress to re-join the campaign army. The thick ring of over twenty thousand Byzantine soldiers awaiting them there cried out in exultation. Emperor Romanus hoisted the purple campaign banner and yanked on his mount's reins, coaxing it up onto its hind legs, cajoling his ranks. '*Nobiscum Deus!*' he roared. '*Nobiscum Deus!*' They thundered in reply. Even the rabble of the magnate armies cheered along with the imperial soldiers.

Apion led the Chaldians to Romanus. 'It is done, *Basileus*. Manzikert is ours once again. One half of the Gateway to Anatolia is under our control.'

Romanus grinned, sliding from his stallion to clasp a hand to Apion's shoulder. 'Aye. Tomorrow, we will rest. And the day after, the two halves of the army will be reunited. Then… Chliat will be taken! These fortresses will be enlarged and bolstered into impregnable strongholds. The eastern passes will be secured for the first time in so many years. Anatolia will flourish once more, safe from invasion.' The emperor said this with tears gathering in his eyes.

A roar from the men shook the land and Apion could not help but cry out with them. All he had fought for since those dark days of his childhood lay before him. But something did not feel right. The emperor's broad smile faltered as soon as he turned away from his men and headed for his tent, flanked by Igor and another varangos.

'*Basileus?*' he whispered, walking alongside. 'Something is wrong?'

'You can read me like you can read a battlefield, Strategos.' Romanus' eyes shot furtively to see who was within earshot, but the men nearby had broken into prayer and song, some indulging in wine to celebrate the relatively bloodless taking of the fortress. 'Our supplies are almost gone, and Doux Tarchianotes has yet to send back the first of the grain and fodder from the fields near Chliat. Indeed, we have had no word from him at all since the army was divided.'

'We will make contact with him tomorrow, hopefully?' Igor tried to assuage the emperor's doubts.

'I pray to God we do, Komes,' Romanus muttered. 'I pray to God we do.'

Apion frowned as the emperor headed inside his tent. Suddenly, like an eerie applause, a nest of bats scattered from the top of Manzikert's keep to dart across the dusk sky. Apion followed their flight, and found that it drew his gaze south, across the flatland, to the darkening outline of the Lake Van mountains far to the south. The navy blue and pink streaked sky betrayed nothing of those lands. Nothing at all. A cool night breeze searched under his armour and chilled his skin.

High up on a lofty shard of rock that jutted from the side of Mount Tzipan, Alp Arslan wrapped the thick bear pelt tighter around his shoulders as the stiff mountain night wind grew and swirled around him. The fur ruffled like his hair and moustache, hanging loose. He absently crunched on the handful of nuts that would be his evening meal, and scoured the north, across the flatland. From this height, he could make out the dull glimmer of torchlight that pinpointed the fortress of Manzikert. His eyes narrowed.

A scraping of boots on rock disturbed him from his thoughts. Bey Taylan and his son, Malik, came to him, flanked by a pair of dismounted ghulam. 'Father, you should come down to the camp,' Malik chattered, glancing up to the snowy cap of the mountain, only a few hundred feet further up from this promontory. 'I have heard that the night chill grows ferocious up here.'

Alp Arslan swigged on his skin of neat wine. 'I will be warm enough,' he muttered darkly.

'They have taken Manzikert, Sultan,' Taylan offered.

'I know,' Alp Arslan grunted. 'And now we must react. It seems that the plains that lie ahead thirst for blood.'

As he looked down to the darkened plain, he sensed Taylan gazing with him. The boy's eyes were lost in thought.

CHAPTER 17

The Lion Circles

Apion loped down from the northern hills, bathed in sweat and dawn light. He had hoped his morning run along that range might give him a glimpse of some activity in the lands far to the south. But he had seen nothing. Just the majestic Mount Tzipan, still and silent, and the bright, sparkling band beyond that was Lake Van. No sign of Tarchianotes' half of the army. No sign of the foraging parties sent south across the plain a few hours before dawn. These kursores had been sent out with a brief to try to make contact with Tarchianotes and to gather up what forage and fodder could be found to tide the Manzikert half of the army over in the meantime. *Ride swiftly*, he thought as he ran onto the flatland and past the walls of Manzikert – the garrison Chaldians cheering him from the battlements.

The siege lines had been deconstructed and transformed into a standard marching camp, straddling the south edge of the fortress mount and enclosing the small brook. Inside, he stopped by a barrel of water and lashed a handful over his sweat-soaked skin. All around, the men were waking for morning roll-call, many nibbling unenthusiastically on their second to last chunk of hard tack biscuit. His belly groaned for his usual breakfast of a hunk of bread and a portion of honey, but the last of the bread had been eaten two days past, and the honey had been finished more than a week ago. He dug out the last morsel from his rations – half a ball of dried yoghurt, almonds and sesame seeds, dropping it in a pot with some water and resting it over the small campfire Sha had kindled at the heart of the Chaldian section of the camp. The yoghurt ball and water blended together to form a thick and nutritious – if scant – portion of stew. He ate slowly, hoping the meal would be enough to see him through the day.

It was then that a shout came from the camp's southern gate. Apion shot to standing, hearing the tone of the sentry's voice. He shaded his eyes from the sun: over the sea of pavilion tents and fluttering banners he saw the returning cluster of foraging kursores. It looked like all of the seventy sent out were present, but some were bloodied. He set down his pot and rushed to the gate.

'Seljuk riders came at us in the lower hills and showered us with arrows,' the lead rider panted, his klibanion damaged where arrows had struck. 'We did not meet with Doux Tarchianotes, but we did manage to gather some food.' The man threw down a few sacks of berries and nuts, others dropping gathered fodder and others had poles draped with shot or trapped rabbits.

'How many?' Apion asked, ignoring the fare.

'The riders? Two to every one of us – maybe a hundred and fifty.'

Apion swung round to see that Igor, Alyates, Philaretos and Bryennios had come to the gate also. Behind them, Romanus strode, ringed by Rus axemen.

'A band of skirmishers?' Igor suggested.

'Perhaps the garrison of Chliat?' Philaretos growled, clearly dismayed by the meagre food gathered by the riders.

'Perhaps.' Apion looked to the south. Still, silent and empty.

'Take a few regiments of your western tagmata, Doux,' the emperor nodded to Bryennios. Then he looked to Apion. 'You should go too. Lead the wing of Norman lancers. Drive off these dogs.'

The emperor leaned in close to Apion, lowering his voice. 'And bring back what food you can, Strategos. This fare will provide each man with barely a mouthful of food.'

'Yes, *Basileus*.'

He hurried back to his tent, throwing on his armour – just his klibanion and helm – foregoing greaves and face veil to aid swiftness. He vaulted onto his saddled gelding, then urged it into a walk to join Bryennios. The Norman riders were assembling nearby, coated from scalp to knee in their mail hauberks, just their pale features visible under the rims and nose-guards of their helms. Each man held a tall and lethal lance.

'Ready, Strategos?' Bryennios cocked an eyebrow.

Apion offered him a wry grin by way of reply.

They rode at a gallop southwards across the plain as the sun rose and grew fierce. Here the grass of the northern hills became sparse, replaced by burnt-gold, dry and dusty ground. Bryennios had summoned a thousand of his western riders; kursores, in effect – light and swift skirmish cavalry garbed in iron-plated klibania and helms, carrying spears and small shields. Apion 'led' the Norman five hundred – in fact they seemed intent on riding ahead of Apion and the rest, barking out in their jagged western tongue.

'Let them win whatever race they think they are running,' Apion snorted, seeing the disgusted look on Bryennios' face. 'If it assures them of their prowess, then what harm is there in it?'

The hills before Mount Tzipan had been but barely visible bumps from the hillsides around Manzikert. Now, as the riders approached, they seemed to grow into mini-mountains.

'It was here, in these first valleys,' the nearest kursoris said, tilting the rim of his conical helm, his face whitening a fraction. This rider had been one of those ambushed at dawn.

Apion looked ahead to the precipitous, green-gold hillsides that sprouted up to present a saddle of land, cast in shade. 'Slow!' he called out.

Bryennios nodded his assent. The Norman riders slowed grudgingly, muttering to one another. They trotted into the rugged valley, seeing nothing but poppies and grass quivering in the breeze, hearing nothing but the echo of their own hooves. They moved about a mile into the valley. Then there was a faint noise.

Apion, Sha and Bryennios shared a wide-eyed look.

'Still!' Bryennios raised a hand.

The Normans' muttering died away and they heard nothing but the whistling breeze and the chattering of the cicadas. Then came again – the distant whinnying of a horse, quickly stifled. The ghostly babble of voices, there and not there at once.

'They're nearby,' Bryennios whispered.

'Aye, listen,' Apion said, lifting his helmet off and covering one ear and then the other. 'It is stronger to the left. They must be there, beyond the fork.' He pointed to the leftmost of two routes at the end of the valley.

Suddenly, the babble ceased.

Bryennios nodded. 'Forward, at a walk,' he hissed.

The left fork led directly east. The late morning sun blinded them as they rode. Apion squinted and shaded his eyes, desperately trying to discern the path ahead. 'Stop,' he uttered flatly.

'Strategos?' Bryennios frowned and his riders halted with him. Unsurprisingly, the Normans continued on ahead, heedless of the order.

'This is a perfect ambush point,' Apion whispered, careful not to let the other riders hear. 'The sun blinds us. And see how the valley narrows up ahead? We should turn around and—'

A whinnying cut him off. He twisted in his saddle to see a dark pack of horsemen spill into the western end of the valley behind them. Seljuk ghazis, more than a thousand of them, rumbling forward at a trot, then breaking into a gallop. Then a roar from up ahead. He twisted to face forward again; another mass of riders washed from the eastern end of the valley.

He set eyes upon the one leading this ambush. An aged Seljuk ghazi. No, he was too finely garbed. Not a mere ghazi, a bey. He glowered at Apion like an angered bear, his brow dipped, his wispy white locks flapping across his face as he lay flat in the saddle and led his men into a charge.

Soundaq?

Apion's mind raced back to his early days in the ranks, to that Seljuk bey he had faced on the hilltop town of Bizye. The proud warrior and his warband had thought to strike the townsfolk down and take what plunder he could, but Apion and his trusted three had seen him off with a fierce mixture of tenacity and cunning. Soundaq's face was creased in fury, mouth agape in a battle-cry shared with the riders he led. '*Allahu Akbar!*'

All around him, the mounts of the Normans and the western tagmata reared and whinnied in panic, their riders bawled in horror, drawing swords and levelling spears. Bryennios hastened to bark them to order. 'Divide the tourma, form a front to the east and to the west!' he roared.

'No!' Apion cried. 'This valley is a snare. We must break free.' He swept his spear up to the steep valley side. 'Break for the hilltop!'

Bryennios took just a moment to concur, seeing yet more ghazis flood into the valley behind Soundaq. An instant later, he had barked out to his men and had them scrambling up the uneven hillside, making for the brow of the valley. Apion was near the rear of the fleeing Byzantine pack. The going was treacherous and many horses stumbled, man and rider rolling back down onto the valley floor where they lay, bones broken, only for the two packs of ghazi to converge from east and west and hack at them. Within a breath, Soundaq and his ghazis then turned their bows upon the scrambling Byzantine uphill retreat. Arrows thumped into the grass and rocks around Apion and the hooves of his Thessalian. Men fell back with cries all around him and the air took on the coppery stench of blood. They were nearly at the brow, he realised. From there they could break from these hills and back onto the flatland. He risked a glance over his shoulder. The majority of the ghazis were content to shoot at them from the valley floor, but a small wedge had broken ahead. Soundaq led them. His eyes were still trained on Apion as if nobody else existed in that valley. His face was set in a chilling rictus as his sturdy mare saw him bound up the hillside, drawing closer to Apion's Thessalian with every passing, frenzied heartbeat.

'I'll have your blood today, *Haga*,' he panted, drawing his scimitar as they crested the valley side and he came to within an arm's length of Apion. 'I'll have what I should have taken all those years ago!'

Apion tore out his own blade just in time to parry, struggling to guide his mount on across the short stretch of plateau as they rode side by side. 'You were once a noble foe. What has happened to you in the years since we last clashed?' he snarled as their blades scraped against one another, each man vying for supremacy.

Without hesitation, Soundaq spat back, 'Nothing, *Haga*… *nothing!*' His face grew crimson with ire as he pushed on his blade, fixed on forcing Apion's blade from his hand or knocking him from his horse. At that moment, the bey employed the strength of a bear. A moment later, the force was gone, the man's face paling. He dropped his sword, clutched a hand to his chest and toppled to the grass, struggling to his knees, gasping for breath. Apion glanced back only to see Soundaq's body slump, his heart ruptured with anger, it seemed. But he gawped at this only for an instant, as the rest of the riders following Soundaq rushed up onto the top of the valley too. Apion dropped flat in his saddle and kicked his Thessalian into a frenzied gallop down the other side of the hill, on after the rest of the Byzantines, racing for the flatland.

The thunder of pursuing hooves faded, only to be replaced by the shudder of bending bows. He swung his shield round onto his back, knowing he would be their primary target, then heeled the mount again and again, bringing it to a frantic charge as soon as he reached the plain. Arrows thwacked down on his shield, glanced from his helm and ricocheted from the mount's scale apron. Many more thudded down in the dust around him. He looked up, seeing that he was catching Bryennios, the western tagma riders and the Normans.

Bryennios turned to urge him on faster, then cried out as two arrows thudded home, finding gaps in the iron squares of his klibanion, also knocking down a clutch of the kursores racing by his side. The next volley of arrows sailed down upon the Normans' hauberks, punching through the mail and felling at least sixty of the western riders.

'Get your heads down, lie flat on the saddle! Shields on your backs!' Apion screamed at the panicked Normans over the rushing wind as they hared north, back across the plain towards Manzikert. Only then did the arrow hail thin.

'They're not following?' Bryennios gasped, blood pouring from the wound on his back where two arrows quivered. 'I'll be damned if they were a small raiding party… or the garrison of Chliat!'

Apion twisted to look back, up to the top of the hill they had just descended. It was now glimmering with silver riders. At the heart of this glittering horizon, a figure stood under the Seljuk golden bow banner. The figure was but a speck in the distance. But even from here, he knew exactly who it was.

Sultan Alp Arslan, the *Mountain Lion*.

'No, Doux. It seems the Sultan has come to the field of battle.'

Bryennios' silence spoke a thousand words. Likewise, Apion's skin danced in a cold shiver. If the Sultan had come to these plains to face the imperial army, then it was a certainty that another had followed.

Taylan, he mouthed, twisting once more and scanning the gathering, thickening crowds of riders up there.

—

Nearing sunset, Apion, Romanus and a clutch of twenty varangoi climbed to the tallest of the northern hills, a safe distance from their camp where they could enjoy a good vantage point across the great plain to view the southern ranges, Mount Tzipan and Lake Van. The only good news to be shared since they returned from the scouting sortie to the south was the discovery of forty barrels of grain inside the cellar of Manzikert's keep. Thus, the men would eat fresh bread tonight. But it was scant solace given Apion and the other scout riders' discovery of what lay only a handful of miles to the south.

'They were there.' Apion squinted, pointing across the deep orange and shadow dappled land to the tiny, almost indiscernible bump that was the valley of the ambush.

Romanus sighed, his unshaven jaw tensing. 'Yet I see nothing, nothing but the coming sunset.'

Apion frowned. 'The arrows in Doux Bryennios' flesh were real enough, were they not?' The western doux was somewhere in the Byzantine camp below, being tended to. Fortunately, his wounds were light, the arrows breaking the flesh but not deeply enough to pierce any organs. He would likely be fit to ride again within a day or so. And the chances were he would have to be.

Romanus' expression grew dark. 'The Sultan was definitely with them? How can a man be cowering in the centre of old Persia and in those hills at the same time?'

Apion sighed, understanding Romanus' ire. He thought of Diabatenus' reports that Alp Arslan had fled back into his heartlands upon hearing of the Byzantine advance. Then he thought of that handsome rider's unexplained disappearance at Theodosiopolis. A dark shadowy truth settled on his thoughts, but he decided not to air them. 'Who knows what really happened between him and Diabatenus when they parleyed. But believe me, *Basileus*, the Sultan is here.'

'Then we must ready to resist what forces the Sultan has brought to the field.' Romanus shook his head with a deep sigh. 'Tarchianotes and his half of the army will be vital – the bulk of my finest cavalry and foot archers. Perhaps the division of the forces might even prove fortuitous – for if we can lure the Sultan's army onto the plains then perhaps Tarchianotes can fall upon their rear.'

Apion nodded, gazing to the south again. He thought of dampening the emperor's optimism, then chided himself. 'Perhaps.'

That night, a waxing moon lit the plain of Manzikert, its light coming and going as grey clouds crawled across the sky on lofty zephyrs. The frantic sortie to the southern hills seemed such a long time ago as Apion wandered between the tents of the various regiments in his tunic, boots and a cloak to keep the gentle night chill at bay. The men prayed or chattered gaily, happy to have their bread, ignorant as yet to what lay in the southern hills. Some had grown suspicious when the emperor ordered a double-strength watch, but none yet knew the full story.

Outside the camp, a small band of Armenian traders had come by this otherwise deserted plain and they stopped outside the camp's southern gate. There were just a few of them, but they brought with them eight ox-drawn wagons laden with trinkets: precious stones set in carved wood, dyed animal hair scarves and fine ostrich feathers for plumage. The Byzantines had little interest in these wares, bar a few who bought up the small amount of prayer ropes the traders had. The Armenian spearmen had browsed the wares with some interest, but the Oghuz had been enthralled by the trinkets, a few hundred of the rugged steppe riders spending hours bantering and bartering with the traders. They even shared some of their bread and wine with the travellers.

Apion headed out to see how they were getting on, taking with him a skin of watered wine. He saw the flat-faced and black-humoured Tamis, leader of the Oghuz wing. The man was squat and sturdy like his fellow riders. He wore black furs on his shoulders, crude leather armour around his torso and an ancient-looking but deadly composite bow on his back. These nimble horse archers — eighteen hundred of them all told including the sixteen hundred or so inside the camp — were the only true archer cavalry left in this half of the bisected army. A vital part of any well-balanced force.

'Ah, *Haga!*' Tamis turned to him, arms out wide.

Apion accepted his embrace. 'Will your men still be able to ride with all these new trinkets?' he chuckled, seeing one Oghuz rider showing off his purchases — a weighty bronze greave, engraved with spiralling patterns, and a thick iron torc around his neck.

'Ah, yes, the horses might need a few more handfuls of fodder to carry that one,' Tamis grinned. Then his smile faded and he beckoned Apion with him on a stroll away from the gathered men and traders and a little further out onto the empty plain. 'Tell me, Strategos, are these rumours I hear true?'

Apion feigned ignorance.

'Come on, I know you are as close to the emperor as anyone. The grain and silage Doux Tarchianotes and his men were to send from the southern mountains — it has not arrived, has it? We have been watching and we saw no wagons.' He stopped and faced Apion, checking he was out of earshot of his men. 'And that sortie today – it was not merely a skirmish with the Chliat garrison, was it? I saw the state of the men who returned – a good number less than set out.'

Apion sighed. 'Tamis, you are a wise and noble leader. You know the swiftness with which fear spreads on the wind of such news. Aye, there is a Seljuk army in those hills,' he looked across the plain to the south. 'But tonight your men and all the others need nourishment and rest – not rumours.'

Tamis nodded, his expression darkening. 'I understand. But tomorrow, we will all be told things as they are, yes? Some of my men think it is only them who are not being told—' His words faded and his eyes bulged, fixed over Apion's shoulder. 'Strategos!' he gasped.

Apion swung round. To the west, the darkness swirled. Something was moving, flitting between patches of moonlight. A rider, then another, then a vast pack, thundering towards the Oghuz.

Seljuk ghazis.

'To arms!' Tamis cried.

'No – get inside the camp!' Apion cried, seeing that there were many of the Seljuk riders. Three thousand, perhaps.

The Oghuz, dismounted, swung round, sure this was some joke, then saw the mass coming for them. They wailed, throwing down their goods, staggering from the trade wagons, some rushing to their horses, others plucking the bows from their backs. Their response was chaotic and all too late. The Oghuz arrows spat forth wildly and without aim. Some riders fell from their mounts in their haste to ride for the nearby safety of the Byzantine camp. In contrast, the Seljuk ghazis unleashed a storm of thousands of arrows on the panicked Oghuz.

Apion threw himself under one of the trade wagons as the hail hammered down. Screams were cut short and bodies thudded to the earth, many twitching or crying out. The wagon shuddered as a shower of the arrows smacked into it – the two unarmoured traders pirouetting and crumpling, riddled with shafts, eyes rolling in their sockets.

The ghazis howled in delight as they swept past, loosing another volley on the remaining eighty or so Oghuz who stood their ground. Over half of these riders were also punched to the dust, having felled only a few of the ghazis in return.

Apion saw the ghazis sweep round, readying to circle and come back again. He pounced on the moment, scrambling from under the wagon, rushing for the camp's southern gate, where the majority of the Oghuz who had leapt on their mounts were cramming to get inside. But something was wrong. Shouts of despair rang up from the men nearest the gate, and cries of pain followed. Apion heard the lashing of iron swords and the shouting of Greek voices. 'Ghazis at the gate! Cut them down!'

No! Apion barged through the mass of milling Oghuz mounts. He pushed through to the front, where he saw the snarling Byzantine skutatoi sentries – a thick triple line of ninety of these spearmen blockading the gateway, punching forward with their lances, more rushing to the call of alarm. In their fear at the sudden rush of cavalry and blinded by the darkness, they had mistaken the retreating Oghuz for attacking Seljuk riders. The Oghuz, blinded by panic at the real mass of Seljuk riders sweeping to and fro behind them on the plain, babbled frantically but went unheard. Man and mount were skewered on Byzantine spears and fell, thrashing. He saw Tamis trying to pull his men back, realising the confusion of the sentries, when a javelin hurled from inside the camp took the rugged Oghuz leader clean through the throat, bringing sheets of blood from the wound. His eyes, hope fading, met Apion's as he toppled from his horse. This only panicked his comrades even more. Some even took to trying to have their mounts leap over the tall palisade wall of the camp. All bar a few of these mounts ended up skewered on the sharpened stakes, thrashing, broken.

'They're our men!' Apion roared over the tumult. The skutatos facing him thrust his spear out again, teeth bared and eyes ablaze, thinking he was fighting for his life. Apion grappled the shaft of the spear and wrenched the man from the spear line. 'They're our riders!' he yelled again. The mist of battle faded from the soldier's face, only to be replaced by a look of horror as he saw the Oghuz for what they were.

'Stop!' the soldier cried, his voice joining Apion's. Buccinas blared all across the camp and the empty tracts between the sea of tents inside became abuzz with men stumbling from sleep, rushing to arms.

By now, the Oghuz were falling away from the gate, racing off into the plain to take their chances there. Panting and bloodied, the sentry line realised what had happened. They lowered their spears, gawping at the dead allies on the reddened earth before them.

'Keep your spears high!' Apion cried, exasperated. 'The ghazis *are* out there, in the darkness.' He fell in behind them, pointing out onto the plain. The drifting clouds had covered the moon, and they could see nothing. The varangoi and a raft of skutatoi now clustered around the camp's southern gate, readying to defend the palisade walls. But for a moment there was nothing. Nothing bar the death rattle of one of the stricken Oghuz on the ground before them.

Then a chorus of howling, wraith-like voices split the darkness along with a thunder of hooves. A sliver of moonlight betrayed eyes, flashing armour and gritted teeth. The ghazi pack swept past the southern gate like an ethereal gust, loosing a cloud of arrows before sweeping away into the blackness again.

'Shields!' Apion roared. This time they listened. Hundreds of Byzantine shields shot up like a brightly tiled roof. The hail battered down, catching out only a handful. Moments later, the men lowered their shields, looking this way and that. Blackness. Then, from the western gate, cries rang out. Apion swung to peer through the sea of tents. Outside the western gate, the ghazis were wheeling away, a rain of arrows hammering down on the tents and soldiers just inside the gate – many not as swift to raise their shields. Again, silence. A short while later, the rain of arrows and chorus of screams came from the eastern gate.

'We must go out to engage them!' the skutatoi komes nearest him snarled, grappling his spear.

'Go out there in the blackness on foot, armed with a spear… against them?' Apion hissed. 'Save yourself time and throw yourself upon your own sword! You stay here, you guard the camp. You are the anvil, remember?'

The man blinked and nodded, his senses coming to him. 'Yes, *Haga*.'

'Strategos!' a gruff voice called out from somewhere inside the camp. Apion looked round to see Igor beckoning him. Romanus was fitting the last of his armour, tying on his greaves.

'How many?' the emperor said flatly.

'At least three thousand,' Apion replied. 'Ghazis, all of them.'

The howling cries of the passing riders sounded again, another volley of arrows – this time wrapped in blazing strips of cloth – reaching deep into the camp, setting tents ablaze and felling men as they ran to and fro, taking one varangos in the eye moments after he had leapt onto his horse. The area where the mass of the magnate armies were camped was in utter confusion, the men of these private armies new to such an attack and bewildered as to how to respond. Their leader, Scleros, fuelled by hubris and panic, roared his men into mindless action with his animal cries. They rushed in mobs to the spots where the hail smacked down, as if they could fight off their harassers by chasing their arrows. Igor lunged forward to stand before Romanus, arms spread, as an arrow plunged into the dirt where the emperor had been about to tread. Moments later, a larger object hurtled down, smacking into the dirt and bouncing to come to a rest before Romanus' feet. The blood and dirt encrusted features of one of Bryennios' riders – felled earlier that day in the valley – gawped up lifelessly, face still fixed in the terror of the wretch's last few moments.

Romanus growled like an angered mastiff, swinging a clenched fist into the air before him. Then, as if to rub salt in his wounds, a thunder of hooves sounded from inside the camp. A pack of the Oghuz riders – nine hundred of them – burst from the area where they were camped, lashing out at any Byzantines in their way, then broke through the spearline defending the western gate and hared off out into the plain, arcing round to the south before vanishing into the darkness.

A skutatos rushed over to the emperor. 'They heard news of Tamis' slaying, *Basileus*,' he gasped. 'They were not for standing with an army who slay their kin. It seems that they have headed south to join the Seljuk forces. Some of them chose to stay, however.' He pointed to the Oghuz camping area, where nearly a thousand still remained, helping to marshal the defence of the camp and fight the blazing fires.

Romanus' top lip quivered in ire. 'Their defection is a blessing. Best that I know the colour of their hearts tonight rather than tomorrow.' Another shower of arrows pattered down only feet from the emperor.

Apion glanced up to the high southern walls of Manzikert, illuminated by torchlight just a hundred feet from the camp's northern gate. 'It is cramped in there, *Basileus*, but safe. We can't all take shelter inside, but I suggest you do.'

'Stow your suggestions, Strategos. I did not march to the edge of the world just to hide,' he snapped.

'*Basileus*, these riders choose not to engage. They know that to attack a fortified camp is folly. They are here to wear us down,' Apion insisted.

'Wear us down?' Romanus frowned.

'For tomorrow,' he and Apion concluded in unison. 'I am certain that they will attack then.'

'If you come to any harm from these rogues tonight, the men will be distraught tomorrow.'

Romanus nodded. 'True, omens are rarely missed by the men of the ranks.'

'But we have to disperse those riders!' Igor insisted as another volley rained down on the area where the mules of the touldon were grazing on fodder. Hundreds of them fell with piercing brays.

'*Basileus*, with your permission, I will lead a counter attack,' Apion said.

'Very well. But do not take unnecessary risks, Strategos. The men will need to see *you* standing with them tomorrow... come what may.' Romanus nodded. 'Igor, bring the rest of the retinue to the fortress.'

Apion turned away, rushing to the Chaldian tents, ducking down under his shield as another storm of arrows smacked down inside the camp. Some of the tents had fallen and caught light from the campfires. Men struggled to douse the fires, and he saw Blastares, Sha and Procopius amongst them. 'Tourmarches!' he bellowed to Sha. 'Summon what archers we have!'

Sha looked up, hesitating for only an instant before spinning round to bark at one cluster of tents. 'Toxotai, form up!' He saw the few hundred Chaldian archers come together. Too few — the other few hundred who should have been there were gone with Tarchianotes' lot.

'Blastares, Procopius, go to the other strategoi and muster their archers too,' he barked. With a nod, they were off, lurching through the chaos.

As bedlam reigned all around him, Apion stood still, his gaze fixed on the darkness west of the camp from where the last volley of arrows had come, his ears trained on the noise beyond the camp. He heard some muffled Seljuk cry, directing the riders. Then the thunder of hooves outside the southern gate, then the twanging of bows and hissing of the next volley. Then the noise moved on to the eastern gate.

He closed his eyes to the gloom of night, and imagined their movements as if seeing the plain from above. An idea came to him.

Taylan kicked his mount's right flank and brought his ghazi wing wheeling round from the western gate. His eyes scoured the orange glow inside the Byzantine camp. They were in disarray. Men stumbled through burning tents, tripped on ropes and fell from their horses as they tried to cope with the deadly hail. They had been sweeping the camp like this for over an hour now – attacking the east gate, the south gate then the west gate in turn – and they each still had one of their four quivers to empty. He kicked his mount into a gentle jump over the pile of some two hundred dead Byzantine spearman lying on the plain. These fools had lost their discipline, bursting from the southern gate to try to snare his riders. They had been peppered with arrows in moments, and the southern gate had lain temptingly unguarded for but a trice.

Tempting for a fool, perhaps, he grinned. His men had suffered only a few casualties from the arrows of the Oghuz they had surprised south of the camp. And it would stay that way, he mused, for these riders of his would be needed tomorrow…

A thrum of another volley of arrows sounded, then the rhythmic thuds of them meeting their targets inside the western gate. Taylan punched the air, bringing his riders wheeling round. 'On, to the southern gate once more,' he cried over his shoulder.

The men rode adjacent to the camp walls, heads and bodies turned to the palisade walls, almost entranced with their work, plucking arrows from their quivers, nocking, stretching, readying to loose. Taylan raised his sword, readying to chop it down as he gave the order: 'Loo—'

Like a storm wind, something hammered into his back, from the blackness to the east. He flew from his saddle and rolled through the dust, winded. He clutched the arrow that was lodged in the scales of his vest, pulling it free to see it had not pierced flesh. He looked up, confused. All around him, the deadly rattle of arrows striking his men down rang out. Hundreds of his riders rolled through the dirt, shafts quivering in their flanks and backs, horses crumpled, thrashing and bloodied. He scoured the blackness of the plain behind them. Moments later, another volley came. He ducked down. Hundreds more fell. He was pinned to the ground as another two volleys came, felling many more of his riders.

There was a brief hiatus. Then, from the blackness, he heard a chant. '*Ha-ga! Ha-ga! Ha-ga!*'

The name curdled in his mind. He snarled, snatching his scimitar and leaping onto his horse once more, readying to charge into the darkness and slay the man who had foiled his sortie.

'Bey Taylan!' A fellow rider grappled his arm. 'Do not! Remember what happened to Bey Soundaq when he lost his discipline?'

'I must face him!' Taylan snarled at the man. But he saw that many of his riders had taken to fleeing south, back across the plain towards Mount Tzipan. He threw up his shield arm to catch the worst of the next volley of arrows. As he wheeled his mount away and to the south with them, his mind spun.

In the blackness, he was sure he heard an eagle crying. He glanced up once, twice and again, his teeth gritted. He saw nothing in the night sky. He remembered the crone from the mustering field at Khoi, felt her words pull at him, forcing him to challenge his every action.

Slay the Haga and break your mother's heart, or stow your blade and let go of this false vengeance.

'You gave me a choice of poisons, old woman,' he roared into the night.

Taylan's roar still rang in the air as Apion stood tall from the spot in the gorse bushes where he and his seven hundred archers had hidden. He looked to the black sky and thanked the waxing moon for staying veiled in cloud and allowing his archers to sneak out here, awaiting the next Seljuk sweep past the southern gate. The ghazi leader had been too predictable with his movements. West, south, east, south then west again – like a dead man swinging on a noose – allowing them to sneak out here while the ghazi arrows rained down at the western gate.

What he had not expected was that it would be his own son leading those riders. He looked again at the composite bow with which he had loosed the first arrow. In the flitting shafts of moonlight, he had only realised it was Taylan after the shaft had left his bow. He had watched, silenced, as the boy had fallen from his mount then righted himself. A swirl of emotions had overcome him as the toxotai had then emptied their quivers and driven the ghazis off. So his estranged son lived on. Might Fate see to it that they could parley in this far-flung plain in the coming days? He allowed himself to imagine talking with the boy, assuaging his anger. He even allowed himself to imagine Taylan speaking of his mother, telling Apion where in the vastness of the Seljuk realm she now dwelt.

Then, as if to rubbish his sliver of hope, he heard Taylan's words from that fraught encounter in northern Persia:

In every dream, in every waking moment, with every step you take on the battlefield, you should beware. I will be coming for you, Haga. I will not stop. And my mother's whereabouts? Never!

One of the archers with him coughed nervously. Apion blinked, then dismissed the men back to the camp. 'Do what you can to stamp out the rest of the fires and repair any damage, then be sure to get what sleep you can.'

The men flooded past him towards the camp, while he turned to face south, the darkness and the flatland. Dawn was barely an hour away. The new day was sure to bring the two great armies face to face.

His eyes fell to the moonlit dust before him and his thoughts spun. A lone eagle's cry pulled his gaze up to the northern hills, behind the camp. A single shaft of moonlight shone on a lone tamarisk tree there. The eagle cry sounded again, from somewhere up there. Apion strode for his Thessalian.

CHAPTER 18

Into the Fray

Dawn on Friday 26th August 1071 threw a pinkish-orange light across the plain. One of the sentries walking Manzikert's battlements was bleary-eyed after the hour or so of sleep he had managed following the chaos of the night raid. He inhaled a lungful of fresh morning air and gazed into the rising sun in an attempt to waken himself, then swept his gaze across the southern flatland, empty bar the dark red stain surrounding the abandoned Armenian trade carts a quarter of a mile outside the camp's south gate. The last shadows of night still clung to the folds of land further south and… he rubbed his eyes once, twice and again, his eyes widening. The shadows were moving. Then the dawn light threw off these last patches of shade and at once he saw what was out there… out there and coming for the Byzantine camp. His face paled and he immediately lifted his buccina to his lips with trembling fingers.

—

Down in the camp, Sha stumbled from his tent at the first blasts of the horn. His mind was still foggy from broken sleep as he looked this way and that: thousands more drawn, weary comrades were spilling from their blackened, still-smoking tents, looking around likewise. His first instinct was to locate Apion.

'What the…?' Blastares grunted hoarsely, storming from his tent with the look of a bear that had drained a vat of bad wine.

'An army approaches,' Procopius croaked, stomping back from the camp gates, throwing a cloak around his shoulders and buckling on his swordbelt.

'Tarchianotes has returned?' one skutatos cried out in hope.

Procopius' stony features and ensuing silence answered the question.

Sha hurried to the southern gate with Blastares. There, from the slight elevation of the camp's walls, he could see it. An army indeed. Like a silvery morning mist, rolling towards the camp from the south. Twenty thousand men if not more. A vast bullhorn of Seljuk riders. A golden bow banner fluttered at their heart. This was not the few thousand who had harassed the camp the previous night. This was the army of the Seljuk Sultan.

'I'd best get my sword then?' Blastares said flatly, his cheek twitching.

Realisation swept over the rest of the camp at that moment. Panicked wails broke out; 'The Sultan is here!' they cried. These laments were only tempered by the barking of commanders and the rattle of weapons and armour being gathered up. A multitude of buccinas keened and men hurried to and fro, all the while the Seljuk line rumbled ever closer. At last, the Byzantine infantrymen and cavalry began to spill out of the camp's southern gate and onto the plain to form up in a line, readying to face the coming foe. When the Seljuk advance came within half a mile of the Byzantine camp, they slowed and stopped. The shimmering bullhorn formation of their army flattened into a wide line. Waiting, watching.

Sha, Blastares and Procopius shot anxious glances at this as they barked the Chaldians into order, readying them to leave the camp and join the forming Byzantine lines outside. Sha eyed his depleted tourma – just two banda of skutatoi and a smattering of toxotai, five hundred men altogether. But they were ready. Likewise, Blastares and Procopius had their regiments in order, helms and armour on, shields and spears clutched, bows and quivers ready. But something was missing.

'Where is the strategos?' he asked his comrades. Glancing up at the Fortress of Manzikert, he could see Romanus, Philaretos, Alyates and Bryennios on the southern battlements, pointing to maps, hurriedly discussing the make-up of the enemy force. No Apion.

'He didn't return to his tent last night after seeing off the Seljuk raiders,' Procopius replied. 'Took to his horse and rode up into the northern hills.' The old tourmarches nodded to the gentle green range behind the camp and the fortress. 'Said he had to talk with someone.'

Sha gazed into those hills. One distant knoll sported a lone tamarisk tree and fluttering tall grass on its crest. Apart from that the range was bare and deserted. Sha felt an emptiness welling inside him as he pieced together Apion's thoughts. Perhaps he had chosen not to face his son in battle. *And damn any man who condemns you for it*, he mouthed, fending off sadness. He turned slowly away from the scene, when a silvery flash from up there caught his eye. On the slopes below the tamarisk tree, a lone rider galloped downhill towards the camp. He could not yet discern the identity of the rider. He did not need to. His face broke out in a broad smile.

'Stand tall, men. Your strategos comes to lead you into battle!'

–

Apion guided his mount down from the hillside, the morning sun prickling his skin and the crone's words swimming in his thoughts.

The storm is upon us, Haga. The answers you seek dance within its wrath...

From his vantage point in the hills he had heard the shock that erupted over the Byzantine camp when first light had revealed the Sultan's dawn move, but he had not shared it. Today had to happen. The two great powers of Byzantium and the Seljuk Sultanate had been on course for this clash for years.

As he rode past Manzikert's walls he saw that the beleaguered camp pitched just outside the fortress was nearly empty – the last regiments of the army were spilling out of the south gate to join the broad and deep Byzantine line facing the Sultan's ranks, orchestrated by the keening buccinas and waving imperial standards. The emperor, Philaretos, Igor and a bodyguard of thirty or so varangoi rode to take their place near a silk command tent that had been erected behind the battle line. Three sections made up the Byzantine line; the centre was composed of the massed ranks of themata spearmen – skutatoi from Cappadocia, Colonea and his own Chaldia – spears bristling, shields interlocked. Prince Vardan and his Armenian spearmen stood with them. The few hundred toxotai were nestled in behind this infantry wall, quivers full, bows strung and ready. The mounted, white-armoured varangoi and a tourma of Scholae riders milled just behind this serried infantry formation. All in, the centre numbered some seven thousand men. And it was bookended by two tight cavalry wings. Doux Bryennios would command the flankguard on the left. He was mounted at the head of his five thousand western horsemen.

Alyates, Strategos of Cappadocia, was to lead the outflankers on the right. There were four thousand riders here. A thousand of them were thematic kataphractoi – armed with lance, blade and mace and wrapped in iron like him, with helms, klibania, greaves and their mounts equally well clad in plate facemasks and scale or baked leather aprons. Two and a half thousand of them were the swifter and more lightly equipped kursores – carrying shields, light lances, spathions, bows and wearing just leather klibania and helms, their horses free of armour. The mail–clad Norman lancers – four hundred strong – made up the right.

Behind this fearsome front line and behind even Romanus' command tent, the mass of the magnate armies were gathering in something more akin to a horde formation than ordered battle lines, infantry standing amongst cavalry, oblivious to the folly of this stance. These private militias had lost several hundred in the arrow storm the previous night, but well over six thousand remained and would form a reserve, Apion realised. They would march some quarter of a mile behind the front line. *To be kept back and used as the blunt instrument they are when the time is right*, he wondered, *or to keep them from disrupting the manoeuvres of the well-drilled imperial troops?*

He saw that Andronikos Doukas sat saddled near Scleros at the head of the magnate army, his hands bound in chains and his head bowed. And he noticed the Oghuz riders who had chosen not to flee during the night were flanking the magnate mass in two wings of five hundred. Perhaps to aid them, or perhaps to police them. Including this reserve, some twenty–two thousand men were ready to face the Sultan's horde.

He rode onto the plain and wheeled along the Byzantine front, headed for the right–centre, his gaze fixed on his Chaldians there. The sharp edge of the anvil. They erupted into a cheer at the sight of their leader. '*Ha-ga! Ha-ga! Ha-ga!*'

He slowed, walking his mount back and forth in front of them, and beheld each of them with flinty eyes. 'Someone told me the Chaldians had come to battle today?' he offered them a wry grin. The men cheered at this, pumping the crimson Chaldian banners aloft. 'They said our ranks were thin and ill-prepared?' The cheers changed into mocking jeers. 'But I see before me nearly two thousand whoresons encased in iron, standing like giants, with the eyes of eagles…' he smashed his fist against his chest, '…and the hearts of *lions*!'

At this, the ranks exploded in unison. '*Ha-ga! Ha-ga! Ha-ga!*' The roar brought stunned looks from the themata nearby, and stirred the other strategoi and doukes into attempting similar homilies.

'Sir!' Sha, Blastares and Procopius barked in unison, mounted at the head of their ranks of spearmen and archers. His trusted three trotted over to converge on him. Sha handed him his greaves and mail veil along with iron garb for his horse. 'I reckoned you'd be in need of these today – I hear you'll be with the riders on the right?' The Malian nodded to the three wedges of kataphractoi on Alyates' cavalry wing.

Apion nodded, seeing his fifty Chaldian riders amongst that number. 'Aye, yet it will feel odd to ride to battle without you three by my side,' he said as he knelt, looking each of them in the eye as he buckled on his greaves. 'This will be more fraught than any encounter we have faced together in the past. While we match the Seljuk number, we have never faced as wily an opponent as the Sultan in a pitched battle before. He is no ordinary foe.' He glanced over the shimmering Seljuk lines across the plain. Some twenty thousand glistening warriors, speartips and fluttering banners slipping in and out of the morning heat haze. 'See how their lines are in three sections.' He nodded to the enemy. 'They match us in shape, but not in composition.'

'True.' Blastares squinted, his bottom lip curling in distaste. 'Not a single infantryman amongst them.'

'Nearly all ghazis. Their mobility will be their strength,' Sha added, sweeping a finger over the light, nimble and deadly cavalry. They wore helms, lamellar, mail or felt coats, carried vividly painted shields, short lances, scimitars and some bore war hammers or axes. To a man they wore the deadly composite bow and several quivers strapped to their backs.

'I see the Sultan's banner, but I do not see him?' Procopius said, shielding his eyes from the now fully risen sun to scour the enemy ranks around the great golden banner.

'There, the Sultan will be watching on from the shade, I am sure.' Apion pointed to a small hummock in the plain a distance behind the Seljuk lines. Atop it, what looked like a silk awning had been set up. Around the base of the hummock, two lustrous rings of soldiers formed a human palisade of sorts. 'Ghulam riders, the shock cavalry of the Sultanate, and no doubt a regiment of akhi spearmen,' he guessed, pointing at the upper and lower rings. He wondered at what words were being shared under that awning right now, and thought of the shatranj game he had played with Alp Arslan some years ago. He imagined the two opposing armies again like the pieces on the board, he and the Sultan looking on, looking for weaknesses. A stiff tension settled over the Chaldian ranks as they noticed their leader's silence.

Blastares broke the silence: 'You know they found a vat of wine in the cellars of Manzikert last night?'

Sha, Procopius and Apion looked at him with frowns.

Blastares' face was granite-serious. Then a craggy grin split it and a sparkle grew in his eye. 'So tonight, when we're back here, united, victory had, let's get utterly shit-faced on it, eh?'

Sha roared with laughter first, Apion and Procopius were quick to follow. The men nearby broke out in laughter too.

'Out there,' Apion smiled, 'I will think of nothing more than the crushing hangover that is to be my reward.'

The buccinas blared once more for final formations. 'Until this day is done, my tourmarchai. Until victory, my friends.' He nodded to his trusted three. The three saluted then turned away, heeling their mounts back to the front of each of their tourmae of Chaldian infantrymen.

Apion trotted over to Alyates' riders on the Byzantine right. There, he dismounted to throw the iron-scale apron and face mask over his mount, stroking its mane as he did so. Next, he set about tying the flexible splinted greaves around his forearms. Finally, he lifted the veil to clip it on across his face. But something caught his eye and he hesitated. The morning heat haze separating the armies flickered. A party was approaching from the Seljuk lines. Just seven riders, wearing not the armour of warriors but the robes of delegates. He saw that the party was headed for the Byzantine centre. They came to within paces of the front then, at some barked command from the imperial command tent, the infantry ranks parted, opening a corridor to let the delegation through. Alyates sidled over just then. 'The Sultan means to offer terms? Perhaps we should lend an ear,' he said, dismounting and beckoning Apion with him towards the command tent.

They arrived at the command tent just as the delegates were dismounting. They were older, grey-bearded Seljuk men, dressed in fine silk yalmas and caps. The lead delegate, draped in gold brocade, moved to stand before the white-and-silver-armoured Romanus, who had dismounted also to sit on a gilded throne, flanked by the great bejewelled campaign Cross on one side and the Icon of the Holy

Virgin of Blachernae on the other. The Seljuk delegate bowed before him.

'Our great Sultan sends you a fine gift, Emperor of Byzantium. He wishes to see all of your men return to their homes unharmed.' Apion noticed that the delegate's voice was booming, so many of the ranks nearby could hear this. 'So you can all be with your wives and children once more.'

Apion's eyes narrowed, sensing the true motive for this parley. He caught Romanus' eye at that moment, and saw the emperor's gaze harden too.

'Disperse your armies, Emperor of Byzantium, and leave these lands. Have your garrison walk unharmed from Manzikert and return to the west. This offer is most gracious and comes to you only once.'

Apion swept his gaze around the nearest ranks of soldiers. He saw many of them charmed by the sudden and unexpected promise of safety. On the cusp of battle, such words always played havoc with a man's heart. He thought of the soldiers who had deserted overnight. He loathed them for it, yet he understood. They had families, no doubt, cherished ones they longed to be with instead of standing to face the Seljuk wrath. He reached a hand inside his purse and stroked the dark lock of Maria's hair. For an instant he envied those craven men, fleeing into the arms of those they loved.

The envoy continued. 'Already, the vast wing of riders and archers you sent to Lake Van's shores have taken this path.' He stopped, a haughty smile spreading over his face as he gazed around the watching men. 'They turned and rode back to the west.'

Gasps rang out. Hundreds of voices whispered.

'Tarchianotes has fled?' Alyates hissed by Apion's ear.

Apion could not bring himself to reply.

'Never,' Romanus insisted.

The envoy's eyes grew hooded, a look of satisfaction settling upon his mottled face. 'Our scouts have been tracking them, and at the last report, those fine forces of yours were still on their retreat to the west, nearly ninety miles away.'

The watching Byzantine soldiers erupted in a panicked chorus.

Romanus' eyes darted, the panic almost taking him too. But he shot up from his chair, silencing the babble, standing tall to glower at the envoy. 'Tell your noble Sultan that we *will* walk from these lands,' he replied in a low growl. A flurry of muttering spread around the crowd. 'But not on this fine morning. No, we will leave these lands only when we are victorious, with Manzikert and Chliat as our prizes, or as spirits, slain on the battlefield as we fight to the last. *To the last!*'

The delegate's earnest and warm expression faded at this, his top lip twitching. The watching ranks had their nascent doubts swept away, many breaking into a defiant, thunderous cheer. The emperor seized the momentary fervour. 'Tell your sultan that we will talk again on the battlefield. Our swords will sing until they grow hoarse!'

The Byzantine ranks erupted now in a lasting, raucous chorus of chanting and cheering, Romanus' glare never leaving the departing delegates as they rode off back to the Seljuk lines.

'That was well handled, *Basileus*,' Apion whispered, sidling up next to the emperor. 'The delegate's words had the men spellbound for a moment there. They even had me.'

'Then they had us all, Strategos,' Romanus flashed a half-smile. 'As he spoke, I saw only Eudokia and little Nikephoros. How I longed to be with them, to guarantee that I would see them again.' He clutched the golden heart pendant as he said this.

'I am certain the Sultan made the offer in the same hope of seeing his own loved ones, *Basileus*.'

'Yet he, like I, cannot be seen to yield. Not even an inch. Each of us has to return to our realm with these lands secured. But only one of us can.'

Apion nodded, knowing full well that Psellos and the Doukas family would be awaiting news of this clash like vultures. Indeed, he mused bitterly, thinking of Diabatenus the missing rider and Tarchianotes the absent doux, they appeared to have invested heavily in a Seljuk victory. 'So what now, *Basileus*?'

The emperor held his gaze, slipping on his purple-plumed battle helm. 'Now, *Haga*, we go to war.'

Atop the hummock in the middle of the plain, Alp Arslan watched the sheepish envoys shuffle to the back of the tent. The Byzantine Emperor's response was not unexpected, yet it angered him greatly. Battle could not be avoided, it seemed. He threw down his green silk cloak, cast off his gold bracelets and neck chains, then took up the white garment he had asked for.

'Sultan!' Bey Gulten gasped. 'This is a terrible omen. Please, don the fine garments that befit you. Not this death-robe!'

Alp Arslan continued to dress in the garment as if he had not heard, pulling it over his iron-plate coat.

'Stand back,' Bey Taylan urged the aged Gulten.

But Bey Gulten insisted again, picking up the Sultan's battle cloak and striding towards him to force it into his hands. 'You mean to inspire your ranks with such a morbid gesture? What kind of man leads his people in such a—'

Gulten's words were cut short by a chorus of blades being ripped from sheaths. He looked this way and that – first at Kilic's dagger, pressed to his jugular, then to Bey Taylan's scimitar, resting on his breastbone. The bey backed away, bowing, his skin paling and sweat spidering down his skin.

'The Sultan will teach you how to inspire men, bold bey,' Taylan hissed.

The bey's nose wrinkled at being spoken to like this. 'Sultan, this boy means to talk to me, a man nearly three times his years, in such a fashion?'

Alp Arslan looked to Taylan and then to Gulten, his gaze distant, his face pinched with tension. 'He may possess just a third of your years, Bey Gulten, but he has thrice your wisdom. Now go back to your riders, you offer me nothing today but a grating voice.'

Gulten's indignation remained buried under his fear of the Sultan. Gingerly, he backed away, bowing. 'Yes, Great Sultan.'

Alp Arslan looped the ends of his thick and long moustache round the back of his neck and tied them there, then he swung around to Taylan. The boy wore a stiff expression, his jaw squared and his tuft-beard oiled and combed. His armour was polished to perfection, Bey Nasir's old scale vest glimmering on his broad shoulders. The Sultan picked up a finely crafted composite bow, slung it over his shoulder and strode to his dappled steppe pony. 'Come, young bey.'

They rode together down the hummock, through the ring of mail- and scale-clad ghulam lancers, and across the short distance north towards the main Seljuk lines.

'You were certain the Byzantines would reject your offer, weren't you?' Taylan asked.

'I do not believe in certainty, Bey. The offer had to be made,' the Sultan replied.

'But their campaign is crumbling. Half of their army fled back to the west.'

'And half remain,' Alp Arslan replied swiftly. 'In equal number to our forces. Their centre is lethal. Should our riders be caught in that spearline in this open terrain, the crows will feast on our corpses before noon.'

'But our riders are swift and nimble, they will not be so slow as to become snagged on their lances.'

'Perhaps, but look at their flanks. Their kataphractoi are their biggest weapon. Should they bring their outflankers round to bear upon our ghazis at the right moment, then we will find ourselves snagged whether we wish to be or not.'

'Bring the kataphractoi, I say, I have sharpened my blade for just that possibility,' Taylan replied.

Alp Arslan shook his head. 'The future of our people hangs in the balance today, Taylan. Yet still you think only of the *Haga*? He killed your father in battle. It was a noble fight in which Nasir fought bravely. Why such thirst for revenge? He is but one of many thousands of blades who we must fight today.'

Taylan's expression grew steely. 'I only know that I *must* face him.'

Alp Arslan eyed the young rider. Taylan's obsession with slaying the Byzantine strategos had grown unwieldy. It was all the boy thought of. Why? he wondered. What was the *Haga* to Taylan but yet another enemy blade? 'I need you to put your mind to the task we discussed, Bey Taylan. The reserves need you to lead them. Now go to them.'

Taylan seemed set to protest, but he sighed and nodded instead. 'Then I will see you in the fray, Sultan.' His gaze grew distant as he peeled away, turning to ride back in the direction he had come, back past the Seljuk command tent and off towards the southern mountains and Lake Van.

The Sultan watched him go, then faced forward as he came to the rear of the main Seljuk battle lines. The three blocks of riders twisted in their saddles and hailed their Sultan, cheering and throwing their hands aloft, parting to let him come to the fore. Their cries made the plain shudder, then they fell silent in expectation.

'Do not look to me as your Sultan today,' Alp Arslan boomed. As he said this, he leapt from the saddle and threw down the ornate scimitar from his belt. 'Give me a warrior's scimitar – a simple blade not weighed down with jewels. And give me a mace,' he cried. Moments later, he plucked a sword and bludgeon from the many proffered and held the weapons up. 'I have come to fight with you today. I am a ghazi, just like you. Whether today brings glory in victory or in defeat, I will share it with you, as one of you.' He leapt back onto his horse and placed his well-weathered battle helm on his crown, the nose-guard slipping into place between his fierce eyes. Then he kicked his mount into a trot up and down the Seljuk front, grasping the material of the shroud in his fingers. 'I come dressed to die, for my life is but a single leaf in a great forest, and I would gladly fall just to see this battle won!'

The roar that this conjured shook the land. '*Allahu Akbar!*'

'Now sound the war horns – take me to *war!*' he bellowed.

—

Apion gawped as the Sultan's battle cry and the roar of the Seljuk ranks echoed then faded. He shook his head, disbelieving, sure it was the heat haze lying to him. The Sultan was dressed in some brilliant white garment… a shroud? The crone's words echoed shrilly in his mind, as if mocking him for ever doubting her.

I see a battlefield by an azure lake flanked by two mighty pillars. Walking that battlefield is Alp Arslan. The mighty Mountain Lion is dressed in a shroud…

For a blessed moment there was only the gentle, whistling breeze, the chattering cicadas and the heat of the morning sun on his skin. He could hear every breath, every thump of his heart inside his carapace of kataphractos armour, every nagging demand for water from his parched throat, feel every trickle of sweat dancing down his skin, the steely touch of the mail face veil that hid all but his eyes. He saw the Byzantine buccinators look to the emperor for the word. He imagined old Cydones by his side, dryly eyeing the wraith of Mansur on the opposing ranks. A poignant smile touched the corners of his lips. He thought of Maria as he scanned the Seljuk ranks. He thought of Taylan.

Let my choices today be the right ones, he mouthed into the ether.

Then the Seljuk war horns wailed. The plain of Manzikert came alive with noise as the guttural roars of men, the keening of retorting Byzantine buccinas, the stamping of boots and the rattling of spears and shields set the earth to tremor. Both armies rippled like two great silver-scaled creatures, caged and raring to be unleashed.

The Seljuk banners chopped down first and the horde poured forth at a canter. The purple imperial banners dipped in reply, and the Byzantine lines coursed forward. The half-mile separating the two sides dissolved as the two iron tides rumbled towards one another.

The infantry in the Byzantine centre moved at a jog, whilst the cavalry trotted to keep pace. Alyates took to encouraging the kursores riders to stay in line and be ready for what was to come. Apion twisted in his saddle to offer his heavier riders a few last words likewise. 'Ride at pace with the infantry and your left flank will be secure,' he cried over the rumble of hooves. 'We will break forward when the moment is right and only then. If we choose the moment well, we can be the key to victory today. For we are the outflankers, the hammer. Our lances might write history on this plain. When the moment is right, we can charge the enemy before us, drive them round and pin them to our infantry anvil. The Seljuk horsemen ahead know this and they quake with fear!'

The kataphractoi roared in approval as Apion turned swiftly to face forward again, seeing the gap was just a quarter-mile now.

'We can ensnare them if we charge now!' one gravel-voiced kataphractos insisted, ranging beside him at a brisk trot, his heels poised to kick his mount into a gallop.

'The moment is not yet here,' Apion growled in reply. 'Now – *stay in line!*'

As the cowed rider fell back, Apion scoured the faces of the approaching ghazi, now barely three hundred paces away. He saw their snarling mouths, their levelled spears, their braced shields. He saw only shaded eyes, and wondered if Taylan was amongst them.

Suddenly, across the Byzantine lines on the left, some commotion occurred. One wing of some three hundred kataphractoi had broken ahead of Bryennios' flankguard, leaving the furious doux howling for their return. The majority of the Byzantine line cheered, eager to see their comrades strike a vicious blow into the Seljuk ranks, especially after the impotence they had felt during the arrow storm the previous evening.

'No!' Apion hissed, seeing this impetuous wedge plunge ahead like a dagger, racing at a full charge for the Seljuk right. The emperor too was signalling frantically for them to return. Buccinas howled and banners waved in futility as the riders bore down on their target.

Then, as if turned by a strong wind and a double moan of the Seljuk war horn, the entire advancing ghazi line swung around into a well-ordered retreat. The kataphractoi wedge drove into the space the enemy had occupied moments ago, the brunt of the charge wasted on thin air. They raced on after the retreating Seljuk riders, but the nimble ghazis melted away before them and reformed behind them like droplets of oil in water. The kataphractoi charge slowed now, the horses tired from the exertion, the impulsive riders realising their folly in being cut off from the allied lines. Worse, each ghazi rider had now stowed their lance and pulled their bow from their back. Those nearest raced to encircle the impetuous kataphractoi and in a heartbeat they had nocked, aimed and loosed. A chorus of *thock-thock-thock* echoed across the plain. At such close range and at such volume, many of the kataphractoi were stricken – arrows aimed for the few gaps in their armour at the knees, eyes and upper arms. Likewise, horses reared up, limbs peppered with shafts. In moments, the wedge of three hundred riders were in pieces. Many dead, many groaning where they had fallen. Another clutch of ghazi swept in to strike down the few who remained, hacking them with their scimitars or knocking them from their saddles and running them through with their lances.

The rest of the Byzantine line watched this, the gap remaining at some three hundred paces as the Seljuk retreat matched the Byzantine advance. Apion looked over his shoulder to the gruff-voiced kataphractos behind him. 'Now, you will stay in line, yes?'

'Yes, *Haga*,' the rider replied sheepishly.

As the Seljuk lines continued to fall back to the south, the emperor gave the signal to slow to a walk. At this, the Seljuks also took to walking their mounts away from the Byzantine advance, keeping the gap steady. Then they twisted in their saddles, lifted their bows skywards and loosed a volley of many thousands of arrows at the Byzantine infantry centre. Every skutatoi heart there froze.

'Keep your shields high, lift them when I say and we will be fine,' he heard Sha bawl from the walking ranks, the Malian watching the dark cloud of missiles that cast the Chaldians in shade momentarily. 'Shields!' he cried. The rattle of iron arrowheads on shields was cacophonous, and vastly outweighed the meaty thuds and yelps of those caught out.

Without hesitation, the ghazis then turned their bows as one to aim at Apion's cavalry flank. The volley rained down on Alyates and his lightly armoured kursores. With a series of guttural grunts and shrieks, those riders were punched from their saddles and mounts stricken likewise.

'Kursores, fall back!' Alyates bawled, snapping off one arrow shaft that had lodged in his klibanion. 'Strategos, you have the front,' he nodded as he and his more lightly armoured kursores fell back behind Apion's heavier riders, out of arrow range.

Apion nodded in understanding, then bawled to his riders as, with a rattling thrum, another dark cloud of Seljuk missiles was loosed. 'They fire from the edge of their range, and their arrows will be lucky to harm you. For you are encased in steel, as are your mounts, slide your shields into your backs, keep moving at a walk… and do not look up!'

'What, why?' the mouthy, gravel-voiced kataphractos behind him grunted.

Apion braced as the arrow hail pelted down all around them. The missiles danced from his helm and armour and the men around him. Only one man fell foul of the volley, a grim, wet, thwacking sound coming from behind Apion's shoulder. He glanced round to see the gravel-voiced rider there gawping upwards, an arrow shaft quivering in his ruined eye socket, the tip buried deep in his brain, blood spilling through his mail veil in gouts. The rider slid from his mount in silence and crunched to the ground, dead. 'That's why,' Apion growled to the others.

'We cannot offer any counter attack?' Alyates spat, riding level with Apion again. His eyes swept along the Byzantine lines as if seeking out some form of answer.

Apion replied curtly. 'That is exactly what they want. Look,' he nodded along the Byzantine lines to the mere handful of bodies that had fallen in the first two volleys, 'they cannot break our lines if we stay together. They mean to anger us into abandoning our formation. If the balance of numbers was not so delicate then we might have been able to charge them, but—'

'But that dog, Tarchianotes, has melted into the ether with half of our army?'

Apion nodded with a caustic gurn.

'Does Tarchianotes realise just what he has done? If I live beyond today, it will be with great pleasure that I track down and slice the cur's wart-ridden, scowling head from his shoulders.' Alyates snarled as he raised his shield, falling back as the next cloud of arrows hissed for the right flank.

Apion braced as the arrows thudded down around him, one jarring his shoulder as it smacked against a lamellar plate there – the armour holding good. 'Think only of the foe before you today,' he called back to Alyates.

The morning wore on and the tense procession continued, the Byzantine line progressing southwards across the plain as a solid front with the magnate armies and the Oghuz riders following a quarter-mile to the rear. The Seljuk riders kept the constant gap between them as they continued their retreat at a walk, loosing fearsome clouds of arrows at leisure. They proved skilled at this, as when the emperor gave the order to slow or speed up even by just a fraction, the Seljuk lines adjusted their pace to maintain the gap at the farthest possible killing distance. Worse, when the Byzantines took to loosing arrows in reply from their own modest companies of archers and archer cavalry, the missiles fell just short of the withdrawing Seljuk host.

Apion glanced over his shoulder, seeing the path they had taken from the camp and the Fortress of Manzikert – now a few miles behind them to the north. The parched plain they had advanced across was sparsely littered with the bodies of the infantry and riders who had fallen to the constant rain of arrows – no more than a hundred though – easy to spot given the clouds of flies that buzzed over the corpses and the vultures that swooped to peck at the flesh. They had some time ago passed by the spot where the headstrong kataphractoi had broken ranks and raced headlong into their own slaughter, and the vultures were thickest there. Another volley of arrows pattered down on Apion's wedge, shaking him from his observations. A missile skated from the rim of his helm, sending a shower of sparks across his eyes.

'Now, they must offer battle!' Alyates said, the young Strategos of Cappadocia pointing just ahead.

Apion squinted through the heat haze to see the hummock in the plain with the silk awning atop it. The Seljuk command tent. The retreating ghazi line had all but backed onto the bottom of this hummock and as the Seljuk riders looked this way and that for direction, the gap between them and the Byzantine advance was narrowing rapidly in their hesitation and their arrow hail faltered. The hummock itself was ringed by akhi spearmen on the lower slopes and a thick cluster of some eight hundred ghulam riders at the top. These iron masked riders were every bit as fierce as the Byzantine kataphractoi. Suddenly, from the ghazi line, the white-garbed Alp Arslan and a handful of bodyguards broke back, up the hill, through the double ring of defenders and into the shade of the awning.

Alyates' eyes scoured the small hill. 'The Sultan took to battle in a death shroud. Now, perhaps, he will find use for it!'

'He wears that garment only to inspire his men to victory,' Apion countered, 'their resolve will only be stronger for it.'

'Let us test that theory, Strategos,' Alyates said, breaking out in a broad grin, his eyes darting to the Byzantine centre.

Apion twisted round to see the source of Alyates' sudden encouragement. There in the Byzantine centre, the campaign cross had been hefted aloft, and the purple imperial banners were being chopped down, signalling both flanks should advance like pincers in an attempt to envelop the ghazi line and the hilltop tent. The buccinas sang to confirm it.

'This is it,' Alyates gasped. 'Take the kataphractoi forward, Strategos, let us seize the Seljuk camp! I will have the kursores rain their arrows on the defenders in support.'

'*Nobiscum Deus!*' the men of the Byzantine line roared as they broke forward, the two wings of cavalry at each end folding round the foot of the hummock in an attempt to corral the ghazi horde there. But the ghazi were swift to break, flooding round the hill's lower slopes and slipping from the closing Byzantine pincers and off to the south. A few hundred fell to Byzantine horse archers, but the rest burst south towards Mount Tzipan in a plume of dust, leaving the hill tent and those guarding it to their fate.

'Ignore them!' some unseen commander bellowed. 'Take the Sultan's tent!'

Apion swept round towards the hill's southern slope as part of the right cavalry pincer. He afforded a southwards glance at the fleeing ghazi. *Too easy?* he wondered. His musing lasted only an instant, the first cries of engagement tearing him back to the hill and the command tent. He lay flat in his saddle and levelled his lance. He saw the triple-line of akhi spearmen halfway up the hummock brace, snarling faces peering over turquoise and tan shields, spear butts wedged into the burnt gold scree for stability. Behind them, hundreds of ghulam riders atop the hummock shuffled, readying to spur their mounts into a downhill charge at their attackers should the akhi line be breached and the Seljuk command tent threatened.

'Break the spear wall!' Apion cried to his kataphractoi wedge and the other two wedges riding just ahead. 'Take one man down and the rest will follow!'

The rightmost wedge of kataphractoi hit the akhi spear line first. A dull, crunching noise marked the shattering of bones on shield bosses and the piercing or crumpling of armour on akhi lances. This first wedge fell back downhill, the momentum lost along with six riders. The second wedge punched into the akhi, desperate to break the hardy ring of defenders. This time, one akhi was run through on the tip of a kataphractos' lance, dark blood showering through the air, the man lifted from his place in the line and carried with the rider on inside, trampling the spearmen in the two ranks behind. But the victorious rider's joy was short lived. A clutch of the ghulam riders rushed down from the tip of the hummock to thrust their spears into him at all angles. His body fell, torn and sheeting blood. Meanwhile the rest of the second wedge found themselves repelled as the akhi line closed up, shrinking the defensive ring by shuffling uphill a few steps.

Apion led his charging wedge at the akhi line next. He set eyes upon one giant of an akhi, moustachioed and roaring, his face covered in battle scars. This foe's face came and went as the dark door pulsed into his vision, rushing for him, crashing back on its hinges, the flames beyond engulfing him.

He felt a dull roar topple from his lungs as he punched his lance through the giant's chest, showering organs and dark blood from the man's back, the tip of the spear tearing the throat of the akhi behind as well and pulling the weapon from his grasp. Trampling over another akhi, he realised he was inside the momentarily ruptured akhi ring with just a handful of his riders. Here, the polyglot cries of war were thick and desperate. He twisted this way and that, seeing the tear-streaked and snarling faces of the other akhi as they lunged for him and his men. One leapt up to slide his spear under the klibanion of the nearest kataphractos. The rider fell and was butchered in seconds, white bone and blood gaping through his mangled armour. Apion felt his limbs move in a numb and sickeningly familiar sequence. In a single motion, he drew his scimitar from his belt and swept it round, hacking the lance tip from one Seljuk spearman, scoring another across that foe's chest and then punching the tip into the next's shoulder. His Thessalian reared, kicked and gnashed, its hooves crushing the face of one foe and its teeth crippling the spear hand of another. Still, the akhi line fought fiercely, desperate to close the breach.

'Hold the breach!' Apion roared, a few more of his riders bursting inside the akhi ring – thirty or so men in total. 'Hold the—' His cry halted as he felt the ground judder. His head snapped round to the rise of the hummock and the tide of iron ghulam riders pouring down from there, their lethal lance tips only paces away and trained on him.

'*Turn!*' Apion bellowed to the smattering of his riders – all engaged in the melee with the Seljuk spearmen. They did their best. Twelve or so managed to swing away from the clash with the akhi and face the coming threat.

The clang of iron upon iron that followed shook the plain. Apion felt his heart thunder as the ghulam riders swept over him and his riders. A lance tip aimed for his heart stayed true until he brought the hilt of his scimitar round on it, diverting it so the spear ploughed through and dislodged a handful of plates from his klibanion, scoring the flesh of his hip. But the sheer momentum of the ghulam rider hit him like a rock thrown from an onager, punching him back from the saddle. As he fell, he dropped his scimitar and grappled at the rider, wrapping his arms around his attacker's torso and pulling the man down with him. They tumbled over and over in the dust as the rest of the ghulam wedge charged on past them. The fallen ghulam rider brought his steel-gloved fist crashing into Apion's face. The thick and familiar crack of his nose breaking filled Apion's head and coppery blood trickled down his throat. Apion swung a knee up into the man's gut to send him sprawling, winded. He leapt up, only to stagger back from the man's sudden recovery and lunge with a scimitar. Instinctively, Apion drew the savagely flanged mace from his belt and the pair circled. He ducked just under the swipe of the man's scimitar then reached up to grapple his foe's wrist and brought his mace sweeping down onto the man's crown. The ghulam's helmet and skull crumpled under the fierce blow. Blood and eye matter spurted from the rider's veil and he at once fell limp and collapsed.

All around him, the screams of Byzantine kataphractoi rang out as the ghulam hacked into them. Apion swung this way and that in the confusion. Through the forest of horse limbs and fallen men he saw that the other two wedges of kataphractoi had come to aid his. They were holding their own, just, and the breach in the akhi line remained open. His fleeting thoughts of barging through the chaos to aid his comrades were scattered by the sound of onrushing hooves behind him. He swung to see a pair of ghulam, lances levelled for his chest, eyes fixed on him. He braced, readying his mace to take one of these curs down with him. At that moment, Igor and a wave of white-steel Varangoi riders broke through the akhi ring just a handful of paces away, and crashed into the flanks of these two riders, dashing and trampling over them. Moments later, the Rus riders were swarming around Apion and hacking down the other nearby ghulam. The varangoi swung their fierce breidox axes to and fro, taking Seljuk riders in the flank and crushing them. Limbs were lopped off and skulls spliced in showers of blood. The infantry of the themata poured in through the gap Apion's riders had made and through the second gap the Rus riders had forced in the akhi ring. Thousands of them flooded onto the slopes of the hummock, cheering in victory. They pulled the ghulam from their mounts, despatching them with swift jabs of their spears and swipes of their spathions, then they turned upon the remnant of the akhi ring. Apion saw Romanus surging through the fray now also. His silver-and-white armour glistening as he urged his army on to the command tent, now only guarded by a clutch of panicked ghulam riders.

A hand grasped Apion's bicep. 'Victory is in sight!' Blastares panted, pointing up to the Seljuk command tent, his face streaked with other men's blood and his chest heaving. The big man ran on with the men of his tourma. Apion saw Sha and the less sprightly Procopius move for the command tent likewise, streams of Chaldian spearmen and archers flooding in their wake. The ghulam there threw down their weapons, and the last few clusters of akhi spearmen did likewise.

A cheer rang out, guttural and desperate. Romanus rode to and fro before the Seljuk tent rousing further choruses of this. '*Nobiscum Deus!*' they cried over and over, all eyes falling on the campaign Cross, being hefted to the top of the hillock by the priests.

Apion sought out and sheathed his lost scimitar, then pushed through the crowds of cheering soldiers to join the emperor. Igor was there, along with Alyates, Bryennios and Philaretos. He heard them conversing.

'We have lost but a few hundred kataphractoi and skutatoi, *Basileus*. This is a decisive victory,' Philaretos enthused, 'and a magnificent one!'

Apion bypassed them, then glanced around the shade of the silk awning at the crest of the hillock. It was devoid of life bar the handful of kneeling ghulam. A few timber chests sat there, open but empty. A table stood, a half-finished cup of red wine sitting beside four daggers dug into the table top, still bearing the torn corners of the map that had been splayed out there. He traced a finger over the cracked oak surface. 'This is not victory,' he muttered to himself, looking south to see that the ghazi lines had withdrawn just a mile or so and now waited there. Galloping to join them was the white-garbed Sultan and his bodyguards.

'But the men need to believe it is,' Romanus whispered, having come alongside him. 'It is a start, but no more.'

'So what now?' Apion asked, looking out from the shade of the awning around the shimmering and parched plain. 'The hottest part of the day lies ahead. Perhaps we should retire to Manzikert to rest the men?'

Romanus shook his head. 'We have taken a regiment of the Sultan's spearmen and a wing of his heavy cavalry. But the man himself and the vast majority of his army still loom out there.'

Apion squinted to the south with the emperor. A heat haze danced on the plain, part masking the thick Seljuk ghazi lines that had withdrawn there. Watching, waiting.

'And Manzikert?' the emperor continued, nodding to the north and the distant outline of the black-walled bastion. 'The fortress offers shelter but little else. It has been stripped bare of the food and fodder we found in its cellars, Strategos. We cannot return there lest we wish to starve or fight on tomorrow as weaker men. We must push on and seize victory on this fine plain today.'

Apion nodded. 'Then push on we must, *Basileus*. But we should be careful, for the Sultan seems eager not to offer battle on this plain.' He pointed to the area a few miles behind the Seljuk mass. 'See how the flat ground breaks up there? Rocky tracts, scree, folds, ditches and hills speckle the land. And then a few miles further on there are the valleys and the mountains that ring Lake Van,' he said, thinking back to the snare in the valley and the snarling Bey Soundaq.

'I will pursue him, but not into those valleys,' the emperor ceded. 'Better starving men tomorrow than corpses this evening.'

Apion looked over his shoulder. There, Philaretos, Alyates and Bryennios were discussing the next moves amongst themselves, and the vast Byzantine ranks were moving down the hummock's slopes, back down onto the plain. Some distance north, he noticed the rabble of the magnate armies still catching up. Nearly seven thousand men. Untouched, untested. A sea of sweating, scowling faces, hands clutching spears, axes, clubs and ornate blades. Scleros was mounted at their head, in his preposterous armour, with the prisoner, Andronikos Doukas, by his side. At that moment, Doukas squinted up towards the awning, his sweating, handsome features glistening like his shackles. 'And what of our reserve, *Basileus*?'

'Let us hope that today does not call for us to use them.' He cocked an eyebrow. 'But they might yet make the difference. They look fearsome enough, after all.' He grinned wryly. 'Now, Strategos, let us focus our thoughts on what lies ahead. Go, help Alyates reform the outflankers on the right. I need you to be ready. For when we engage with the Sultan's horde – and engage we must – I need you by my side.'

The Byzantine advance and the cautious Seljuk retreat continued as the afternoon wore on and soon the hillock with the awning – like the Fortress of Manzikert – was but a bump in the northern horizon behind the Byzantine line. Now the rocky majesty of Mount Tzipan and the surrounding green hills and valleys loomed over them, less than a mile away. As they came onto the rougher ground leading to these hills, the march was plagued by the rasp of parched throats and the stench of drying blood. But still they marched, slowly, steadily, driving the ghazi line back onto the first of the coarser terrain. Still though, the ghazi arrows came in rhythmic showers, and handfuls of Byzantine men were felled by each volley.

'Soon they must run short of arrows?' Alyates panted, riding near Apion.

'No, they each carry three, sometimes four quivers. They will have enough to loose upon us until dusk,' Apion replied, ducking as the latest volley smacked down around them.

'Then we will accept their surrender at dusk!' Alyates grinned, plucking a shaft from his shield and throwing it down.

Just then, a stiff northerly breeze picked up. It was at once cool and fiery, throwing up stinging particles of hot dust. A thick cloud of this dust billowed up and shot across the ground towards the ghazi line. The ghazi line, walking south but twisted in their saddles to look and loose north, were cloaked by this dust cloud. Their next volley faltered, arrows driven askew by the gust, pattering harmlessly into the ground. Most of the archers gagged and yelped at the stinging dust, wiping at their eyes, coughing and spluttering. A raucous cheer rose up from the Byzantine lines and the priests took to lifting the campaign Cross and the Holy Virgin of Blachernae as if claiming responsibility for nature's intervention.

'Ah, dusk, dawn or on this fine afternoon,' Alyates beamed. 'What does it matter when God is with us?'

Apion pulled a wry smile. 'If God was with us, then he would have struck Tarchianotes down with some foul pox before this campaign set out. He would have sent Diabatenus' horse tumbling into a gully. He would have torn the heart from Psellos when he was a child. Thank the men of our ranks, not God.' He pointed to the infantry in the Byzantine centre. There, Sha led the Chaldians in continuing to scoop up dust in the bottom lips of their shields, tossing it in the air to be caught by the northerly bluster. The men of the other themata and the Armenian spearmen had followed suit. His lips played with a smile as he watched Sha rally them to continue. The Malian was a strategos in all but name, he realised.

But Alyates did not hear his words. 'Look, they come to battle, at last!' the Cappadocian Strategos cried.

Apion followed Alyates' gaze. Indeed, the ghazi riders were sending out packs of riders from their retreating line. Pockets of a few hundred wearing cloths and silks across their faces to protect them from the stinging dust. They swept towards the Byzantine lines, then veered out towards the flanks.

'Outflankers, ready!' Alyates bellowed to his kursores.

'Harry them,' Apion said to Alyates, buckling his veil in place again. 'My kataphractoi will engage, but only if you can draw them close enough to our lines. We must not be drawn into the rocky tracts,' he insisted, looking to the ever more jutting and jagged folds of land that surrounded each flank of the Byzantine march.

The first pack of Seljuk riders darted for the Byzantine right like a flock of swallows, coming with light lances levelled as if to charge Alyates' kursores riders, then, at the last, hurling their spears like javelins and wheeling away. These weighty lances punched a raft of the more lightly armoured kursores from the saddle and a few kataphractoi as well. Alyates led the kursores forward in pursuit, trying to corral the ghazis before they could slip away. The nimble Seljuk riders were swift though, especially with the strengthening wind at their backs.

'Pull back!' Alyates snarled after a few hundred paces as the ghazis swept up and over one fold of shrub and dust-strewn land to disappear into an unseen dip beyond. A few riders raced on oblivious, and Alyates roared at these. 'I said pull back!' He loosed an arrow that whizzed past one disobedient rider's ear to reinforce the message. Soon, the kursores were back with the right flank.

'They will not tolerate constant harassment, Strategos. And nor will I,' Alyates growled, seeing the next pack of ghazis coming for them in the same formation. The sight was the same over on the left flank, where Bryennios' men were being pulled from their lines by these small packs.

'I know. I feel it too. But they must. If our cavalry flanks start disintegrating into these shallow valleys in pursuit of a few hundred riders, our centre will be exposed. And we don't know what lies in those valleys.'

Apion scoured the land ahead. Just a half-mile onwards, the folds grew more severe and then the steep, green-sided valleys rose up, many of them already pooled with shade as the sun worked its way towards the western horizon. It was a confused and maze-like terrain. He glanced to the Byzantine centre, hoping Romanus would stay true to his plan of retreating instead of entering those valleys. The northerly gust from earlier had now picked up into something of a gale in these corridors of land, circling and sweeping around their legs, pulling on their shields, seeing their banners pulled horizontal, rapping in the squall. And the dust now stung every eye in the battle, Byzantine and Seljuk alike.

The ghazis continued to retreat in their lines, sending out small packs to continue the harassment. Now Alyates began to lose his cool. The Cappadocian Strategos roared and waved his riders on after the next harrying ghazi pack, chasing sixty of them up to the brow of one gentle valley.

Apion watched the kursores go. When they slipped over the brow and out of sight, the breath stilled in his lungs. *No, you fool!* A heartbeat later, the clash of steel and cries of men sounded from beyond that brow. Apion's blood chilled. Moments later, the kursores reappeared, Alyates leading the retreat, a hundred or more of his riders missing, many more bloodied with gaping wounds. Pursuing them in a frantic gallop – instead of the sixty ghazis they had gone off after – were some fifteen hundred of these riders.

'Ambush!' one rider cried.

Apion's eyes widened, fixed on the lead ghazi. He saw the shaded features under the conical helm, the scale vest, the broad shoulders. *Taylan?* he mouthed, feeling all else drain from his thoughts. Then the lead ghazi held his head high and the dimming sunlight revealed the snarling, scarred features of an older warrior.

'Riders, fall back!' Apion cried, stirred from his trance. Alyates and his kursores joined the rest of the Byzantine right in flooding back from the ghazi charge. As one, they bent in behind the infantry centre as if to take shelter.

'Refuse the flank!' Apion bellowed as he passed the Chaldian infantry at the right of the Byzantine centre. Sha, Blastares and Procopius acted immediately, bringing the Chaldian front swinging back like a great arm to catch the ghazi charge. The ghazis were riding too hard to pull out of their pursuit, and hundreds of them ran onto Sha's spear line and the volley of rhiptaria loosed from it. Blood shot up as man and mount were run through and screams rang out as riders were catapulted from the saddle.

Those ghazis who had slowed in time hurried to turn and flee back to the main ghazi line. But as they swung their mounts round they saw only Apion and the cavalry of the Byzantine right sweeping back out from behind the infantry lines and arcing round, blocking their path back to the south.

Apion focused on the bold Seljuk riders, trapped between Sha's spear line and his own cavalry charge. *Anvil and hammer!* he mouthed through gritted teeth as the powerful gale seemed to help him on his way. He grappled his spear tightly and welcomed the flames of the dark door. Then his wedge smashed into the confused sprawl of Seljuk riders, driving them back onto the Chaldian spears, breaking them utterly. He lanced through one man, felt his mail veil being torn off by the hand of another, then felt the others melt away before him. In moments, the brave ghazi ambush of some fifteen hundred riders was little more than a third of that number. Those who could broke south in disarray, Byzantine missiles raining down all around them and Greek jeers ringing in their ears. But a chorus of laments rang out from the Byzantine left. Apion squinted through the dusty evening haze to see that a similar Seljuk ambush on Bryennios' flankguard had been successful. They had gone too far in pursuit and had not managed to recover the situation. Hundreds of kataphractoi and kursores lay in broken heaps as the victorious ghazi band over there swept away to the south, whooping and punching the air in delight as they moved to re-join the main line of slowly retreating Seljuk riders.

'We must turn around,' Apion growled over the howling wind, wiping the gore from his face, seeing the sun sliding away.

'Aye, the valleys are growing steep and the light is fading,' Alyates agreed, his hair matted with blood, his arm torn badly from a Seljuk blade.

'Let me speak with the emperor,' he said.

Alyates nodded. 'Be swift, Strategos. You are needed here.'

Apion nodded briskly, then kicked his mount into a gallop across the Byzantine front, heading for the centre. The Chaldians, the Armenian spearmen and then the ranks of the other themata lofted then waved their spears and banners like wheat stalks in a breeze to salute him. '*Ha-ga! Ha-ga! Ha-ga!*' they chanted.

Apion heard nothing of them, focusing only on Romanus, ringed by the Varangoi, with Igor and Philaretos by his side. He barged through, the Rus axemen recognising him soon enough. '*Basileus*, we must end this pursuit.'

'Yes we must,' Romanus admitted, his cobalt eyes defiant, his flaxen locks whipping in the gale. 'The sun is almost gone. Worse, I fear the ambuscades we have stumbled over so far are but a hint of what lies further south.'

Apion followed the emperor's gaze. The land ahead was treacherous, with tracts of volcanic rock jutting from the valley floor like waves in a foaming sea, churning in the squall. Overlooking this rough ground was a jutting outcrop of rock. A clutch of silhouetted figures watched from up there. One was crouched, wearing a Seljuk war helm and a white shroud, billowing in the wind. Alp Arslan. Beside him was another, broad shouldered, the setting sun's halo dancing from his outline, shimmering on the scales of his familiar vest. *Taylan?*

'Our riders will crush the Sultan's forces tomorrow, then,' Romanus boomed, disguising well his doubts over how they would feed themselves tonight. 'Bring up the banners, signal across the lines for an ordered retreat,' he called to his signophoroi. 'We are to return to the camp.'

For the briefest of moments, Apion felt a wave of relief. Then, from high above, an eagle shrieked. A piercing, chilling shriek of warning.

Alp Arslan watched the Byzantine manoeuvre studiously from the rocky outcrop, crouched on one knee, smoothing his moustache, the gale singing around him like an army of wraiths. In the broad, uneven land below, the purple imperial banner had been raised aloft, then turned to face northwards at the tune of three buccina blasts. Like a great silvery creature coming about, the Byzantines halted. Spears were raised, shields clattered and men turned about face as they readied to march back to Manzikert and their camp. In response, his ghazi line had now halted their slow retreat just under the jutting hill, their commanders looking up, waiting on some signal from him and his best men.

And now I must choose, Alp Arslan mused. *Retire for another day of battle tomorrow, or risk an attack upon the Byzantine retreat?* He looked to the purple-pink dusk sky, streaked with scudding clouds, and wondered if it was woefully late to ask for Allah's wisdom. Grain and fodder in the Seljuk column and in the granaries of Chliat was all but gone. A day of hesitation might be a death knell to them all. He thought of all that his rival, Yusuf, might do with news that he had failed in this long-awaited clash with the Byzantine Emperor.

'Sultan, what should we do?' Bey Gulten asked. 'Why do they turn?'

'It is just as it was at the Cilician Gates,' Taylan said flatly. 'The emperor turns because he fears the night.'

'He turns,' Alp Arslan growled, 'because he is not a fool.'

Taylan paced over to Alp Arslan and crouched by his side. 'My riders are fresh, eager. Give the word, Sultan.'

'You want to lead your riders into a spear wall?' Alp Arslan gestured towards the men who would form the rear of the ordered Byzantine retreat – readying to pace backwards and present their spears and shields at any minded to attack. 'You would lead your riders into a pit of fire just to strike him down, wouldn't you?'

Taylan balked at this, his dark locks whipping across his face. 'I… I must face him. I am Taylan bin Nas—'

'Bey Nasir once told me that he and the *Haga* were like brothers. They swore to die for one another.'

Taylan looked away, scouring the slow turnaround of the Byzantine lines. The dusk light betrayed the tears building in his eyes. 'I miss him. He loathed me but I miss him every day.'

'Bey Nasir loved you. He loathed himself for being unable to show it. It destroyed him.'

'No, the *Haga* destroyed him.'

Alp Arslan grasped his shoulders. 'His hatred is what destroyed him. In the end he ran onto the *Haga*'s blade, despite his old friend trying to spare him. Why do you waste your life, trying to repeat such folly?'

Taylan's eyes provided an answer before his lips moved. 'Because Nasir was not my father.'

Alp Arslan frowned. 'Then who…' His words trailed off, the glint of dusk light in Taylan's green eyes enough to piece it all together. Until now, he had thought Taylan to be just one of that rare breed with bright eyes that came about every so often amongst his people. 'No!'

Taylan nodded. 'It is true.'

Alp Arslan's eyes widened, his very marrow chilling. 'You are the *Haga*'s son?'

'Aye,' Taylan said, standing tall. 'And now you know. I am the bastard who reminded Nasir each and every day of his shame.'

The Sultan searched for the right words to reply. The gale screamed around them. 'Taylan, if there was one thing Bey Nasir would have wanted for you… it would be to unburden you of these troubles.' He saw the confusion in the boy's eyes, then grasped his shoulders. 'Let go of the past, let go of…'

Just then, a shrill Greek voice cried out from the Byzantine lines, below: 'The emperor has been slain!'

Alp Arslan and Taylan were torn from their exchange, both men's eyes shooting to the source of the cry.

His retinue hurried to crane over the edge of the jutting outcrop with them, gawping, their eyes disbelieving at the sight of the Byzantine lines – in chaos, the neat rear-facing spear line of moments ago disintegrating. And the cry sounded again by many others.

'The emperor has fallen! God has deserted us!'

Nobody there spoke for some time, until Taylan broke the spell:

'Now, Sultan, you must give the word. Set my White Falcons loose.'

Palladius the toxotes tilted the wide brim of his hat up and squinted up at the front-centre of the Byzantine line, the wind stinging his eyes.

He saw the furiously flapping imperial standard turning round and heard the buccina blasts. An ordered retreat? This was unexpected. A tense hiatus was followed by concerned murmuring. It seemed that none had expected this.

Men pushed and shoved all around him, eager to get into their positions. This would see the majority of the army turn to face north, while the current front ranks would remain south facing, but march backwards to present shields and spears against any attack from the rear. It required composure, discipline and perfect timing to execute.

He saw that many of the men were craning their necks to catch sight of the emperor, keen to see him confirm this order. He heard the men nearby rally their ranks with cries of 'About-face! Ordered retreat!'

Here at the back ranks of the Colonean Thema, Palladius had seen little of the battle so far, merely watching the front ranks of the infantry centre suffer the constant barrage of Seljuk arrows. He had been paid a fine campaign purse just to do this. Now, however, he saw an opportunity to make a far larger purse – a sum that would see him able to afford a villa in the Bithynian countryside and leave behind the squalor of his Colonean shack. He heard the continuing concerned babble from the ranks and filled his lungs. Then he let loose a cry that echoed above all others and above the gale:

'*The emperor has been slain!*'

There was a momentary silence, then chaos broke out all around him. Men echoed the cry and laments broke out. He smiled and pulled the rim of his archer's cap down to hide his face. He had always had a strong voice. Now he could use it to call upon his slaves in his new villa.

Apion swung round at the cry, his blood turning to ice, sure he had misheard over the squall. Then it was repeated, once, twice and then again, spreading like a wildfire through a dry forest.

'The emperor has fallen! The Seljuks have his head!' In moments, the ordered retreat had descended into panic. Skutatoi who had already turned to face north believed the cries and – fearing that some Seljuk attack had penetrated into the men behind them and slain their glorious leader, broke for the north. As soon as the first few did this, panic grasped the others. Men trampled over men, shouting, cursing. Some fell, snapping their lances, spraining their ankles, being trampled by their comrades. In moments, the tidy, ordered centre had disintegrated into a swarm of fleeing men, breaking around those who stood firm. Even the men marching in reverse to cover the rear seemed shaken by the cries, some fleeing too despite seeing that the emperor was in fact nearby, alive and well amidst his ring of varangoi.

Apion spun to meet Romanus' disbelieving gaze. 'Raise the banner, call to them, show them you are well!' he cried. Romanus was already waving the purple banner frantically, having snatched it from the signophoroi to perform the duty himself.

But still riders and archers continued to flee for the north, blind to the truth and fuelled by panic. Of the centre, only the Varangoi, the Chaldian Thema and the Armenians with them held their fragmented lines, though many were on the verge of panic, seeing the chaos that had erupted right next to them.

'Sir!' Sha cried over the thunder of boots and laments and the howling wind. 'What's going on?'

'Maintain the retreat, Tourmarches. Blastares, Procopius – keep the men at a steady retreat and bring them together to close the gaps!' Apion yelled.

But beyond the Chaldians, he saw Alyates crying out to his riders. The kursores had seen the centre crumble and break for the north and they too had set off in panic – many hundreds of them – and this left a glaring gap between the remaining outflankers and the infantry centre. He flicked his gaze to the Byzantine left; Bryennios' western tagmata riders had kept their discipline and were holding their lines, but for how long?

'*Basileus*, we can still retreat well if we form a narrower line and pull our remaining men together. The left is good, but the right is about to break.' He glanced this way and that. In these few panicked moments, the Byzantine front line had thinned drastically to just seven thousand men – more than six thousand having broken into flight. 'If we can stabilise this retreat, we can rally the deserters back to us.'

But Romanus' gaze was fixed on a point beyond Apion's shoulder, his hair blown back from his suddenly pale face by a furious gust of wind. 'Then by God, Strategos, bring them together!'

Apion swung round on his saddle to look south. The thick ghazi line, having spent the day retreating, now stowed their bows and instead took up their lances, swords and war hammers. They had scented the blood of the hugely weakened Byzantines and were now coming for the kill. He saw the Seljuk war horns being raised, ready to signal the charge, when he noticed something else from the corner of his eye. High up on the valley side to the Byzantine right, a dark smear emerged. A fresh wing of ghazis. They spread out like an iron wall up there, poised like a glinting dagger at the Byzantine flank. Most wore striking white falcon feathers jutting from the front of their helms and they clutched clusters of arrows in their knuckles, bows already nocked.

'A reserve,' Apion gasped, counting some five thousand of them.

Igor gazed with him. 'God have merc—' His words were cut short by the wailing Seljuk war horns that brought these fresh ghazi riders flooding down the hillside like demons, heading straight for the ailing Byzantine right flank. At the same time, the ghazi front on the rugged valley floor coursed forward. Both fronts raced as if to gnash like iron jaws on the beleaguered Byzantine ranks.

'*Allahu Akbar!*' the horde cried as one, causing the valley to quake.

Apion swung his gaze between the two walls of advancing enemy, then saw that the Byzantine right was about to suffer the first blow: an arrow storm from the hillside ghazis. 'Shields!' Apion roared over the squall, waving desperately at Alyates. But the Cappadocian Strategos was still desperately trying to organise and calm the horsemen on the right, and the thick hail of arrows struck the life from swathes of them. Crimson mist puffed into the air only to be swept and swirled around in the gale. Men slid from their saddles, limp, arrows jutting from necks and eyes, horses toppled, thrashing. Apion drew breath, readying to ride over to aid Alyates in the expected hiatus before the next volley. But the next volley came just a heartbeat later, and the next as soon again, the white-feathered ghazis standing tall in their stirrups and loosing like demons as they swept down to thunder through the gap between Alyates' riders and the infantry centre, like a knife prising open a clam. The feathered riders then swooped round on the Byzantine rear. A shower of arrows smacked down before his Thessalian and the beast reared in fright. It was then that Apion saw the lead rider of the white-feathered ones. And the leader's piercing green eyes sought him out across the fray too. *Taylan*.

The boy closed one eye and took aim… but hesitated.

Apion, frozen, saw the torment dancing in the boy's open eye.

Then Taylan loosed.

The shot was true and powerful, and Apion jerked his head to one side instinctively, the missile tearing his cheek. He struggled to calm his mount as it again rose up on its hind legs and he lost sight of Taylan. Before he could seek him out again, the charging main line of ghazis drove into the Byzantine front. A terrible song of bone, flesh and iron filled the rugged land as broken bodies were tossed into the air, the ghazis ploughing deep, red furrows into the Byzantine lines. Apion was barged back, a Seljuk speartip clashing into the shield on his bicep, and another two riders hacking at him with their swords. He parried desperately. Seljuk riders swarmed in every direction, iron flashed all around and Seljuk arrows battered down without mercy.

'We are too few – bring the reserve forward!' he heard Igor cry distantly, frantically waving the imperial banner to bring the seven-thousand-strong rabble of the magnate armies – still halted some quarter of a mile to the north – into the fray. After all their inactivity so far, they would have a vital role to play. And the banners were waved to the two wings of Oghuz riders who flanked them too. But would they rush to save an emperor whose men had unwittingly slain their brethren in the confusion by the trade carts the previous night?

Apion swept his scimitar across the throat of one determined attacker, chopped the arm from the next then kicked another to the ground. In a heartbeat of respite, he glanced to the emperor, fighting desperately alongside Igor and the varangoi just a handful of paces away. The golden heart pendant on Emperor Romanus' breast sparkled in the ailing light, swinging with every sword stroke, the thick and merciless hail of Seljuk arrows dancing from his armour. It was then that the gale picked up like never before, filling the valleys, keening around the battle as if to sweep away the souls of the fallen.

The crone's truth rang now like never before.

At dusk you and the Golden Heart will stand together in the final battle, like an island in the storm.

Andronikos Doukas gawped at the horde of some twenty-five thousand Seljuk riders just a quarter of a mile ahead, swooping and darting, cutting through the Byzantine ranks with their lances. And there were the white-feathered ones too, circling, loosing a constant storm of arrows at an incredible rate.

'They're going to be butchered,' he gasped, his shackles rattling in the fierce wind.

'And they want us to come and be butchered with them, it seems,' Scleros, the trident-bearded magnate general remarked glibly, pointing to the emperor's banner rapping in the gale and being waved frantically.

Andronikos eyed Scleros, seeking to understand the man's intentions. He seemed anything but eager to heed the command. Indeed, when the nine hundred Oghuz riders near the magnate ranks burst into a gallop and hurried to the emperor's aid, this one still hesitated.

The wind whistled, the battle sang and not a soul amongst the magnate ranks spoke.

'Aye, well, we should be swift,' Scleros said at last. Then he turned to Andronikos. 'Give me my banner, wretch,' the man snarled, pointing to the black standard he had given Andronikos to carry.

Andronikos heeled his mount over to Scleros. He thought of home in Constantinople at that moment. Of his father. His black-hearted, loutish and loathsome father. The man had been a bully both to him and to his mother, each taking beatings that would leave them bruised and whimpering. Now his father languished in some grim Bithynian backwater – exiled from the seat of power he so coveted. He held up the standard with his shackled hands. Scleros snatched at it. Andronikos did not let it go.

Scleros scowled in confusion. 'Give it to me, fool. The emperor calls upon us.'

Andronikos grinned, then, with a flash of silver, whipped his wrists up, throwing his chains around Scleros' throat then wrenching them tight at the nape of the man's neck, drawing it as fiercely as he could. Scleros' ludicrously plumed helm fell to the ground. He thrashed and gagged, his face turning purple as he pulled at the chains, great clumps of oiled hair coming loose from his beard as he did so. His eyes darted over the nearest of his riders, who watched on impassively.

'They will not come to your aid, you old fool,' Andronikos grunted, yanking the chains just a little tighter. 'They are my men now.'

When Scleros fell limp, Andronikos threw the corpse to the ground, then held up his chained wrists in expectation. Another of the chief magnates ranged forward and swung his sword down, cutting through the bonds.

Andronikos stretched his arms and flexed his fingers. 'Damn, but it feels good to be free.' Then he hefted the magnate banner and swiped it overhead, bringing them about face and leading them away from the battle at a canter.

He gazed into the western horizon, grinning, an edge of madness in his eyes.

I hope you appreciate this, Father.

CHAPTER 19

Island in the Storm

Every man in the beset Byzantine ranks cried out in lament, as word of the rearguard's desertion spread. This only spurred the encircling Seljuk host to attack with renewed ferocity, spilling around them, swords, axes and spears swinging and cutting, innumerable arrows raining without mercy. At the heart of the Byzantine ranks, Apion held his shield overhead, arrows battering down upon it. He glanced northwards through the chaos, seeing Andronikos and the magnate armies melt away. Their last hope of reinforcement. Gone. *You foul-hearted dogs!*

He fought on numbly, knowing that the few hundred brave Oghuz would not be enough to turn the battle. The rugged steppe riders swept around the outside of the battle, showering the ghazis with arrows in an attempt to relieve the pressure on the trapped Byzantine ranks.

The battle raged on as the last slivers of light began to fade. Soon, any semblance of opposing lines had evaporated and the two forces were entangled, men fighting men in single combat, small pockets of comrades taking on groups of their foes.

Apion caught sight of his trusted three and his Chaldians, fighting like giants in the crush of bodies nearby. He saw they were struggling, saw the Seljuk cavalry had them pinned. 'Ya!' he cried, kicking his mount into a charge. He threw down his spear and plucked out his scimitar and mace, then surged towards his men, cutting through their attackers.

'Come on then, you *whoresons!*'

Sha and his tourma of Chaldian spearmen had managed to form some semblance of a defensive huddle, but the press of the surrounding ghazi noose pushed the breath from their lungs, and they were being driven back pace after pace such was the pressure, their boots ploughing a furrow in the dust.

A pair of siphonarioi had managed to ignite their fire canisters, and the thunder of Greek fire rolled across the din of the storm, the orangey flame driving back a section of the Seljuk front. Riders screamed and toppled as thick black smoke roiled in the air. For just a moment, the pressure was eased, then the first siphonarios was peppered with Seljuk arrows and toppled. Moments later, the second was struck down and his canister was punctured by an arrow too. The canister erupted, spilling a blanket of flame over Byzantine and Seljuk alike. The screams were harrowing, yet only a few heartbeats later, the fire died and the Seljuk cavalry thrust forward and the crush resumed. They pressed like demons, their lances skewering swathes of the brave Armenians. Prince Vardan took to swiping his long sword at them, determined to drive them back. He cut down four or more of the riders before he disappeared under a flurry of hacking Seljuk swords and spouting blood. Moments later, the Armenians were all but broken.

'Hold!' Sha screamed over the din of the storm and the battle, jabbing his spear up into the chest of one hulking ghazi. He looked to his left and right, seeing that big Blastares and old Procopius were faring little better. Each of them and their tourmae were but islands of men now, surrounded by the ocean of ghazi riders. He filled his lungs and roared. 'Chaldians – come together!'

Blastares was first to react, forging a path through the melee with gusto. The big man had lost his helm in the action. His scalp was torn from some spear wound and his face awash with a nightmarish mask of blood. But his eyes gleamed and his anvil jaw jutted defiantly as he swept his spathion at the riders before him. He parried an axe blow then brought his spathion round to cleave the attacking man's axe hand clean off, before prizing the weapon from the severed hand and promptly leaping to lodge it deep in the rider's face. The clutch of two hundred or so that remained of his tourma came with him, inspired by his utter lack of fear.

On the other side, he heard a bitter tirade cutting through the din and the gale. 'I'll use your guts to string up a trebuchet,' Procopius snarled, hobbling with the aid of his spear, swinging his sword this way and that to cut a path towards Sha, 'then I'll use it to hurl your balls into the Eternal Fires of Chimera!' he finished, sweeping his spathion across the throat of one ghazi then punching it into the crotch of another.

At last, the remnants of the three Chaldian tourmae came together as one.

'The army is in pieces,' Blastares gasped, slotting into place by Sha's right, adding to the desperate spear wall.

'What do we do?' Procopius panted, coming to stand by the big man.

Sha looked to his close friends. These two had been pillars of the Chaldian army for years. Never had they looked so lost. Never had Sha felt so adrift. 'We do all that we can,' Sha said.

'Aye,' Blastares grunted. 'All that we can. As it has always be—'

His words were cut off by the hissing of an arrow and the *thunk* of splitting flesh. Blastares clutched at his throat, blood leaping from where the shaft had punctured. The big man clasped a hand to Procopius' shoulder, then slid down, under the hooves of the advancing ghazis.

Procopius gawped, grappling to retrieve his friend's body. 'No!' he cried, seeing his comrade's corpse churned into the reddening mire. The aged tourmarches set eyes upon the Seljuk who had loosed the arrow, nocking his bow and aiming for his next victim.

'Forgive me, sir, but I must leave my place in the line,' Procopius rasped in Sha's ear.

'Stand firm, Tourmarches!' Sha demanded, swiping out to deflect a jabbing Seljuk spear.

'I am already dead,' Procopius cried, pulling up the hem of his klibanion to reveal the deep gash in his thigh. Black blood was washing down his leg. 'One of those bastards got me. I have moments, at most. Let me spend them well. Let me take the cur who killed the big man.'

Sha parried a spear thrust and nodded, cursing the tears that stung behind his eyes. 'Do what you must, old horse, and do it well,' he croaked.

With that, the old soldier barged forward, leaping up at the ghazi archer, barging him from the saddle and into the mush of bone and blood. Sha saw old Procopius straddle the ghazi then choke the life from him. Moments later, the mortal struggle was obscured by the advancing Seljuk crush and a flurry of flashing Seljuk blades.

Sha fought to banish the anguish from his chest. He heard his own battle cries as if from another, and felt his every spear thrust numbly. When the spear was torn from his grasp, he fought on with his spathion, barging his shield up and hacking at everything that came his way. Moments later he realised he was one of just a handful of Chaldians remaining. A searing pain raked down his thigh. He swung to see a Seljuk spear lodged there, then cried hoarsely as it was torn out. He fell to one knee, his vision spotting over and his strength leaving him, the battle noises growing distant. In his fading vision, he saw Apion on his Thessalian, coming to save his men, kicking out at the ghazis surrounding him, swiping his old ivory-hilted scimitar at all who tried to cut him down.

'Fight on, *Hagu*. I pray you find your peace,' Sha mouthed before he toppled into the gory mire.

Palladius' vision jostled as he fled with the many other Byzantine soldiers. He had been swift to run after his false cry. *Get clear of the battle, think of nothing else.* But already his mind was turning to the imperial loot that sat, barely guarded in the camp outside Manzikert. If he ran fast enough, he might be one of the first back there. He could have his pick of the jewels and fine silks there. And that was even before he picked up his purse from Psellos. Elated, he stretched his stride and overtook fleeing comrades, throwing down his quiver and bow. He let loose a whoop of joy as he burst ahead of the foremost runaway. But a dark splodge in the corner of his eye spoiled the moment. Riders were overtaking him.

Bastards! He thought. *They'll get the best of the loot before me!* A moment later, he realised they were not Byzantine riders, but a clutch of ghazis who had broken away from the battle in the foothills to pick off the Byzantine deserters. There were thirty or so in this pack. They raced ahead of him, then swung round and charged back, coming head-on at him and the fleeing soldiers. The lead rider leaned to the right of his saddle and held out his scimitar, his feral eyes fixed on Palladius.

'No,' Palladius panted, slowing, waving his hands. 'I'm not your enemy.'

The rider lay flatter in the saddle, rode harder.

Palladius' eyes widened. 'No, there is gold.' He pointed frantically to the north, in the direction of the camp. 'There is go—'

It was an odd sensation. A sharp, biting pain where the ghazi blade scythed into his throat, then a dull clunk where it sheared bone and ripped out through the back of his neck. There was no feeling after that, just a whoosh of air as the world seemed to spin violently around him and a thud as he landed on the dust. He blinked, wondering why he was at eye level with the feet of passing men. Then he noticed a headless body standing where he had been just moments ago, blood spouting from the neck.

The body crumpled and the life slipped from Palladius' head. The din of the battle he had fled raged on.

—

Apion's face dripped with gore, his sword hand and every inch of his blade glimmered red and his Thessalian's skin was slick with sweat and blood. Arrows battered from his helm, shield and armour relentlessly and the gale threw up sprays of blood like some gory ocean. He brought his mace up and across the face of one ghazi, smashing the man's jaw and crushing his face, then brought it round to crumple the chest of another. He slashed out with his scimitar at the next few who came at him, then found himself with a precious instant of respite. He panted, hearing his heartbeat drumming in his ears, seeing the faces of his trusted three. Lost. Cut down before he could reach them. He buried the blade-like sorrow and swung his mount round, parrying frantically as he tried to make sense of the battle.

All he had known, all he had been taught about warfare, strategy and tactics by Cydones and Mansur meant nothing now. There were no formations, no ordered lines, no options. Just a seething tide of ghazis pressing in on the archipelago of Byzantines. Bryennios and his cavalry had fought well, it seemed, clustered by the emperor's left, but many had fallen. The varangoi had dismounted and were now standing valiantly around Romanus, Igor swinging his breidox axe tirelessly at all who tried to breach their roughly formed square, his face and white armour spattered red.

A wing of ghazis surged for the Varangoi square, forging a path towards the emperor. One chopped his scimitar across Igor's breastplate, another swept his blade across the Rus' shoulder, cleaving deep into a gap in his armour and leaving his axe arm hanging uselessly. But the warrior took up his weapon in his other hand and swung it out regardless. Yet the next blow tore out the Rus' throat. The old, gruff axeman sputtered lifeblood and looked around as his last moments of life ebbed away. A heartbeat later, he was gone, but his staunch resistance had allowed the varangoi either side of him to close up the gap in the square, and the ghazis were rebuffed in their attempts to get to Romanus. Amongst them was Alp Arslan, the great warrior Sultan's sword held aloft and his mouth agape in a battle cry, his white shroud soaked with blood. The next ghazi surge pressed one side of the Varangoi square back until it was on the verge of collapse.

'Ya!' Apion yelled, guiding his mount through the heaped bodies, the clusters of fighting men and the mire of blood to aid the tenacious Rus in their last stand. He veered away from swiping blades and ducked under jabbing spears. Then, suddenly, his world was thrown into chaos. He heard the agonised whinnying of his Thessalian and felt the gelding fall away under him. Earth and sky changed places as he tumbled through the slick of blood and bone. Dazed, he staggered as he tried to stand, clutching his head, realising his helm had been lost in the fall. His scimitar had fallen too. Worst of all, he saw his Thessalian breathe its last, crippled by the spear that had been hurled into its chest, piercing its heart. He looked on numbly, seeing the light in the beast's eyes dim.

All around him, men fought with their blades and with their bare hands. The hundreds fighting for their lives around him seemed oblivious to his presence. They barged around and past him, splashing a filthy mix of blood and earth up at his face. He gazed through the forest of horse legs and saw his scimitar, a few paces away, in the mire. When he reached out to lift it, an arrow sliced through the air before him, punching into the mire and quivering.

He swung round to meet Taylan's glower. His son was mounted, only paces away.

When another ghazi rider raced for Apion, sword hefted, Taylan swept up a hand and the rider pulled out of the strike then raced on into the fray.

Taylan slid from his saddle, thumping down into the blood-wet earth as the struggle raged on around them. He dropped his bow then prised Nasir's helm from his head and threw it to the mire, letting his dark locks billow in the whipping wind. His brow was dipped like an angry bull's, his eyes glimmering like jewels in the dusk.

'You saved me?' Apion said, flashing a glance to the ghazi who could have slain him. Likewise, many more skirted past, eyeing Apion as if to strike then thinking better of it upon seeing that Taylan was already facing him.

'Perhaps only so that I could slay you myself,' Taylan replied, one corner of his top lip flickering. He drew his scimitar.

'Perhaps?' Only now Apion could see the young man's face was streaked with recent tears. 'Unlike when we last met, you do not seem so sure this time?'

'You killed my true father, your armies sacked my home in Hierapolis. You stole my soul...' Taylan growled over the squall.

Apion saw the knuckles of Taylan's sword hand flex on the hilt of his scimitar, then he eyed his own blade – still jutting from the ground. 'I wished for none of that. I, like you, am just a leaf in this storm of war.'

'But my mother,' Taylan snarled.

All of Apion's senses pricked up. His son looked him in the eye.

'She did not want this,' Taylan continued. 'Not for Bey Nasir, not for me.'

'She has a good heart, Taylan. One of the few who do.'

'Don't you speak of her!' Taylan barked, lifting his scimitar to point it like an accusing finger. The wind blew his locks across his face and part-masked his gritted teeth.

Apion raised his hands in supplication. 'Tell me she is well, Taylan,' he cried over the din. 'Tell me she is happy. Tell me this and I will not seek her out anymore. Tell me this and we need not clash swords.'

Taylan looked along the length of his scimitar and frowned, his sword arm quivering. 'Then what would be my purpose?'

'You can be a good man. Do not let a quest for revenge stain your life like it did mine and Nasir's.'

Fresh tears darted from Taylan's eyes. Slowly, he unbuckled Nasir's scale vest, the armour jacket crunching to the ground.

'Taylan, what are you—'

'I am unshackling myself of the past,' he said with a weak smile. 'The shame, the anger, the hatred...'

His words shuddered to a halt and he staggered forward, his back arching and blood lurching from his mouth. A wiry-bearded older Seljuk swept past on his mount, reaching down to wrench his thrown axe from between Taylan's shoulders. 'Where is your hubris now, whelp?' the older rider spat, a sneer wrinkling his blade-like features.

The man's victory was short lived. Apion swept up his scimitar and brought it chopping round on the rider's belly. The blade cut through the man's mail shirt and sliced open his flesh. He toppled from the saddle, screaming, then scrambled up onto his knees, desperately trying to scoop his steaming, spilling entrails back into the wound – scraping up blood, earth and slivers of flesh from other bodies in the process. Devoid of feeling, Apion strode over to the man, who glared up at him, mouthing some kind of plea. With a swipe of the scimitar, the man's head was off, gawping as it rolled through the mire.

He heard a distant cry: 'Bey Gulten has fallen!'

Apion stumbled through the fray to the prone Taylan. He fell to his knees and cradled the young man, lifting him from the filth. The snarl was gone, replaced by a look of fear. He looked every bit a fifteen-year-old boy, breathing his last on a battlefield.

'She is… she needs you,' he spluttered, the colour draining from his face and his pupils dilating. 'Go to her. Be swift… tell her I'm… sorry.'

'Where is she?' he gasped.

But there was no reply. He felt the boy's body relax, a last rattling breath escaping his lips. He stared into Taylan's lifeless eyes, hearing the boy's last words over the screaming, gnashing of mounts and rasping of iron nearby. Tears blurred his vision and his chest racked with a sob. His trusted three were gone. His faithful old warhorse had charged its last. The emperor's army was on the brink of destruction. And now his son lay dead in his arms. Surely now he too was to die on this field. The truth he had sought about Maria would die with him.

'What is left?' he mouthed, feeling bloodspray settle upon him.

It was then that he heard a desperate cry from amidst the pocket of Byzantine resistance. 'Do not lose heart!'

He looked up. The voice was unmistakable. Emperor Romanus. Apion lay Taylan down and stood tall. A short distance away, the writhing mass that had been the Varangoi and the remainder of Bryennios' cavalry wing were now clustered together in a desperate last stand. A few thousand other men still held out in pockets here and there, despite the relentless press of Seljuk cavalry. A pair of ghazi riders circled around him at that moment. He levelled his scimitar and swept up a discarded shield, seeing they each had their bows trained on him. But the lead rider looked down at Bey Taylan's body and then at Apion, then flicked his head towards the nearest cluster of Byzantine resistance. 'I saw what happened. Go, join your comrades. Fight your last. You deserve to die in battle at least. We will tend to Bey Taylan's body.'

Apion backed away, panting, giving the man a brisk and earnest nod. He turned and hurried for the cluster of varangoi – now in a swiftly shrinking circle. These Rus – barely a hundred of them – swung their axes valiantly. Seljuk bodies fell back in swathes, cleaved open or deprived of limbs or heads, only for many more to replace them. He saw a gap that had been forged in the circle, and, just before the varangoi had a chance to close it, he rushed for it, tumbling into the tiny patch of ground within. At one edge of the circle, Romanus tugged on the reins of his rearing stallion, swiping out at the attackers, aided by Bryennios and a clutch of his cavalrymen. The emperor's armour was battered and gore-coated, his helm lost and his hair matted with blood. Then, with a flash of steel, the *Golden Heart*'s mount was struck down, peppered with Seljuk arrows. The emperor sunk out of view.

'No!' Apion cried.

Romanus thrashed in the blood-soaked earth, desperate to free his trapped leg from under his dying mount. Apion and a pair of varangoi wrenched him out by the shoulders and to his feet.

'Get me armour,' Romanus growled over the whistling gale, unbuckling his ornate white-and-silver breastplate. 'Proper armour.'

A varangos came to him with an old iron klibanion – the lamellar armour jacket of the ranks – and a simple conical helm, before rushing back to the tight defensive circle.

'*Basileus?*' Apion frowned.

'What use is splendid cavalry armour when you are to fight on foot?' Romanus offered him a flash of a grin that did well to mask his fear. This man was the figurehead of all the Seljuk army were here to conquer. His head would surely be a prize sought by every blade coming for them.

Apion did not protest, clasping a hand to the emperor's shoulder as he buckled the klibanion and helmet on. The vicious squall circled around them with a howl as if it had come to battle too, and the relentless arrow hail thickened further, striking men down in swathes. 'I will be by your side to the last, *Basileus*.'

When a pair of varangoi cried out, lanced by Seljuk spears, and fell from the circle, Apion and Romanus leapt into the breach as one. The wailing storm buffeted them, arrows danced from their armour and the Seljuk blades were relentless, and they fought with all they had. Apion parried, swiped and cut out, feeling his sword arm tremble with fatigue, knowing he had little left to give, sensing that this last stand was about to fall. The hundred varangoi became thirty, and all too quickly just a handful. Soon, he felt Romanus press up back-to-back with him and realised they were but two. He felt the vibrations of a defiant war cry shake his bones. Then a Seljuk axe cut down across his cheek and sliced the skin open there. A heartbeat later a spear punched into his klibanion, puncturing his flank. He faltered, falling to one knee, blood lurching from the wound. He felt Romanus, at his back, sink to the ground too. The emperor clutched his forearm, an arrow having pierced his wrist, knocking the spathion from his grip. Weaponless, Romanus tried to barge out with his shield. Apion swiped weakly at those who came at the emperor. His parry was swept aside with ease, and a Seljuk shield rim cracked against the bicep of his sword arm, shattering the bone. He roared in agony, barely seeing the scimitar that scythed for him, the flat of the blade crashing against his temple.

He fell back into blackness, hearing pained cries all around him as the Byzantine resistance collapsed. Cries for mercy rang out from the pockets of men who fought on. A Seljuk war horn spoke next. It sang across the battlefield, echoing through the hills and into the near-dark sky. The Seljuk victory cries were relentless.

CHAPTER 20

Amongst the Dead

The southern end of the plain and the valleys around the foot of Mount Tzipan reeked of death. The moonlight betrayed thousands of glistening corpses and flocks of crows – heedless of the night – who descended to tear at the still-warm flesh. The gale had died not long after dusk, as if satiated by its feast of souls.

Alp Arslan picked his way sombrely through the carpet of dead, the night chill searching under his bloodied shroud and the armour underneath. Around him, his men set to work on laying out the bodies for burial and disarming the remnant of the Byzantine army.

He came to Bey Taylan's corpse. The boy's skin was as pale as a westerner's now. He was laid out on his back, as if placed there, his eyelids having been closed. The Sultan's heart hardened as he realised the boy must have faced his father after all.

'Spearmen,' he called to a passing pair of akhi who carried a ghazi body. 'How did Bey Taylan fall?'

The akhi bowed. 'Great Sultan. He died with Bey Gulten's traitorous axe in his back.'

Alp Arslan's blood cooled. 'Then bring that dog to me——' He stopped, seeing the spearman's gaze switch to another body, disembowelled and headless. This body had been offered no care – neither laid out straight nor reunited with its head.

'The *Haga* destroyed Gulten, moments after Bey Taylan had fallen.'

Alp Arslan felt a long-lost emotion claw at him. Sorrow tightened his throat and ached in his chest. A boy had died before his father. Many more mothers and fathers would be without their sons too. He thought again of his newborn son, and of Malik, growing into a fine battlefield leader. How long would they have in this world of endless war?

'And the *Haga*?' he asked.

The spearman looked up, setting down some other body. He looked this way and that, across the piles of dead, over to the masses of Byzantine prisoners. 'It is hard to tell, Sultan. Every man we come to wears a mask of blood.'

Alp Arslan laughed a chilling laugh at this. Utterly mirthless. 'Don't we all, brave akhi? Don't we all?'

He walked on, hearing the weary salutes of his men, seeing the wounded writhing in agony – far too many to be treated by the few physicians in his ranks. He entered the valley south of the battle-field, skirting Mount Tzipan's eastern face. Here, the akhi spearmen were putting together a rudimentary timber corral and herding the Byzantine prisoners inside. Here, they could be guarded more easily and would have access to a small brook that trickled through the space.

Further on, he came to the wide, flat area where his army had made camp. In the heart of the sea of tents and torches was an obscenely large yurt. Nizam stood at the entrance and Kilic was there too, there for him as they always had been. They offered him no words of congratulation or solace, Nizam simply handing him a flask of wine.

Inside alone, he felt the silence claw at him. The space was adorned with a few simple chairs on a raised timber platform, a post to which his pet falcon was chained, and a small table with a shatranj board and a platter of fresh bread and dates. He had never felt less like eating.

He tore off the bloodied shroud and threw it down, unbuckled his swordbelt and armour and drew a green silk cloak around his shoulders. A shrill whistle brought his hunting dog into the tent and to his feet. Then he sat on one of the chairs, supping at the wine, smoothing the dog's sleek, dark coat and gazing out through the tent flap into the darkness. When dawn came, the flask was empty. It was then that he noticed a party approaching. An excited rabble. Akhi spearmen jostling around a beleaguered Byzantine. They led this one by a rope tied around his neck.

Alp Arslan sat up, leaning forward on his chair, the fog of the wine dissipating at once. More and more of his men gathered around this prisoner. Soldiers, still stained with the filth of battle. Beys and noblemen, washed and in clean robes. They spilled inside the tent under Kilic's glower, eagerly forming an audience, awaiting the pris-oner.

When the prisoner was brought inside, Alp Arslan eyed him. A mere spearman, his hair a knotted mess of blood and dirt, his face black with dust and his lamellar vest clad in a layer of gore. The ropes shackling him had chafed his neck and wrists, and one hand was encrusted with the blood of what looked like an arrow wound. A sorry sight. Despite his condition, the man's azure eyes blazed with defiance.

'Sultan, we bring you your prize.' The foremost akhi stepped forward. 'The Emperor of Byzantium.'

Alp Arslan threw his head back and roared with laughter. 'Then you have been had, brave akhi, for this is not the great Romanus Diogenes!'

The prisoner's gaze dropped to the floor, his nose wrinkling and his jaw stiffening in ire. Alp Arslan cocked his head to one side, noticing the gold chain peeking from the collar of the man's armour. 'Bring me another prisoner,' he said.

The akhi frowned, then nodded hurriedly and slipped from the tent. The audience murmured in excitement. The akhi returned with a Byzantine foot archer. This wretch was scrawny, with a tattered, bloodied tunic and teeth like tombstones. The archer stumbled in, trembling, looking all around him like a cornered animal. Then his gaze swept over the lone Byzantine spearman. At once, the man's eyes bulged and he dropped to one knee, bowing. '*Basileus!*' he gasped.

The audience broke out in a babble of excitement. Alp Arslan looked on the lone spearman with interest now. 'Is it really you?'

Romanus looked up, his features drawn and weary. 'The victory is yours. So do what you will with me and be swift about it... had the situation been reversed I would not hesitate to put you with the dogs in a lead collar.'

Alp Arslan cocked an eyebrow. 'Now I have no doubt that it is you, *Basileus.*'

'Bow before your new master!' one bey snarled, striding forward to grapple Romanus' shoulders. Another bey came forward to help him. 'Kiss the ground before the Sultan's feet!'

Alp Arslan tensed, seeing the pair as jackals, knowing their thirst for blood was not yet satiated. Romanus shrugged them off with a swing of his broad shoulders, and a pair of watching akhi instantly grabbed for their sword hilts, ready to intervene. At this, Alp Arslan shot to standing, knowing he had to act. He brought the back of his hand raking across Romanus' face. Once, twice and again. This brought the Emperor of Byzantium to his knees, spitting blood from his split lip. The offended beys and the eager akhi pair stepped back, pleased at this sight. The Sultan then lifted a leg to place the sole of his boot on Romanus' shoulder.

'From this moment, Emperor of Byzantium, I am your master,' he said. He scanned the sea of gleeful faces watching this, then clapped his hands together. 'Now, leave us!'

He watched them go, then when the tent was empty, he nodded to Kilic, who stepped outside too and drew the tent flap over, leaving him alone with Romanus.

He lifted his scimitar from the pile of his dumped armour, then walked back over to the kneeling Romanus, eyeing the sword. 'The blade is still sullied with stains from the battle,' he said, placing it on Romanus' neck. 'But I envy it, for while the blade might be cleaned this morning, I will remain tarnished.'

Romanus frowned, then started as the Sultan flicked the blade up deftly, slicing through the ropes on his neck. With another lick of the blade, the wrist ropes fell away too. 'Come, sit with me.' He beckoned Romanus up then sat on his chair again.

Tentatively, Romanus rose.

Alp Arslan held out a square of silk. 'Clean the blood from your lips, and know that I struck you only to appease my men.'

'What is this?' Romanus asked, sitting, his eyes darting as if expecting some sudden attack.

'Did you mean what you said? Were the situation reversed, you would have me in chains with the dogs?' Alp Arslan asked.

Romanus snorted. 'Were the situation reversed, I can only guess at what I might do. Mercy, torture… what does it matter? I will never know now.'

'It befits a man to understand that good fortune can swiftly be turned upon him. Allah alone knows how close I have come to falling to those baying dogs.' He flicked a finger at the space where the audience had been standing, the eager acolytes who he knew secretly supported his rival, Yusuf. 'Thus, I will not have you subjected to torture or punishment. Perhaps then fortune may spare me any such fate should I find myself in your position in future?'

Romanus nodded gingerly, the frown on his brow fading only a fraction.

'You are confused?' Alp Arslan asked.

'I look around your tent and see a reflection of my own. I find myself at ease in your presence. Many of my courtiers – even the few noble ones – told me you were a mindless blood-drinker, a foul-hearted cur.'

Alp Arslan cocked an eyebrow. 'I drink only dark wine, and too much of it. And as to the nature of my heart,' he shrugged, 'aye, at times, I have done foul deeds.'

'Then perhaps that is the lot of any sultan, emperor or king,' Romanus said, his gaze saturnine. A silence hovered as both men gazed into their own thoughts. 'So what is to become of me?' Romanus said at last.

Alp Arslan pulled the small table round between their chairs. He poured a cup of water for Romanus and pushed the dates, bread and yoghurt towards him. 'In the years that have been and gone, I would have gladly kept you as a hostage, a trophy of sorts. A brave and noble ruler of Byzantium reduced to a mere slave at the Sultan's court.'

Romanus' lips narrowed.

'Then our great empires did battle yesterday after so many years of posturing, raiding, taking of cities and burning of homes. What did yesterday tell me?' Alp Arslan leaned a little closer to Romanus. 'It told me that you are indeed brave and noble. You stood with your men until the end, when you could have fled on your stallion and broken free of the carnage.'

'I stood firm because I was the last source of hope to my men!' Romanus insisted. 'I stood my ground because I had nowhere to flee too. Yesterday was my last hope. You, Sultan, are a wily and powerful foe. But you do not know of the enemies who hover at my back like crows, waiting to swoop upon my failures. Even now, word will be on its way back to Constantinople, to laud my disaster. The lords and nobles who have long sought to depose me will rejoice.'

Alp Arslan held Romanus' gaze. His sparkling azure eyes were earnest, resolute. In them he saw his own features reflected – as weary and battle-stained as the Emperor of Byzantium's. 'Then despite our differing faiths, our opposing cultures, our clashing wills, we have much in common. I saw what happened yesterday. My armies did not win a great victory – the traitors in your ranks handed it to me. Your reserve was strong enough in number to have repelled or broken up my forces. Had they not turned from the battle and left you to your fate… I might well have been a prisoner sitting in your tent right now, under the walls of Manzikert.'

Romanus' weary features cracked into a desert-dry half-grin that did not come close to reaching his eyes. 'But you point out only a fraction of the treachery, Sultan. When I marched east, my armies numbered some forty thousand men. Yet half of those men forsook me before we even came to battle. I sent them to Chliat and never saw them again.'

Alp Arslan sighed. 'We came to these plains, braced to face such a number. I am more certain than ever that, had they stood with you, then our roles would be reversed right now.'

Romanus chuckled mirthlessly at the notion. 'And the treachery did not end there. In the battle itself, when I gave the order to retreat at dusk – some black-hearted dog spread the rumour that I had been slain. That is why my lines foundered and fell apart.'

Alp Arslan sighed and let his head drop. His thoughts drifted to his nightmares. The skeleton mountain and the gory rain. 'Sometimes I fear we are blighted with a certainty of blood. Every summer when the lands grow lush and verdant, abound with life, we seem determined to march with our armies, to cut it down and soak the dirt in blood. What happened yesterday was grim indeed, and as I sat here alone in the night, I asked myself the same thing over and again: could it have been avoided?'

Romanus frowned at this. 'Then tell me, Sultan… tell me one thing. Why did you reject my offer?'

Alp Arslan shook his head. 'I don't understand.'

'When you were besieging Aleppo, I sent my fastest rider to you, with a scroll.'

'I received no scroll, met no rider of yours. I merely had a threat passed to me from a rider of my own. He said you were set to seize these lands then march down the Euphrates valley and penetrate my heartlands.'

Romanus shook his head, sadness wrinkling his face. 'There was a scroll. It outlined a peaceful swap: Hierapolis for the Lake Van fortresses.'

Alp Arslan's eyes darted. He recalled the haze of the wine that had muddied his thoughts on the day that messenger had come to him. The wine and the anger at his failed sieges of Edessa and Aleppo had catastrophically clouded his judgement.

Romanus dropped his head into his hands. 'What use is it complaining about dice that have already been cast? Their willingness to betray me is a sign of my weakness as a leader. Had they believed in me then—'

'Had they believed in anything other than gold, *Basileus*,' Alp Arslan cut in, 'then they might have stayed loyal.'

Romanus looked up, frowning. 'You know of Psellos and his scheming?'

'I have heard of the rogue that festers in your capital like a boil.'

'He is in exile now – though not for much longer, I suspect.' Romanus shrugged, a cheerless laugh escaping his lips.

'Regardless, his ilk are well known to me. Did you know that this year, I have escaped two attempts on my life and narrowly averted a coup by jealous emirs and beys? And it is but August – so I fear another is due soon.' He chuckled dryly. He saw Romanus' gaze was studious, as if trying to uncover some hidden agenda. 'My point is this, *Basileus*; once my forefathers spoke to me of their dreams of conquering all Byzantium. I know now this will never happen – not in my lifetime anyway. Thus, the game we must both play is one of balancing power. That balance can be fierce and sweeping, swinging to and fro and leaving tracts of dead in its wake. Or it can be stable. You are a tenacious foe, but a virtuous one. I fear that should another usurp your throne, then I will have a far less noble opponent on my borders. So you will return to your capital, and secure your throne.'

Romanus' eyes widened.

Alp Arslan shrugged. 'There will have to be some token tribute, of course. Ten million nomismata, shall we say? And give me Hierapolis, Edessa, Antioch and, of course, Manzikert.'

Romanus' face paled visibly, even through the soot and dirt of the battle. 'Sultan, you overestimate the health of the imperial treasury greatly. Barely a million nomismata lie in the vaults, and much of that is owed to the mercenaries in the armies.'

'Then we will come to some form of arrangement,' Alp Arslan ceded. 'But the cities – they must be sworn over to the Sultanate.'

Romanus' brow knitted. 'Such concessions would mortally weaken my hold on the imperial throne, Sultan.'

'To fail to achieve those prizes would severely weaken my hold on my own throne, *Basileus*. What would my people say if, having achieved victory over Byzantium, I let you walk away and keep all of your holdings?'

Romanus nodded, stroking at his jaw in thought. 'Perhaps we can defer the transfer of the cities? Allow me to march back to

Constantinople and see that my throne is safe? Then those great walled settlements can be given over.'

Alp Arslan felt instinct nag at him. 'Some men make grand promises when faced with the tip of my blade, only to spit on their word when they are far away,' he said, his eyes narrowing. But Romanus' gaze was unerring, resolute. 'But you are not one of these.' He picked up the water flask and supped from it. 'Let it be as you say.' He held out a forearm to Romanus.

Romanus clasped it. 'A balance of power it is. Perhaps the most wretched thing about today, Sultan, is that it has taken until now for us to speak like this.'

They talked on for the rest of the morning and on into the afternoon. Romanus spoke of little Nikephoros, and Alp Arslan of his own baby boy. They talked of their homes, their lives in simpler times, their wishes for how things might be.

It was late afternoon when at last they grew short of conversation. Alp Arslan stood. 'Now, *Basileus*, you should bathe and wash the grime of battle from your skin. Then you can eat and rest here until you are ready to travel west. I will assign a wing of one hundred ghulam riders to see you and the remnant of your army safely back into your own lands.' He clapped his hands.

A pair of akhi entered the tent to escort Romanus. As he left, Alp Arslan's eyes fell upon the shatranj board. An earlier thought came to him again and he called after Romanus. 'And what of the *Haga*?'

Romanus turned round. 'The Strategos of Chaldia? He stood with me until the end.'

'I expected nothing less,' Alp Arslan laughed. 'But did he survive?'

Romanus' face fell into a curious expression of sadness and fondness. 'He lives. We have spoken since – in the prison pens. It seems that he lost more than most in the fray.'

In the prison pen, Apion sat wearing his bloodstained, faded red tunic, head bowed, his amber-grey locks dangling over his face and the afternoon sun burning his neck. He stirred only to fasten the bloodied bandage wrapped around his torso then scoop water with his good hand from the brook over the blunt fracture in his arm. It was bruised and swollen, and the arm was still numb and hanging limp. Still, the water stung like vinegar, and his body shuddered at the sensation. He looked up and around those seated with him; of the seven thousand who had not fled in the chaos of the ordered retreat, some twenty-six hundred men had survived. A few hundred varangoi, Bryennios and maybe a third of his cavalry wing – stripped of their mounts, weapons and the best of their armour – plus Alyates and a hundred or so of his riders. Apart from that, there were clusters of themata infantrymen, most of them mortally wounded. They sat with their heads bowed, faces filthy. Some sobbed, some prayed, others gazed into the dust before them. It had been this way all the previous night and today. Mercifully, the bodies on the nearby battlefield had been cleared away and the crows had nothing left to scavenge on. Only clouds of flies remained, buzzing in the late afternoon heat over the remaining bloodstains. Some four thousand Byzantine men had fallen there in the dusk light, and probably the same number of Seljuks. The bloodstains were drying. Time would see new grass sprout and mask the red earth. In just a few seasons, would anyone even know what had happened here?

He saw the faces of his trusted three behind his closed eyelids. Sha, the diplomat, one of the few who could see reason even in the heat of battle. Blastares, the big infantry lion who had helped Apion develop the callous skin of a soldier in his early days in the ranks. Old Procopius, the artillery master. The wily old bastard who could prise open any fort or city like a clam. Each of them friends, brothers. All gone. He felt his heart swell with emotion. 'I should have been by your side.'

Then he thought of gruff Igor, the loyal varangos axeman who had fallen in his duty, protecting the emperor to the last. 'Had you been given a choice, you whoreson, you would not have had it any other way,' he mouthed with a sad half-grin.

Then he thought of the Chaldian ranks. Many hundreds of them dead, having suffered the worst of the casualties. Sha's baritone words echoed from memory then: *many widows we make of waiting wives, with so little thought we squander men's lives.*

And his memories came round – as he knew they would – to Taylan. What a foul mixture of confusion and pain the memory of the lad's dying moments brought to him. Taylan had confronted him as he swore he would. But something had changed in the lad since their first confrontation outside Mosul. At the last, it seemed, the boy understood. Apion closed his eyes, desperately trying to block out the image of that scowling old bey who had cut his son down. 'If we had been afforded time, in some place far from this war, then things might have been different.'

He looked up into the sky, wondering if the crone was listening to him. But there was nothing.

Just then, a crunch–crunch of boots shook him from his thoughts. He looked up to see a pair of akhi hauling the rough timber gate of the prisoner pen open. One carried a basket of bread loaves and began handing them out to the prisoners. The other was scanning the sea of faces, then stopped, staring straight at Apion. 'You, come,' the man beckoned.

He walked numbly, barely giving thought to what was to happen to him. When he was led inside some vast tent, he drew his gaze up and across a familiar sight. A shatranj board. Behind it sat Alp Arslan. The Sultan offered him a weary smile.

'Sit, *Haga*.'

'I will sit, but please, do not use that name,' he said, taking a seat, 'I am dog-tired of it now.'

'I understand,' Alp Arslan replied. 'To a young man, war is like a pretty young lady. He chases her. Only when he has her in his grasp does he see her for the hag she is, and by then it is too late...' His words trailed off and he shook his head.

'That may be the case for some, Sultan. For me, there was no chase. War consumed my life when I was a boy.'

Alp Arslan nodded in acquiescence, then tapped the shatranj board. 'Remember when we started this game?'

Apion frowned, seeing that the layout of the pieces was familiar. 'You preserved the board from that night, after the taking of Caesarea?'

'I do not like unfinished business. It irks me. Drives me to drink too much wine,' he chuckled dryly. 'Though after yesterday, I feel I am finally tired of the lustre of all things red.'

Apion shrugged and moved a pawn with his good arm, taking the Sultan's war elephant. 'Then let us end our dealings, Sultan. I find that most of my affairs are winding up before my eyes, so let us be done with this game.'

Alp Arslan's eyes narrowed. He lifted his vizier out from the back line. 'You are not known for acting in haste,' he said, eyeing the path this move had opened to Apion's king. It would take several moves, but it was there.

'What am I known for, Sultan? What are you known for? The *Haga*, the *Mountain Lion*. Bitter soubriquets indeed. Merchants of death, that's how they will remember us,' Apion said, lifting his war elephant out and across to strike at the Sultan's knight. He lifted the Sultan's piece off the board without ceremony.

'That was something of a reckless move, Strategos,' the Sultan frowned. 'Perhaps you should take more care?'

'Why? All that mattered to me has crumbled around my feet. All those I cared for have been slain. I told you this before and it is ever more true now. The empire I fought for is at your mercy. My comrades are dead. My son…' He stopped, the words choking in his throat.

Alp Arslan stood, moving over to a small chest at the side of the tent. He produced from it two sets of armour. One was Apion's own, stripped from him upon his capture. The other was equally familiar. A scale vest and a fine conical helm with an ornate nose-guard. Nasir's armour. Taylan's armour.

'You may want these things. I had them found and brought to me.'

Apion eyed Taylan's armour. 'You know that Taylan was my…'

'I found out only too late. At least it allowed me to understand the boy.'

Apion nodded, a weak smile failing to disguise his sorrow.

'Now take them, Strategos.' Alp Arslan thrust the garments into Apion's good arm. 'Our battle is over.' He waved a hand across the shatranj board as if dismissing it. 'This unfinished game will irk me no longer.'

Apion stood too. 'And what is to become of me, the army and the emperor?'

'Your emperor will ride from here in a few days. He plans to gather his armies and secure his throne.'

'You are not keeping him in bondage?' Apion frowned.

Alp Arslan shook his head. 'I have discussed this at length with him. Suffice to say that territories will be ceded, but it is imperative that he remains on the throne. I have suffered nightmares of blood fields and skeleton soldiers since I was a boy. Now I find them a waking reality. Together, your emperor and I can change this. We can oversee an era of peace. No more border raids, no more war in these lands. I am tired of it, Strategos.'

'I hope with all my heart this comes to pass, Sultan. But do you realise the enormity of your victory. Are you aware of what will happen now, back in the imperial capital?'

Alp Arslan's gaze grew weary and distant. 'The snakes of Constantinople will come out to feast, or so I understand.'

'They will. The emperor's next moves will be crucial. Unfortunately, I will be of no use to him as a soldier, not for some time.' He gingerly clasped a hand around his shattered arm.

'Ah, yes,' the Sultan mused, eyeing the bruised, swollen arm. 'My physicians will fit a splint to the wound. But I do fear it will take a long time to heal. Be sure though that when you are well, you will be swift to your emperor's side.'

'I will,' Apion said.

'But for now, you should take Taylan's things home.'

Apion glanced down at Taylan's armour and then frowned. 'I have long forgotten what home is – bar a draughty barracks or some lonely citadel chamber.'

Alp Arslan frowned. 'You misunderstand. I mean you should take them to *his* home. To his mother, Lady Maria.'

He left the Sultan's tent, numb, staggering past the pair of ghulam guarding the entrance, through the sea of yurts, campfires and ghazi riders grooming and tending to their wounded and exhausted ponies. Alp Arslan's words continued to echo in his mind.

He made his way back to the prisoner pen, and saw that Romanus was there. He had bathed, he was well and he was dressed in a clean Seljuk yalma. The Sultan had also given him a grey steppe mare, and a wing of ghulam riders were helping to marshal the Byzantine prisoners into ordered ranks, even handing them their lances and shields back.

'Strategos!' Romanus beamed. He hid the shame of the defeat well. 'You have heard what is to happen?'

'I have,' Apion smiled, shaken from his stupor. He tried to seek words of encouragement and avoid dwelling on the loss. 'Now your true enemies will have to step into the daylight after their years of subterfuge.'

'We are heading west, back to Theodosiopolis. There, we will take stock of what is left of the ranks. Next, I will gather an army of allies.

Alyates thinks he can muster another few thousand men. Bryennios might be able to convince a Pecheneg horde to fight for us too. Philaretos will ride for Melitene and rally what soldiers he can. Then, and only then, I will return to the capital. I will do all I can to ensure the throne is not lost.' He looked down to Apion's crippled arm. 'It pains me that you will not be able to ride at arms with me. But when you are well, you will join me?'

'If what I hear is correct – that peace in the borderlands can be had if your agreement with the Sultan is upheld – then yes, I will be by your side as soon as my wounds are healed. Until then, I have other affairs that I must see to.'

'So be it, Strategos. Until we meet again,' Romanus said.

'Wherever that may be,' Apion said in reply, clasping his good hand to Romanus' outstretched forearm.

The emperor heeled his pony round to lead the Byzantine soldiers from the Seljuk camp, across the plains of Manzikert and off to the west. As the chain of riders and then infantry snaked out after him, Apion watched them fade into silhouettes, framed by the dropping sun. Then, as the last few soldiers departed at the tail of the column, a hand clasped onto his shoulder.

Apion swung round. A coal-dark face beamed at him, tears darting from the eyes. 'Sha!' he gasped.

The Malian said nothing, simply embracing Apion. When he pulled back, Apion saw that he balanced on a crutch, an angry wound peeking from behind a thick bandage on his thigh.

'I thought I was dead, Strategos, I truly did. A Seljuk rider cut through my thigh and my strength left me in moments. Then came darkness like no sleep, then a grey, lifeless land. I only woke a few hours ago, found myself lying amongst corpses. The *skribones* had left me with the dead while they tended to those they thought they could save.'

Apion looked either side of him, at the other few stragglers. Two men with dirt and soot obscuring their faces. One tall and hulking, the other stooped. *Blastares, Procopius?* But a shaft of sunlight revealed the pair as two young skutatoi from his Chaldian ranks.

'I too have seen them amongst the living,' Sha said, reading Apion's thoughts, 'when memory intertwines with hope.' Sha reaffirmed his grip on Apion's shoulder, then nodded to the burial grounds to the east of the camp. 'They died like they lived. As lions.'

'As lions,' Apion repeated.

The pair gazed at the burial grounds in silence. It was Sha who spoke next: 'I was going to ask you if you would be coming with us, Strategos. But I know you better than most. I can see that sparkle in your eyes again.'

'I know where Maria is, Sha. No more searching,' he said. 'I shall return after the winter.'

'Then go,' Sha said, pulling away from Apion to keep up with the tail of the column, the two young skutatoi flanking him and helping him in his movement. The Malian turned to cast back a valedictory salute and offered him a broad, white-toothed smile. 'But do not be gone too long. These lands need you, *Haga*.'

Apion watched Sha go, joining the others in the sunset. *I hope with all my heart they do not, my friend.*

Then a voice spoke beside him in the Seljuk tongue. 'Byzantine? The Sultan said you needed a pony for some journey to the south?'

Apion looked to the lithe akhi sentry and then to the dappled steppe mare whose reins he offered. 'Aye, I do,' he said, taking the reins and gazing to the navy blue, star-speckled south.

Rain battered down over the Bithynian villa. Inside, a slumped varangos' chest rose and fell in the bubble of lamplight by an open bedchamber door. Psellos crouched in the night gloom within the chamber, waiting, eyes fixed on the slumbering Rus axeman. The fool had grown complacent after months of this uneventful exile guard duty. Now, Psellos thought as he stood tall and drew the dagger he had fashioned from an old plough blade, he would learn a lesson that might serve him well in the afterlife.

He crept forward, hoisted the blade and then tensed, ready to swing it down onto the varangos' neck. *Freedom, wealth... power!*

But the Rus' shovel hand shot up, catching his wrist. The Rus' eyes shot open too, as if awakened by the scent of his impending death. He twisted Psellos wrist until the bone cracked. Psellos let out a yelp, falling to his knees as the blade clattered to the floor. The Rus stood to tower over him, a disdainful glare in the big man's eyes. 'You think we have forgotten what you are, snake?' A dull rumble sounded outside. Psellos frowned. The big Rus frowned too, glancing to the nearest shutter. *Thunder?* The shutters rattled and burst open, lightning streaking across the sky.

The Rus frowned and turned away from the shutter. 'Now you will return to your chamber, and you will dwell upon what brought you here. You will wallow in a life without purpose. You will remember the many who died at your command.' The varangos' teeth ground together. 'Like my brother, the palace guard who breathed his last on your torture table…' He brought up his axe, resting the edge on Psellos' throat. 'Only when you repent for all you have done – then, I might swipe the head from your shoulders.'

Psellos felt fear snaking across his skin. Then lightning flashed again. This time he saw something from the corner of his eye. Outside, through the flapping shutters. Horsemen, riding up the estate path towards the villa's main entrance, illuminated in the storm light. *A change of guard at this late hour?* Thunder rolled across the night sky, and he heard something else. A muted clatter of iron, then the creak of the main door opening, some way down the hall.

The varangos frowned. Psellos frowned. Footsteps rattled on the flagstones just behind the big Rus. He swung round just in time to see the cluster of Numeroi spearmen rushing for him. They drove their already-bloodied spears at his chest, running him through and driving him back against the wall, piercing his flesh and bone. Blood lurched from the Rus' lips and his eyes darted over the scene. Psellos looked to the rain-sodden soldiers, his eyes glinting in the lamplight. 'Can it be true?'

The leader of the numeroi nodded. 'Diogenes' army was crushed at Manzikert. He was taken in chains by the Sultan then released like a mangy dog. Now he wanders the eastern lands like some beggar, pleading for men to stand with him. Constantinople is ready for a new master.'

At that moment, John Doukas wandered from his own chamber, bleary-eyed from sleep, but a feral grin spreading across his face. 'Then it is finally time for a Doukas to sit on the throne once more?'

'I have two fresh mounts waiting on you outside,' the leader of the numeroi said. 'We can be back in Constantinople within days.'

Psellos' mind spun at the possibilities. He looked to John, seeing the oaf's eyes alive with thoughts of the throne. *No*, he mused, *your usefulness as my puppet has waned. Perhaps a younger Doukas might serve my ambitions better?*

The speared Rus gurgled where he was pinned, his arms outstretched in some vain attempt to exact revenge. Psellos stooped, picked up his dagger, then plunged it into the varangos' left eye. He watched the light dim in the man's remaining eye, then swung to the villa doorway. 'To Constantinople, then.'

The rain lashed them as they rode. It was cold and came in sheets. But no amount of this chill deluge could cool the fire on Psellos' chest. It had burgeoned when they first mounted, and now it blazed like the fires of Hell. He felt the familiar writhing in there. The burrowing. The gnawing. With a shaky hand, he reached under the fold of his robe and touched the wicked lesion. This time, something more than putrid flesh came away in his fingers. He withdrew his hand and frowned, unable to discern the lump he held in the gloom. Lightning flashed overhead and he saw it then. A lump of pure-white breastbone, slivers of rotting flesh dangling from it, writhing maggots feasting on these tendrils.

He tossed the morsel away in fright, then set his sights on the west. Somewhere beyond the horizon lay Constantinople. All he had longed for. He had his freedom. Now he could seize his wealth, his power. With the world at his behest, surely no illness could best him?

An eagle's cry sounded from somewhere in the storm. That was answer enough.

'Ya!' he cried into the night storm, trying as best he could to fend off the fiery terror in his breast.

CHAPTER 21

Home

The midday sun blazed over the city of Mosul. Maria sat in the shade of a date palm by the water font in the walled courtyard of her modest villa, coaxing a sand martin down from the fronds overhead. The bird issued an endless chorus of plaintive song as it weighed up the offer, its tiny head cocking this way and that in judgement. She stood, gently humming the tune her father had once used to soothe her to sleep. The lilting tune harmonised with the bird's. At this, the creature fell silent, then hopped onto her palm. She sprinkled a dash of sesame seeds on the heel of her hand and watched the bird feast happily. It was then that her gaze fell upon the font. She saw her reflection in the water's surface and – not for the first time in these last months – wondered at the sight. The grey strands were all but gone. The weary lines around her eyes were absent. The gauntness that had come with the growth was but a memory, replaced by a chubby roundness of her cheeks, reminiscent of her lost youth. She moved her free hand down to her abdomen. The growth itself had shrunk to the size of a walnut.

'You gave me a gift, old woman,' she whispered into the ether. 'A gift of life. Yet I must enjoy it alone?' she said as the sand martin finished its feast and fluttered back up into the palm fronds. Nasir was but a memory. Taylan would not be returning home – she knew this now. This villa he provided for her was all she had when the physician had allowed her to leave the hospital. Empty, silent, still.

She thought again of her childhood, before war had riven her life and those of so many others. She thought of the young Byzantine boy her father had brought home to the farm, and the lazy days they had spent together in the sun-baked valleys by the River Piksidis. *What became of those days, Apion?* she mouthed.

Just then, the scraping of a boot sounded behind her. She turned, realising she was not alone. In the archway leading inside the villa, a tall figure stood. With the sun at his back, she could make out only his battered iron helm and the three eagle fathers jutting from the crown. His broad shoulders were draped in a crimson cloak. In the shade that was his face, she thought for just a moment that she caught sight of his eyes – like two glittering green gemstones. She swung away and grappled the edge of the font, her breath coming in short gasps.

He moved up behind her, placing the hand of a heavily bandaged arm on her shoulder. She looked down in the water's surface to see her reflection and, by her shoulder, the features of another. Sun-burnished and scarred skin, a battered nose, an iron-grey beard. Age and war had ravaged him. But the boy from her youth shone through in those emerald eyes. At once she was overcome with fear that if she looked away or disturbed the water's surface, the image might vanish. But a deep voice broke the spell:

'Maria, I… let me look in your eyes.'

She turned to him, slowly, then rested a hand on the chest of his battered klibanion and looked up at his troubled features. 'You thought me dead for many years. For that I have felt shame, almost every day.'

'It was surely for the best that I did not know you were alive. In the years we have been apart, I have not been the kind of man any woman would want to be around.' His eyes reddened as he said this. 'But I must first speak of another,' he said, his shoulders sagging as he unstrapped a parcel of cloak and armour from his shoulder. 'Taylan, he—'

'Taylan is dead,' Maria finished for him flatly. 'I knew this the moment he rode from here to join the Sultan's army. I knew this despite word coming back that the Seljuk armies won a great victory. I knew this before his riders came to confirm it.'

Apion sighed. 'Know that at the last, he knew the answer did not lie in striking me down. It was the jealous eye and the honed blade of a rival bey that felled him in the end. I tried to save him… I…'

A long silence passed. Maria and Apion gazed upon one another. Tears spilled down Maria's cheeks first, and then, like rain touching a desert creek for the first time in years, Apion followed suit.

When they embraced, they lost themselves in a fit of sobbing, holding each other tight, sharing the pain of all that had gone before, since those long, lost days on the farm. They sunk to their knees by the font. The sobbing ebbed away and eventually ended. But there they remained, holding each other, at peace for those blessed few moments.

The last days of late summer drifted by, with Apion and Maria rarely leaving the villa. She tended to his wounded arm, seeing that the bone was not healing and so putting it in a fresh wooden splint. They spent almost every day of autumn in the courtyard, talking endlessly, bringing their shared days at Mansur's farm back to life. At nights they simply lay together, Apion sheltering Maria, his good arm around her waist and his gaze marvelling at the nape of her neck. As the weeks went by, he found the feeling returning to his arm. Now he could clasp objects in his hand and hold them for a few moments before the muscles would spasm and he would drop them again. But at least it allowed him to hold Maria properly. It was a dreamlike existence and it was only when they entered the garden one morning to find a light frost on the tiles and stones that they realised it was winter. In this cold, Apion noticed how his old wounds and scars ached – something he had never noticed in his youth. On these winter nights, he and Maria huddled together by the hearth, logs spitting and crackling as they fought to fend off the fierce night chill. Some weeks later, Apion removed his arm splint. The bone was healed. He flexed and unflexed his fingers in delight, the spasm did not come. But still he frowned, seeing how withered the limb was.

'I doubt I'll be able to lift a fork with this, let alone a shield,' he chuckled. He saw Maria's face fall at the words. He looked over her shoulder and saw the neat pile where he had laid down his armour and helm upon arriving here. It had gathered a thick layer of dust. 'But I have no wish to hold sword nor shield,' he said, fixing her with an earnest gaze.

'Then hold me, Apion,' she whispered, drawing the chord of her robe and letting it fall to the ground. Her beauty was only magnified by the dancing firelight, accentuating every curve. He tore off his tunic and seized her, pressing his lips to hers, feeling her fire-warmed bare skin against his. That night, the fire had long dulled to ashes before they fell back from their lovemaking.

The seasons seemed to pass like days, and when they were awoken one morning by a dawn chorus, Apion realised spring was upon them already. He rose, taking care not to disturb Maria from her slumber. He threw on his tunic and took up a handful of blueberries from the table in the hearth room. The tart berries reinvigorated his senses and shook the sleep from his mind. He strolled out into the garden courtyard, scooped water from the font and slung it across his face and hair, knotting his locks back in a rough loop as he did so. He looked up and around the brightening sky and heard the first hustle and bustle of the streets outside, beyond the garden's walls. Market day, he realised, hearing lowing oxen and the grinding of cart wheels on the street. The traders and citizens were already about their business after the winter lull. In these last months he had left the villa only to fetch food. That was all they needed. It had seemed that this life could last forever. Just then, a lilting song sailed through the air. The morning call to prayer. Apion enjoyed it for its melody – as he had done most days. He wondered at the strength of those who had managed to hold onto their faith throughout all that had happened. The Byzantines and the Seljuks. Two peoples, two faiths, one god. For so many years he had been unable to think of God with anything but spite. Today, he felt no urge to scowl or scorn. He looked up and scanned the sapphire sky above the minarets, lost in thought. 'Your lessons are harsh indeed,' he whispered, 'but what can we ever become, lest we learn from them?'

It was then that he heard another noise from outside; the crunch-crunch of military boots and the rustle of iron vests. The noise was like a blotchy cloud passing over the morning sun. It brought back memories of his oath to Romanus. *And what of Sha and my comrades?* He frowned, realising he had already been away longer than anticipated.

'You want to go back, don't you?' he heard her words from the doorway as if they were his own thoughts.

He did not turn to look at her, wishing he could spirit away the truth.

'Do not be afraid to say it, Apion,' she said, stepping out into the sunshine to rest a hand on his still-weak arm. 'Indeed, in these last months with you, I have often thought that perhaps we should both return to where it all began – to my father's farm?'

His ears pricked up at this. 'You would come with me?' He held her by the shoulders.

'We have talked of the old place so much, Apion. It seems only proper that we should go there,' she smiled.

Joy surged around his veins at the notion. To return to Chaldia, to the farm in the Piksidis valleys? There they could make a home, enjoy the peace that was to come from Romanus' and Alp Arslan's agreement. There they could honour the many lost and fallen by seeing out their years in tranquillity. A peaceable life in the borderlands, with Maria at his side. *Are these not the two things I have dreamt of?*

She returned his broad grin with one even more infectious. They embraced and he inhaled her scent – sweetness mixed with the warmth of sleep. Once again, her mere presence took away his aches and pains. He stroked her hair as they remained locked together. But he noticed that there was something different about her. Her dark, sleek locks had more grey hair than in previous weeks – far more.

He stood back, not too concerned about time's efforts to annoy him. 'Come then,' he beckoned to the shade of the arched door leading into the villa, 'let us go inside and see what we might need for such a journey.' He led her by the hand, but a yelp halted him in his tracks and her hand fell away from his.

He swung round. Maria had fallen to one knee, a hand pressed to her belly and her face contorted in pain. 'Maria?' he gasped, crouching by her and cupping an arm round her shoulder.

The pain drained from her face and she waved him away. A look of realisation seemed to come over her then, followed by a sudden soberness. She stood tall once again, disguising another wince, before summoning her smile back. 'Come on then, let us plan our journey home.'

–

On their last morning in Mosul, Apion ventured out into the city. He was gone for some time and when he returned, Maria seemed concerned.

'I was worried something had happened,' she said as the dying notes of the call to prayer floated across the city. 'Where were you?'

'Visiting someone I used to know,' was all he said. He pulled her close and kissed her forehead, dispersing the frown. 'Now let us go home.'

The journey was relaxed, their ponies travelling just ten or twelve miles per day at a gentle trot along the dusty tracks of Persia and then northern Syria. This gentle pace had been the plan at first, but then it had become a necessity when Maria's stomach pains became ever more regular. Just over a week into their journey, the pains became so fierce that Maria was unable to sit upright in her saddle, and so they were forced to stay at an inn for three days.

'Ride for Mosul,' Apion instructed the skelf-like young Seljuk rider he had met at the inn, dropping three silver dirhams into his palm. 'Find the physician at the city hospital. Tell him that Lady Maria needs the chalky mixture once more. Ride fast and I will pay you this much again on your return.'

The boy rider nodded and sped off to mount his pony then kick her into a gallop to the south. Apion watched the lad go, then turned back to the inn — a simple timber building, one amongst a small collection that had sprung up around this Seljuk waystation on the north road. He came back to the room inside, where they were staying, and heard Maria's whimpering. *Why didn't you tell me?* he mouthed, closing his eyes and halting, trying to stave off the tears there before he rounded the doorway and came into sight. The growth in her belly had burgeoned in these last few days. From nothing, it seemed, it was now the size of an apple. He steadied himself and entered the room, sat by her side and helped her to drink chill water from a skin.

When the rider returned with the powder for making the healing paste, it seemed to swiftly rid her of her pains, but the growth did not subside. Still, she could ride again, and that was something. So they set off once more at an ever more gentle pace. Whenever Apion suggested stopping early, finding a place to stay so she could rest, Maria would dismiss the idea out of hand. 'You fuss like an old hen, Apion. We set out to go home, so let us go home.'

It was late summer, nearly a year after the Battle of Manzikert, when Apion and Maria crossed into Byzantine territory. They had travelled across the Seljuk border regions, through the no-man's land of blessedly shaded mountain passes, then on into the Byzantine Thema of Colonea. The burnt-gold hillsides of this region were devoid of thematic dwellers, it seemed, just the odd distant plume of some trade wagons breaking the hazy skyline, and the occasional deserted farmhouse. But no sign of strife, Apion realised. In his convalescence and this journey with Maria he had been utterly cut off from his military life and had no inkling of what had occurred in this last year. He flexed and unflexed his arm. The break had healed well and the muscle had returned. He had taken to lifting gradually larger burdens over and over at the end of his morning runs, and now the weaker arm was once more in balance with the other. *Fit for holding and swinging a sword?* he thought, looking to the parcel of his arms and armour — unworn for over a year — tied to the saddle of his pony. Then he glanced to Maria by his side. Her skin was slick with sweat and her hair seemed straw-like as well as grey. She was ill, regardless of the healing powers of the paste. *And has she not seen enough of those she loves falling to the sword?* But when he remembered his promise to Emperor Romanus again – *I will be by your side as soon as my wounds are healed* – he realised a choice lay before him. He could not merely return to the farm with Maria and be happy. For then he would be breaking his oath to the emperor. But by upholding this oath, he would be spiting Maria, throwing salt in all the lesions in her heart.

'Ach,' he muttered, swiping a hand through the air before him, 'let the journey provide the answers!'

They travelled north and west just a few miles a day, allowing Maria plenty of time to eat the healing paste and to rest well. It was November when they finally crossed into Chaldia, and that month was drawing to a close when they reached its heartlands and arrived at the banks of the Piksidis. Just a few miles downriver lay Mansur's farm and all the memories they both shared. The terracotta and gold shrub-speckled hillsides sparkled in the morning sunlight, dusted with a light frost. The waters of the river babbled like an old friend, welcoming them. He turned to Maria, unable to fend off the warm smile that their surroundings conjured.

'By nightfall we will be there—' He stopped, his face falling. Her eyes were nearly closed, her lips tinged with blue, her head lolling. 'Maria!' he cried, leaping from the saddle of his pony and scooping her from hers, then laying her down by the reeds at the river bank. He hurried to dig out the hemp sack of white powder. Then, with fumbling hands, he crouched in the shallows to fill his water skin before tipping a splash of it into an empty bowl and adding some of the powder. He stirred the mixture with a spoon, then cradled Maria's head, resting it upon his legs and bringing the spoon to her lips.

'If you love me,' she croaked, summoning just a hint of mischief to her voice, 'then you'll throw that damned paste in the river.'

'But Maria, you have to—'

'Just hold me, Apion,' she sighed. Moments later, she was asleep. Apion threw a woollen blanket over her, then watched her chest rising and falling and sought out his next actions.

A rumble of approaching hooves stirred him from his worry. He looked up. A lone kursoris on a white gelding hared down the valley side and then came charging along the riverbank, towards him. The man was Chaldian, going by the crimson triangle of cloth he had tied to the end of his spear. Apion rested Maria's head gently down on the grass and reeds, then stood. This was the first Byzantine soldier he had seen in well over a year. Instinct told him that the rider would recognise him and halt at once, but the young kursoris seemed set to knock him down and ride onwards.

'Whoa!' Apion yelled, waving his arms, at last pulling the rider from his trance. The lad was barely sixteen, Apion realised. He wore a conical helm with a brim to shade his eyes, and an ill-fitting leather klibanion vest. His eyes were wide with agitation.

'Move aside, old man!' the rider barked. 'I have an urgent message to deliver!'

It hit Apion at that moment. His faded and frayed tunic, his grey locks and his haggard features. Thirty-seven years' worth of scars and bitterness. 'You don't know who I am, do you?'

The rider frowned, eyeing him. 'No, and nor should I care. Now step aside.'

Apion lunged forward, grappling the reins from the boy's hands and wrenching the gelding towards him. The boy's hubris left him at once. 'Know that I have lost more than most in the wars that have ravaged these lands – and then you will know enough of me. Now, you can go on your way soon. But first water your mount – it is close to exhaustion.' He nodded to the froth gathering at the horse's lips. 'And while your gelding drinks, you can tell me – what is happening? Is there some trouble in the border themata?'

'The border themata?' The boy frowned, then a look of realisation overcame him. 'You don't know?' he gawped, sliding from the saddle and leading his mount to the shallows before turning back to Apion. 'The border themata fell some months ago. The empire is in flames! Malik Shah and his Seljuk hordes have poured into the heart of Anatolia. His words set fire to the hearts of his men, and were oft repeated as the Seljuk riders rode through our broken cities, chasing us into the hills: *All of you be like lion cubs and eagle young, racing through the countryside day and night, slaying the Christians and not sparing any mercy on the Byzantine nation.* What men are left of our thematic armies fight on, but they are in disarray, pressed back to the coastal strongholds of Anatolia.'

Apion's heart turned to ice. 'Malik Shah leads this army of conquest?' he repeated, thinking of Alp Arslan's son. The previously solid promise of peace between Alp Arslan and Romanus seemed to evaporate in his hopes at that moment. 'The Sultan allowed this?'

The boy blinked, still struggling to comprehend. 'Where have you been, old man? Malik Shah *is* the Sultan.'

Apion frowned. 'Then Alp Arslan—'

'Slain by a rival. Some traitor called Yusuf was to be shot through with arrows for his plotting against the old Sultan. But somehow, the man smuggled a concealed dagger to his own execution and managed to leap up and tear out the *Mountain Lion*'s throat before he was cut down by the Sultan's bodyguard.'

The words rang in Apion's head, refusing to settle. His thoughts turned to Constantinople, to the *Golden Heart*.

'What of the emperor?'

The boy spat on the ground, his nose wrinkling. 'The emperor brought all this upon us. Had he adhered to the concessions and the peace proposed by Alp Arslan, then none of this would have happened. Instead, he refused, sent Malik Shah foul letters, and then he cowered in terror when the son of the *Mountain Lion* roared in reply.'

Apion bristled at this. Romanus would never do such things. He was sure there was some mistake. Then he realised there was. A mistake on his part. 'Romanus is no longer our emperor, is he?'

The boy's look of disgust faded and he offered Apion an apologetic look, shaking his head. 'Just weeks after the battle at Manzikert, the Doukids rose from exile and swooped upon Constantinople. They marched upon the Imperial Palace, arrested Lady Eudokia and seated Michael Doukas on the throne as their puppet emperor. They raised armies to intercept Romanus Diogenes in his attempts to return to and secure the capital. Twice they clashed and twice Diogenes' forces were routed. Many Byzantines have died on the swords of their kinsmen in this last year. Our armies were in tatters and the Doukids took to inviting rogue Seljuk hordes to the battle, to side with them for gold and glory. Those same hordes now take our cities for themselves and side with Malik Shah once more.'

'And Romanus Diogenes?' Apion asked.

The boy shook his head. 'I was there in his ranks at the last clash with the Doukids. He surrendered in order to see his men spared, and he himself was promised no harm would come to him. Yet his men were slaughtered as soon as he had given himself over – I was one of the few to escape. Then they treated him like a pauper, tying him to

an ass and leading him back to the capital like that, pelting him with
rotten vegetables. Finally, his eyes were put out with hot pins.' The
lad's words faltered. 'They say the infection that followed was vicious,
his eye sockets festering. They say the dog, Psellos, sent him a letter
congratulating him on the loss of his eyes. It was only merciful that the
emperor succumbed to an infection in his eye-wounds within weeks.'

Apion heard the lad's words as but an echo. The *Golden Heart* was
gone and his fierce but noble adversary, the *Mountain Lion*, gone too.
Two great leaders who had hoped to end the struggle. Hope was dead.
'So Psellos and the Doukids... have won?' he stammered, imagining
Psellos and John Doukas perched like vultures either side of Michael
in the heart of the palace.

The rider sat straighter in his saddle at this. 'Won? Never! Aye,
Diogenes' supporters are scattered, and many of his best generals are
wanted men. Doux Philaretos holds out – he has control over the city
of Melitene and has gathered a strong mercenary army to defend it
in the hope that one day he might be able to overthrow the Doukids.
And Bryennios now fights in the west, trying at once to regain Thracia
for the empire and to remain vigilant to the Doukid assassins who are
known to want his head. But while they live on, others were not so
fortunate. Alyates of Cappadocia fought in one of the battles against
the Doukid armies. He was hunted down on the battlefield and had
his eyes gouged from his skull with rusty tent pegs,' the lad said with
a shiver. 'And then there is the *Haga*. No one is sure what became of
him. Some say he fell at Manzikert. Others are sure he will one day
return from some exile. All pray that he does.'

Apion held the lad's gaze. 'And where are you headed now?' he
uttered numbly.

'South, to rendezvous with an Armenian army raised by Doux
Philaretos. With them we might be able to stave off the Seljuk advance
on Trebizond,' the boy said, remounting his gelding and kicking it
round to face south.

'Then ride on, lad. Ride fast.'

The rider moved off at a trot. 'And you, old man, be wary, for Malik
Shah's war bands are circling in this part of Chaldia – they mean to add
it to their rapidly growing conquests!' he threw back over his shoulder
as he kicked his steed into a gallop.

Apion watched the rider disappear in a dust plume, then turned
back to Maria. His heart wept at the sight of her and the storm of

thoughts raised by the boy-rider cleared. Her usually dusky skin had a blue-ish pall about it, her cheeks were gaunt and her breathing shallow. He scooped her up and hugged her close, longing for the coldness in her skin to be gone. He lifted her onto the saddle of his pony and climbed up there behind her, clasping his arms around her waist and holding her there. With that, he kicked his mount into a gentle walk for the valleys to the north.

'We're almost home,' he whispered into the nape of her neck, his voice cracking.

It was late afternoon. Mansur's farm was but a few valleys away. The pony swayed as he walked, his gaze fixed on the uneven scree of the riverside. He felt Maria's every heartbeat on his back, heard her weakening breaths. He looked to Maria's pony that he was leading along with them, then let go of its reins. It slowed and then fell back, grazing and drinking from the shallows. A moment later, he heard a familiar cry from high above. An eagle's cry. He did not look up, knowing the sky would be empty.

'It has been a cursed day,' the crone said, coming into view in the corner of his eye. She walked alongside, where Maria's pony had been. Her withered, knotted frame jostled as she stepped along on the scree. Her face was long, more drawn and aged than ever, and her wispy white locks seemed almost translucent.

'Is this what I fought for?' Apion replied numbly. 'Peace in these lands and my love by my side was what I sought. One is lost and the other is...' He clasped a hand to Maria's waist more tightly.

The crone sighed. 'What matters is that you did all you could to save these things that were dear to your heart. What matters is that you tried.'

'She told me you came to her. You drove off her illness. Can you—'

'Her time was long ago, Apion. I used what strength I had left to interact with this world in order to give her long enough. To give you long enough. For you both to meet again.'

'Then our year together was a gift from you?' He frowned, tears stinging behind his eyes. 'What kind of gift is it to give someone the chance to watch their loved one die?'

'I understand your pain, Apion, believe me I do. If you had walked this world as long as I have, you too would lose count of those who slip away before your eyes. Love and loss are inseparable. One must learn to love while they can, and accept the loss that must come. I know you two have shared great love in this last year. Now must come the loss.' She bowed her head as if expecting some pained retort.

But Apion reached out and clasped a hand to her shoulder. 'Thank you,' he whispered.

They walked on in silence and came to a familiar hill. Atop it was a beech thicket and a rocky cairn with an ancient Hittite etching of the *Haga* on it – the two-headed eagle emblem just as ancient as those days when Apion had first set eyes upon it. He clutched Maria's hand again, remembering the first times they had sat up there together as children. And then in their adolescence, the first time they had made love. His mind flashed with many more long forgotten memories as they climbed the hill, knowing that just beyond the brow lay the valley and Mansur's farm. A place he had not visited in seventeen summers. He wondered at that moment: for all that had happened in those years, what had he achieved?

Apion's eyes darted. 'What is to come next? What will become of the empire, of these lands?'

'Ha!' the crone uttered. 'You should know well by now not to ask me such questions!'

'Then tell me at least, that those who brought about so much strife and bloodshed will not go unpunished.'

Wordlessly, she reached up to touch his hand. His head swam and for a moment he felt warm all over, the aches and pains of the ride gone from his body. His vision swirled and he was spirited from the present. He saw before him the throne room in Constantinople. Young Michael Doukas was seated upon the gilded chair. Beside him, as he had feared, were two figures: Psellos and John Doukas. But there was a shadow behind them. Another figure. A eunuch dressed in white, his eyes sparkling with malice. Moments later, he saw John Doukas being dragged in chains, tossed into some dank and foul, lightless dungeon. The cur screamed and bellowed until the door to his cell was bolted shut. His screaming grew weak as his hair sprouted and whitened, his skin puckered and eventually, life deserted him. In the end, he was but a pile of dust and bones, long forgotten in that miserable underground cell. Then he saw another scene. This time it was Psellos, lying in a bed of silk sheets in some fine chamber. But the advisor was writhing in agony, his face white and his skin shrivelled like some over-ripe fruit. His screams were shrill and piercing, and only abated when the physicians came over to tend to him. They drew open his robes to reveal a black, rotting hole the size of a small shield, dominating his chest and belly. Each of the physicians stepped back, aghast and heedless of what to do. For it was as if a lion had gouged away Psellos' flesh and cleaved out a great portion of his breast bone. Maggots squirmed in the rotting wound, with pink-red organs losing the battle against the putrefaction. At the centre of the wound was a weakly pulsing heart... encrusted in dried matter and as black as night. A cluster of maggots writhed here, like a besieging army at a city's walls, hungry to pierce the organ and feast upon it. The advisor's eyes were aflame with terror.

'The blackest of souls will reap the darkest of harvests,' she said solemnly, her words cutting through the vision.

Then he saw the throne room again. Now there was just the white-robed eunuch standing by Michael's side, more vulture-like even than Psellos and Doukas. *Nikephoritzes*, a sibilant voice hissed in his mind. The eunuch and Michael's imperious look faded, however, when an angry babble echoed from outside their chambers along with the smash of iron, the crackling of flames and the bash of doors being barged down. Both men adopted looks of utter panic. The vision swiftly changed. Now it showed a black-robed Eudokia on a verdurous island in the Propontis, standing over two tombs – Romanus' and that of their son, Nikephoros. She gazed beyond the tombs and across the placid turquoise waters to the distant walls of Constantinople. There, men cheered from the battlements as the Doukid banners were torn down. In their place, golden standards were raised. They bore an image he refused to believe. A double-headed eagle, talons-sharp, wings extended – identical to his stigma. A cry rang out from within the capital's walls. Kom-ne-nos! Kom-ne-nos! Kom-ne-nos!

The crone lifted her hand from Apion's, and at once he was drawn back to the present – the stillness of the Chaldian hilltop, the chattering cicadas and the crisp November air. His mind raced over myriad thoughts, then settled on one. The boy on the dead man's horse. The lad from the mustering fields of Malagina. 'Alexios? Alexios Komnenos will oust the Doukas family? Or is this another of Fate's games?'

'Fate is a powerful beast, but he cannot dim the light in a man's heart,' the crone said. 'While good men stand firm and refuse to buckle under tyranny, corruption or lies… there is always hope. Always.' She smiled. 'Your words, Apion. With those words you have sown a bright seed. Just as Mansur and Cydones guided you, Alexios now strives to achieve all you hold dear, to one day realise Romanus' ambitions of ridding these lands of war. He talks of the legend of the *Haga*, the one who stood with the emperor at Manzikert to the last… then vanished from history. You went to war, Apion, you faced your boy – when it would have been so easy to take another path. Your choices gave you those last moments with Taylan, this last year with Maria, and they have fired the heart of the boy, Alexios. Had you chosen differently, then none of this would have come to be.'

His mind danced over the fading flashes of the vision, then his breathing and heartbeat slowed again. 'Then all that has gone before has not been in vain.'

'No. It has been a savage road to walk, but it has been the right one,' the crone said. 'And now your journey is almost over.'

Apion eyed the approaching brow of the hill, then clasped Maria's hand. It was colder than ever.

'Now, I must leave you. I have a journey to make. Someone needs me to lead them… through the grey land,' the crone said, dropping back a little. Apion twisted in his saddle, offering her an earnest nod. 'I have often talked of choices,' she called after him. 'Shortly, you will have another to make. Once again, the right choice might seem the hardest. I know you will choose well. Farewell, Apion.'

The lone eagle screeched, unseen, high above.

He rode on, clasping Maria's waist tightly. He guided the pony over the brow of the hill, then on at a walk down the hillside, towards the tumbled ruin of Mansur's farmhouse on the valley floor. The fields were overgrown and long untended, and the tracks were thick with weeds, but to Apion it was finer than any palace or villa he had set eyes upon before. He squeezed Maria's hand, but she did not respond. He realised the faint whistle of her breathing had faded away, and the weak thud of her heartbeat had stopped too.

'We're home,' he whispered.

The sun was halfway set when Apion put his spade to one side. He had buried Maria beside the old mound marked as Mansur's grave. He sat before the graves, cross-legged, his pony nuzzling into his neck in search of attention – and fodder no doubt. He reached up absently to stroke its muzzle, the distraction welcome and helping to fend off the ferocious waves of sorrow that clawed at his chest. They came again and again, like a crashing tide. He glanced over to the ramshackle ruin of the farmhouse, and wondered what his next steps might be. It would take some months or years even to repair the place. He looked to the pile of his armour, crimson cloak, helm and Mansur's old, ivory-hilted scimitar and reasoned that he might be able to sell the set for some coins to aid the restoration. In his mind's eye he heard Mansur's gravelly voice bark in protest, and this brought a pensive smile to his face.

It was then that he heard a snorting of distant mounts and a jabbering of voices. Seljuk voices. He looked up. There, on the hill-side, three ghazi riders trotted down towards the farmstead.

'Ride on,' Apion muttered under his breath, 'there is nothing for you here.'

But they came closer. The leader was mean-eyed with a cold grin. His two comrades looked over Apion and the ground nearby, clearly keen on any sort of plunder to be had.

'Give me your armour, grey dog!' the leader snapped in broken Greek, flicking a finger at the heap by Apion's side.

'Like me, my armour is old and in dire need of repair,' he scoffed in reply using the Seljuk tongue.

The leader's eyes narrowed at this. 'Regardless,' he replied in Seljuk now, 'you will hand it over.' Bows creaked as the two other riders sought to underline their leader's threat, taking aim. 'You have moments, dog. Make your choice!'

Apion looked up, seeing the greed in the lead rider's eyes. He realised then it would be the easiest thing to let these curs slay him, to be free of his sorrow, to be unburdened at last of the struggles of this land. Perhaps somewhere beyond this life he might find Maria? But the crone's words would not leave him be.

Once again, the right choice might seem the hardest.

At that moment, something else came to him. Something almost forgotten. A dark, arched doorway, hovering in the blackness of his mind's eye. No flames, just darkness and utter silence. He looked to the hilt of the scimitar and the handle of his battered old shield, each just an arm's length away. Then he beheld each of the archers, his emerald eyes shaded under his dipped brow. Finally, he flicked his gaze to the lead ghazi, and offered just a crooked, mirthless half-smile.

EPILOGUE

It had been over two years since the Battle of Manzikert, and by late August, Anatolia had suffered one of the bloodiest summers ever known. Civil war between the reigning Doukids and their opponents had torn the empire apart. Sultan Malik had capitalised on the chaos, his armies swooping in to seize almost all of the Anatolian heartland. And the Sultan had rallied to his cause the many mercenary steppe riders employed by the warring Byzantine factions. Nearly every inland city and fort now bore a golden Seljuk banner. Only Doux Philaretos' splinter empire in Melitene held out against the Seljuk tide, and only the fortified coastal cities remained in imperial hands – Tarsos, Sinope, Antioch… Trebizond.

On one blistering hot, late afternoon, the gates of Trebizond swung open to let a party of scout kursores race inside. Sha watched from the battlements as they dismounted at haste. The lead rider called up to him.

'Sir, the Sultan's siege army is gone from our land. I am sure of it. We did not sight them anywhere along the route of our patrol,' the rider yelled. Relief was etched in the man's face and danced on his words.

'Then we are likely to make it until winter without the threat of another siege,' Sha replied. 'Take your riders to the barracks. I have set out six skins of wine for you. You have earned them.' The riders broke out in a cheer, drowning out their leader's formal reply. In moments, they had dissolved into the barracks.

Sha turned back to look beyond the battlements and out over the green hills and cliffs of northern Chaldia, only now expelling a sigh of relief himself. He thought of the previous summer when a thick horde of Seljuk riders and siege engineers had camped outside Trebizond's walls. Only a network of pottery-filled pits had put paid to the advance of the rams and siege towers and spared the city. He looked up to the skies and mouthed a silent thank you to the spirit of old Procopius who had taught him that ruse some years ago. He drew out his dagger and examined his reflection in it, seeing the many white hairs now dappling his stubbled scalp, and the thick scar welt that ran across the bridge of his broad nose. 'Cah – as old as Procopius and as ugly as Blastares,' he chuckled, his heart swelling at the thought of his lost brothers. He looked in over the city. There, under the shadow of the citadel hill, Tetradia and her children had lived through their grief. 'I've looked after them well,' Sha whispered, imagining big Blastares by his side. He made to walk along the battlements, but winced, his leg twisting awkwardly. The wound from the Battle of Manzikert had healed and allowed him to ride well, but had left him weak in his stride. He grappled the stick that he loathed and used it to support his weight as he walked. 'Ha – and I have the limp of the *Haga*!' he chuckled dryly, remembering those early days when Apion had first enlisted, hobbling with the aid of some iron brace on his knee. Suddenly, as if conjured by the mention of the name, a flash of ginger startled him as Vilyam leapt up onto the crenelated wall top, purring and butting his head against Sha as he walked with the Malian.

Sha stopped and stroked the corpulent cat's ears, looking to the south and wondering what had become of his old friend, unseen and unheard of in those two years since the great battle. 'Sometimes it is best to live in wonder,' he mused, pushing away logic and reason. A gentle breeze bathed him then and rippled the petals of a poppy growing in a nook on the battlements. The sight conjured a forgotten memory. The Chaldians on the march. He, Apion, Procopius and Blastares at their head, resplendent and fearless. Blastares in a mischievous mood: *Hold on. Are you calling me a bloody flower?* The four of them erupting in belly-laughter. Sha could not fend off a smile as the memory faded.

Just then, a scuffling of boots stirred him. It was the lead kursoris rider. Sha shot him a confused frown. 'The wine is no good?'

'It is like nectar, sir. But there was something else I wanted to tell you. I didn't want to shout aloud. When we were on patrol, far to the south near the old Chaldian borders, we did sight one small Seljuk warband – fifty or so ghazis. They were heading north-east, most probably to plunder the farmlands east of these walls.'

Sha's shoulders tensed. For all Trebizond's walls could hold out against the Seljuk armies, those vital farmlands were easy prey. Immediately, he began thinking over how to organise the few men at his disposal to cope with this incursion. But the kursoris continued before his thoughts could fully form.

'We tracked them for hours, but we lost sight of them.' The kursoris' eyes narrowed and he shook his head. 'But when we saw them again, they were in flight. Some bore arrows in their flesh. Each wore a look of terror.'

'Fleeing? From whom?' Sha asked. 'Your riders were the only imperial soldiers outside this city's walls.'

'I don't understand it either, sir. All I know is they were turned away by some foe before they made it to our farmlands.' The rider shrugged. 'Then, later in the day we came to a Seljuk village even further south – unwalled, without warriors. They were just farmers. They offered us salep and bread. We saw that they had acquired Norman war horses to plough their fields. When I asked where they got them, they said they had taken them from the Doukid Norman mercenaries who sought to sack their village last month.' The kursoris shrugged. '*How?* I asked, seeing that they had only hoes and hunting bows by way of weapons. The village leader smiled when I said this, told me how a man had helped them, shown them how to defend themselves. He showed me caltrops and spike pits hidden in the ground around the village. Then he showed me how the farmers had been taught to stand in a spear wall, each of them bringing tall, sharp lances from their homes – weapons they had made under the direction of this man.'

'One man?' Sha asked.

The kursoris shrugged. 'Just one man. A haggard sort with pale skin and the tongue of both a Greek and a Seljuk. It made me think of…' The rider's words trailed off and he shook his head. 'It just reminded me of the past.'

Sha's breath halted in his lungs and he considered his next words carefully. 'Do not trouble yourself with it. These lands are vast and full of surprises. Now go, return to your comrades and enjoy your wine.'

'Thank you, Strategos,' the rider beamed.

'Don't call me that,' Sha said softly, shaking his head. 'The themata have fallen and the age of the strategoi is over. They are all gone.'

'Yes… sir. It's just old habits, you know?' the kursoris grinned, before turning away to hurry back down into the city and to his men. A ribald tune soon erupted from the barrack blocks.

Sha turned back to look out over the Chaldian landscape, tears gathering in his eyes, a broad grin lifting his face and a spark of hope swelling his heart.

'All gone,' he whispered into the ether. 'All but one.'

Author's Note

Dear Reader,

Writing Apion's tale has been a massive part of my life for these last four years. In that time I've immersed myself in Byzantine history, travelled to parts of the old empire and even taken up running in an attempt to understand the hero of the tale and the world he lived in. Apion, of course, has lived only in my imagination (and hopefully now, yours too), but the world I had him endure was very much based on my historical research. As always, I feel it is my duty to discuss the main areas where I have deviated from fact or speculated where detail has been thin on the ground.

Emperor Romanus Diogenes granted the Black Fortress at Mavrokastro to a mercenary Norman general, Crispin, around 1068. Crispin's brief was to protect the border doukate that encompassed Chaldia and the lands immediately east of it. Instead, he took offence at something — possibly lack of reward or title from the emperor — and began hoarding the imperial tax levy and harassing any who tried to bring him to heel. I have exaggerated his brutality (the eyewitness historian, Michael Attaleiates, states that Crispin did not harm any Byzantines until they tried to attack his men), but there is no doubt he was a rogue. After a few failed attempts, he was finally captured and sent into exile, only to be recalled by the Doukas family in 1072 for the civil wars against Romanus. Indeed, Attaleiates attests that Crispin personally saw to gouging out Alyates of Cappadocia's eyes with rusty tent pegs, before dying of poisoning shortly afterwards. Incidentally, my depiction of Apion instructing his men to use the menavlion (a weighty, extremely lengthy spear usually made out of a sapling tree trunk) against Crispin is little more than a nod to his understanding of past military tactics — the menavlion was a vital part of the 10th-century military machine engineered by Basil II.

The 1069 campaign saw Romanus Diogenes set off for Lake Van, crossing the Euphrates near Romanopolis with the intention of taking

Chliat from Seljuk hands. He was but days from achieving his goal when he heard news of the arrival of a Seljuk army at his rear and of the fate of Philaretos Brachiamos and the rearguard he had left stationed at the river's western banks. Thus, he had to swing his campaign army round and pursue and harry the marauding Seljuks around inner Anatolia. The Seljuks made it as far west as Iconium, besieging that city before swinging back round towards Cilicia. It was here that the Byzantines managed to finally strike back at their foe, calling upon Armenian allies to pelt the fleeing Seljuk horde from the heights of the Cilician mountains. Anatolia was free of the raiding army, but Romanus' stock was low with the people of the empire. They had watched their taxes being poured into the armies, while the cities were neglected. Thus, Romanus elected to remain in the capital the following year, in an attempt to remedy the situation.

In 1070, I have depicted Romanus selling off his lands and possessions in order to stage games in the capital and appease the people. This is speculative, but I think it helps illustrate the man's desperation. He knew he needed to buy time in preparation for a future campaign that could bring lasting victory and security. Part of his plan was to despatch Manuel Komnenos on an intermediary expedition in his stead, to fend off any Seljuk incursions while he stabilised affairs at the capital and prepared for the next year's campaign. The disaster which befell Manuel Komnenos' army near Sebastae is all too true, though history has it that Manuel actually escaped captivity (with the aid of a turncoat Turkic commander by the name of Yunus), as opposed to being freed to bring word of Sultan Alp Arslan's taking of Manzikert. But Manzikert (and effectively all of the Lake Van region) did fall into Seljuk hands that year, and this only fortified Romanus' convictions that a decisive campaign to seize those holdings was essential.

The year 1071 began with the exile of John Doukas and Michael Psellos – sent from Constantinople to some remote villa in the Bithynian countryside (note that the suggestion in the story that Psellos or his minions burnt down the Palace of Blachernae is purely this author's imagination). With the city clear of his greatest foes, Romanus now set out on his grand campaign to finally seize the Lake Van fortresses.

From the beginning, the expedition was riddled with ill omens. The blood-red comet, the grey dove on the sea voyage across the Hellespont and the snapping of the imperial tent pole at Helenopolis all sparked fear in the hearts of the army. Perhaps, for once, they did not have God's blessing? Worse, something seems to have happened to Romanus after they set out from Helenopolis. He began acting very oddly. His hovel camp on the hills above Malagina, his sudden bursts ahead of the imperial column and his outrageously provocative behaviour at the banks of the Halys must have come close to destroying morale. My only thoughts were that he was either maddened by the pressure of the campaign, or that he had been poisoned. I chose the latter as it seems he was suddenly 'himself' again after they crossed the Halys — more in keeping with a poisoning that had been stopped than some chronic and worsening mental state. That said, the rhinokopia incident happened not at the banks of the Halys as I have described, but at Manzikert itself, many weeks later, so perhaps poisoning is too simple an explanation.

Regarding the make-up of the 1071 campaign army, I have tried to juxtapose the various accounts of which regiments of tagmata, themata and foreign mercenaries were present. The numbers in each corps are a best estimate to fit my choice of the forty thousand who set off from the mustering ground at Malagina. The murkiest aspect of the campaign force was that of the magnate armies. The term itself is the best fit I could find to describe the men who formed the treacherous rearguard. Some sources identify them as the Hetairoi, a pseudo-tagmatic corps composed of mercenary or non-imperial troops. The historical sources describe Andronikos Doukas leading these forces. Andronikos was a proven military man, but I simply could not overlook the fact that he was a member of the Doukas family, and so I had to portray him as riding in shackles.

The campaign route through Anatolia is as true as I could ascertain, passing the imperial cities of Dorylaeum, Amorium, Ancyra, Caesarea, Sebastae, then taking the northerly pass into Armenia via Theodosiopolis (you can see the full map on my website). Here, or shortly after they left this abandoned city, the army split in two, one half going to secure the lands around Chliat, the other to take Manzikert. Alp Arslan's movements at this time are also as close to the history as I could determine, with the exception of his siege of Edessa — the sources state that the siege took place in April, not June as I have suggested.

Romanus Diogenes' offer to Alp Arlsan of a swap of Hierapolis for the Lake Van fortresses might have fended off battlefield conflict that year, but it seems that something odd happened. History has it that Romanus offered the exchange once, then again in a somewhat demanding, insulting tone. I opted to modify this, instead having the messenger Leo Diabatenus (a true historical figure from the events of 1071 – though almost certainly not a Hippodrome champion), poison the message and ensure that Alp Arslan, already enraged – the anecdote of the black veil around the tower at Aleppo is quite true – would march to Manzikert and to war.

Friday 26th August 1071 is a date that is scorched into history. Some believe the defeat at Manzikert was the single event that broke the Byzantine Empire. Others reckon the battle was a bloodbath that saw the empire's armies reduced to nothing. In fact, it was neither of these things. But it was a grievous blow to the image of imperial invincibility and a catalyst for the disastrous sequence of events that followed.

The battle was a fraught clash indeed and many lives were lost – though not as many as some estimates once suggested. It is thought that the Byzantines lined up on Manzikert's plains with anything between 20,000 and 40,000 soldiers, and the Seljuks faced them with a similar number. I have adopted the lower end of this scale as I find it more feasible given the lack of manpower available at the time (considering the 1070 disaster and other recent military losses). Modern estimates show that probably only as much as 20 per cent of each army fell or were captured in the battle. But the Seljuks won and won well. How?

Well, the telling factor was treachery rather than the tactical nous or ferocity of the Sultan's army. The perfidious behaviour of Joseph Tarchianotes in his flight from Lake Van (though there is much debate over whether he had an 'innocent' reason for fleeing back to imperial territory without telling anyone) left Romanus Diogenes with just half of the army he had set out with. Still, Romanus' numbers matched the Sultan's on the day of the battle. It was only at dusk, when the call for an ordered retreat descended into chaos, that the tide turned. The false cries of the emperor's death sent the lines into panic and flight, exposing huge gaps to the onlooking, probably dumbfounded Seljuk army. The loyal regiments who stayed with the emperor and tried to repair the collapsing retreat were swamped by masses of ghazi warriors. If Andronikos Doukas had come to the emperor's call, the day could yet have been saved. Instead, he calmly led the Byzantine rearguard from the field. The battle was lost at that moment.

History details several days before the battle, where the Byzantines were camped outside of the newly taken Manzikert. I have omitted some of this time period to keep the narrative (hopefully) flowing and engaging. In particular, on the day when Apion, Bryennios and their riders go south, across the plains and into the valleys in search of the Seljuk raiders who shot upon their foragers, the sources tell of a secondary advance in aid of Bryennios, led by an Armenian horseman named Vasilakes. Unfortunately, it seems Vasilakes had been in the sun too long that morning, for he charged blindly at a feigned Seljuk retreat. His cavalry were cut to pieces in the southern valleys near Mount Tzipan and he ended up in captivity. Also, the sources have it that there was a day in between the Seljuk night attack on the Byzantine camp and the battle itself, whereas I have the battle coming the morning after the attack.

Moving on to the days after the battle: it seems that most of the Byzantine armies (those who fled or deserted and those who stood) survived to fight on in the ensuing civil wars between Romanus Diogenes and the Doukas family. And it was these civil wars that truly broke Byzantium. Romanus fought with what forces he had left and after his ignominious death, Philarctos fought on against the Doukas family, carving out a rebel empire around Melitene – it is even thought that he might have converted to Islam at this point! Bryennios fought on against the Doukids also, albeit politically (at first, anyway). Determined to seal his place on the throne against these men and others, John Doukas welcomed mercenary Seljuk hordes into Anatolia, promising them riches if they would support his cause. Instead, when the Byzantine factions had exhausted each other, the Seljuks decided to claim the imperial heartland for themselves. Worse, having deposed Romanus Diogenes, the Doukas family dismissed the peaceful handover of land and cities that Romanus had agreed with Alp Arslan. This incited Malik Shah – after he had acceded Alp Arslan to the Seljuk throne – to urge the many Seljuk warbands from his lands and into Anatolia, firing their blood with the following rhetoric:

All of you be like lion cubs and eagle young, racing through the countryside day and night, slaying the Christians and not sparing any mercy on the Byzantine nation.

I have described Malik Shah's conquests occurring in the first few years after Manzikert – mainly to tie in with Apion's journey home. In reality, they were spread over the next six to eight years.

Certainly though, by 1081, Byzantium had lost her heartland and Anatolia was a largely Seljuk dominion. It was the start of the decline of the empire. But, as the crone showed Apion, the age of heroes was not quite over. Alexios Komnenos (the lad who, as the sources have it, turned up at the 1071 mustering camp at Malagina, eager to fight, only to be turned away by Romanus Diogenes for his own safety) led what has come to be known as the Komnenian Restoration, halting the Norman advance into the Balkans and stabilising the losses in Anatolia. The following centuries would be bumpy indeed for the empire, especially with the arrival of the crusades at the end of the 11th century (something the Byzantines welcomed… at first), but Alexios Komnenos is thought to have strived for the ideals of secure borders and a strong army once held dear by Romanus Diogenes. Regarding my description of Alexios Komnenos ushering in the use of the double-headed eagle as the icon of the empire; this is speculative, although the symbol did grow in prominence in this period and was firmly in use in the centuries that followed. One theory is that the symbol was adopted from the many ancient Hittite rock carvings of the mythical *Haga* found throughout Anatolia.

As for the delightful pairing of John Doukas and Michael Psellos (both of whom I have admittedly painted in an extremely unfortunate light), their time hovering by the imperial throne came to an end when an even more noxious individual – a eunuch by the name of Nikephoritzes – managed to gain the favour of Emperor Michael Doukas, poisoning the young emperor against Psellos and John.

John ended up in exile once again, dying there without the power that he had coveted for so long. Psellos' end is uncertain. One theory is that he died of a grotesque illness in throes of unearthly pain. This fate seemed fitting for the loathsome and clandestine kingmaker I have portrayed him to be.

Regarding the Seljuk Sultanate: in the first volume of the trilogy I depicted the expansion of Seljuk territory as inexorable and the peoples within unified. The previous volume and this one try to examine the reality of the situation: Alp Arslan faced many of the domestic challenges his Byzantine counterpart did, including opposition factions, assassination attempts, tensions amongst an ethnically diverse people and a constant need to prove his worth as the leader of this great world power.

Apropos the Seljuk armies: I have portrayed Taylan 'inventing' flat-bottomed stirrups. These almost certainly had been around for some time by 1071, but I wanted to highlight the expertise in horse archery the Seljuk riders had honed so well. Likewise, Taylan's White

Falcons' practice of wearing raptor feathers in their helms is something the original Seljuk steppe peoples had once practised many years previously. As the Battle of Manzikert saw Alp Arslan throw off the trappings of the armies he had assimilated in his time (the Persian artillerymen, lancers and spear infantry) and fall back to the guile of the ghazis – the closest thing to those original steppe riders – I thought the return of the falcon feathers was rather apt.

There are probably many more points for discussion, but I'll leave it at that. Please do feel free to get in touch if you'd like to chat over any other details or theories.

Usually at this point, I would inform you when you could expect the next volume in the series. But instead I have to bring the curtain down on the story of 'Strategos'. Apion's tale is over, yet the journey in telling it is one I will never forget. Thank you from the bottom of my heart for taking that journey with me.

Yours faithfully,
Gordon Doherty
www.gordondoherty.co.uk

P.S. If you fell in love with Byzantium and the tale of the Strategos of Chaldia, please help others to do so also – a short review on Amazon is the best way of spreading the word, and I'd be most grateful if you could write one. In fact, if you do leave a review on Amazon, drop me a line at my website to let me know, and I'll send you a free ecopy of *Legionary*, the opening volume of my other series, as a token of my appreciation.

Glossary

Adnoumion: The great Byzantine mustering. This usually happened at Malagina, near the Zompos Bridge by the River Sangarios in Bithynia.

Akhi: Seljuk infantry armed with long anti-cavalry spears, scimitars, shields and sometimes armoured in lamellar, leather or horn.

Archiatros: Byzantine physician.

Armamenta: State-funded imperial warehouses tasked with producing arms, clothing and armour for the armies. They were usually situated in major cities and strongholds.

Ballista: Primarily anti-personnel missile artillery capable of throwing bolts vast distances. Utilised from fortified positions and on the battlefield.

Bandon (pl. banda): The basic battlefield unit of infantry in the Byzantine army. Literally meaning 'banner', a bandon typically consisted of between two hundred and four hundred men, usually *skutatoi*, who would line up in a square formation, presenting spears to their enemy from their front ranks and hurling *rhiptaria* from the ranks behind. Banda would form together on the battlefield to present something akin to the ancient phalanx.

Bandophoros: The standard-bearer for a Byzantine *bandon*.

Basileus: The Byzantine emperor (feminine: *Basileia*).

Bey: The leader of a Seljuk warband or minor army.

Breidox: The battle axe used by the *Varangoi*.

Buccina: The ancestor of the trumpet and the trombone, this instrument was used for the announcement of night watches and various other purposes in the Byzantine forts and marching camps as well as to communicate battlefield manoeuvres.

Buccinator: A soldier who uses the *buccina* to perform acoustical signalling on the battlefield and in forts, camps and settlements.

Chi-Rho: The Chi-Rho is one of the earliest forms of Christogram, and was used in the early Christian Roman Empire through to the Byzantine high period as a symbol of piety and empire. It is formed by superimposing the first two letters in the Greek spelling of the word Christ, chi = ch and rho = r, in such a way to produce the following monogram:

☧

Daylamid warriors: Fierce and rugged warriors from the mountains of northern Iran. It is thought that they may have fought with twin-pronged spears (though many argue that this is a mistranslation and that they actually fought with double-edged blades).

Dekarchos: A minor officer in charge of a *kontoubernion* of ten *skutatoi* who would be expected to fight in the front rank of his *bandon*. He would wear a red★ sash to denote his rank.

Dinar: A golden Seljuk coin.

Dirham: A silver Seljuk coin.

Djinn: Islamic demon.

Domestikos: A title afforded to the man in charge of the eastern or western half of Byzantine military affairs.

Doux: One of the titles for the leader of a Byzantine *tagma*.

Dromón: Byzantine war galley with twin triangular sails. Capable of holding up to three hundred men.

Droungarios: A Byzantine officer in charge of two *banda*, who would wear a silver★ sash to denote his rank.

Fatimid Caliphate: Arab Islamic caliphate that dominated the area comprising modern-day Tunisia and Egypt in the Middle Ages.

Foulkon: The Byzantine heir to the famous Roman *testudo* or 'tortoise' formation.

Ghazi: The Seljuk light cavalryman, a blend of steppe horse archer and light skirmisher whose primary purpose was to raid enemy lands and disrupt defensive systems and supply chains.

Ghulam: The Seljuk heavy cavalryman, equivalent to the Byzantine *kataphractos*. Armoured well in scale vest or lamellar, with a distinctive pointed helmet with nose-guard, carrying a bow, scimitar and spear.

Haga: A ferocious two-headed eagle from ancient Hittite mythology. Also the basis for what would become the emblem of both the Byzantine Empire and the Seljuk Sultanate.

Kampidoktores: The drill master in charge of training Byzantine soldiers.

Kataphractos (pl. kataphractoi): Byzantine heavy cavalry and the main offensive force in the *thema* and *tagma* armies. The riders and horses would wear iron lamellar and mail armour, leaving little vulnerability to attack. The riders would use their *kontarion* for lancing, *spathion* for skirmishing or their bow for harrying.

Kathisma: The imperial box at the Hippodrome in Constantinople. This was connected directly to the Imperial Palace via the Cochlia Gate and a spiral staircase.

Kentarches: A Byzantine officer in charge of one hundred Byzantine soldiers or the crew of a *dromon*. A descendant of the Roman centurion.

Klibanion (pl. klibania): The characteristic Byzantine lamellar cuirass made of leather, horn or iron squares, usually sleeveless, though sometimes with leather strips hanging from the waist and shoulders.

Komes: An officer in charge of a *bandon* who would wear a white★ sash to denote his rank.

Kontarion: A spear between two and three metres long, the kontarion was designed for Byzantine infantry to hold off enemy cavalry.

Kontoubernion: A grouping of ten Byzantine infantry who would eat together, patrol together, share sleeping quarters or a pavilion tent while on campaign. They would be rewarded or punished as a single unit.

Kouropalates: A general appointed to lead a Byzantine military campaign in the emperor's stead.

Kursoris (pl. kursores): Byzantine scout rider, lightly armed with little or no armour.

Menavlion: A weighty, thick and extremely lengthy (11 feet or more) spear used to repel cavalry charges.

Nomisma (pl. nomismata): A gold coin that could be debased by various degrees to set its value.

Numeroi (sing. numeros): A Byzantine imperial *tagma*, stationed in Constantinople. They guarded the prisons, the walls, the site of the Baths of Zeuxippus and parts of the Imperial Palace.

Pamphylos (pl. pamphyloi): A small, round–hulled Byzantine cargo ship, used typically to transport horses and artillery.

Portatioi: A shadowy subset of the *Numeroi*. It is thought that they were employed as torturers.

Protoproedros: Title of a senior Byzantine court official.

Rhinokopia: Cuttinf off the nose – a method of punishment for criminals in the Byzantine Empire.

Rhiptarion: A short throwing spear. *Skutatoi* carried two or three of these each.

Salep: A hot drink made with orchid root, cinnamon and milk.

Shatranj: A precursor to modern–day chess.

Signophoroi (sing. signophoros): Byzantine standard bearers for the *tagmata*. They would carry the sacred purple-and-gold banners on campaign.

Siphonarioi (sing. siphonaros): Operators of Greek–fire throwing siphons. They operated large siphons mounted on towers or walls, and it is thought that they also carried smaller, hand–held siphons into field battles.

Skribones: Byzantine medical personnel who would carry the dead and wounded from the battlefield.

Skutatos (pl. skutatoi): The Byzantine infantryman, based on the ancient hoplite. He was armed with a *spathion*, a *skutum*, a *kontarion*, two or more *rhiptaria* and possibly a dagger and an axe. He would wear a conical iron helmet and a lamellar *klibanion* if positioned to the front of his *bandon*, or a padded jacket or felt vest if he was closer to the rear. *Tagma* skutatoi may well all have been afforded iron lamellar armour.

Skutum: The Byzantine infantry shield that gives the *skutatoi* their name. Usually kite- or teardrop-shaped and painted identically within a *bandon*.

Solenarion: A wooden channel that can be fitted to a standard bow to create a rudimentary crossbow. This allows quick aiming and firing of short, weighty darts.

Spathion: The Byzantine infantry sword, derived from the Roman *spatha*. Up to a metre long, this straight blade was primarily for stabbing, but allowed slashing and hacking as well.

Strategos (pl. strategoi): The *themata* armies of Byzantium were organised and led by such a man. The *strategos* was also responsible for governance of his *thema*.

Tagma (pl. tagmata): The tagmata were the professional standing armies of the Byzantine Empire. They were traditionally clustered around

Constantinople. These armies were formed to provide a central reserve, to meet enemy encroachment that could not be dealt with by the *themata*, and also to cow the potentially revolutionary power of those regional armies. They were well armoured, armed, paid and fed. Each tagma held several thousand men and was composed exclusively of cavalry or infantry. In the 11th century AD, some of these tagmata were moved closer to the borders to deal with emerging threats. In addition, a raft of smaller, 'mercenary' tagmata were formed in these regions, comprising largely of Rus, Normans and Franks.

Thema (pl. themata): In the 7th century AD, as a result of the crisis caused by the Muslim conquests, the Byzantine military and administrative system was reformed: the old late Roman division between military and civil administration was abandoned, and the remains of the Eastern Roman Empire's field armies were settled in great districts, the themata, that were named after those armies. The men of the themata would work their state-leased military lands in times of peace and then don their armour and weapons when summoned by the *strategos* to defend their thema or to set out on campaign alone or with the *tagmata*. The manpower of each thema varied vastly, with some able to field only a few thousand men while others could muster as many as ten or fifteen thousand men. The diagram at the front of the book depicts the structure these forces would be organised into. In the 11th century, the thematic system was in steep decline, with the *tagmata* gradually taking over as defenders of the borderlands.

Touldon: The baggage train that would follow and supply a Byzantine army on the march.

Tourma (pl. tourmae): A subdivision of a Byzantine *thema*, commanded by a *tourmarches*. Each tourma was comprised of some two thousand soldiers of the *thema* army and encompassed a geographical subset of the *thema* lands.

Tourmarches (pl. tourmarchai): A Byzantine officer in charge of the military forces and administration of a *tourma*.

Toxotes (pl. toxotai): The Byzantine archer, lightly armoured with a felt jacket and armed with a composite bow and a dagger.

Varangoi (sing. varangos): An elite infantry unit of the Byzantine army, employed as personal bodyguards to the emperor. These axemen were primarily Rus or Germanic, and were thought to be both loyal and fierce in battle.

Yalma: A close-fitting, long-sleeved and knee-length silk shirt worn by Turkic peoples.

—

*The use of a sash to denote rank is backed up by historical texts, but the sash colours stated are speculative.